BOUND BY

A Tale of Love, Loss, and
the Inescapable Pull of Fate

R. MB. PEARSON

To H. T.

The cycle turns, from frost to flame,

Breathing life, love's gentle claim,

Drifting down from dreams untold,

Where hopes take wing,

and hearts grow bold.

-JORDAN SLOAN

Gift or Curse

Raoghnailt

JUNE 1970
LEVITTOWN, PENNSYLVANIA

The Scottish Highlands have a way of revealing the truth, and those with *An Dà Shealladh*—the gift of two sights—were revered and feared equally. This gift had been passed down to Raoghnailt through generations of her Scottish lineage. Tonight, it called to her once more, slipping into her dreams, weaving seamlessly into the fabric of her slumber.

She stood in a modest bedroom, a silent observer. A frail woman lay in a rented hospital bed at home, barely able to move, her teenage son tenderly feeding her. But each bite was a monumental effort; chewing was a battle against fatigue, every swallow an agonizing ordeal.

"One more bite, Ma. Please?" The boy's voice cracked, eyes filled with desperation.

The woman shook her head weakly. "I'm so tired, honey... I miss your father. He's waiting for me."

"Shhh...," he whispered. "You promised we wouldn't give up."

Raoghnailt's heart ached for him. She was a mother now, too—her daughter, Rainey, just a few months old—and the thought of leaving her behind was unbearable. This lad was too young to carry such a burden. His shoulders sagged under the weight of it all—his mother's illness, the empty house, the loss of his father. He was barely holding on.

Raoghnailt saw his eyes glisten with unshed tears as he set the tray aside and adjusted her blankets and pillows with the quiet efficiency of someone who had done it countless times. He lowered the bed's headrest, unaware of the tiny spark that flickered from the electrical socket behind it.

"I'll be in my room studying, Ma. I've got finals tomorrow. Here's the bell where you can reach it."

He bent to kiss her goodnight and whispered, "I love you, Ma."

But the woman was already slumbering.

Raoghnailt moved closer, feeling the weight of death settle over the room. She gently touched the woman's forehead, whispering a Gaelic blessing to ease her pain. The woman wouldn't make it through the night. Her son—he should be by her side when she drew her last breath.

As she turned to leave, something—a flash of light—caught the corner of her eye. Embers had dropped onto the carpet and ignited into low flames within seconds.

Raoghnailt cried out. She ran through the house, searching for the boy, calling out for him.

Where are ye, lad? Yer Mama is in trouble. Hurry!

Her voice echoed, hollow and powerless. She was only an observer. No one could hear her. Raoghnailt tried one more time to use her voice.

"FIRE!"

She shrieked and jolted awake in her husband's arms, flailing in panic. Tono cupped her face gently.

"Rae, look at me," he whispered. "You're safe."

She blinked, still shaking. This vision was different—too real, too vivid.

"No, my love. There is no fire. There, there..." Tono comforted, holding his wife tightly while caressing her hair. "We are all fine, Rae. Everything is just fine."

"Rainey. Where's Rainey?"

"She's in her room sleeping, sweetheart. Shhh... hush now, or you'll wake her."

Raoghnailt clung fiercely to her husband, wanting to believe it wasn't real. But she knew.

"'Twas a vision, Tono," she sobbed. "I dinna ken the mother and her lad in the dream. She burnt tae death, *duine-cèile*. An' the lad saw t'all. Something will happen to Rainey."

"Shhh..." He comforted her shaking body, coaxing his wife to go back to sleep. "Nothing will happen, love. I'm right here. We can talk about your dream in the morning, alright?"

Having had a late night at their restaurant, Raoghnailt persuaded Tono to go back to sleep. She then quietly rose and tiptoed to her baby's room.

Chubby four-month-old Rainey was sound asleep in her crib, her pouty mouth parted, breathing quietly. Raoghnailt reached down to pick her up, cradling her warm, cuddly body. Then, she settled into the nearby rocking chair to croon a lullaby in Gaelic.

Raoghnailt thought of her prophetic dream, its vividness and haunting scene. She had never been sent a vision of someone she didn't know or recognize, nor a place she had never been, and never about suffering or tragedy happening in the present.

She was aware her *An Da Shealladh* revealed not only the future but also the present. As she glanced at the small electric clock on her baby's dressing table, its second arm sweeping past midnight, she knew the tragedy was still unfolding. And with each ticking second, she felt herself pulled back into the vision, the scene growing clearer—the young man she'd seen in her dream, rescued from the flames. Third-degree burns covered his arms, chest, and parts of his face, where the skin had turned a sickly, waxy gray in places. He let out a howl that pierced the air, not from the pain of his injuries but from seeing his mother's form lying on a gurney covered beneath a white sheet from head to toe, emerging from the charred remains of their home.

From the edges of her vision, she glimpsed a young reporter furiously scribbling every detail as the chaos unfolded. His pen raced to capture it all. Every tortured detail, from the acrid smoke burning his throat to the boy's agonizing wail that split the night. This was his moment, his first major story, the one that would launch his career and carve his name into the pages of the big city newspapers. But no triumph could erase the memory of this night, the night when a son's tortured eyes watched his mother ascend in flames.

A cold shiver crept up Raoghnailt's spine, shaking herself back to the present. She pulled her baby tighter to her chest as if shielding her from an unseen menace. The boy. The reporter. Two strangers she had never known now seemed tethered to her child's fate, their paths winding toward her daughter's future in ways she could barely begin to understand.

CHAPTER 1

Raine

JANUARY 2000

NEW YORK TO NEW HAMPSHIRE

I bought a Jeep Wrangler. A red one.

As I cranked its ignition, the engine's growl echoed through the silent parking garage, sending tingles in anticipation of adventure and a new life ahead.

They called January 1, 2000, 12:01 a.m., Y2K, and the doomsayers predicted the world would end. Computers' internal clocks would come to a complete stop. But then nothing happened. The world didn't collapse. Mine? *Kaboom!* It was completely shattered.

It has been trauma after trauma since that fateful day in December '98 when my life took a dramatic turn, taking over as head of the ad agency, working tirelessly to bring it the success that would have made Peter and his partners proud of me. But after discovering the lies and the duplicity a year later... And Jim. God, I could barely say his name without vomiting. The man was my mentor. I trusted him with my life. He was like a father to me. What he did to me after the company's New Year's Eve party to celebrate our IPO? I shudder every time I think about it. And Luke? I thought he was my friend.

I couldn't take it anymore. I had to get away from the city. I needed a fresh start, somewhere far from the sordid memories that resurfaced with every city corner I turned.

While warming up the engine, I lowered the driver-side visor to check myself in the tiny mirror, turning my face left and right, taking in this shocking new profile I'd brashly decided on just yesterday. My revoltingly long dark chestnut hair that spoke of elegance and sophistication when I was Peter's wife—gone. In its place, a bob cropped short to my ears and bangs trimmed straight across my forehead just below my eyebrows. Vivienne, my best friend, said if I spiked my hair with gel, I would pass for a Japanese punk rocker.

"New Hampshire or bust," I said aloud. Easing the clutch to back the Jeep out of its parking spot, I shifted forward to slide down the corkscrew ramp and headed out onto the pre-dawn-darkened streets of Manhattan.

God! It had been years since I'd driven with a manual transmission. With each shift of gears, I felt in control of my life once again.

By the time I reached the George Washington Bridge, dawn was breaking, and from my rearview mirror, I watched New York City's skyline recede. I cranked up the radio, singing with Tom Petty, belting out *Won't Back Down,* and continued northward where a changed landscape and respite beckoned.

Once I crossed New Hampshire, the scenery changed from the clustered housing developments of the Boston suburbs to the stark contrast of granite mountains rising alongside the highway.

When signs for Durham appeared, I exited and drove down a two-lane country road that wound through isolated farmlands and quaint little colonial towns, following signs to the tiny college town where I would live—for a year.

As I pulled into Main Street and parked in front of the real estate office to pick up house keys, I took a moment to survey the town I'd only seen once last summer.

Durham thrived on the presence of the University of New Hampshire, which absorbed much of the town's real estate. Its campus flanked one side of Main Street. On the other side, small businesses clustered together—the real estate office, tavern, pizza joint, hardware store, etc. There was also a quaint Amtrak station where the Downeaster trains headed south to Boston or north to Portland, Maine, stopped for passengers. That was pretty much it for "downtown" Durham. Everything else around it was farmland and wildlife refuges.

"Mrs. Garvey. Welcome to Durham." Cora, the real estate agent, greeted me as she retrieved a set of keys. "Your utilities have all been turned on, and as your lawyer instructed, we had it inspected and cleaned. The report shows the house is sound, and the plumbing and heating are all working. I sent your lawyer a list of all the other things that need attention. I trust you've read it. Nothing major. They were mostly cosmetic."

I nodded, all good to know I could stay in the house tonight. When I reached the sole traffic light at the edge of downtown, I made a right onto Mill Road and downshifted to climb the gently sloping street. After passing just a handful of houses on my left, I pulled into the driveway of my 'new' old house.

Sitting in the Jeep, I wondered how the Callahans and their four kids ever managed in this thousand-square-foot, two-bedroom, one-and-a-half-bath house. Built in 1932, it had been in the family until the late Edwina Callahan moved to a nursing home ten years ago, refusing to sell to anyone. It was her first home, and she wanted it to shelter another young, loving family in the way it did hers. Left empty and unsold, the house deteriorated into its current state—dirty white paint peeling from the clapboard siding, a sagging front porch with missing spindles resembling a toothless grin. When she died a couple of months ago, her heirs wanted it sold as-is ASAP. I swooped in, offered cash, and a fast closing.

It was so rundown that no one wanted it—except me. I saw its potential and the hope for renewal.

That night, huddled inside a sleeping bag in an upstairs bedroom, I listened to the clang and bang of the ancient radiators, followed by a soft hiss of steam trying to warm the drafty room. It sounded unfamiliar, but the gentle heat radiated comfort as if whispering, *"Shhhh... Everything will be fine."*

As I lay in the darkness, hundreds of miles from New York, the memories came unbidden, making me wonder if getting away was the right decision. It gave credence to the phrase, *'You can run, but you can't hide.'*

I had initially planned to walk away from it all, step down as CEO, and just fuck it. But Vivienne, who was not only my best friend from childhood but also my company's investment counsel, pleaded with me to reconsider.

So I agreed to one year. And if a year from now I still wanted to quit, she promised to help me with an exit strategy that would be more orderly than my harebrained, reckless decision to run away and everything be damned.

I broke into a gut-wrenching, rib-wracking cry. I called out to my parents, whom I missed so much since our estrangement. Yet I couldn't bring myself to reconcile with them despite the chasm of our separation for nearly a decade.

Peter.

I whispered into the darkness, raw pain beneath my breastbone stabbing hard.

I loved you. I loved you so very much.

Burying my head in my pillow, muffling the choking sobs, I asked again.

Why?

CHAPTER 2

Raine

I was five years old, stomping around our yard in pink mud boots, holding a small watering can painted with white daisies, while my mother planted juniper saplings around our house. I was charged with watering the shrubs after she'd burrowed each one into the earth. After the fifth plant, I was getting bored, so I asked her why we had to plant so many trees around the house. My mother knew that if she didn't answer me or tried to brush me off with some lame response, I'd pester her to insanity.

"Rowan trees hae magic, *mo nighean*. 'Twill protect oor house an' oor faimly," she replied in her thick brogue, referring to the junipers as the Rowans that grew in Scotland.

I had been a precocious child of two when I learned to speak in complete sentences without the typical baby babble. Before I was three, I held intelligent conversations with adults. The speed with which I grasped knowledge surprised, if not terrified, my parents. My thirst for answers was unquenchable. To shut me up, they bought me a set of Grolier's Encyclopedia, which I read from A to Z before I was even five.

"How can these trees protect us when they're so little?" I raised my eyebrows and looked at the saplings, which were no more than twelve inches tall and had thin, delicate stalks. I'd even made a grand gesture of raising my arms exclaiming, "This makes no sense whatsoever."

"They'll soon grow tae be big and strong, Rainey," she said patiently. "Ye'll see."

"But I read in the encyclopedia that it takes ten or more years for a juniper to grow tall," I argued. To friends and family, I was cute when I acted like five going on fifty with aplomb. To my mother, I was exasperating.

I heard her sigh. That was when she must have considered that I had the intellectual maturity to understand the gravity of her reason for planting this particular tree and why she wanted them around our property.

"Awright. Since ye're now a big lassie, I'll tell ye. When ye were but a wee bairn in me arms, the fae of *An Dà Shealladh* visited me. They took me awa' from here, tae this house where a lad was carin' for his sick mam."

It sounded like she was telling me a fairytale. But at five, I understood my mother's mystical power passed down from her Scottish highland ancestors, allowing her to see the present and future. Only my father and I, and my mother's family back in Edinburgh, Scotland, knew about this 'gift' of hers. What she saw were people's destinies. Premonitions. And thus far, every single one she's foretold has come true. My father has always believed in her gift. I never really thought it was anything special because I'd been aware of it at such a young age.

"T'laddie, he was nae more than fifteen or sixteen. He should hae been havin' the time o' his life wi' his mates, playing football, doin' foolish things. Instead, he had tae care for his mother who wis verra sick."

I listened with rapt interest. She kept her focus on the planting, not wanting me to see her eyes glistening at the memory of her vision.

Halfway through, sadness gripped her, choking off the rest of her story, unable to continue. She didn't have to. I easily figured out what had happened afterward, and my bottom lip quivered. Sensing my fear, she picked me up and held me tightly. Over her shoulder, I gazed at my father's restaurant next door to our house and thought of all the open flames that blazed from several stoves during the dinner service.

"Ye're not to worry, Rainey. It were nae us in the dream, but even as they're yet small, the Rowan trees will protect us, *mo chridhe,*" she said.

She set me back down and said, "Now, give this one a wee bit o' water an' make sure ye soak the roots well. We'll plant th' rest o' th' trees aroun' yer Da's restaurant in the morn an' he'll be safe, aye?"

I nodded, feeling satisfied with her comfort and assurance as she brushed a tear that rolled down my cheek.

What she didn't tell me was how her vision portended a dark omen that would one day define my destiny.

CHAPTER 3

Raine

DECEMBER 8, 1998
NEW YORK, NEW YORK

S omething was wrong. Very wrong.

"Shit!" I mumbled, twisting in the bedsheets. Peter was still lying next to me, dead asleep. "Sweetheart, are you okay?"

I felt a gnawing fear when he didn't respond to my gentle nudge. Peter was always up at four a.m., and it was already six. In the nine years I'd known him, he always roused himself without an alarm, hit the gym, and would be at the office by now.

I knew he'd been more tired than usual lately. But with the campaign, I'd brushed it off as added stress. Today, however, was not the time to oversleep. He would announce that he was running for senator at a live press conference tonight.

"You go on," he finally mumbled when I shook him again. But he'd gone right back to sleep. I reset the alarm to seven a.m. to ensure he didn't sleep later than that.

I left Peter, still tangled in the sheets, and rushed through my morning routine, my mind racing. By the time I stepped into the office, I was working to ignore the tension tightening into a hard knot in my stomach.

My assistant, Timothy Hong—aka Timmo—a sharp Columbia grad followed me armed with a pen and yellow pad, reading off my agenda for the day.

"Okay, I sent the volunteers to the library," Timmo started, reading from his notes. "Al's supervising them. The background equipment was delivered last night. I'll be there to ensure the tech works while the cameras roll. Corinne has the caterers ready for the Read Aloud Ball."

"What about Peter's campaign posters?" I asked, sipping a Starbucks Grande coffee that Timmo, bless him, had picked up for me before I even arrived. His efficiency has been a godsend.

"Not ready yet," he said.

"Yikes! What's the holdup?"

"Software glitches in graphics. Should be ready in an hour."

"I need to show them to Peter before we send them to the library," I said, flipping my wrist to check the time, frowning slightly, wondering if Peter had finally woken up.

"It'll get done on time," Timmo said reassuringly.

"Great! Is that it?"

"I took care of your voicemail messages, except for one. A woman. Her message was in a foreign language. It's not Asian. Not European either." Timmo puckered his brows in thought. "Maybe Scandinavian? I don't know. It wasn't like the other whacky calls you've gotten before. She didn't sound crazy. More like...desperate to reach you. I saved it for you if you wanted to listen to it."

"What time was the call?"

"Four a.m. Her accent was pretty thick, but she didn't leave a number either."

I shook my head. "Nah, I don't have time for this. Delete it."

By eleven, Peter still hadn't shown up at the office. I called the apartment—no answer. I tried his cell phone. No luck.

"Carty, where's the boss?" I asked our chauffeur, who'd been with us for as long as I can remember.

"I took him to the Montclair headquarters on Park Avenue. He said he'd be done around ten," Carty said.

I frowned.

Montclair? Who's at Montclair? Was this a new client?

"Okay, thanks, Carty. Please tell him to call me as soon as he's done?"

I buzzed Rosemary, Peter's secretary, to see if she had any details on his calendar for Montclair.

"He just asked me to block off an hour and a half on his schedule this morning. Didn't say with whom or where," Rosemary said.

I checked with Greyson Thorne next. Greyson, head of sales, was Peter's right-hand man and the likely successor who would take Peter's place when he left for public office.

"Is Montclair a new client? A prospect?" I asked over the phone.

"Not that I know of," Greyson replied.

It was well after lunchtime when I finally heard from Peter.

"Oh my God, where've you been?" I asked, pacing my office.

"Caught in traffic. Is everything ready for this evening?"

I considered how he quickly deflected my question. I hated it when he did that. I knew he meant well, not wanting me to worry, and after almost ten years of marriage, I'd gotten used to it—well, most of the time.

"We have the posters that need your final approval," I replied, resigned once again to his cool disregard for me.

"Good. I'll be there in a few minutes," he said, then abruptly hung up.

When Rosemary finally alerted me to his arrival, I rushed to his office, carrying the posters, making sure not to damage the delicate foam boards.

Always looking like the proper English marm with her hair in a chignon and reading glasses perched on the bridge of her nose, Rosemary was in Peter's office taking her usual notes the old-fashioned way—in shorthand. I barged in unannounced and propped the posters on the ledge against the window.

"What do you think? This is Luke's creative genius. See the light blue single brushstroke silhouette of a mother reading to a child? This will be Read Aloud's new logo."

My finger traced the brush stroke. "Every night, read them a story," read the tagline in bold serifs.

I showed him the second set of posters featuring Peter reading to a child on his lap. "These are for your campaign," I explained.

The tagline was "Championing future generations. Garvey for Senate."

When I worked on the creative, I wondered with a pang if he had wished the child model we'd hired was ours instead. I know I did. Peter and I have been childless for all nine years of our marriage for reasons we'd never explored.

"We should have TV ad production underway in another couple of weeks," I said excitedly.

When Rosemary left, he walked toward the posters and skimmed them. He hadn't looked at them for more than ten seconds when his intercom buzzed. Returning to his desk to pick up the phone, he glanced back and said, "That will do, Raine."

I noticed a brief flicker of something in his eyes—was it weariness? Anxiety?

Before I could ask, he turned to the speaker phone, his voice strained. "I'll take the call, Rosemary... Ermata! Darling!"

Peter smiled upon hearing the voice of his largest campaign contributor on the line.

"Fine," I grumbled.

He turned around, his finger on the mute button.

"Raine, it's getting late. Don't you have to be somewhere?" he said in a clipped tone, then returned to his call.

Crestfallen, I gathered up the posters and left. So much for trying to talk to him about what happened this morning—his oversleeping, the meeting at Montclair, and what's been going on with his health. But that terseness in his voice meant we were not discussing anything.

A flurry of activity and the phone's incessant ringing kept me from dwelling on Peter the rest of the afternoon, but I couldn't shake the gnawing worry. He'd been so distant lately, his vibrant energy dimmed by something he wouldn't share.

It was nearing five when I finally leaned back against my chair and released a deep breath. I had missed lunch, and the faint throbbing at my temples threatened to balloon into a full-fledged stress headache. I couldn't help but wonder if the campaign was too much for him. He'd always been my rock, but now he seemed so fragile, and I felt helpless watching him slip away.

When someone rapped on my partially closed door, I growled, "Go away."

But an undaunted Luke poked his head in.

"Hi," he said, leaving the door open and leaning against the jamb.

I mumbled a greeting while popping four ibuprofen capsules, chasing it with water.

"That doesn't look good," he said, eyeing the open bottle of pills.

Silverman & York Advertising was the third-largest in the country, still privately held by Jim York, Peter, and Luke Henes. Luke and Peter, however, went back to their undergrad days at NYU.

"I hate seeing you like this, you know," Luke said, folding his arms across his chest. "You work too hard."

Born in China but adopted as a baby, Luke Chen Henes was S&Y's chief creative officer. He looked like a younger version of my Japanese-American father. Both were tall with broad shoulders, which was uncommon among Asians.

I always thought Luke had a thing for me, but in deference to my husband—his best friend—he'd never said a word or acted on it openly. He'd always been there for me, as a true friend. When I arrived in New York, Luke gave me insight into the man I married. When I started working for the agency, he stood ready to lend any assistance.

"I don't think I work any harder than anyone else on the payroll, Luke," I said, sinking back into my chair and rocking it slightly. "You know this is too important for Peter."

"No one gets as stressed out as you do. This is supposed to be a fun place to work, kid," he joked.

"Comes with being married to the boss, I guess. Expectations are different."

"Yes, but there's no reason to be such a boor to you," Luke replied with sadness.

"It's okay. I'm used to it. Anyway," I said, switching topics. "He didn't say much about the posters. But I think he liked your creative with Read Aloud. I know I do."

Luke shrugged and laughed. "Well, that's Peter. He'd have let us know if he didn't like it."

"Well, I love what you created, and I'm sure the board at Read Aloud will too. Speaking of which, I should get going," I said, checking my watch.

"It'll all go well," Luke said, backing away from my office. "They'll love Peter, and you'll be dazzling with him."

"I wish you'd come," I said, knowing it was futile to suggest it. Luke always bowed out of public events. He was an artist at heart and would have been happy if he could spend his days painting by the River Seine in Paris.

He shook his head. "Raine, you know I hate going to those things. Don't worry, I'll catch you on TV."

I could only smile back weakly before he turned to leave.

I decided to check on Peter before leaving. His door was ajar, and I noticed him pacing, rubbing the back of his neck to ease the tension. Sensing my presence when I walked in, he turned around.

"Heywood, come see me in about ten minutes," he said over the phone, then hung up.

He ushered me in, closing the door behind me.

Unexpectedly, he folded me in his arms and held me so tight that I gasped, taken by surprise. Within that tight embrace, my world stood still as he stroked my back, burying his face at the base of my neck. His breath against my skin brought back a rush of memories.

I pressed my cheek against him, sniffing his jaw. It was the same after-shave he'd worn the day he first held me when I was just a nineteen-year-old freshman at UCLA. Goosebumps ran up my spine. He still made me tingle. God, I'd missed this from him.

I brushed my fingers through his hair and felt its dampness. His neck felt cool, maybe even a bit clammy. A wave of worry washed over me. He'd been avoiding the doctor for months, insisting he was stressed. Something was off. I looked up at him, unsettled.

"Are you alright?" I finally asked in a barely audible whisper. "You've been so tired lately. I'm worried, Peter. I wish you would see a doctor."

He pulled away, drawing me in with his gaze.

"I'm fine, sweetheart," he whispered.

Before I could say more, he lowered his lips to mine lightly. The kiss lasted only a fleeting moment and slowly released me.

I looked at him, puzzled. Peter was still so handsome, with those blue eyes that always melted me. But I knew something had changed him the past year-and-a-half. He was thinner, his face gaunt. I had chalked it up to the stress of his upcoming campaign for office. Though now, he just looked so sad. And I didn't know why. He wouldn't tell me why whenever I pressed.

"Why don't I wait for you?" I suggested with concern and a gut feeling he shouldn't be alone.

"No, I'll meet you at NYPL," he said, cutting me off and gently pushing me away. Just like that, he'd returned to his calm, distant self.

"Why not?"

"Don't argue with me, Raine," he snapped. "I don't have to be there until eight. On the other hand, *you* need to be there for both of us. Now go."

When he opened the door, the general counsel, Marc Heywood, was waiting outside.

"Come on in, Heywood. Raine was just leaving," Peter said, clearly dismissing me.

As I walked toward the elevator, a heavy silence settled around me, Peter's coldness pressing down like a weight I couldn't shake. The unanswered questions swirled—his distant eyes, erratic moods, and unspoken secrets that had built a wall between us. For a brief second, the cryptic voicemail flitted through my mind, a shadow of something I'd overlooked. But I pushed it aside, unaware that this—this moment—was the last time I'd ever see my husband alive.

CHAPTER 4

Nick

DECEMBER 8, 1998
NEW YORK, NEW YORK

The New York Tribune newsroom buzzed constantly with news and commentary. Low-barrier cubicles divided the space into departments—business, sports, crime, and education—each identified by banners hanging above the desks. Televisions suspended from the ceiling broadcasted twenty-four-hour news networks, ensuring no event went unnoticed.

Nick considered himself fortunate. After winning a Peabody for his piece on Phil Hartman's tragic murder by his wife, his portrait was deemed significant enough to be included in *The Tribune's* "Gallery of the Greats" on the executive floor with other legendary journalists who'd also been winners.

But not tonight. He'd agreed to cover the cop desk for a friend—a fellow reporter who had tickets to the hockey game. Still, it felt good to get involved in breaking news occasionally. Nick thought the crime beat always got him back down to Earth. He hadn't done this in quite a while—years, in fact—since he'd subbed for someone else's shift. It would be like the old days, chasing cops and robbers, raging fires in the Bronx, shooting in the ghettos. But first, dinner. Nick chuckled as he settled himself at his buddy's crime desk with a slice of pizza and tuned in on the Rangers game. Same game his pal was at, that bum.

Scanners on his desk bantered back and forth. Dumpster fire at Grand Central, a traffic accident on Broadway, and an attempted robbery at the Citibank ATM in Chinatown. A series of beeps in coded sequences would filter through intermittently, signaling various distresses for fire and emergency. In New York City, none of those warranted so much as a raised eyebrow. Nick ignored them and focused on the game while chewing.

The Rangers ought to beat the crap out of the Devils. Sure enough, Wayne Gretzky was about to steal the puck from Martin Brodeur when Sheila Bidlingmaier, the night editor, grabbed the remote control and flipped the channel over to the news, raising the volume.

Nick was about to mouth off, "what the fuck," but stopped short when WABC's Rob Hanrahan came on.

> *"We've just learned that advertising billionaire Peter Garvey failed to appear at a press conference this evening to announce his run for senate. As of now, no one knows of Garvey's whereabouts, but authorities are taking his disappearance very seriously. Jennifer Liu reports live at the New York Public Library on Fifth Avenue."*

Liu's sweet face came on, mic in hand, facing the glaring spotlight in front of the camera.

> *"Thank you, Rob. Senate hopeful Peter Garvey has not appeared at his scheduled press confer-*

*ence to officially announce his candidacy. I spoke
with his campaign manager, Rick Wolcott."*

The camera switched to a closeup of Rick Wolcott, trying to appear calm.

"I fully expect him to be here. I'm sure there's a logical explanation for his delay. We should know soon."

As the TV droned on, Nick laid his pizza on a greasy paper plate and turned to the scanners, raising the volume. He also turned up the local police scanners while keeping his other ear tuned to the TV for more reports of Garvey.

After ten minutes, Nick frowned. The scanners should have been buzzing with chatter about the missing Senate nominee. In his twenty-plus years as a reporter, Nick knew that when the airwaves went silent, it meant one thing—something big was happening, and the cops were scrambling signals or switching to secure channels.

He picked up the phone and called his detective pal, Lieutenant Richard Molino. It was great timing because Molino was en route to the Garveys' apartment. "Nickie, I can't tell you what's happening because I don't know," Molino said. "I got the call from the guy's partner. I think Garvey's home, but that's all I know until I get there."

Nick didn't press for more. He picked up his keys and hollered to Bidlingmaier, "I'm off to Sutton Place to check on the Garveys."

Luke

DECEMBER 8, 1998
NEW YORK, NEW YORK

Luke had just dumped the empty container of the take-out dumplings he had for dinner. Twisting open another beer, he settled into his armchair to watch the special broadcast of Peter's big announcement. Instead, he heard WNBC reporter Grady Wallace come on for breaking news.

> *"Senate hopeful Peter Garvey has not announced his candidacy for U.S. Senator and, according to sources, missed his press conference, which was scheduled at 8. Reporting live at the New York Public Library is Elisa Kwan. Elisa?"*

Luke didn't need to hear the rest before dialing Raine's cell but got no answer. He tried Jim, who said he'd sent Raine home to check on Peter, while the senior partner tried to keep the event from turning chaotic with innuendo and rumors. Luke didn't wait. He grabbed a coat and, within seconds, was outside hailing a cab.

Sitting anxiously in the back seat, he tried Raine's cell phone again without success, then called Jim back.

"She's not answering, Jim," Luke howled. "I'm on my way to their apartment. Ten minutes tops... Yeah, I'll keep you posted."

Despite the light traffic, it seemed an interminable trip as they passed block after painful block. Save for diners, delis, and bodegas, most of the retail shops on First Avenue were gated down and darkened, although a few storefront windows left their blinking Christmas lights.

When the cab approached the building, he noticed a couple of reporters and a cameraman chatting about by the entrance. As the taxi slid to the curb just past the building entrance, Luke pulled his knitted hat below his ears and raised his winter coat collar to hide his identity as best he could. He hopped out and walked briskly toward the glass doors where the doorman, who thankfully recognized him, quickly ushered him inside, but not before a reporter called out, "Sir, do you live here? Can we talk to you?"

"Thanks, Johnny." Luke nodded to the doorman in relief.

"You're welcome, Mr. Henes."

"Have you seen the Garveys come home yet?" Luke asked Johnny.

"Mr. Garvey came home an hour ago, but Mrs. Garvey arrived just a few minutes ago. She came in the side door. I guess she was trying to avoid those reporters out there. Don't know why they keep asking if they are here. Did something happen?"

Luke released an audible sigh. At least they were both home. He would go up to make sure everything was all right.

"I'm going to find out, Johnny. Hope you didn't talk to the reporters."

"Never, Mr. Henes."

"Good."

With his copy of the elevator card and front door keys, Luke made his way up to the penthouse floor.

After trying the doorbell three times and hearing no response, Luke slowly unlocked the door and poked his head inside.

He scanned the room. Finding only Raine's purse on the hallway table, Luke called out.

"Raine? Peter?" He walked inside and closed the door behind him.

He heard a voice... like someone was singing and it was coming from the bedroom.

"Hey, guys? Everything all right here?" Luke followed the crooning, feeling more relieved that they were home.

But the relief evaporated when Luke entered the bedroom, his breath catching in his throat as the sight hit him like a punch to the chest.

"Oh my God!" Luke stood frozen in disbelief as his eyes traveled to the ceiling, gasping at the horror he saw when he spotted a segment of rope dangling from an exposed beam.

Raine sat on the floor, clutching Peter's limp body against her, her voice barely a whisper, singing a lullaby in a language Luke didn't recognize. A knife glinted on the floor beside a severed length of rope, like some dark afterthought. Her eyes, glassy and unseeing, were locked in a distant gaze as she rocked Peter, her trembling voice begging him—pleading for him—to wake up.

"Oh, Raine, love, I'm so very sorry." Luke knelt next to her, choking the tears that flowed without restraint as he tried to take Peter from her arms, but she wouldn't let go.

Luke sprung to action, grabbing his cell phone, calling not 9-1-1 but a detective friend, Rich Molino, from the NYPD.

"Richie, it's Luke. I need you. It's an emergency. It's Garvey, and it isn't good. Get an ambulance and tell them to wait by the back door. I'll have maintenance meet them there. Richie, please hurry and watch out for reporters outside. No sirens or flashing lights."

His next call was to the doorman, instructing him to have maintenance meet an ambulance by the service entrance and keep it quiet.

When Molino arrived with the EMTs pulling a gurney behind them, Luke knelt beside Raine and wrapped his arms around her shoulders.

"Raine, sweetie, let the paramedics take care of Peter now," he whispered, his voice breaking. "It's going to be okay. I'm here."

She rose with him while the paramedics took over, checking Peter's pulse for a heartbeat, then noting the time to record his official time of death.

She was rigid as a board, her expression hard and unreadable, while they loaded him on a gurney, covered his body with a white sheet, and wheeled him away. Staring into space, Raine was unable to answer Molino's questions. Luke somehow managed to choke through what he knew and how he found them. They checked the apartment thoroughly, brushed for fingerprints, and found no foul play. It was a sad and tragic end to his closest friend's life.

When Raine started shaking and sweating, one of the medics checked her heart rate and blood pressure.

"Mrs. Garvey, you're having an anxiety attack. I want you to take this pill. It's a mild sedative. This will help you relax and get some sleep," the medic said, then turned to Luke. "Somebody should stay with her."

Luke nodded, and after everyone had left, he took stock of the place, still in shock and disbelief. Molino's guys had removed the remaining rope and taken the kitchen knife as evidence. Once a charming feature of the prewar building, the exposed ceiling rafter now cast a dark shadow over the room. Luke shuddered at the thought of Raine continuing to live here, surrounded by memories that would haunt her. Something about Peter's death felt off, but now wasn't the time to delve into those suspicions. His priority was Raine.

He walked to the liquor shelf and poured himself a stiff drink. Before he took a sip, he shuddered uncontrollably as his tears flowed again, not only for the loss of his best friend—but also for the woman he loved, who would now be irrevocably broken.

CHAPTER 5

Ron

Despite the damp, chilly temperature, the sun felt warm to Ron as he stood on the front porch of Frank Murdoch's house with Goober in tow. It was the winter semester break, and he was house and dog-sitting for the dean and his wife while they soaked up some rays on Sanibel Island.

"He's the lucky dog as far as I'm concerned, Goobs," Ron said to the mutt, patting him for sitting still while he snapped on the leash. Goober didn't care that his owner had gone to a tropical island without him. So long as someone took him for a walk, fed him, or played with him with a stick, he was happy.

Leash in hand, Ron let Goober lead the way through the Oyster River trail behind the campus where the mutt could sniff out little critters and other scents along the way, and do his business.

After a two-mile hike, Ron and Goober emerged onto Mill Road then strolled down the sloping street heading for the old Callahan house. He didn't know why, but something about the neglected structure always drew him. It was love at first sight for Ron, and he'd vowed to buy the house one day and bring the old dame back to her glory days.

Once he graduated and successfully defended his dissertation in the fall, he'd be done with school and be appointed full professor. The college fund his late father had left for him and his sister would be distributed, and Ron would have enough to buy the house with his share.

He'd envisioned restoring every piece of woodwork, stripping, cleaning, and polishing every beam and cornice till it gleamed. The house was a dream born from the visions the fae had sent him. A vision of him by a crackling fire, on a plush rug with pillows strewn about, making love to his future wife. Her face was a mystery, but he imagined her to be beautiful and kind, someone who could see beyond his dorkiness and love him for who he was.

But as he got closer, Ron stopped in his tracks, yanking poor Goober from charging ahead. There was no missing the blazing-red Jeep Wrangler sitting in the driveway. It looked brand new, with temporary license plates, so Ron couldn't tell where it was from.

No, No, please. Let it not be sold.

But the *for-sale* sign was gone.

"Looks like someone's moved in, Goobs," Ron said, his heart sinking. The retriever mutt with his floppy spaniel-like ears yelped, resisting Ron's tug on the leash.

"One sec, Goob. I know it's time for your breakfast."

He searched for movement inside the house, scanning from the front room to the top floor. But the high sun only reflected the cloudless sky against the dirty panes.

Who would have bought such a rundown shack? Was he someone who also wanted to restore the house? Or was it some speculator looking to fix the place with shabby contracted work then flip it for a quick buck?

Goober barked while a deflated Ron sighed and turned to leave with his four-legged companion.

Raine

JANUARY 2000

DURHAM, NEW HAMPSHIRE

I awoke from my grief-laden sleep to strange but cheerful sounds. Crawling out of the sleeping bag, I walked to the window to check out my new world. Sparrows perched on the branches of a maple tree outside my bedroom window were arguing noisily. I heard bells pealing from a nearby church, and a dog barked. I was definitely not in New York.

Through the hazy windowpanes that begged a good cleaning, I squinted against the rising winter sun and watched my garrulous, feathered tenants take off. On the street below, I saw a young man surveying the house with his dog on a leash. His head tilted upwards as if looking straight at me. I tried unlatching the window but couldn't raise the sash; it wouldn't budge. I noticed layers of paint sealing it shut.

Making a mental note to add replacement windows to my growing list of house renovations, I pulled on a pair of drawstring pants underneath my T-shirt and went down to make coffee. Then someone banged on the door.

"I'm coming!" I yelled, thinking it was the guy with the dog.

Jeez, he should learn to knock more gently.

Instead, a huge, burly man filled my doorway and said gruffly, "You ordered a two-ton dumpster?"

"What?" I asked, looking confused. But when I tiptoed to look beyond his shoulder and saw the green container with BIG BOY HAULING painted on its side, I remembered that I had asked the realtor to order a dumpster. I hastily nodded and signed the receipt where he marked X.

I looked around for the guy with the dog, but they had already left. Oh well, I shrugged. It was time to get to work.

But first...coffee.

In the tiny kitchen stood an old butcher-block table and stool—the only piece of furniture that the owners left behind. I sat on it, sipping my coffee, letting my mind drift back to a time when I was twelve, and my Scots-born mother had whisked my father and me to the remotest part of the Highlands so far north as to be removed from nearly all civilization and anything connected to technology. My Da, as fathers were referred to in Scotland, had suffered a minor stroke from the stress of running his high-profile restaurant in Beverly Hills catering to the high-brow Hollywood crowd and *culinerati*. His cardiologist said he was fortunate. There had been no damage to his heart. This time. But he wouldn't be so lucky again if he kept the same pace and put pressure on himself. I'll never know how my mother convinced my *thick-haided* father to get as far away from LA for a month.

Her family owned a cottage in Kirtomy, about a two-and-a-half-hour drive north of Inverness. It had once been a bothy that sheltered travelers who sought shelter from a storm in the old days. This one was perched on a small hill overlooking a landscape dotted with farmhouses in the distance. From the front, the house faced a stretch of lazy pastoral fields with Scottish white highland cattle, while the back porch overlooked the North Sea. On a clear night, you might see the

Strathy Lighthouse in the distance, winking its light to warn ships off its rocky shoals.

A path carved among the wild, fragrant Scottish heather led down to a pebbly beach where, on warm days, it was pleasant enough to enjoy a quick swim in the shallow tidal pools.

Despite its size, the house had a cozy living room with an overstuffed sofa and two armchairs flanking a stone fireplace. A dining table with six chairs sat on the other end near the kitchen.

I remember my father falling in love with it despite its tight footprint—unusual since he was used to the six-hundred-square-foot kitchen at his restaurant. This one had a small electric range, a deep farmhouse kitchen sink, and a woodblock counter connecting the sink to a peninsula with two stools meant for breakfast. Here, he was most inspired to create new dishes and plating designs and would test them on my mother and me, requiring none of the fancy tools of the trade.

Those memories now inspired my vision for this house. I ran my hand over the worn butcherblock table and let my eyes wander around the kitchen, picturing its transformation and renewal. Already, it felt like home, which made me wonder.

Could I really do this? You know, live here? As in, like, forever?

CHAPTER 6

Raine

JANUARY 2000

DURHAM, NEW HAMPSHIRE

"Can I help you?"

A man wearing an apron with the *True Value Hardware* logo embroidered across his chest noticed me fiddling around in the tape section—electrical, masking, painting, Velcro, and even the lowly Scotch tape—frowning in confusion. Why so many different kinds?

"Yeah, if you've got a few minutes," I said, turning to the man who spoke to me.

He was maybe in his fifties, with only the faintest wrinkles when he smiled. Judging by how he peered *down* at me above the spectacles perched on the bridge of his nose, he must have been at least six-foot-five. With the UNC baby-blue ball cap he sported, I'd bet he played on the hardwood with the legendary Tarheels.

"I moved into the house on Mill Road, and it needs work," I said, retrieving my notebook and pen from my tote bag. "I took some notes on what I would like to do. Since I've never done this, could you tell me what I need?"

"You bought the old Callahan house?" Then he whistled when he glanced at my notebook.

"I know I'm new at this, but I want to try. I've got some how-to videos..." I trailed off, sensing his disbelief, worried he'd snort and send me off to hire contractors instead. My eyes must have looked woeful and pleading because then he smiled.

"Okay, tell you what. Let's break down your list and see what you can do today. Then you can come back for what's next."

"Thank you! I appreciate it." I sighed with relief.

"I'm Tye McBean, by the way," he said, holding his hand out. "I'm the store owner."

"Raine Garvey," I replied, shaking his hand.

"Nice to meet you, Raine," he said genuinely.

"You played for Carolina?" I asked, pointing to his cap.

"Point guard. '76."

"I'm Tarheel born and Tarheel bred, and when I die, I'll be Tarheel dead," I chanted the famous Carolina cheer, eager to show off some sports knowledge.

Tye laughed. "You a fan?"

I grimaced. I'd be damned if I would admit I was a Tarheel fan.

"Bruins," I replied with UCLA pride, even if I'd only attended for a semester.

"Oooh... them's fightin' words, young lady. I might have to upcharge you for being anything but a Tarheel fan." He winked at me.

"Oh, puh-lees. It's not like I was a Blue Devil fan." I rolled my eyes. The Blue Devils of Duke University were a bigger nemesis for Carolina than UCLA.

We both laughed at our sports rivalry silliness.

"So you're from LA?"

I nodded. "Originally. But I've lived in New York for ten years, until yesterday anyway."

"What brings you to Durham?"

I considered his question, wondering how much of me I wanted to reveal, then replied. "Sabbatical. I needed a break. I wanted to see if I could do something different."

"Welcome to Durham. Now, let's get back to your list." I was glad for the topic change.

After spending a few hundred dollars, Tye helped me remove the back seat of my Jeep and offered to hold it to make room for all my purchases—including a wheelbarrow, which he assured me I would need.

He shut the tailgate and gave it a couple of slaps to signal that everything was set, then shouted, "Remember, if you need something or run into a problem, just call me."

"Don't worry. I get the feeling this place will be my second home," I quipped, waving as I slowly pulled away from the curb, taking care not to jostle the precariously propped wheelbarrow on top of all the shopping bags of tools and supplies that filled the back of the Jeep.

Just as I pulled away, an orange Mazda Miata slid into the spot I'd just vacated.

Cool car. Cute driver. I glanced back from my rearview mirror and eyed him as he climbed out of his car. *Oh, and uhm... yeah, sexy too. Wait, was that the same guy I saw earlier this morning with a dog?*

All that talk of college sports and now ogling a cute young driver in a sports car made me feel like I was nineteen and back at UCLA. As if ten years of my life in New York never existed.

Ron

JANUARY 2000

DURHAM, NEW HAMPSHIRE

R on couldn't miss the distinctive red Jeep Wrangler pulling away from the curb in front of the hardware store, a
wheelbarrow teetering precariously over a load of supplies.

"New kid on the block," Tye said, catching Ron's questioning look, his gaze lingering longer as it drove off.

"Must be. I saw the Jeep this morning at the Callahan
House. Same one?" Ron finally turned to Tye.

"Yeah, the new owner," Tye confirmed while Ron followed
him inside.

"Wasn't there talk of a New York developer buying the
place?" Ron asked.

"She's from New York. I don't think she's a developer
because she intends to work on the house herself."

"By *herself*?" Ron tried to hide his surprise. "Does she know
what she's doing?"

"Yes, by herself, and no, she's never done any renovation
work. She's got some ambitious plans. I started her on the
simple stuff. We'll see. Gotta give her props for trying."

"Huh," Ron shrugged, grabbing a pack of batteries. He
was dying to gossip but played it cool.

Despite what Tye had said about the new owner doing all
the work herself, it seemed farfetched. Probably married, or
has a boyfriend, Ron thought.

"Dinnae be a numpty. Ye're being sexist, like," the fae
chided, their voices weaving into his mind unexpectedly and
interrupting his thoughts. It was annoying, really. Ron resisted
rolling his eyes in front of Tye. Stupid *An Dà Shealladh*.

Of all the gifts he might have inherited from his Gaelic ancestors, this was the most useless. Instead of his forbearer's towering Viking height, hairy broad chest, and angular jaw, he was under six feet tall, with no chest hair, and was baby-faced to boot. Instead, he got the gift of Two Sights, which was maddening because if something were destined to happen, there would be nothing he could do to change its course.

Leannan Sith, Maighdeann-mhara, and Baobhan Sith were the fae that sent him visions in his sleep. They guided his destiny. Well, Gaelic folklore says they were beautiful but evil. To Ron, they were like having three benevolent Scottish aunts. They loved him, but they were mischievous. And they nagged. It was so not funny.

He quickly paid for his merchandise and left before he could say any more.

He was tempted to return to the trail he and Goober followed this morning to spy on her unloading her Jeep. She would need help unloading, and he could offer to assist. Then maybe she'd invite him inside, and he could see what it looked like, probably depressing him further of the lost opportunity to own the house. But if she was cute...

"What's wrong wi' ye? Ye sound like a creepy stalker," nagged the Siths.

Jesus Christ! It was way too early for them to be scolding him.

Raine

R emoving flooring was not difficult. Still, it was tedious and back-breaking, what with pulling every nail that tacked the rug to the baseboard. Tye never warned me there would be hundreds of them.

I spent six hours groaning and grunting to pull up carpeting rank with years of pet urine and dislodging sections of underlayer and padding glued down for decades. Then with a large Exact-O knife—one of Tye's many suggested tools—I started cutting the shag rug into twelve-inch squares, loaded them onto the wheelbarrow, and wheeled them to the dumpster.

I was hot, sticky, and dirty, but I stripped the floors in the living and dining rooms to bare wood, saving the kitchen linoleum for another day.

After sweeping up the leftover debris, I knelt and ran my hand over the wide oak planks, carefully avoiding splinters. The golden hue peeking through the haze of leftover adhesive made my chest swell with relief and pride. What an indescribable sense of accomplishment I felt. This was an even bigger deal than the day my company went public. The manual labor and physical exhaustion that made me ache all over was like a drug-inducing high.

I rose to stretch my spine backward. Time for a long soak in that claw-foot tub in the upstairs bathroom, the one room in the house I fell in love with and didn't require any renovation.

For now, Peter, New York, and all that mess were the furthest from my mind.

CHAPTER 7

Raine

JANUARY 2000
DURHAM, NEW HAMPSHIRE

Despite the falling temperatures, I decided to walk to town for dinner. I wanted the fresh air and the stretching of tight calf muscles and limbs from today's exertion. Bundled in a long, puffy winter coat with a hood, fur-lined boots, and gloves, I trudged toward Main Street. The cold felt clean and refreshing, contrasting the day's labor.

The campus was quiet, with students still on winter break. Shops were closed, but a pizza joint and the old tavern were well-lit.

I surveyed the university in twilight, its scant but modern buildings sprawled on acres of ground. This school was nothing like the vast UCLA campus where I'd once spent my freshman year. Durham unwound in the evenings while UCLA revved up at night.

1989. God, that was a lifetime ago.

The small, bright neon signs gracing the tiny windows and the weary front door made Joplin's Jazz Tavern look like a cheesy dive, but it was homey and inviting. Only a few cars were parked in the empty lot, although I spotted the orange

Miata again. I mean, how many pumpkin-colored sports cars could there be in this town?

Inside, the warmth from a woodstove welcomed me. A few young guys—probably grad students—hung out at one end of the bar while Nina Simone's *Feeling Good* played softly. I chose a stool a few seats away from them.

"What can I get you?" asked the short-bearded bartender, setting a cocktail napkin before me.

"What's local?" I asked.

"Mad Viking," he said. "Madeline Aegir brews it in Portsmouth. And she's a true descendent of a Norwegian Viking. Hence the name."

"A woman brewer? I'll go with the Mad Viking then."

"Good choice. Can I see some ID?"

I pulled my wallet from my coat pocket.

After checking my license, he smiled. "You don't look a day over twenty-one."

"Aww, you're sweet to say that."

"Hungry?" he asked after serving my beer.

"Starved. Whatever's cooking smells luscious."

He walked to the end of the bar to retrieve a menu and handed it to me.

"My wife, Rosie, is the resident chef, and she makes a mean chowder that will keep you warm to your toes. Thick, hearty, with a dash of Tabasco to keep the clams jumping."

"How can I resist that? A bowl of chowder then," I said, handing the menu back without looking further.

"You own this place?" I asked while I took in the woodwork of the counter.

"The bar has been in the family for three generations. I've been working here since I was sixteen, then took over almost fifteen years ago. Pop-pop still comes in now and then to 'supervise,'" he said with air quotes and an eye-roll but laughed.

"Nice. Very classy yet homey," I said.

One of the guys at the bar teased, "You callin' Jops classy? You must be new."

I turned to the group and smiled. "Yup, just moved here."

"Yeah?" asked the bartender, Jops.

"Yup, up on Mill Road."

"I noticed your license says you're from New York. So you're the one who bought the Callahan house?" Jops raised his brows. "Please tell me you're not living in it right now, are you?"

"I am. It's not so bad. Electricity's on. It's got hot water, heat, and a flushing toilet." I replied, rapping my knuckles softly on the bar. "I've already started working on it."

He eyed me with skepticism. I couldn't blame him. Heck, I'd be skeptical of myself too.

"I thought you were a freshman at UNH. You look too young to be a homeowner fixing an old house."

"Wow, I'm flattered. You probably say that to all the coeds who come here," I smiled.

One of the guys from the group heckled, "Yo Jops, you flirting? Rosie won't like it."

"Shut up, Fritzso," Jops replied, then turned back to me. "Ignore him. Fritzso's a goofball. I'm Ken Joplin, by the way. No relation to the legendary jazzman."

"Raine Garvey," I said, shaking his hand.

"So you're really going to work on the house yourself?"

"As much as I can," I said proudly, taking another swill of my drink. "I got all that ugly carpeting out of the living and dining room already. Gorgeous flooring underneath. I intend to sand it. I have a long way to go, but one day at a time. Like Tye says, baby steps."

"Ah, you've met Tye McBean. He's a good guy to know if you intend to do renovation work. If you need an extra hand, let me know. I did the inside of this bar myself," Jops boasted.

"Impressive," I said. "I might take you up on your offer."

I spotted a young woman, probably Rosie, peering through the kitchen's pass-through. She was sliding a steaming bowl of chowder with a buttered roll on the side. I waved at her, and she waved back.

"I take it that was Rosie?" I asked Jops as he set my chowder and roll before me.

"Love of my life and my stomach," Jops said, laughing.

"Smells amazing," I said, sniffing the steam from the bowl.

"*Bon appétit,*" he replied, then turned to the guys and left me to enjoy my meal.

As I ate, I noticed one of them watching me. I recognized him as the Miata driver. He was cute. *And* sexy with his shoulder-length hair framing his baby face. He reminded me of a rocker dude I had a crush on when I was in high school, but I can't remember the band's name now. The way he avoided my eyes though, made him seem awfully shy. I returned to my chowder, smiling, feeling something I hadn't felt in a long while—butterflies.

Ron

JANUARY 2000
DURHAM, NEW HAMPSHIRE

Ron couldn't keep his eyes from Durham's newest resident. That brief glimpse of her this morning didn't prepare him for how attractive she was. Sophisticated and polished, she leaned lazily over the counter, arching her back in a way that seductively accentuated her figure, like a cat stretching from a nap.

Her bangs fringed just above her brows, not hiding those hazel-amber eyes. Ron pulled a swig of beer, ignoring his buddies' banter until Ed waved a hand in front of his face.

"Earth to Ron. Yo!"

"Yes, you were saying?" Ron finally shifted his attention to Ed, who, along with Fritzso, had been his best friend since they were on training wheels.

But Ron's gaze drifted back to the woman, ignoring his buddies. She tipped her beer, lengthening her neck, then tasted her chowder, her eyes closing in bliss. He imagined her with that expression under him—naked.

Get yer mind oot o' the gutter, lad. Ron heard the fae nagging again.

For someone who was so introverted around women, he couldn't figure out why he was thinking lustful thoughts. But something about her drew him beyond physical attraction.

Ron tried to convince himself that his interest in meeting this bewitching new homeowner was self-serving—he wanted the house. If he ingratiated himself to her, she'd give him first right of refusal when she returned to New York. He was almost too confident that she would soon get frustrated with renovating the house and leave town, although that thought seemed to depress him. Did he really want her to go?

Ed noticed Ron's focus.

"Well, hell, just go talk to her," Ed said, nudging him.

Ron blushed and mumbled something, lowering his gaze.

Ed cupped his ear toward Ron. "What's that? Your 'attractive female anxiety disorder' kicked in?"

Ed's loud tease made Raine turn. Ron glared at Ed while Fritzso stood up.

"Well, in that case," Fritzso started, "I'll go introduce myself."

Ron gripped Fritzso's shoulder firmly, keeping him in place.

"Okay, pal, I'll give you twenty-four hours. Then she's mine," Fritzso declared, raising his hands.

Ed interrupted, "On that note, it's time to go, kids. School night for us professors."

Ron saw Raine look up at them again as if she was about to say something. But then Ron panicked. Quickly pivoting to Ed, he said, "Yup, let's go."

As he stumbled past her, he found it oddly familiar and mildly disturbing that he caught her scent. It gave him the sense of being in a field of flowers rather than inside a beer joint.

Once outside, Fritzso turned to Ron and reminded him, "Twenty-four hours, pal."

"She's too good-looking for you, pig. Look at that gut!" Ed remarked.

Fritzso swung away to avoid Ed's fake punch.

"Hey, the ladies love my six-pack," he laughed, patting his muscled midriff.

Ron ignored the wisecracks. He waited for his friends to drive away before starting up his car. While the engine warmed up, he saw Raine exit Joplin's Jazz, pulling her hood up.

"Uhm... Hi!" he called out, cranking down his window.

"Oh, hi!" she responded.

"Are you, ah, walking home?"

"Yeah, it's not far."

"D-do you want a ride?"

Ron sensed her hesitation.

"I mean...it's safe around here, but I'd feel better if you got home safely. Or, I could, um, walk with you?"

Jesus, why was he stuttering so badly?

She chuckled.

"Jops knows me," he added, hopeful.

After a moment, she rounded the car and slipped inside.

"Thank you so much," she said, rubbing her hands. "I hope I'm not taking you out of your way."

"No, um... you're not."

As he drove her home, darkness enveloped them. He felt a spark of energy between them and wondered if she felt it too. Her tentative smile told him she did. But before she could say anything else, he was pulling into her driveway.

"Hey, thanks again," she said quickly. "You saved me from freezing to death."

Before he could reply, she jumped out and ran to the house.

Crap! He scared her. Within the five-minute drive from Jops' to her house, he wondered what he might have said or done to make her run off like that.

Baffled by her abrupt departure, Ron could only shake his head as he backed out of the driveway.

Raine

JANUARY 2000

DURHAM, NEW HAMPSHIRE

"Hey, thanks again," I quickly said. "You saved me from freezing to death."

Before he could say anything, I jumped out of the car and ran to the house.

Once inside, I immediately regretted running off like a scared mouse. He must have thought I was a weirdo for my rather hasty exit. I didn't even introduce myself or ask his name. That was rude of me.

After he left, I stumbled in the dark through the partially demolished house and reached for a bottle of single-malt scotch. I filled a Styrofoam cup with a shot and sipped it slowly, savoring the smoky spirit and then feeling it course through my veins, warming me up.

In the dark, I tried to conjure up Peter's face. Instead, the shy man who gave me a ride home tonight kept intruding on my thoughts. Through the blur of aching memories, his warm brown eyes felt comforting. Even healing.

Was it time to let go of the past? To forgive? But how could I forgive something when I still didn't understand why Peter chose suicide? Certainly not for the lies that came after.

CHAPTER 8

Raoghnailt

DECEMBER 1998
BEVERLY HILLS, CALIFORNIA

She heard the snap—a sharp, sickening crack so violent it jolted her awake, a guttural howl tearing from her throat. Deep in sleep beside her, Tono bolted upright, instinctively reaching out to calm her flailing arms.

"Rae, wake up!" he urged with concern as he tried to pull her back from the nightmare's grip.

Raoghnailt pushed her husband away in a panic and began frantically packing a suitcase.

"Somethin' verra, verra bad's gonnae happen tae Peter," she cried, her voice trembling. "The lass needs me, Tono. I must go tae her."

Tono followed, grabbing his wife by the shoulders and gently forcing her to face him. His eyes searched hers, seeking to ensure she was truly awake.

"Rae, sweetheart," Tono said, "what did you see?"

"I dinna see it. I only heard it—a crack, like his neck breakin', and then silence. He's goin' tae die. Tonight. We must get tae Rainey an' warn her."

Raoghnailt's body trembled with grief threatening to drown her. Then, the weight of ten years of regret settled heavily on them. The memories of harsh words and the bitter estrangement with their only daughter came flooding back.

"*I fucking hate you!*" Her daughter's last bitter words still echoed in Raoghnailt's mind. The years of distance and silence have not erased them from her memory.

Tono pulled Rae into his arms, his own heart breaking as he held her close. For several long minutes, they clung to each other until her shuddering finally began to subside.

"Rae, in all these years, she hasn't returned our calls," Tono whispered, his voice raw with emotion. "Even if we went to New York, would she want to see us?"

"We have tae try, Tono," Raoghnailt insisted, her voice barely a whisper. "We can go tae her office where she an' Peter works. They have tae let us see her."

Tono hesitated, then gently suggested, "Why don't you try to reach her mind?"

Raoghnailt nodded, a flicker of hope in her eyes. "If her mind's open..." But she knew too well that Rainey had previously blocked her telepathic messages.

"We can also call her office in the morning," Tono suggested, trying to ease her distress. "Right now, that's all we can do, Rae. If *An Da Shealladh* says it will happen tonight, you know we cannot stop it."

Tono was right. She shook her head in despair and cried again. Laying her hands on his chest, she pushed Tono away gently, "Ye go back tae bed, *mo ghràdh*. I'm sorry I woke ye."

Tono sighed, kissing her forehead softly. "I've told you before, you should never be sorry. I want to be with you when you have a bad vision like this. Especially when it's about Rainey."

"Aye, I'm fine now. Ye barely had an hour's sleep and hae tae wake soon. Ye need yer sleep," she urged softly. "I'll make meself some tea then follow ye soon."

"Are you sure you'll be alright?"

Raoghnailt managed a slight nod, nudging him back to bed.

Once he was settled, she quietly slipped on an overcoat, her mind too restless for sleep or tea.

Before stepping outside, she called and left a message on her daughter's office voicemail—in Gaelic—hoping she would get it in time.

"A nighean, na fàg taobh do fhir an-diugh. Cùm ris, agus na leig às do làmh." My daughter, do not leave your husband's side today. Stay with him, and do not let go of his hand.

Her words carried the weight of a mother's love and a seer's warning without revealing too much, hoping against hope that her daughter would receive it.

Outside, the cool night air bit into her skin as she walked to a small clearing in the backyard, just past the towering juniper trees she and Rainey had planted twenty-five years ago. She looked up at the stars, rare to see in the light-polluted sky of Los Angeles.

A floodlight spilled a warm, incandescent glow across the hillside, illuminating the rows of rainbow chard, their stalks ready to burst into vibrant orange, yellow, and red colors. They would soon be ready for whatever Tono would create for the winter menu.

Hearing a rustle of footsteps in the wild brush at the edge of the property, Raoghnailt froze. A chill raced down her spine. She pulled her robe tighter, her senses heightened, alert for intruders. Even if she thought that anyone reaching their hillside home in the dark would have likely been killed. The steep drop covered in thorny desert bramble bushes was nearly impossible to scale. Then she gasped as a shadow approached.

"Whit in the name o' aw that's holy, Uncle Angus! Whit on earth are ye daein' here?" Raoghnailt sputtered, pressing a hand to her heart to calm its frantic beating.

"Now, is tha' a way tae greet yer uncle, lass?" Angus replied with a warm chuckle, stepping into the light. "It's been a wee while, after all."

Dressed in his traditional woolen kilt of the MacDonald of the Isles tartan, Angus looked as strong and youthful as she remembered him from childhood. The vibrant red of his kilt, crisscrossed with stripes of dark green, black, white, and yellow, was as striking as ever. Around his waist, his sporran gleamed in the light, and his woolen hose, tied below the knee, led down to his ghillie brogues. He held a long wooden staff, the kind he had once used to hike the rugged Scottish Highlands.

"Shall I put on the kettle?" Raoghnailt asked, her voice still trembling.

"Och, lass, dinna worry yersel' wi' the tea," Angus said, his tone gentle as he approached her. "There's a sadness in ye that runs deep, an' I could feel it across the veil."

Raoghnailt lowered her eyes, the weight of her sorrow threatening to overwhelm her. But Angus tipped her chin up to meet his gaze. He looked at her with the same steady eyes that had once guided her through the early days of her visions when *An Da Shealladh* first came to her. He was her mother's brother, also blessed with the gift, and it was from him that Raoghnailt inherited her magic.

"Aye, lass, I ken ye've seen it—Peter's end. The vision's come tae ye, has it no'?"

"Nae, Uncle. The fae sought tae spare me the sight. Still, I canna shake it. How can I just stand by an' do naught for me bairn?"

Raoghnailt's voice broke and sobbed quietly. Angus pulled her into his arms, letting her cry as he had done many times before, offering the comfort that only he could provide. When her tears subsided, he moved her face away to look straight into her eyes.

"Listen tae me, Raoghnailt. 'Tis a heavy burden, the sight, but ye ken well 'tis no' yer place tae meddle wi' what's been shown tae ye. Ye called to yer bairn tae warn her, but she'll still choose no' to listen tae ye."

"But Uncle, if there's a chance tae save him—and to save Rainey from the pain—how can I no' try? How can I let it happen?"

"Lass, I ken yer heart's in the right place, but ye must remember, there's a greater plan a' werk. Ye ken Peter's a troubled soul an' tis his choice to join his mither. 'Tis his destiny an' 'tis no' up tae us tae alter it."

"An' Rainey? I canna jes stan' by an' watch her suffer."

"Fer Rainey, the pain is part o' the path she must walk. But ye've tae trust in the wisdom o' the fae an' her own strength. The lass is strong like her mither, aye?"

"I want her tae come home, Uncle," Raoghnailt whispered, her voice breaking again. "She's been awa' too long. She'll be needin' her mama."

"When the time comes, she'll come home." Angus's voice was warm with conviction. "And when she does, ye'll be here, as ye always have been. But fer now, ye must let things happen as they're meant to."

Angus guided Raoghnailt to sit on the nearby garden bench, then knelt before her, taking her hands.

"Rest yer weary heart, ma bairn. One day, the hurt will fade away, an' the fae will fill ye wi' joy. 'Twill come soon, aye? Now there's something ye can believe in." Raoghnailt closed her eyes. She didn't remember falling asleep on the cold marble bench, but in her dreams, she felt Tono's strong arms lifting her and tucking her back into bed while she called out to Raine.

"Tha d'fhearann ort an rathad a choiseachd nad aonar. Fanaidh tu làidir. Ach cuimhnich, bidh mi an-còmhnaidh còmhla riut, ge bith càite a bheil thu. Thig dhachaigh, mo nighean."

CHAPTER 9

Raine

DECEMBER 1998
NEW YORK, NEW YORK

I heard my mother. She called to me the night Peter died. I vaguely remembered being given a sedative while the EMTs laid Peter on a gurney, pronounced him dead, and then wheeled him away. It was that dreamless sleep when my mind was wide open that she spoke to me in Gaelic.

You're destined to walk your path alone. Stay strong. But remember, I will always be with you, no matter where you are. Come home, my daughter.

I didn't know what she meant by "the path I was destined to walk alone." All I could see at that moment was a huge boulder in front of me, with no clue how to move it or see what's behind. I wasn't gifted like my mother. Then I remembered Timmo telling me about a voicemail in a strange language. I wondered if that had been my mother, perhaps warning me because she knew Peter's death was imminent. It was too late for regrets.

The next few days passed in a fog. I felt numb, sleepwalking through the arrangements for Peter's funeral. I couldn't even cry.

It should have rained that day. Instead, the sky was a vast expanse of cloudless cerulean, mocking my sorrow. Only a few black limousines and sedans lined the narrow driveway leading to the mausoleum at Nazareth Cemetery in Radnor, Pennsylvania. The service inside the Van Rostum crypt, where his grandparents' ashes were also interred, was brief. I struggled to mourn for Peter. How could I mourn a death I didn't understand?

On the two-hour drive back to New York, my thoughts returned to that dream. My mother's voice had been so clear, pleading with me to come home. For a moment, I considered it. But then the memory of the day I left my parents nearly ten years ago hit me—how they had hated Peter and fiercely opposed our engagement. I thought my father would hit me that day as if falling in love with Peter was a terrible crime. The sharp pain of missing them quickly turned into resentment.

When I arrived at Jim's home in Fieldston, that resentment had settled into a familiar numbness. I needed to get through the next few hours, and then I could disappear into the solitude I craved.

I stood at the reception line, mindlessly accepting sympathies. I mingled and made polite conversation. But after an hour of holding my pasty smile, I snuck away to Jim's study. Finding it empty, I sank into a leather wingback chair, kicked off my shoes, and tucked my feet under my legs. This had been Peter's favorite chair when he visited, brandy in hand, talking shop with the elder partner. Lulled by the fog of memories, I dozed off.

I wasn't sure how long I'd been asleep when I felt a warm, alcohol-laden breath against my face. I opened my eyes to find Jim's face hovering close, with the scent of brandy. Startled, I sat up, forcing him to step back. His proximity unnerved me, but I brushed it off, embarrassed at having dozed off so casually.

"Hi." He smiled as I stood to search for my shoes.

"God, I'm sorry," I said, resisting the urge to stretch. "I didn't mean to fall asleep. Has everyone left?"

Jim nodded. "I asked Silvey to prepare the guest room. You should go upstairs and get some rest."

I checked my watch—almost eight p.m. I'd been up since four this morning after a restless night. No wonder I'd dozed off.

But I shook my head. "Carty's waiting outside. He can take me home," I insisted, gathering my purse.

"Raine, I'm sure it's hard to sleep in the same room where Peter..." he began.

"Hung himself?" I coldly finished his statement.

"I'm sorry."

"I'm fine! Stop with the sympathies already, or I'll scream!" I said, raising my voice. Immediately, I regretted the outburst. "I'm sorry."

"I think I understand what you're going through," Jim said. "I smashed a glass against the wall in this room when Helen died."

"I'm sorry," I repeated, mortified by my behavior. He'd been kind, helping with the funeral and the reception. But I was exhausted. Still, he stopped me as I headed for the door.

"Raine, I know this is bad timing, but..." he hesitated.

"Is something wrong?" I asked.

"I'm concerned about our clients, particularly the ones Peter brought in. They are our largest clients and the lifeline of the firm. We can't have them thinking we can't service their accounts without Peter. I'm also worried about the competition taking advantage."

I shouldn't have been surprised. So, people who offered condolences today also circled like vultures, ready to poach the spoils?

"I also noticed that snake Nick Coelho, from *The Tribune*, was here. I don't know how he got in, but I guarantee he's sniffing around for news," Jim said, taking a final swig from his brandy snifter. "I won't be able to find a new CEO immediately, Raine. These things take time.

"Take a couple of weeks off, but you need to return to the office," he continued. "Talk to the clients, reassure them that the work won't suffer. Tie up loose ends Peter left behind. Finish what's undone and keep things running until we find someone to fill his spot. You can ask Grey, Luke, me, or even Rosemary if you have questions."

I was baffled. Peter had an army of vice presidents qualified to step in. Jim must have suspected my bewilderment. He walked up to me, touched my arms, and ran his hands down their length. When I stiffened, he hesitatingly let go and turned to pour himself another drink.

"Honey, others may think they can take over Peter's job, but you're the only one I trust. The only one I know who won't harvest the accounts and leave for another firm—or start a new one. And I know you know Peter's accounts as well as he did."

I winced at his use of "honey." He used it casually with the office staff, but something in his tone didn't sound harmless.

"Shouldn't you be the one taking over?" I asked.

"I'm not an ad man, Raine, but I've watched you work. You have an impressive ability to absorb knowledge and expertise quickly, which means you have a keen sense of our business as much as Peter did. He never acknowledged it, but I have.

"You've worked with our clients before, so you're in the perfect position to help smooth the transition for them."

I took a moment to consider Jim's request. But really, it was a no-brainer. I could bury myself in work, immerse myself in the challenge of keeping the company afloat, avoid grief, keep the pain locked up, throw away the key, and never ever again cry.

I pursed my lips and replied, "I don't need two weeks. I'll be in on Monday."

Nick

DECEMBER 1998
NEW YORK, NEW YORK

Nick watched Raine slip away from the guests as murmurs of speculation and whispers of opportunity wafted discreetly around the room.

Nick liked to think he still had journalism ethics. But when the CEO of *The Tribune* passed her invitation to Garvey's funeral reception to him, he couldn't resist. He assured his editor he wouldn't bother anyone with his trademark in-your-face questions, but that didn't mean he couldn't pick up a story or two.

Amidst the somberly dressed crowd, Nick Coelho moved quietly, blending in as he tuned into the speculation about the impending leadership change and the agency's uncertain future.

"It's anyone's guess what Raine will do since she stands to inherit his entire estate."

Nick's ears perked up at the mention of Raine. He edged closer, swirling his cocktail, catching conversation about clients considering jumping ship. He filed away the details in his head, knowing they would make excellent leads for a follow-up story.

It was nearly eight on a Friday evening, so Monday would be soon enough for him to make calls, verify his info, get quotes, and then contact the agency's PR hack to see if he could get a direct line to York—or, better yet, the widow herself. He was certain he could catch them off guard.

But when Monday rolled around, Nick was greeted by the morning edition of the *Wall Street Journal* on his desk, its glaring front-page headline stopping him cold.

Raine Garvey Appointed Acting CEO of Silverman & York.

He'd been blindsided. He knew this was her doing, and she'd one-upped him. She wasn't the demure trophy wife the public thought she was. No, the cunning Widow Garvey had played him at his own game. Coelho-zero, Garvey-one.

CHAPTER 10

Ron

JANUARY 2000

DURHAM, NEW HAMPSHIRE

"Well?" Fritzso poked his head into Ron's office in the basement of James Hall, where all UNH science faculty had their offices—in shoebox windowless rooms.

"Well, what?" Ron asked, looking up from his old beige Macintosh computer.

Fritzso looked at his watch. "T-minus seven hours before I can ..."

"I gave her a ride home last night," he said, interrupting Fritzso. Now, maybe his buddy would leave him in peace.

"*You what?*"

Ron leaned back in his chair, threw his arms behind his head, and propped his feet on the desk, looking smug.

"You heard me."

"Fine," Fritzso mumbled, walked out, and strode down the hall toward Ed, whose head was poking out of his office, obviously waiting for news.

When Fritzso brandished a twenty in his left hand and raised it high, Ed, wearing the widest grin, caught it as his pal walked by.

Witnessing the scene, Ron yelled at them. "You guys suck!"

Raine

"*Ahhhhhhhhhhhhhhhhhhh!!*"

After finally loosening the nut connecting the kitchen faucet to its water supply, water squirted right into my face. Then, I hit my head against the bottom of the sink before I finally found the shut-off valve.

Good job, Raine.

I'd been trying to move the whole sink unit away from the wall so I could finish peeling off the rest of the old kitchen floor linoleum. It looked easy on video. The sink didn't seem too heavy to drag away from the wall. But now I was sloshing in a big puddle.

Another lesson in renovation: things were not what they always seemed.

"Shit!" I cussed at the heavens and the gods of home improvement.

The extent to which I could quickly grasp knowledge clearly didn't extend to plumbing. I dropped the giant wrench on the floor with a bang in frustration and grabbed a towel to dry myself off as best as I could before picking up the phone, keeping my fingers crossed that a local plumber would be available.

After snagging one who promised to stop by later in the afternoon, I grabbed my keys, wallet, winter jacket, and raced to Tye's store. I didn't even care that I was covered with black smudges from my hands up to my elbows and all over my sweatshirt.

"Cheer up, Raine. Gordon said he can be here next week to pick up the sink and range," Tye said after calling a vintage kitchen equipment restorer in Vermont. "He'd said it would take about a month, so you'll get it back around February. And that's assuming the weather holds. I mean, it is still winter, and it does snow here. Like, a lot."

"Thanks for reminding me, Tye," I grumbled.

Sensing my dejection, he piped up. "I have an idea. You can start sanding the living room and bedroom floors. You'll be done when Gordon arrives to remove your sink and range. Then, you can remove the old linoleum, sand the boards underneath, and start painting.

"Unless you're planning to do a lot of cooking, you can probably get away with just using a microwave and one of those camping cookstoves. Or, if you want, I've got guys who can do it for you if you've had enough."

"Nah... I've already conceded the plumbing to a pro. Let's get started with sanding, shall we?"

Sanding wasn't nearly as traumatizing as plumbing. My skill wasn't perfect, and there were a few uneven ridges in some areas, but overall, it wasn't a bad job. When I started applying a clear coating, the glow that shone right through made all the heartache and disappointment worthwhile. Finally, walking barefoot over the beautifully polished oak planks felt heavenly.

A week later, I'd stopped by Tye's to pick out my paint and painting supplies. After loading them onto my Jeep, I drove to Joplin's Jazz for lunch. I hadn't been back since that first night I moved into town. Maybe I could ask about the shy rocker dude who gave me a ride home that night.

"Hey there, Sunshine," Jops called out as I pushed open the heavy oak doors of the tavern. I loved how he called me "Sunshine," the opposite of my name.

It was well after the lunch rush, and the bar counter was empty.

"Hungry?"

"Starving!" I said, perching onto a stool.

"What's your pleasure?"

"I hear Rosie's burgers and fries are out of this world."

"How do you want it?"

"Medium-well, no cheese; tomato and lettuce on the side."

"You got it. Anything to drink?"

"Scotch. Double. Neat."

Jops raised a brow, walked to the kitchen to place my order, and then came back.

"So, you're either celebrating or you're sulking." He poured two shots of the golden liquor with a hint of cold water to bring out its smoky essence. Scotch is one of the many things I love about my Scottish heritage.

"Definitely celebrating. My floors are finally done! And now I am on to painting."

"Way to go, Sunshine. Want some help with the painting?"

"You offering? I won't say no, you know."

"Then you got yourself an assistant. I'm off next Tuesday."

"I'll take whatever help I can get, and Tuesday sounds great."

Then he pointed to the bruises on my arm and bandages on my three fingers.

"Battle wounds?"

"That's one way to describe them," I said, looking at my elbow.

"How'd you get that one up there?" He asked, pointing to the bluish-black bruise on my left temple.

"Hmmm..." I debated revealing why because it was embarrassing.

"Get into a fight with the sander?" Jops teased, coaxing me to spill it.

"I was trying to drill a hole through a beam in the basement to install a junction box. When I squeezed the power drill, my head turned with it and smacked right into the rafter. I had no idea that could happen."

Jops released a boisterous laugh that echoed around the room. He pulled himself a Corona on tap and raised his glass to my scotch.

"Well then, here's to your battle wounds, Sunshine."

I forgot to ask about the shy rocker dude with long hair.

Ron

JANUARY 2000

DURHAM, NEW HAMPSHIRE

If he was honest with himself, Ron was attracted to Durham's newest resident for reasons other than the house. Ever since that night, he'd given her a ride home, he must have creeped her out because something sparked between them during that short ride—and they both felt it.

Whenever he would park his car at the faculty lot, instead of heading for James Hall, he would detour toward her house, determined to knock just to say hi. A friendly call. Nothing more. But each time, he'd get cold feet.

He'd hoped he would see her at Joplin's again. No such luck. Or at least not when he and the guys were there together.

"She comes at lunchtime," Jops said after Ron mumbled whether anyone had seen Raine since that first night she'd strolled into the bar.

Ed and Fritzso perked up and turned to Ron, which heated his face.

"Wait, haven't you guys hooked up yet?" Ed asked.

When Ron said nothing, Fritzso pounded his fist on the counter, "Dammit it, Dude. You said you gave her a ride home that same night. Did you make that up?"

"I did give her a ride home," Ron spat back defensively.

"And?" Ed and Fritzso choroused, staring at him, waiting for an answer. Jops was chuckling while pouring three glasses of wine for his waitress at the bar's service counter.

"I didn't say I stayed over," Ron blurted out.

"Okay, but didn't you ask her out?" Fritzso demanded.

When Ron remained silent, Ed pressed him, "Did you *at least* get her number?"

Ron shook his head in defeat.

Jops watched Ed and Fritzso pile on poor Ron.

Fritzso muttered to Ed, "Did I just lose a twenty for nothing?"

"I think we need some intervention here, right, Jops?" Ed glanced at the bartender, who was entertained by the exchange.

Ron looked morose. He hated it when his friends would tease him about his lack of courage when asking women out on a date.

"Well, I'm helping her paint the house on Tuesday," Jops said.

"Wait, what?" said all three guys almost in unison.

"I'm coming with you," Fritzso volunteered instantly. "What about you, Ed?"

Fritzso was clearly *not* asking Ron.

"Name the time. I'll meet you there," Ed replied.

"Dang it, guys! You know I have labs on Tuesdays," Ron said, deflated.

He turned to Jops and asked, "Can we do it tomorrow?"

"Ron, Tuesday's my day off. So, I can't tomorrow. But you can do me a favor," Jops offered. "Since you're free, can you bring her the eight-foot ladder I have in the back? She could use it now since she picked up the paint yesterday. She'll probably get started before I have a chance to get there next week. Maybe you can see if she needs help."

"Sure!" Ron perked up while Ed and Fritzso struggled to contain their sniggers.

"So how exactly will you bring the ladder over in your pumpkin?" Ed reminded Ron.

He looked to Jops, who rolled his eyes.

"Fine. You can use my pickup."

Perfect, Ron thought. He now had a legit reason to knock on Raine's door. Maybe he'd bring his boombox. They could rock out while they painted. He mentally sorted through his CD collection—Radiohead, Tom Petty, maybe a little Alice in Chains? Would she go for that, or would it be too dated for her?

"Well, buddy, you've got a big day ahead tomorrow. I think you should call it a night and get some beauty rest," Ed teased, slapping Ron on the shoulder.

"I'm going to get you guys for this," Ron muttered while he rose and paid for his drink, glaring at them. As soon as he left, he knew they'd be making bets on his sorry-ass dating life again, but he didn't care. Humming the words to "Creep," he walked to his car, dreaming of slow dancing with Raine to the song, smearing her nose with paint, and finding the perfect moment to kiss her senseless.

Raine

JANUARY 2000

DURHAM, NEW HAMPSHIRE

I wanted some music. *Loud* music.

Yesterday, I drove to Rochester, about fifteen minutes away, and bought one of those fancy 300-megawatt Bose systems with a multi-CD changer at Best Buy. I intended to shuffle the songs and play them loud.

I excitedly loaded CDs from the '80s: Tears for Fears, Tom Waits, Journey, Bon Jovi, Def Leppard, and Melissa Etheridge, all from my high school years.

With a canvas drop cloth covering the newly finished floors and edges taped, I opened a can of paint—white with a dollop of sunshine yellow. The smell filled the air with a sense of renewal, a new beginning. I was filled with excitement.

This house is going to look amaaazing! But first... *Maestro, music, please.*

When I hit play, *Shout* from Tears for Fears exploded through the house at near wall-shattering levels.

I couldn't help but let the music wrap around me, my heart pounding to the beat of the thumping bass. Then I fingered the strings of the aggressive riffs from Bon Jovi's *Runaway*, simulating Richie Sambora's talent on the electric guitar, bobbing my head and letting my bangs fly around my face.

With my paintbrush as a pretend microphone, I sang along to Melissa Etheridge's *I'm the Only One,* seductively shaking my shoulders to the beat like I was singing to a fan in the front row of my concert. As the bass filtered through me, I was transported to a time when Vivienne and I tooled around in her brand-new Porsche Carrera with the top down, belting out the song at the top of our lungs.

I could almost hear Vivienne's laughter. I allowed myself to forget New York, Peter, and the pain and just lost myself to Cyndi Lauper's *Girls Just Wanna Have Fun*. I surrendered to the joy of who I once was—the bold, loud, daring, and fearless (and sometimes bratty if you asked Vivienne)—Raine 'Nish' Nishiseki.

CHAPTER 11

Raine

MAY 1989
BEVERLY HILLS, CALIFORNIA

"I hate my fucking life! Get up, Vivi. It's eleven."
This wasn't the first time I barged into Vivienne's room, yanked open the curtains, and let sunlight flood her dark sanctuary. I'd been doing this since we met in fifth grade, and just because we'd graduated high school a week ago didn't mean we had to start acting like adults.

"Jesus Christ, Nish. What the fuck is your crisis now?" Vivienne groaned, pulling the covers over her head.

I plopped down on the old Victorian settee she'd rescued from someone's trash in Beverly Hills last year. Shoving aside four days' worth of clothes, I huffed, "My parents bought me a used econobox for graduation. Arrrrgh!" I shrieked. "Why couldn't I have been born to normal parents?"

Vivienne peeked under her quilt, "What are you talking about?"

"If you get your lazy butt out of bed, I'll show you that piece of junk they call a car parked in your driveway."

"Do I have to?"

Vivienne had never been a morning person. Getting her out of bed before noon, especially on weekends or holidays, was like waking the dead.

"We are not poor," I stated, embellishing my drama with exaggerated hand gestures as if I were performing Hamlet on stage. "I didn't even ask for anything as flashy as your Porsche. All I wanted was a new car. But nooo. I come home to find some used Toyota Corolla in the driveway. A dull, drab, *gray* Corolla. The ultimate insult is my parents standing there, smiling, telling me it's mine!"

Vivienne squirmed under the quilt, trying to block me out, but I was on a roll.

"'What's wrong wi' the car?'" I mimicked my mother in her accent. "How could she not know? Then my dad says, 'It'll get you where you want to go. You don't need a new one.' Ugh!

"It already blows that I can't go to Columbia for journalism," I continued ranting and pacing the room. "They said UCLA was just as good because it's close to home, and I could commute. I got that stupid scholarship. 'Why pay good money to go to a school so far away?' And my mother had to add, 'Ye can have a perfectly decent education in town for free!' Meanwhile, everyone else in our class is heading out of town for college, and I'm stuck at a state school, commuting in a *gray* Corolla! Somebody, please take me away from all this! If my Prince Charming walked into this room and asked me to run away with him, I'd do it in a New York minute!"

Vivienne finally gave up the fight, tossing aside the quilt. "Nish, you are such a dramatic bitch."

"Easy for you to say," I pouted, sinking back into the settee with a sigh. "You got the car you wanted. Hell, you got the car I wanted!"

"So fucking what?" Vivienne shot back, suddenly clambering out of bed. "I got the car because my dad feels guilty about not spending time with me. He didn't even show up for graduation. He's in Morocco filming another blockbuster."

"I know. He sent you those gorgeous flowers," I exclaimed, rolling my eyes.

"But *your* parents were there! And I was happy they were there for me too."

Wow. Way to make me feel like a selfish brat.

"Don't you realize you have everything? Now, where are my cigarettes?" she grumbled, rummaging through the pockets of a discarded pair of jeans on the floor for her cigarettes and lighter. Just as she was about to light a stick, she paused, changed her mind, and tossed them on the dresser.

"Shit! I've been trying to quit. Now look what you're making me do. I'd take your parents—and your gray Corolla—any day."

"What?" I asked, stunned. Did she really say she'd take my parents? Was she nuts?

Vivienne Oliver, the epitome of cool, daughter of an Oscar-winning director, envied my life? What was she talking about?

"I love you, Nish, but sometimes you can be such a juvenile, especially when you complain about your parents," she said, heading for her bathroom. She returned with an ashtray, eyeing the cigarette again. I quickly snatched them and flushed them down the toilet.

"Hey!" she protested weakly. "You suck."

I stared at the ceiling, suddenly feeling guilty for coming to her for sympathy. I wanted her to validate my feelings, to tell me I was right and my parents were wrong. But now I felt a lecture coming.

"Your parents cheered for me at graduation. They invited me to join you for dinner afterward. They gave me a Mont Blanc pen to sign my name in style when I became a lawyer. I had no idea what I wanted to do with my life until that night. Thanks to your parents, now I know."

Yes, the fancy Mont Blanc pen, while I got a gray Corolla.

"Did you know I used to dream of being part of your family? Of being your sister? That my parents were dead, and yours had adopted me?"

"Be careful, Vivi. My grass only seems greener from your side of the fence. Do you really think it's better being the daughter of cheapskates who are so overprotective? You have all the freedom you want while I'm constantly restricted."

I was stretching the truth because, after Vivienne's drug overdose scare, my parents took her in whenever Stanley was on location and kept a watchful eye on her. She lived with us, shared the same curfews and chores, and thrived under their care. She loved my parents, and they loved her right back. Gone were her wild ways as she strove to please them. In school, she stuck next to me, studying as I did, never dating because I wasn't allowed in high school, and strove to stay away from the vagaries of bored rich kids our age who had gotten her in trouble. Still, my parents hadn't objected to her dying her hair blue, wearing black lipstick and an eyebrow piercing. So unfair.

Vivienne released a deep breath as if blowing out smoke, presumably to relieve the craving.

"Nish, this conversation is too deep for me this early in the day," she said, pulling on a pair of jeans. "Come on, I'll give you the keys to the Carrera, and you can drive me down to DiNardi's for coffee."

I smiled, grabbed the keys she dangled before me, and declared, "Then we'll take the top down, play loud music, and sing our brains out all three hundred miles to Carmel. We'll get a hotel room and stay over. And we won't tell my parents until we get there."

CHAPTER 12

Ron

JANUARY 2000
DURHAM, NEW HAMPSHIRE

R on heard the thumping bass long before he turned Jops' pickup into Raine's driveway. Pulling the ladder from the truck bed, he kept glancing at the house, unsure if this was the right place. The pounding music was so ear-splitting he doubted anyone could hear the doorbell, let alone his knocking.

"Come on, Raine, open up!" Ron yelled as loud as he could while hammering against the door.

It wasn't as if he didn't enjoy loud head-banging rock as much as the next Gen-Xer, but peering through her front window, the woman was in her headspace, dancing around, and wouldn't hear an explosion if it went off in her front yard.

He tried waving frantically to catch her attention. But then, when the band Journey started its riff on "Don't Stop Believing," Ron began to panic.

"No, no, no, Raine. Not Journey. Anything but Journey," he cried out loud. Jesus, she couldn't have such bad taste in music, could she?

It wasn't that he hated the band. But their music to Ron just made his ears cringe. If he didn't leave soon, he would have a full-blown migraine.

Frustrated, Ron jumped back in the pickup, tires screeching, cursing the faes as he sped away.

Raine

JANUARY 2000
DURHAM, NEW HAMPSHIRE

A bove the din of my fantasy rock concert, I was startled by the sound of screeching tires. I turned to the window in time to see the rear of a truck pulling away. *What was that all about?*

I turned down the volume, opened the door, and noticed a ladder propped against the side of the house. I frowned.

Weird.

Must have been Jops. "Thanks for the ladder. But why didn't you knock? I was home," I said when I rang him.

"You're welcome. Ron dropped it off," Jops said.

"Who's Ron?"

"The guy who gave you a ride home the other night?"

"Oh, him! I didn't hear *him* knock."

"I doubt you could've heard anything over your music," Jops laughed. "He said he knocked as loud as he could."

"Yikes! He must think I'm insane."

"Nah, he was sorry he missed you."

"Well, tell him thank you for me. Are you still coming over Tuesday?"

"Yup. Ed and Fritzso are coming too. We'll knock out the painting in one day."

"Thanks, Jops. You guys are the best." I paused, then asked, "Hey, is Ron coming too?"

"Unfortunately, he can't make it. But Ed, Fritzso, and I will be there on Tuesday."

After hanging up, I felt a little disappointed. Jops, Ed, and Fritzso were great, but there was something about Ron that intrigued me besides his cuteness. I didn't know why.

It was hard to believe how much the house had transformed. With the floors polished and the walls painted—thanks to Jops, Ed, and Fritzso—it was slowly becoming mine. It wasn't just a house I'd bought, it was a space I was shaping with my own hands.

By mid-February, with temperatures stubbornly in the thirties, I gave myself a well-deserved break for my thirtieth birthday. I would celebrate the Scottish way—a fire crackling warmly in the fireplace, a shot of single malt scotch, my soft flannel pajamas, Vivaldi's *Four Seasons* streaming softly through on the sound system, and the comforting pages of *Outlander*—perfect. I nestled into a vintage stuffed armchair—the first piece of furniture I'd bought for the place—and let the novel transport me to another time and place.

I'd barely sat for five minutes when I heard a soft knock. I peered out the front window and spotted two cars parked by the curb and an unmistakable orange Miata in my driveway.

"*Surprise,*" shouted four guys at the top of their lungs when I opened the door, startling me. I clutched my heart and closed my eyes, then heard them all shout, "*Happy Birthday, Raine!*"

There was Ron, looking like a rocker in jeans and a UNH hoodie, probably feeling like an idiot, standing at my door with flowers, a bottle of wine, and a goofy grin. Behind him were Jops holding three pizza boxes, Ed carrying a six-pack, and Fritzso as himself.

"Oh, for chissakes! How the hell did you even know?" I cried with my hands covering my blush.

"Come on, Raine. Let us in. It's freezing out here," Fritzso called out.

"Okay, okay." I held the door open, gesturing them inside. "You guys are nuts."

I ushered everyone to the kitchen while I ran upstairs to quickly change into jeans and a pullover, brush my hair, and smear lip gloss to color my pale mouth.

When I returned, Ron handed me a nosegay of blue flowers and a bottle of wine.

"Oh my God! Scottish Bell Heather. Where in the world did you get these? And at this time of year?"

"I hope they're okay," he mumbled shyly.

It was more than okay. How did he know they were my favorite? I was so delighted that I pulled him into a tight hug, which startled him as he tentatively hugged me back.

He looked so cute when he blushed.

After ceremonially lighting three candles on the pizza— one for each decade of my life—and me blowing them out awkwardly, I asked, "Okay, so who did the police search on my birthdate?"

"Guilty," Jops admitted. "You showed me your ID, re-member? Since you haven't been coming by at night, we de-cided to bring the celebration to you. Besides, it's also a wel-come-to-the-neighborhood that's long overdue."

"You're sneaky."

"I see you've already started celebrating," Jops said, notic-ing me putting my scotch in the mini-fridge to save for another time and accepting the red solo cup he'd poured wine into.

"Yes, until I was rudely interrupted," I teased back.

Jops laughed as his eyes fell on my newly installed Magic Chef vintage range. "Oh wow! It arrived."

"Yup. This morning, along with the sink. Gordon did good work—it looks brand new."

"Don't let Rosie see that, or she'll start wanting one for the house," Jops said with a grin.

"Speaking of Rosie, where is she?" I asked.

"She's unfortunately closing tonight. But she sends her birthday wishes."

"Well, I'll have to rescue her and invite her here for a girl's night out on her day off. I'll cook for us to give her a break."

"Wait, what about us? How come we can't tag along?" Fritzso asked.

I rolled my eyes at Fritzso's antics. He was goofy—flirtatious but harmless. I felt Ron's eyes on me, but he stood apart, unsure whether to join in.

"If you're good, Fritzso, maybe I'll invite you over..." I mocked.

"What do you mean 'if I'm good'? Didn't I help you paint?"

"I seem to recall you doing more... supervising?" I shot back, making Jops and Ed burst into laughter.

Turning to Ron, I asked, "We missed you at my painting party."

Before he could respond, Fritzso interrupted. "So what are you going to make for the beautiful Rosie?"

I was amused by Fritzso's obvious attempt to keep my attention on him. He liked to play the ladies' man, and while he was good-looking, he was too much of a player for my taste.

"Well, I make a mean ramen," I said. "From scratch, not the packaged stuff. I noticed no ramen noodle houses in Durham, so I'll make my own."

"Oh my God, I love ramen. Please, please, please save some for me?" Fritzso pleaded dramatically.

"Where did you learn to make ramen?" Ed asked, grabbing another slice of pizza.

"My father owns a restaurant in Beverly Hills. That's where I'm from originally."

"Wait, are you Chef Tono's daughter?" Jops asked, his eyes widening in recognition. "Rosie and I read about him in a restaurant trade magazine. The Shogun, right? Michelin star-rated restaurant in Beverly Hills."

"Yup, that's me," I admitted, though I didn't want to get into the subject of my parents. Thankfully, Ed steered us away from that topic.

"So you're from LA?"

"Born and bred. Go Dodgers!" I grinned.

The room filled with simultaneous groans, except for Ron, who was chuckling to himself. He was determined to stay in the background, and I wondered why.

"Please, Raine. I thought we were friends," Ed joked, pretending to be scandalized.

"You wound me," Fritzso added dramatically. "I guess this relationship is over before it even had a chance."

If I had eyes in the back of my head, I would've seen Ron rolling his.

Fritzso took my hand and kissed it theatrically. "Swear off any teams but the Red Sox and Patriots, and we might have a chance."

I jerked my hand away, pretending to wipe off his kiss. "Eww... Begone, the lot of you! I'll have to cleanse my house of your evil thoughts."

Ron burst into laughter, a full-bodied, bent-over kind that made me grin.

"He speaks," I teased as he tried to sip his beer, only to choke and dribble some down his chin.

"You okay, buddy?" Ed asked as Ron embarrassingly grabbed a paper towel to clean up.

The guys stayed for another hour, sharing stories about their youth. I learned they'd all grown up in the same neighborhood and attended the same schools until college. Fritzso had gone to Notre Dame on a football scholarship, while Ron and Ed stayed local, majoring in geology at the University of Michigan. A career-ending injury had sent Fritzso back to Ann Arbor, where he joined Ron and Ed. After graduation, Fritzso and Ed moved to Durham to pursue their master's and doctorate at UNH, while Ron spent a year at Hamrlio University in Iceland.

"So you left Iceland to join these two here at UNH? Why? Too cold? Bad breakup?" I teased.

Ron's expression darkened, making me instantly regret my words. "Sorry, didn't mean to pry," I said, turning to toss my empty cup in the trash.

"Looks like I'm giving you back your twenty," Ed mumbled to Fritzso.

"What twenty?" I asked, curious.

"Nothing!" Ron thundered, glaring at his friends.

I raised my eyebrows at Jops, who raised his hands in surrender. "Don't ask me."

Okay, private joke among the three amigos.

"Well, it ain't over till it's over," Fritzso replied, nudging Ed.

Sensing the perfect moment to end the evening, I announced, "Yes, it is. It's late and time for you guys to go."

"But the night is young," Fritzso protested.

"I've got a date with a Scottish Highlander," I teased, eager to return to my book. "Thank you all for celebrating my birthday with me."

As I ushered Jops, Ed, and Fritzso out the door, Ron lingered behind. When we were alone, he pulled me into a warm embrace, his lips close to my ear. "Happy birthday, Raine," he whispered.

His mouth was so close to mine, and for a moment I thought he might kiss me. Instead, he leaned his forehead against mine, studying my face as if searching for something.

"What?" I asked, pulling away, suddenly self-conscious.

Instead of answering, he kissed my forehead softly. "Goodnight, Raine. Sleep well." And then left.

What was that all about?

Ron

F ritzso and Ed stuck their heads into Ron's office and announced, "We're headed to Raine's house in an hour. You coming along or what?"

Ron's head shot up. "What? When did you guys decide to do this?"

"Just now. Jops remembered it was her birthday. The love of my life is turning the big three-oh," Fritzso teased.

"Fuck you, Fritzso," Ron said in jealousy. But that just sent Fritzso and Ed into hysterics, as if the state of his love life was some private joke.

Ron quickly left his office and drove to the supermarket, grabbing a bottle of wine. He spotted a bunch of blue flowers that still looked fresh, wrapped in clear cellophane with a lavender bow. He brought them to his nose and instantly recognized the scent—hers. This would be perfect.

When they arrived at Raine's house, he hadn't expected such an effusive response from her. She pulled him into a tight embrace when she handed over the flowers, making him flush with surprise and pleasure. But as he held her, he sensed a wave of unhappiness from her that left him bewildered.

Throughout the evening, he kept a small distance from the group, leaning against the kitchen counter as he watched her socialize. Raine was full of confidence, laughing with Jops, Ed, and Fritzso as if they were old friends. But unlike them, he lingered in the background, almost in awe of her self-assurance. Yet, behind that poise, he sensed a woman who was hurting.

After everyone said goodnight, Ron stayed behind, hoping for a moment alone with her. He gathered his courage and pulled Raine into his arms, anticipating a long, lingering kiss. His lips hovered close to hers, feeling the warmth of her breath, the softness of her skin. He wanted to kiss her, to comfort her in a way that words couldn't. When as he held her, the overwhelming torment he sensed from her soul again hit him like a wave. The depth of her sorrow held him back. It wouldn't be right.

Ron had always been sensitive to others' emotions. As an empath, he often felt more intensely, more deeply. It was both a gift and a curse. At that moment, Raine's pain was almost too much to bear. He knew he had to try to absorb some of it. She needed relief, even if she didn't realize it.

When he pulled away, he gave her a soft, reassuring smile, kissed her forehead, and whispered, "Goodnight, Raine. Sleep well."

He left, hoping she felt a little lighter, a little more at peace. As he walked away, he couldn't shake the feeling that he'd done the right thing, even if it meant holding back his own desires.

Raine

After Ron left, I shook my head, perplexed, and returned to the kitchen to tidy up. I grabbed the coffee pot with my flowers, inhaled their scent again, letting its fragrance fill me, then took it upstairs and set them in my bedroom.

I thought about him. I felt his yearning to kiss me but then held back. Instead of feeling spurned, I felt a wave of calm and peacefulness wash over me. My heart no longer felt quite so heavy.

When I went to bed, the anguish in my heart seemed lessened, if not gone, and replaced with a sense of stillness. As I slipped into dreams of Peter and our beautiful times, another memory surfaced, one that shaped my romantic ideals long before I met him.

CHAPTER 13

Raine

JULY 1984
LOS ANGELES, CALIFORNIA

When my mother moved to the US to marry my father, she embraced many American traditions—her apple pie recipe, hotdogs, and the Los Angeles Dodgers. Oh, and Robert Redford.

I was fourteen when she took me and Vivienne to see *The Natural* when it was first released. My mother was giddy as a schoolgirl who couldn't stop chattering about the forty-eight-year-old actor who was once her heartthrob as a teenager, and I found her dreamy-eyed crush on him infectious.

Quite a few people must have felt the same way as I eyed the long line to get tickets.

"You know, I bet Uncle Stanley could have given us a private screening at his house," I announced, fidgeting like an earthworm on a fishhook. I was not one for patience.

Uncle Stanley was Vivienne's father but given my parents' old-fashioned insistence on respect for elders, anyone older by more than ten years had to be addressed as "auntie" or "uncle" until I reached eighteen. As a Hollywood Oscar-winning producer, he and Vivienne lived in a mansion with a mini theater where he often had private screenings. All we had to do was ask.

"Raine, ye'll not be acting a snob. Yer Da and I raised ye better, *leanabh*," my mother scolded.

"That's alright, Auntie Rae. I like watching movies at the theater. The screen is bigger," Vivienne interjected. I wasn't sure if she meant to save me or embarrass me.

As the lights went down, the movie opened with a scene of a young boy running through the fields to chase a fly ball with his glove. He ran after it, face up to the sky, all that golden flax hair flying. But it wasn't until it cut to Redford that I understood why my mother was so infatuated. My eyes locked into that same face, soft blond hair, steely blue eyes, an angular jaw, and a melt-your-socks-off smile, which made me giggle in my seat, causing a shush from Vivienne and my mother.

I was still wistful when we walked out to the theater lobby. As Vivienne and I waited for my mother to use the restroom, my eyes rested on a large poster of Redford dressed as he was in the movie. Vivienne noticed.

"Eww, Nish, he's so old," she said.

"Shut up, Vivi."

When Ma came out, I asked her to buy me the poster.

"I'm putting this up in my room, at the foot of my bed, so I can say goodnight to him every night," I giggled. Vivienne cringed.

A year later, my father wondered if I was starting to blur my fantasy from reality. I'd overheard him talking to my mother about it.

"What's with Rainey and her obsession with Redford?" he asked.

"She's fifteen, Tono."

"I don't know. Doesn't seem healthy. She talks to him in her room. She doesn't even go out with boys her age."

"Tono, ye won't let her date boys."

My father pulled my mother into his arms.

"You know why, Rae. This is Hollywood. So much fakeism," he said.

"Fakeism?" My mother pulled away slightly with laughter glinting in her eyes. "Is tha' a werd, luv?"

"You know what I mean. This is Hollywood, Rae. It's all illusions. I don't want her falling for something that's not real."

"I ken ye're afraid," My mother said. "But we hae tae accept that she'll leave us. Let's jist enjoy her time wi' us. She'll be awa' soon enough."

As I watched my father tighten his arms around my mother, I was unaware of her vision and their looming fear of my destiny—the one that would inevitably crush their hearts. Little did I know, their fears about my infatuation were tied to something more profound—a desire to protect me from heartache.

By the time I entered UCLA as a freshman, my parents, and even Vivienne, thought I'd gotten over my idolizing Redford. Maybe. But then I met him.

Well, not exactly. But definitely, he was the man of my dreams.

"Dress smart 'cause this guy's big time, Raine," said Scott Jackson, *The Daily Bruin's* editor-in-chief. "I normally wouldn't give this assignment to a freshman, but you've got experience with hard news interviews, so I expect you'll give it your best shot, right?"

I sneered at the six-foot-eight African American communications senior who played forward for the Bruins on the hardwood. He held back the press release, eyeing me skeptically, but I knew he was kidding.

"Gimme that," I said, grabbing the press release and read it aloud.

"Peter Garvey, CEO of advertising giant Silverman and York in New York City, to speak on the state of the advertising and media industry."

"The networks would be there," Scott warned as he regarded my fashion grunge—an oversized t-shirt, baggy Bermuda cut-offs, and sockless feet wearing white Keds.

I knew what he meant—I had to look professional.

Of course, the day of the press conference, the weather threw a wrench into my plans for dressing to kill. The skies opened in an angry downpour when I stepped out of UCLA's campus shuttle bus. I had no umbrella (what native Angeleno owned one anyway?) or a raincoat.

So much for the white shirt I had painstakingly pressed the night before and the pleated gray wool skirt fresh from the cleaners. Once I entered the air-conditioned confines of the Carey Hall Auditorium, I felt I could use a tight wringing. My damp shirt clung to my back, and my waterlogged pumps squished with each step as I approached the stage where a few people stood by the podium.

I recognized Dean Clay LaForce and John Anderson, one of the school's benefactors for whom the school was named. The portly dean with a receding hairline and full beard stood there looking business-like, hands dug deep in his pants pockets, casually rocking on his heels in a stance set to impress Garvey. So did Dr. Anderson, whose elbow rested on the podium while his other hand made gestures as he spoke to the guest, the man with irresistible blond hair. The kind you wouldn't mind running your fingers through. I felt my skin tingle against my clammy shirt.

"H-hello," I called out, tiptoeing halfway up the stairs so they would not be looking down on me.

I hesitated to walk across the stage to where they stood.

"I'm Raine Nishiseki from *The Daily Bruin*," I announced, finding some confidence.

The dean stared back impatiently. I felt he was feigning ignorance about my appointment.

"Scott Jackson arranged for me to interview Mr. Garvey at 3:30." It was already 3:33 p.m. My precious time was ticking away.

Still no response from him. "Six-foot-eight forward, Number 43...,"

"I know who he is," replied a testy Dr. LaForce. "You can come back at five."

His tone rankled. I may not look my best but damn it, I had an appointment with Mr. Garvey, and I aimed to keep it, soggy shoes notwithstanding.

That's when the man with the golden hair turned to look at me.

"I'm... I-I'm uhm, on deadline? And I have a class at, uhm, four?" I stuttered with a Valley Girl accent.

I was still a few feet away from them, yet I could feel his eyes transfixed on me and he was making me nervous.

"Well, we mustn't keep the press waiting," the New York man replied, "Will you excuse us, Dr. La Force?"

I took a deep breath as he approached me, his height looming nearly a foot above my head. He touched my back and led me back down to the seating area. His hand was shorting my spinal nerves. I was sure he could hear my heart thrashing about and skipping beats.

"Hi, I'm Peter Garvey."

I slipped my soggy palm into his outstretched hand, instantly feeling his firm grip. When he covered my palm with his other hand, I bit my lower lip to quell my nerves.

Oh, that sandy flaxen hair, the bangs that casually fell across his forehead. I discreetly blew out a sigh. If I were in a nineteenth-century Regency romance novel, I would swoon.

"I'm Raine Nishiseki of *The Daily Bruin,* the university newspaper. So nice to meet you, sir," I finally uttered.

Dr. La Force and Dr. Anderson excused themselves with the promise to return after precisely ten minutes, reminding Garvey that they intended to start on time.

We sat in the front row together. I cleared my throat and crossed my legs, a calculated move to establish a sexual power dynamic and take control. I was in charge. The move was not lost on him as his gaze briefly rested on my legs. But when our eyes met, our sustained eye contact fostered a connection and intimacy, intensifying a potent form of flirtation from him. It should have felt intrusive. Instead, I felt flattered.

"You're not here to talk about the state of the advertising industry, Mr. Garvey, are you?" I asked while retrieving my notebook and pen.

"I'm not?" He merely sat there, with his honeyed smile focused on distracting me.

"Tell me if I'm wrong. You're here to listen to the new center's plans and decide whether it's a worthy cause for your checkbook, right?"

"I don't know. I think I was just about to find out before you walked in," he answered.

He sounded sincere, but I needed more.

"I see." Quickly, I flipped the page of my notebook to check the next question.

"You're gorgeous, you know," he said, rendering me tong-tied for a moment.

His eyes moved to my mouth. Then his body shifted slightly forward and his lips tilted faintly at its corners. He was challenging my self-control, daring me to resist his magnetism.

"Excuse me?" I finally said, my face heating up. He would win—if I let him. I reminded myself this was the oldest trick in politics—men interviewees lobbing flattery to fluster women reporters. "That's a statement clearly *not* for the record. Mr. Garvey, I have seven minutes left to wrap this up. No, six," I said after checking my watch. "Can we please go on?"

"You're very good at what you do. I think you'll have a bright future as a journalist," he said.

"Not if we don't continue," I replied dryly. "I'm sure you must have heard about the new center and the dean's plan to fund it with bequests. A couple of New York investment bankers have already ponied as much as fifteen million between them. With Dr. Anderson's four, Dean LaForce has nineteen of the twenty million he needs for the project. Are you going to write a check for the balance?"

If he was surprised, he hid it well.

"Listen, this is the first I've heard of this. But I would love to learn more from you," he said with that self-effacing smile. I felt he knew more than he wanted to admit to the press.

"Have dinner with me tonight? We'll have more time, and you can tell me all about it. I'll give you all the answers you need for your story."

Wide-eyed, I stammered, "D-dinner? B-but wha-what about Dr. La Force and Dr. Anderson?" Wasn't he going to have dinner with them so they could schmooze him into bestowing some money for the school?

"Don't worry about them. I'd rather hear it from you. Can you push your deadline?" he asked.

More than ten minutes with Mr. Gorgeous? It was tempting. And dinner? Oooff. Christ, I was in deep trouble with this man. But he could also simply be putting me off.

I stood up and picked up my backpack. I noticed LaForce and Anderson walking toward us. I felt stirrings of disappointment. I had failed to get the interview I desperately needed.

"Tonight, you can take as much time as you want," Garvey said as if reading my mind.

He must have also sensed my hesitation. Taking hold of my arm as he propelled me toward the door, he spoke with conviction, "DiNardi's on Rodeo Drive at seven."

I stopped and turned to face him. "You're a busy man, Mr. Garvey. I understand things can arise at the last minute, and this interview isn't your priority."

I tore a sheet of my reporter's notebook and scribbled my number, handing it to him.

"This is my beeper number. You can reach me anytime. Should you need to cancel, I'll understand, and we can interview by phone. This story is very important to me. I hope you're not just trying to dodge the press," I finally said with more confidence.

"Raine?" And yet, that voice had me spellbound when he said my name.

"When I say I'll be there, I'll be there," he said self-assuredly, but he still kept my number.

"I'll call my editor," I said, holding my breath. I was completely slain.

I called Vivienne for fashion advice, hoping she would be at her dorm at Harvard.

"How could I possibly think of wearing anything I own to go out on a date with such an important man," I cried.

"Go on to the house. Nobody's home, and Priscilla will let you in. Feel free to rummage through my closet," she said encouragingly. My excitement was contagious, and I could tell she was thrilled for me. She knew who Peter Garvey was and she couldn't believe it herself that he'd asked me out to dinner.

"It's all professional, Vivi. Not exactly a date," I reminded her.

"Sure, Raine. And you're going to dress in a business suit?" Ha! She knew me so well.

"You don't know how much this means," I said.

Then, without my asking, she added, "Hey, Nish?"

"What?"

"Take the Porsche," she offered. "Might as well have somebody use it."

"Are you serious?"

"Sure, I'm serious. There's a spare set of keys on the top of my dresser," she said excitedly. "Hey, Nish."

"What?" I expected her to give me the standard line— don't go fast, don't scratch it, or I'll fucking kill you.

Instead, she giggled, "I want details."

We cackled like schoolgirls back at St. Joe's. Back when life was uncomplicatedly fun.

Vivienne's closet was a treasure trove of fashion. I ran my fingers over the fabrics, finally choosing the Donna Karan black leather mini skirt that rode further up my thighs than it did hers because I was an inch taller than Vivienne. I knew I was purposely dressing seductively.

I pulled on a body-hugging tank top to match the mini skirt, then slipped on a lightweight oversized pullover with a wide neckline that drooped over one shoulder, revealing the tank top's strap. Then, I slithered my feet into plush Ferragamo alligator short boots lined with cashmere, which felt like a million bucks.

With the spare keys in hand, I stepped into the Porsche. The engine purred while I pushed the button to lower the top. I drove away, shifting aggressively, feeling bold and confident as my hair whipped around me, the city lights of LA blurring past. I couldn't help but smile, the anticipation of the evening ahead mingling with the thrill of the drive. The engine's growl, the feel of the leather steering wheel beneath my fingers, and the exhilaration of the speed all combined to make this moment unforgettable. Tonight was going to be amazing.

Throughout dinner, Peter kept a hand over mine while he ate with one hand, and I toyed with my pasta. I asked him personal questions. Where are you from? What were your parents like? Where did you go to school? How did you get to New York? I hoped I could memorize what he said because I wasn't about to break the moment by writing down our conversation.

Who was this man sitting before me? A man who was pursuing a romantic interest in me. But he would either candidly reply with light humor or brush my questions aside. Not enough for a story. Instead, he wanted to know more about me. And I was only too willing to do the talking.

I told him about my parents, my father's Nisei family, and my Viking Gaelic mother. They met in Edinburgh when he was a student at the University of Edinburgh, and when he returned to the States to start his restaurant, she'd followed him.

"When my mother first saw my father, she told me they were meant to be together. So she pursued him." I gave him the abridged version of my parents' love story because I did not want to bore him with the long, adventurous tale of their romance, and I did not want to divulge my mother's ability to foresee glimpses of the future.

"You're a romantic, aren't you?" he asked with those glimmering blue eyes.

I could only smile, but my reddening was a giveaway.

I'd never blushed as much as I had that night. How foolish I must have seemed to him. Naïve, stupidly believing in love at first sight. How ignorant of worldly things I must have appeared. Peter had been jetting to exotic places with various lovers in every port. And I was what? A teenager? I'd never even had a steady boyfriend. I still harbored romantic notions of what it would be like to find the man of my dreams. To fall in love. I could never fit in Peter's mind as someone he'd pursue, and yet here he was.

"You look stunning tonight, Raine," he said, kissing my knuckles, and when he looked at me, soft and lingering, his gaze veiled a smoldering heat of desire. How was he so relaxed and calm if he felt the same way I did?

When he walked me to the car, he kissed me full on my lips. No one had ever kissed me like that. Like a grown woman. His tongue slipped to touch mine then swirled it around. It made me breathless. I felt his urgency, his need to claim my body as he leaned me against the car, and I responded with frightening swiftness. I would have said yes if he had asked me to go to bed with him. But he kept his control, which I found admirable, even if I didn't think I would ever see him again.

Vivienne

DECEMBER 1989
HARVARD UNIVERSITY, MASSACHUSETTS

As Vivienne listened to her best friend moon over the dashing billionaire, her mortification grew. Raine was so smitten she couldn't see the forest for the trees.

"He's my Prince Charming, Vivi. I found him. And if he asked? I'd follow him to the ends of the Earth," Raine said, breathless over the phone after her date with Peter Garvey.

"I fucking hope you aren't serious, Nish. This doesn't sound like you at all," Vivienne giggled nervously. "You're the biggest man snob I know."

"That's because I was waiting for someone like Peter. I've been waiting for him my whole life."

Vivienne paced her dorm room at Harvard, wondering what kind of spell Peter had cast on her best friend. This wasn't the Raine she knew.

"*Ni-iii-sh!* For fuck's sake, listen to me," Vivienne implored. "You've never experienced being in love. Not really. You're infatuated and you are setting yourself up for a huge heartbreak. Snap out of it. You're scaring me."

"Come on, Vivi," Raine cried, her tone indignant. "Why can't you be happy for me? I can't believe you don't get where I'm coming from."

"*Omigod, please,*" Vivienne said anxiously. "You don't know him—not on a deep, emotional level. Christ, he treats women like playthings."

"What? How can you say that?" Raine interrupted, her voice sharp. "Viv, you don't actually believe what the tabloids say about him, do you?"

"I don't," Vivienne said, her frustration mounting. "But..."

She wished this were just mindless girl talk, like when they'd swooned over Keanu Reeves. Peter Garvey was real, powerful, and dangerous. His presence would eclipse Raine, reducing her to another conquest in his long line of them. Raine was brilliant, capable of great things—she was Peter's equal. But Peter didn't see anyone as his equal. He would crush her, and Vivienne couldn't bear to watch her best friend give up everything for him.

"Look, he's going back to New York. If he says nothing, then fine. I'm just stupid. But if he wants me in New York, I'm going," Raine insisted.

"You're being delusional. What makes you so sure he's serious about you?"

"Because he's the one, Vivi. *The. One.*"

Vivienne shuddered as if a dark shadow had passed, sensing that this conversation marked the beginning of a fracture she was helpless to stop. She was about to lose Raine in the most profound and painful way she had ever thought possible.

CHAPTER 14

Peter

DECEMBER 1989
LOS ANGELES, CALIFORNIA

I f there ever was the perfect model for the cover of *GQ Magazine*, Peter Garvey was it. Towering at six-foot-two, muscled from regimented workouts and a weekly game of squash, he exuded a combination of rugged charm, athletic prowess, and a magnetic presence. Peter rose to prominence as a hard-nosed, ambitious executive in the cutthroat field of advertising and media, with political aspirations of one day holding the country's top job. And though he currently didn't have a steady relationship with any one woman, his name was often linked with various ladies of the society set—debutants, divorcees, and widows alike.

When he set his goals, he singularly focused on each one to achieve them. For Peter, there was no plan B.

He'd called to have his appointments canceled for the next few days and stayed holed up at the company residence in Malibu, juggling some work and other matters that occupied his mind. He'd walked along the coast contemplating—no, formulating—*The Plan*.

He'd just turned thirty-five, and if he aspired to move into politics over the next few years, he'd need a wife. But she couldn't be just any woman. She had to be stunningly beautiful. Not a Hollywood celeb good-looking, but one with an understated beauty. Eyes that were mysterious and a face that could mesmerize. Not Asian exotic. Peter hated that word because it conjured up images of submissive geisha girls, which made him cringe. But he also eschewed the stereotypical apple-pie midwestern Caucasian as too ordinary. And Peter never thought of himself that banal.

He wanted someone...without equal, beyond compare. A woman who would make all the other guys in the room jealous of him when she was on his arm. And there was Raine.

She'd occupied his mind since the night they had dinner. He'd kissed her long, hot, and wet, which revealed her ingenue and that she was pure as the first snowfall on a New England wintry day.

She wouldn't have skeletons in the closet. And that had to apply to her lineage. No family scandals, huge debts, or financial losses. They would be upstanding citizens in the community and all that jazz. His partner in New York would confirm this.

He'd also wanted someone healthy, no secret diseases or problematic genes in the family. She seemed to have all her teeth white and straight with no gaps or imperfections, sporting a smile that could melt even the most hardened soul. His partner would know where to get all that information, privacy laws notwithstanding.

Plus, Peter wanted someone who would be whip-smart, sharp-witted, sophisticated, and educated without the ambition to succeed professionally. He wanted perfection. He wanted Raine.

And if he were lucky and remained symptom-free in the next ten or so years, there'd be a good chance he hadn't inherited his mother's gene for the disease that had claimed her life so tragically at such a young age. Then he and Raine could start a family. He was confident Raine would be fertile enough to have two or three of his children. That was the image he had in mind, the picture-perfect First Family. Only time will tell.

That was *The Plan*. And it had to be strictly devoid of any personal feelings.

Having skipped shaving for three days, his chin felt scruffy as he impatiently waited for his partner to call.

It was nearly noon in California but late in New York when Jim York finally called.

"Thanks, Jim. That's perfect," he said over the phone.

"One more favor?" Peter quickly added before his partner hung up.

"I'd like to get married at Jardin Malanga...

"Tomorrow... Yes, it has to be quick...

"I don't want to return to New York with just a girlfriend or a lover...

"She would have to be my wife. Her parents may join us, not sure... I haven't asked her yet... Yes, I'm confident she'll say yes... How do I know? She has that look... You know, starry-eyed, head in the clouds..." Peter recalled how she'd gazed at him over dinner, all dreamy and blushing.

"I need to take advantage of that moment... She's too much in love with me. I'm proposing tonight... No, I have no feelings about this one way or another. It's all transactional... I know, but that's how it has to be... Jim, if I don't close on this deal with Raine as my wife, who knows when I'd find another one who'd fit the bill? And I'm not getting any younger, you know."

Peter held a cordless handset in his ear, pacing the room, then paused to stare at the view through the vast expanse of glass that framed the wild Pacific Ocean.

"I know I'm not giving you and Helen much time to pre-pare, but if I wait too much longer, I'd lose her... I've already wasted three days getting this all together. I know it's fast, and yes, we could do a civil service courthouse marriage, but I still want her to have a beautiful wedding with all the trimmings. When you meet her, you'll understand..."

Peter was now smiling to himself. He could already see Raine as his blushing bride.

"I think if you call her high school alma mater... St. Jo-seph's in Bel Air. I'm sure a small donation would convince the nuns to release the yearbook, and you can see what she looks like. Oh, it's a recent photo. She's only nineteen. Her picture would have been taken just this past year.

"It has to be now. I'm not waiting... No, no prenup..." There was a long pause before Peter responded firmly, "Jim... no prenup, and we are not discussing it. If anything should happen to me, I want her to get it all. That's final... Thank you for taking care of this. And thank Helen for me... See you soon."

And with that, he'd hung up. All the rest of his plans were unfolding like a perfectly choreographed ballet. The internally flawless three-carat diamond ring, custom designed and set on raised solitary prongs surrounded by encrusted diamond chips, arrived yesterday by overnight courier from Tiffany along with its matching white-gold bands. He'd looked at her fingers long enough on their first night at dinner to know she was a size three-and-a-half—such delicate and soft hands.

It had been three long days since he'd taken her to dinner. That was long enough of a wait. He wanted his wedding band on her left finger. Tomorrow. She would belong to him and him alone.

There was just one problem. A *huge* problem. Despite the dispassionate way he'd planned to woo and propose to Raine, he was falling madly in love with her. But he wouldn't admit it because that was not part of *The Plan*.

Raine

DECEMBER 1989
LOS ANGELES, CALIFORNIA

"You're going to do what???"

I winced at Scott's bellow.

"The new center. This would make a much better piece than Garvey's boring talk yesterday." I tapped my fingers, waiting for the laggard computer to power up.

"Raine, you can't do that! We've already covered the new center," Scott cried in a panic.

"This is different. It's about LaForce's funding for the center. The guy's got just about one hundred percent of the cost from private investors and donors, with Garvey possibly pitching in his mullah for a cool million. So, I saw the dean this morning and got the details."

When I walked into the Bruin's newsroom that afternoon, I owned up to Scott and told him what happened.

Sort of.

How could I admit to having dinner with Mr. Gorgeous Blue Eyes but not interviewing him when I had the chance? So I pivoted and cajoled my way into Dean Laforce's office this morning for the details on the center. He was irritated and threatened to throw me out. But sweet talk and layers of flattery, and I had LaForce singing like a canary.

"You did? Now that's news!" Scott said excitedly. "Big news!"

"He's waiting for word from Garvey about whether he's getting that last bit. I said I needed it by six tonight. He seemed confident he'd get it so the school could break ground in the spring. Even if Garvey doesn't come through, getting that last million using debt ain't so bad. And he said we can go on the record with the donors' names."

Scott's eyes lit up. "Good job, Raine. Make sure your story leads with the money and the scheduled groundbreaking. Can you give me enough to fill a fifteen-inch column right now?"

"On it."

"We'll put it on page one if the money comes through. It'll be your first front-page break, kiddo," Scott said as he leaned over my shoulder, reading what I'd started.

I finished the story, but then there was the excruciating wait for LaForce's phone call. The last hour crawled, minute by minute, second by painful second. We were coming on to six o'clock.

"We can't wait much longer, Raine," Scott warned.

"Wait! We still have a couple of minutes."

He waited barely ten seconds when he pronounced, "That's it. We can't wait."

The phone's shrill on Scott's desk pierced the room. I grabbed it before Scott could.

"*Daily Bruin...* Hello, Dr. LaForce?" There was a discerning pause and silence in the newsroom where everyone held their collective breaths. "Thank you so very much. Yes, it's running on Page One."

"Let's go!" Scott yelled to Colleen, who'd been waiting to lay out the final Page One section.

"*Yes!*" I screamed. I jumped. I pumped a fist, danced the twist, and high-fived Scott.

I'd gone out with the rest of the Bruin staff to celebrate the newfound respect I'd earned from each of them. I could be well on my way to making it in this business.

The next morning, I'd picked up a copy of the day's edition with my front-page story. And there was Peter's press photo, smiling at me, my heart sinking that this may be my only memory of our time together. I would save this issue forever. Being in love sucked.

"What's the matter, Raine? Faculty profile stories not so exciting?" Scott asked when he'd heard me sigh for the fifth time in an hour.

"Yeah, we need a crime to happen."

Two days after my first page-one story, the high that I'd felt began to subside, which drove me back into pining-for-Peter mode. I could hear Vivienne's I-told-you-so reproach. I hated that our last conversation didn't end on the best of terms. It had hurt that she didn't believe I could attract someone like Peter. That he was the one for me.

"Want to take a stab at this? Rising number of campus parking tickets?" Scott broke my thoughts.

I made a twirling gesture with my finger. *Yippee.*

I powered down my system and left for finite math class.

"I'll take a look at it when I get back," I said with such cynical enthusiasm.

I walked out of the newsroom, pausing to say hi to a couple of friends passing by, barely paying attention to where I was going when I bumped hard into a man carrying the most enormous bouquet of blood-red roses I'd ever seen.

"Oh gosh, I'm so sorry," I said. The bouquet was so large I couldn't see who was holding it.

"Delivery for Raine Nishiseki." I froze, recognizing the voice. The man of my dreams lowered the bouquet slowly, revealing his unyielding blue eyes and a smile.

"Peter!" I was breathless, flustered.

I looked around to see if anyone noticed us. The hall was empty, which meant everyone was in class. And I was late. I bit my lip, fingered the long bangs away from my face, and tilted my head to look at him.

"When did you get back?" I was in no hurry to get to class.

"I never left, sweetheart. Had some things to take care of."

He'd called me sweetheart? He'd come back. To see me. I felt the heat rise to my face.

Even without a suit and tie, Peter was strikingly handsome. In his tailored charcoal blazer, crisp white Oxford shirt, slim-cut navy chinos, and polished leather loafers, he embodied a perfect mix of sophistication and effortless confidence that left me breathless. It was hard to believe he was here to see a silly coed dressed in vintage Madonna Village rags rummaged from the bins of a thrift shop.

"Did you miss me?" He flashed his famous million-dollar enchant-the-client smile.

I had my hand pressed against my heart, laughing nervously to dispel my tizzy.

"You have no idea," I replied animatedly.

"So when can you get away?" he asked, sounding rather impatient, as I took the bouquet from him and inhaled the sweet fragrance deeply.

I looked around to see if anyone from the newsroom followed me. Forget *The Daily Bruin*. Forget the rest of my classes. Peter was here. That was all that mattered.

When we reached the parking lot, he waved at a man leaning against a stretch limousine. As soon as the black, shiny car pulled up, Peter waited for the chauffeur to climb out and open the door for us. A few people were ogling us. I didn't care. I felt like a princess, and my royal coach had arrived.

"Malibu Beach," he commanded through the glass partition.

"It's too nice of a day to spend it all indoors. Wouldn't you agree?" he said, turning to me.

"Uh-huh," I muttered, catching him looking at my mouth, knowing he would kiss me next.

"I've missed you too," he said, gathering me in his arms to show me how much.

We struggled to break away from showering each other with kisses when the long nose of the limousine pulled up to a solitary house that overlooked the crashing waves of the Pacific, a vast estate perched on a rocky ledge.

"It's a corporate residence," Peter said as we walked inside.

I sensed how comfortable he was in his lavish surroundings as I observed him stride around the house as if this was his primary residence.

"Come," he said, reaching for my hand. "Let's go down to the water and watch the sunset."

When we reached the bottom of the ridge, we shed our shoes. He rolled up his pant legs. Together, we walked barefoot along the crystallized sand of the coastline. There was a nip in the breeze that made me shiver slightly. He noticed and slipped off his blazer to put around my shoulders. Then, protectively, he wrapped an arm around me, keeping me close to him. I felt safe and warm in his embrace.

"What's New York like, Peter," I asked as I stared at the flaming horizon, wondering if East Coast sunsets blazed the way they did in California. Did the Atlantic roar like the Pacific Ocean?

"It's a big city. Noisy, very busy. Everyone is always in a rush," he said.

"Sounds exciting," I replied.

"For some, it might be. It takes a certain kind of person to love a city that hustles twenty-four hours a day."

"I've never been to New York," I said.

"Never?"

I shook my head.

"I'm not sure stopovers count," I said, recalling one summer I spent with Vivienne in Paris. Her father's private jet had stopped in JFK to refuel.

"I thought maybe I'd travel after graduating, get my master's at Columbia, and intern at NBC with Connie Chung and Peter Jennings if I'm lucky. Maybe see you—if you remember me, have time for me," I teased. I paused momentarily, taking in his lack of a reply, wondering if he took my dreams seriously or just heard the hopeful ramblings of a girl in love. But he only pulled me closer and kissed me on my forehead. As we continued walking silently, I wondered if I'd said something wrong by sharing my dream.

"You would love New York," he said at last, his tone warm but vague, and said nothing about my ambitions.

"Yes, I'm sure I would," I replied without hesitation, bitterly recalling my parents' adamant refusal to let me go to Columbia.

I couldn't tell what Peter was thinking. But whatever it was, I felt even more determined to go to New York after graduation and seek him out. I'd be twenty-one. Surely by then, my parents wouldn't stop me from pursuing my dreams.

Peter stared out at the ocean, suddenly pensive.

"Is something wrong?" I asked when he stopped walking. Thoughts of him pushing me away, saying goodbye because he couldn't see a future with me, struck, and fear crept up my spine.

He took the palms of my hands, turned them up, then kissed each on the inside.

"I'm falling in love with you, Raine," he said above the roar of an incoming wave that crashed against the shore.

I was keenly aware of the icy froth lacing my ankles, yet I made no move to seek drier ground, for at that moment, there was only Peter, the hammering of my heart, the feel of his arms around me as he pulled me closer.

"I know this is happening fast. And I don't think I've ever believed that love at first sight was possible until I met you at the Carey Auditorium. You took my breath away. I couldn't concentrate on the interview."

My hand flew to my heart, willing it to stop palpitating. Had I taken his breath away despite looking like a drowned rat the day we met? Tears threatened to spill, wondering if what I was hearing was real.

I looked away, but he turned my head and lifted my chin, willing me to meet his eyes.

"I love you," he said, sealing his declaration with a burning kiss that was wet, slopping, insistent, and urgent. The kiss elicited a moan from my breath as the sun dropped into the ocean, and I tumbled into that abyss called love.

We made love that late afternoon in the big beach house with the sunset dipping into the horizon. It was my first time, and he was so gentle, sweet, and caring to ensure that I felt every bit of pleasure as he had. Amid the rapid beats of our hearts, I couldn't help but cry.

"Hey, what's wrong? Did I hurt you?" He asked as he rose and rested his head on his elbow, looking at me with concern.

"No. Everything's perfect. You've made me so happy, Peter. I've never felt like this before. I don't want it to end. But I know you have to go back to New York," I said, brushing away tears, trying to sober up from the drunken trance of my emotions. Peter laughed softly in response.

"Oh, Raine. My darling, darling silly girl," he said, rolling on top of my naked body, scrutinizing me seriously. "I do love you. And by that, I mean we will never end, sweetheart. Like your parents, we'll have our happily ever after."

A distinct robin's egg-colored Tiffany box appeared in his hand as if by magic. He flipped it open and said, "Raine, will you marry me?"

I gasped, wordless, staring at the glittering three-carat solitaire diamond. *Marriage?* I'd barely gotten used to his declaration of love. I was still basking in the warmth of our lovemaking, which was so new and beautiful.

Voices of reason echoed around my brain. *What? Wait, this is wild. It's nuts. Too fast, Raine. Your parents would never agree… Look at the size of that fucking rock! Wait till I show Vivienne.*

I was in love with Peter. I never wanted to let him go. And I wanted my happily ever after with him. With that, there was only one answer I could give.

He went for my mouth again, slipping the ring on my finger, swallowing anything else I might have had to say, then grazing his lips downward, increasing my desire, worshiping my body, and bringing me to that explosive edge of the world. I let myself fall over without any fear. We made love again while the rumble of waves outside the window crashed on the shore in rhythm with our lovemaking.

My parents had warned me that I would experience heartbreak if I wasn't careful about whom I gave my heart to. But feeling Peter's love, hearing his vows of a future together drenched with nothing but the joy consuming me, they had to be wrong. Yes, everything was unfolding too fast. But, like destiny, how could it be anything but real?

Still, when I tell them, they're going to fucking kill me.

CHAPTER 15

Peter

DECEMBER 1989
LOS ANGELES, CALIFORNIA

Inside the comfort of the company's private jet in flight crossing the country, he tried to catch up with his work, but Raine kept intruding on his thoughts, interrupting his concentration in a way he couldn't control.

She now slept peacefully aft of the aircraft, where a settee was converted into a comfortable sleeping alcove. His gaze intermittently wandered over to where she lay, pondering whether he had been too rash, unfair, or demanding. After all, she was only nineteen, and he'd just uprooted her from her parents, the only home she'd ever known, to follow him as his wife, pledge her life to love only him.

It felt right to ask her to marry him now while she had eyes only for him, believed in him, and trusted him. She had been pure, untouched, unjaded, unaffected. And when he took her virginity, there would be no way he would let anyone else possess her. No, he could not have left LA without her.

But that scene with her parents tugged at him. The tears she cried when her father disowned her. Peter had expected Raine's parents to give her the world when they'd asked for their blessing to marry. He was appalled to witness the anger, the insults, the agony they'd inflicted on their only daughter, particularly her father, whom she adored the most.

He thought of his parents. They would never have disowned him. And he would have given the world to see his mother live one more day. To tell her he was sorry he couldn't save her. Sorry that she had to suffer.

Although the chances were slim, the malevolent gene that took his mother's life may not manifest in him. No, he could not have waited as Raine's parents had wanted. Life was too short, and regrets too long.

Anticipation welled inside him because he would hear Raine pledge her vows tomorrow, as he would. He would slip that white gold band on her third finger, lock it behind her diamond engagement ring, and then she would belong to him. Only him.

He dropped his pen and walked toward the back where she lay sleeping. Carefully, not waking her, he lifted the hand that bore the solitaire diamond. He stroked the glittering rock between his fingers and whispered his silent vow while she slept. He promised to give her the world. He promised he would die trying.

Raine

DECEMBER 1989
LOS ANGELES, CALIFORNIA

Despite the Gulfstream's luxury, I slept fitfully, haunted by the hateful confrontation with my parents. Their spiteful accusations and my father's desperate pleas replayed in my mind, inescapable and clear.

"Why? I don't understand, Raine. Does this fool blind you so much? Can't you see how illogical this is?" My father had argued, then turned to Peter. "She's only nineteen, Mr. Garvey. And you're what, fifteen years older than her? I don't think you understand what you're asking her to do."

My father addressing Peter like I was a child made my cheeks burn with humiliation.

Kneeling before my father, my hands on his knees, I pleaded, "Da, I love him. Remember how you and Mama fell in love? Why can't you see that I'm capable of the same?"

But the look of stoicism on his face hurt deeply. I couldn't get through to him and neither could I see his point of view. My mother, usually the quiet mediator, held my father's arm tightly. She squeezed it occasionally, a silent plea for calm. Her eyes, however, were fixed on Peter, searching his face as if trying to place a familiar puzzle piece, as if she had known or met him before. And then I watched her expression dissolve from recognition into fear.

She faced me with a mixture of sorrow in her eyes, resigned to the fact that I was going to leave no matter how much she and my father pleaded for me to stay.

"Raine, we've always wanted the best for ye, and we're scairt. Scairt ye might be making a mistake that ye can't undo."

My father, however, rose from his armchair and shook his head in frustration, as if to declare this conversation was over.

"If you love her, you'll wait for her to finish school," he told Peter.

"I can enroll at Columbia," I countered. "I've been accepted, remember? It was my first choice, but you insisted I stay in LA with you and Mama. Now, I have a reason to be in New York. I want to be with Peter, as his wife. Please, Da, why is that so wrong?"

"Raine," my father's lips quivered, trying to temper his rising fury. "For the love of God, you've known him for three days! Do you even realize he's a known playboy?"

"That's not fair, sir. I can't help what the press writes about me. But that's not who I am. I am not asking Raine to be my lover. I'm marrying your daughter. I'm giving her my name. I have never said that to any woman before."

My father ignored him and shook my shoulders. "I'm trying to protect you from getting hurt. I know this man will do that. No! I won't allow it."

He won't allow it?

Memories of dutiful obedience flashed through my mind—hours spent poring over textbooks, the loneliness of skipped parties, the tight-lipped nods of approval from my parents. Back then, I had obeyed without question. I'd always followed their rules, never cutting school, keeping my grades up, and agreeing not to date until college. It was what they expected, and I conformed. Their rules had been my compass, guiding every step. But this time, things were different.

I'm nineteen!!!

As if reading my thoughts, Peter calmly kept his fingers entwined with mine.

"Raine's nineteen and old enough to decide. She says she loves me, and I love her. I promise to take care of her. I wish you'd give us your blessing. She loves you so much and it will hurt her if you don't."

My father asked Peter to leave so he could speak with me alone, as if that would have changed my mind.

"I won't leave here unless you tell me to, Raine. I'll just be outside waiting in the car." He'd kissed my hand, and I hesitatingly let it go.

When Peter was out of earshot, my father asked, "Have you had sex with him, Raine?"

The words struck me like a blow, my cheeks burning with shock and anger.

"*What?*" I whispered, my voice trembling with disbelief.

"You heard me!" His voice boomed with impatience. My mother squeezed his arm, imploring calmness.

"Tono, enough," she said firmly, placing a hand on his chest to steady him.

When he asked me that question, I spun around, a torrent of fury twisting my features into a snarl. The words that erupted from me were sharp, vicious, and unfamiliar, even to my ears.

My chest heaved with each ragged breath, my heart a wild drumbeat in my ears. The words spilled out, dripping with venom.

"That is none of your fucking business, old man. *How dare you!!!*"

My mother cringed as my ultimate disrespect for them hung in the air when an unspoken chasm opened between us.

"I am not your little girl anymore. You can't just demand me to respond. I have a right to my privacy."

"You live in my household. You are my business, Raine," he roared.

"Then this conversation is over. I'm leaving." I threw up my hands and went to my room to pack some things.

"You walk out that door, then don't ever come back. You will not be welcome here."

I gasped and felt that I was tumbling into a gorge of darkness. I had to get out of there. I stepped inches from my father's face and spat, "I FUCKING HATE YOU!"

His hand rose to strike, and I crouched in fear, screaming until Peter burst in and I flew into his arms."

"Tono, don't!" My mother begged, pulling him away.

"You were going to hit me? *You were going to hit me???*" I was breathing hard, my heart pounding, and finding the courage borne of an all-consuming hatred for him.

Disbelieving that I had driven my father to the brink of hitting me, I watched his red face crumple in disgust. With himself, or me? I didn't care. He took one last look at me, then stormed out, slamming the door so hard it shook the house.

My mother approached me, lifted my chin, and raised my now tear-streaked face to hers. She had looked straight at me with that hard Clan MacDonald pride.

"Ye've made up yer mind, *mo charaide*, and none shall change it. Go and hurt yer Da and me no more. Make yer own way in the world alone. Ye're fated to leave us heartbroken, and it will be many years before we can heal from the pain ye've caused us."

She'd made no move to hug or even say goodbye. I had run out the door, leaving Peter behind, when I heard him speak with my mother.

"I'm sorry you and Mr. Nishiseki feel that way, Ma'am. I hope you won't hold a grudge against Raine... life's too short for that."

When Peter joined me outside, he wrapped his arm around me, warm and steadying.

As we settled in the limo, he reassured me it didn't matter if I hadn't packed anything. He would take care of it all. I would have absolutely nothing to worry about. And that was just fine by me. I wanted nothing that would remind me of my past, who I was, where I'd come from.

From that day forward, I would take on my married name and become Raine Garvey.

Raoghnailt

DECEMBER 1989
BEVERLY HILLS, CALIFORNIA

Raoghnailt stepped into her daughter's now-empty bedroom and let out a piercing wail, her heart shattering into pieces too small to ever be whole again. Tears blurred her vision as she touched Raine's cherished belongings—a tennis racket, the trophy she brought home when she won the school tennis championship match. Her gaze fell on a poster of Robert Redford, and she caught her breath, startled by how much he resembled Peter. She hadn't known then, but that poster hinted at the path Raine would take, the choices that would lead her to this moment.

Her fingers lingered on the guitar strings. She once strummed to pop music, but it will remain silent. Raine had always been unpredictable, as wild as her name—soft and nurturing one moment, dark and stormy the next. She and Tono tried to temper her wild streak without breaking her spirit, teaching her to choose wisely, hoping it would change the course of her destiny. But they had failed. And what they hadn't foreseen was how much heartbreak her decisions would bring or how long it would take for the wounds between them to heal.

Sitting on Rainey's bed, Raoghnailt stilled her mind and called upon the fae of An Dà Shealladh—her Uncle Angus.

"When will my baby girl come back?" she implored in Gaelic, tears soaking the pillow she now hugged, inhaling the sweet scent of her daughter's shampoo—Scottish heather.

The only response was a faint, distant whisper—patience. But patience wasn't enough. The fae offered no visions of her daughter's future or comfort. She felt lost, tossed into a turbulent sea beneath a dark sky, with no stars to guide her and no sign of a safe harbor. She had no choice but to let Rainey go as she was fated.

Raoghnailt rose slowly and walked out, closing the door behind her. The soft click of the latch was like the crack of a heart too broken to ever heal.

CHAPTER 16

Raine

DECEMBER 1989
JARDIN MALANGA, GUADELOUPE

Peter's whisper cut through my exhausted slumber. "Raine, sleepy head, we're here," he cooed, brushing strands of hair from my face as the jet's turbines hummed to a stop.

"Where are we?" I muttered, rubbing sticky tears from my eyes.

"Take a deep breath. What do you smell?" As the door opened, a warm breeze filled the cabin. I inhaled deeply.

"Ocean," I replied excitedly, recognizing the tang of salt and the spicy scent of sea life. "What time is it?"

"Time to go. They're waiting for us," Peter said, reaching for my nervous hand.

As I disembarked and stepped onto the tarmac, the breathtaking island of Guadeloupe stretched before me, an emerald jewel nestled in the heart of the Caribbean Sea. In the distance, perched high above the cliffs where the sea and sky blurred into a seamless horizon, stood a grand old-world estate. Jardin Malanga.

A couple approached us with welcoming smiles, their elegance and poise evident in every step.

"Raine, meet Jim and Helen York," Peter said. The warmth in their eyes put me at ease, even though their polished presence reminded me of how out of place I felt in this world of privilege.

After the introductions, Peter turned to me, his expression serious but soft.

"I'm heading back to New York for a few hours. You'll be in good hands with the Yorks." Seeing my surprise, he said, "Don't worry, sweetheart. I'll be back this evening. I can't wait to marry you."

He kissed me lightly. Then with a final reassuring smile, he boarded another sleek jet, leaving me disoriented and confused on the tarmac.

Sensing my bewilderment, Helen slipped her arm through mine, steering me toward a waiting car. "Don't worry, Raine. He'll be back in time for your wedding. Meantime, we'll be busy preparing for your big day."

I forced a smile, nodding mechanically.

From the back seat of the Jaguar, I watched the gentle waves brushing the Caribbean shoreline while Jim navigated the car into a narrow road that wound upward toward an elegant house perched on a hillside. As I walked through the front door, I was awestruck. Thoughts of Peter's departure faded as I absorbed the breathtaking views and opulent surroundings.

"Come, let me show you to your room," Helen offered cheerfully as we entered the house. We climbed a wide set of stairs, and when we reached the landing, she ushered me through one set of double doors.

"This is your dressing room, bathroom off to the side."

I stepped inside, feeling like an intruder in someone else's life. The room was filled with clothes—elegant dresses and delicate lingerie, all in my size. Helen must have noticed my hesitation, and she smiled kindly.

"Peter described you perfectly," she said. "I had fun shopping for you. Don't worry. You'll have a stylist in New York to help you build your wardrobe, but these should do for now."

I nodded, not trusting myself to speak. The reality of the changes in my life was sinking in, leaving behind everything I knew and stepping into a world so different from my own.

"One of the local seamstresses from Basse-Terre will arrive this afternoon and bring you a collection of designer bridal gowns to try on. Peter wanted the best, and you'll love the designs." I hadn't even thought of a wedding dress. My mind was spinning, trying to keep up with everything happening around me.

If the dressing room had been impressive, the bedroom was staggering. I found myself standing amid a semi-circular atrium unblocked by walls or posts. From where I stood, there was glass everywhere, all around, and even the ceiling seemed like nothing but the clear blue sky.

On the island's northern side, I could see La Soufriere, a four-thousand-foot volcano, shrouded in an eerie unmoving vapor of hot mist, quiet for now, but knowing it smoldered thermal liquid rocks from the boiling belly of the Earth.

Helen suggested brunch by the pool, and if I wanted to swim, I would find a bathing suit among the things she'd picked out for me.

"But we'll understand if you'd rather rest. I know it's been a long flight and an exhausting day for you. There's a button by your bedside. Press it if you need anything, and it will buzz downstairs in the servants' quarters. Caton will see to your needs."

I thanked Helen and took a moment to absorb my surroundings, the weight of everything settling in. This wasn't the wedding I'd dreamed of as a little girl. Vivienne's absence felt like a gaping void, her voice from our last conversation echoing sharp and unforgiving in my mind. But I couldn't call her. I didn't *want* to call her. I could already hear her disapproval, feel the weight of her judgment, and maybe I was afraid she'd fly out and drag me back by the hair.

As I thought back to the moment I'd left my parents—the hostility, the sharp, painful words exchanged—I knew this was *my* choice. I wasn't just chasing a fantasy. I had chosen this path and was determined to prove to myself—and everyone—that I was destined for this.

Peter

DECEMBER 1989
JARDIN MALANGA, GUADELOUPE

He hated leaving her on the island, but business couldn't wait, and the client was too important to ignore. Still, as Raine watched him with those wide, questioning eyes, he felt a tug he hadn't expected—a feeling he quickly buried beneath the weight of responsibility. It couldn't be helped. The call had come in mid-flight from an important client that even his most trusted right-hand man couldn't handle in his place. The client was one of the agency's largest accounts, filling the company coffers with more than $50 million in fees every year, and was now threatening to bid their advertising out to other firms. The client wanted to see Peter personally.

Time was tight. Peter would barely have enough time to land, freshen up at a hotel, and return to the regional airport for the meeting. The client had already scoffed at meeting in "Podunk" New Jersey, so Peter placated him with the promise of golf and a steak dinner at the Posthouse, where they served two-foot-long Tomahawk ribeyes—tomorrow.

He wouldn't tell his client that he was getting married tonight. It was nobody's business but his own. Still, he was glad the client relented because he could return in time for his wedding that evening.

He couldn't wait to see Raine in her wedding gown. The anticipation alone would make getting through this meeting difficult. But then, he'd also have to tell her there would be no honeymoon. It would have to be later. Much later. Peter shook his head, brushing aside his romantic musings and disappointment. For now, Raine would have to understand and embrace the world in which he lived.

Raine

DECEMBER 1989
JARDIN MALANGA, GUADELOUPE

The cliffside infinity pool rippled back, reflecting the azure sky. At its edge, water cascaded down the ravine to a stream that flowed into the turquoise Atlantic Ocean.

I dove into the water, the shock of cold invigorating. I bottom-fished for as long as I could hold my breath, twisting and turning, playing with make-believe mermaids, before I shot straight up, breaking the surface with a big splash.

I was startled to see Jim standing by the pool.

"How long have you been standing there?" I asked, feeling strangely naked.

"Not long. You seemed to know what you were doing."

Swimming to the poolside, I took the towel he offered, feeling self-conscious about the string bikini Helen had picked out. I struggled to dismiss his lingering gaze over my skin, convincing myself he only admired me respectfully. After all, I was his partner's bride-to-be.

"Where's Helen?" I asked.

"Seeing to lunch, I presume," he replied. "She'll be along shortly. How about a tour of the grounds before lunch?"

Pulling on a matching robe and slipping into flip-flops, we followed a cobblestone pathway that opened to a lavishly landscaped garden with flowering azaleas and brilliant celosias.

"This plantation home has been in my family for over two centuries," he began. "We grew sugar, exporting it as a commodity for decades."

Wet blades of grass tickled my ankles as we strolled.

"Do you have a large family?" I asked.

"Just Richard and Silvia, a sister who's a physician at Stanford. Helen and I have no children but many nieces and nephews."

"How'd you get into advertising?"

"My uncle, Max Silverman, owned Silverman Advertising. I joined after getting an MBA. But I never liked managing accounts. So when Uncle Max left me the agency, I brought Peter in to grow it. That's why he owns two-thirds of it. I plan to retire soon and return here to Jardin Malanga."

"You have a rich family history," I said.

We talked until we reached a cliff's edge, taking in the sea unfurling toward Les Saintes.

When we returned to the pool area, Jim asked, "Raine, how much do you know about Peter?"

I hesitated, unsure how to answer.

"I suspect not much," Jim said, reading my silence. "Peter keeps his past to himself. I want to make sure you know him before you take your vows."

I frowned. "Are you trying to discourage me?"

"It wasn't fair of him to rush you into marriage," Jim said, his tone strong. "You're only nineteen." I started to protest, but he stopped me. "No, listen. Peter has demons that drive him to succeed. If this marriage doesn't work, it could destroy him—and you. I begged him to work out a prenuptial agreement, but he refused. After meeting you, I see why. He's really in love with you."

His concern touched me. "Jim, I know I'm young, but I love him. I gave up everything to be with him."

"I know. And that scares me," he said.

After the congestion of Los Angeles, nighttime on the island was eerily quiet of civilization. The only sounds came from the krik-krik-krik of crickets, the summer singing of cicadas, and a symphony of croaking frogs. I sat in the back of the Jaguar with Jim and Helen as we drove through the darkness. When we reached the edge of the beach, a small chapel stood in solitude. It was pitch-black outside save for a million candles glowing inside the chapel. Their flickering cast off a soft amber radiance the color of a topaz jewel. For music, I marched to the only sound that could be heard: the gentle waves rolling with the tide.

He stood against glimmering candles, smashingly handsome in a suit and tie. His baby-blue eyes were soft and filled with love, gazing at me draped in designer Galia Lahav's ivory crepe wedding dress that I chose for its halter-style simplicity and classiness. It had fit so perfectly without alteration, hugging my subtle curves. Its high front slit revealed my long bare legs raised by a pair of impossibly high satin heels. I left my long hair hanging down and clasped one side behind my left ear with a cluster of tiny island flowers. I felt tall, elegant, sophisticated, subtly seductive, and sexy without a trace of the teenage coed that I was just yesterday.

I walked the short aisle alone. When I reached the altar, I gave my bouquet to Helen, took both of Peter's outstretched hands as we said our vows, and, with conviction, embraced my destiny.

I did not miss my father.

CHAPTER 17

Ron

A VISION OF HIS FUTURE
KIRTOMY, SCOTLAND

"Let's go-o-o-!!" Mackenzie hollered. Her voice carried on the gentle breeze as she tugged at Ron's hand, urging him down the sloping field of blooming Scottish heather. The vibrant blossoms filled the air with its sweet fragrance, and the landscape rolled out toward the sea, where they would picnic and swim in the tidepool.

The morning sun cast a warm, golden light over everything, making the scene feel almost dreamlike. Ron's heart swelled with life and joy as he watched his daughter's excitement. How had she grown so fast? She was already five, and every day, she seemed more independent and so full of life.

He glanced back, shielding his eyes from the bright sun, to check on his wife, who followed behind with their two-year-old. The child's chubby legs moved clumsily alongside her mother's. His wife's belly was gently rounded—she was four months pregnant with their third child. He squinted to make out her face, but the sunlight obscured her features.

Then, further down the field, he noticed a figure dressed in white, her long silver hair shimmering like spun silver. Recognition stirred in his heart.

"Granny!" Ron called out. He lifted Mackenzie into his arms and ran toward his grandmother. He hadn't seen her in ages, but she looked exactly as he remembered—radiant and full of life.

Ron set his daughter down when they reached her and embraced his grandmother's open arms. The familiar comfort of her soft bosom brought back memories of childhood summers spent at his grandparents' Michigan farm.

"You're here," he said, breathless with excitement. "You look beautiful, Granny. I've missed you."

"*Agus tha thu a' coimhead gu math, mo ghille,*" she replied likewise to Ron, her smile as bright as the sun, speaking in the Gaelic of her homeland.

"Thank you, Granny. I am well," Ron replied. It was from her that he had inherited the *gift of two sights*. It was also from her where he learned to speak Gaelic fluently.

Skye Ailsa MacKenzie, born and raised in the Highlands, had followed her adventurous spirit to London, where she married Sir James Reginald Mitchell of the Royal Navy. Her Scottish family disapproved, but Skye trusted her visions, which had foretold her marriage to an Englishman and a life far from home. Ron admired her bravery and felt a deep connection to his Scottish roots, stronger than his English or American heritage.

She looked down at the small child beside Ron.

"Mackenzie, this is your great granny, *a ghrá,*" he said, introducing his daughter.

"Why, look how bonny ye are, a *leanbh beag,*" Granny Skye cooed, embracing the child who eagerly leaned into her.

Ron glanced over his shoulder, searching for his wife and younger child. They were still coming down the hill, but their faces remained indistinct, like a mirage.

"I want you to meet her, my wife, and our younger daughter, Amee," he said, a frown creasing his brow. Why were they so far behind? Why couldn't he see her face clearly?

"What's the matter, Ronnie?" Granny Skye asked, lifting his chin with a gentle hand. She ran her fingers through his hair just as she had when he was a boy. "I see ye're troubled."

"I have two daughters and another child on the way. I see my wife coming down the hill, yet I can't see her face. Who is she, Granny? My vision hasn't been very clear."

"*Gar-mhac*, of course, ye ken who she is. Ronnie, all ye hae tae dae is look at yer daughter's eyes. Look at her bonnie wee face, *mo ghil*. Does she no' look like her mither?"

Ron studied his daughter's face more closely, noting the shape of her eyes, their almond tilt, and how they sparkled with life. How had he not noticed before?

"Her name is Ouisgé, a child of Highland blood, like yersel'. But her heart bears many scars. Ye must heal those wounds, Ronnie, before she can truly see ye. Trust in yer sight, lad—it's more powerful than ye ken."

Mackenzie squirmed in his arms, and when he set her down, she grabbed his hand, pulling him toward the beach.

"Let's go, Da. I wanna go swimming!" she shouted, her voice rising in the wind, and Ron could only run with her.

"Wait! We need to wait for your ma and your sister," he said, pulling back to slow her down, but his voice seemed lost in the wind until the shrill of his clock radio rudely woke him to Journey's "Don't Stop Believin'."

Ron opened one eye and reached over to hit the snooze button, wondering if he'd been drinking the night before to have changed the station to one playing that godawful Journey song.

Then he remembered his dream. Were the fae trying to tell him something? Well, whatever it was, he sure wasn't going to be ready for it.

Raine

MARCH 2000
DURHAM, NEW HAMPSHIRE

By March, cabin fever had set in. Though it was still sweater weather, I could ditch heavy jackets, gloves, and hats for a hoodie. The days were lengthening, and the outdoors beckoned.

Under the carport, I set up an old table from the garage, contemplating cutting some wooden boards I'd ordered from Tye for my kitchen shelves. Handling a circular saw didn't seem like a big deal, but the moment I let it touch the board pinned beneath my knee, it jerked violently. I jumped back, miraculously keeping the contraption from flying overhead.

I set the now-quiet saw on the ground like a sleeping baby. Why hadn't I thought to have these boards precut at the lumber yard? Feeling foolish, I stared at the saw, wondering how those women carpenters in videos kept such a steady hand.

I jumped at the sound of a menacing dog's bark that seemed so close behind me ready to pounce.

"Good God, you scared the shit out of me!" I exclaimed, spinning around to see Ron standing there with his dog.

"Sorry, we didn't mean to interrupt," he said, patting the dog's snout. "Goober's harmless."

I let out my breath, one hand over my chest, willing my heart to slow. I smiled at him, then at his mutt. I approached the pooch, let him sniff my fist, and then patted him.

"Uhm, you need help with that?" Ron asked, tilting his head toward the saw on the ground.

I turned to look at it. "Uhm ...I don't think so. Thanks anyway," I lied, too embarrassed to admit that I *did* need help.

I rushed to pick up the tool again but found the cord tangled around my ankle.

He loosely tied Goober's leash on a corner post of the carport, scruffed his neck, and ordered him to 'stay.'

"Here, I'll show you how to use this," he said, walking over to untangle the cord I had stepped on. "Got an extra pair of goggles?"

"You can use mine," I said, taking them off and handing them to him.

"Keep them," he said, then put on a pair of sunglasses that made him look like a Hollywood celebrity. "This will do for now."

He wasn't going to just demonstrate—he was going to make me do this myself, with his guidance. Positioning me before the board, he handed me the saw and leaned against my back. I felt his warmth, and though I'd expected to be a nervous wreck, his presence was surprisingly calming.

"Place your left knee on the board," he instructed, his voice steady and reassuring. "Now, hold the saw like this." He guided my right hand, his fingers firm over mine, and flipped the switch with his thumb. As the saw buzzed to life, the vibrations resonated through both of us. He held me steady as we moved slowly along the penciled line, the blade gliding through the pine in a smooth, controlled cut. The moment we finished, I let out a breath I didn't realize I'd been holding. "Phew! That wasn't so bad after all."

"Now, try it on your own," he said. "Don't worry, I'll watch and make sure you get it right."

After my second cut, I got the hang of it and finished the rest of the planks. He picked up two boards. "Would you like me to set these inside the house?"

I nodded. He carried them to the kitchen floor and returned for the rest.

"Do you need help putting them up?" he offered, looking at the space on the wall where I intended to install them.

Before I could answer, Goober's barking went off like an alarm.

"I guess not today," he sighed. "Somebody wants his breakfast."

"Yeah, I don't think you should keep him waiting," I said.

"I'll stop by again, or you can call me," he said, jotting down his number in my notebook that lay open on the butcher block table.

I walked him outside. "Thanks for helping with the saw and carrying the boards. I appreciate it."

"No sweat," he said, untying Goober. "I'd get earplugs if I were you. The noise can be pretty loud."

"Okay."

"I'll see you around. Come on, Goobs," he said, walking away.

Inexplicably, I wished he could have stayed longer.

Ron

When Ron left Raine the evening of her birthday, he'd sworn he would stay away from her. She had a lot of emotional baggage. He really didn't want to deal with anyone with all that drama. And her taste in music? Well, he didn't want to even think about that. He'd already convinced himself that they weren't suited for each other.

And then his granny visited him in a vision. Yeah, that was more than a fleeting dream. It was definitely a vision. But like all other visions he's had, they always spawned more questions than answers—a cryptic hint instead of a clear path. It was maddening, but if the fae weren't going to spell it out, then fuck it. He'd rather not get involved.

Yet, as he sat staring at his computer, the cursor blinking, waiting for him to continue with his dissertation research, Ron couldn't stop thinking about that morning, seeing Raine wrestle with the circular saw. She clearly had no idea how to handle it and would end up in the emergency room. He had to do something, didn't he? Ron tried convincing himself he was gallant in saving Raine from serious injury—a damsel in distress.

He could have done her a favor, cut the boards, and left. But, noo-oo. He *had* to teach her, which meant leaning against her, guiding her hand across the plank. The feel of her, the scent she wore, the tool's vibrations made him want to...

Ron shook his head to clear his thoughts. But then he ended up staring at his phone like a lovesick teenager, waiting for it to ring. Why, for fuck's sake, had he given her his number?

Raine

MAY 2000
DURHAM, NEW HAMPSHIRE

Standing outside my creaking porch, I cupped my mug of coffee and took stock of the overgrown gardens. Decades-old azalea bushes in full bloom, burning colors of brilliant pink and deep purple, bordered the walkway in the front yard. Forsythia limbs haphazardly budded yellow blossoms with wild abandon, like a woman's long frizzy hair in a humid heat wave.

The house where I grew up hugged the side of a mountain in Beverly Hills, overlooking sweeping views of LA. Instead of leaving the sloping landscape behind our house barren and unkempt, my parents had planted over an acre of produce, which my father used in his restaurant. The gardens were my mother's domain, and I always helped her. It was one of my assigned "chores."

While I didn't develop a passion for gardening like my mother, I enjoyed the work immensely. Creating a life of beauty for food was quiet and fulfilling, and I missed this while living in New York.

I had no experience renovating houses, but looking at my neglected yard, I thought I could do something I'd enjoy.

After a visit to Tye's with enough gardening materials to relandscape the White House, I hunched over with a spade in my front lawn, turning over the brown earth, soft from a recent spring shower. The effort exerted into pulling old dead plants and stubborn weeds, tilling the soil by hand, felt rejuvenating. It reminded me of when I would sit with my mother, plastic spade in hand, and listen to her gardening lectures embellished with Gaelic folklore in her thick Scottish brogue.

"Ye hae tae push the dirt in and tamp it doon, mo charaide. Else the bad faeries will find their way in and mak' a home in the roots. Ye'll no' hae any flowers t'all."

I really should call my mother. Talk to her about the flowers I'd picked to line my well-worn brick walkway. The mulch I would use to enhance their growth and color, doing everything I'd learned all those years ago when she thought I wasn't listening.

I would ask her to get Da on the phone. Tell him about the house I was restoring and how I'd learned to spackle and plaster wallboard. The Malley bolts I used to hold up a medicine chest that I hung in the kitchen, which served as my spice cabinet, were like the house in Kirtomy. Tell them both how New York was. How hard I worked to rise in business and make a name for myself. Tell them Peter was dead. Tell them both how he killed himself. How I'd found him...

Suddenly, the sun felt hot, and the air was stifling. I rose to get inside the house for a drink of water, but the sudden movement sent the blood rushing from my head. Before I knew it, spots of pink and yellow were blotting my vision, and the ringing in my ears wouldn't stop.

Breathe, Raine.

CHAPTER 18

Peter

"*Altissima quaeque flumina minimo sono labi.*"

That was the caption beneath Raine's yearbook picture when she'd upset the varsity tennis championship match, unseating four-year team captain Vivienne Oliver.

Peter recalled that picture vividly. Raine, then just eighteen, was sweaty but suffused with unbridled joy as she hoisted the two-foot trophy above her head. He had initially failed to grasp the Greek idiom's inference—Still Waters Run Deep.

When Peter was vetting Raine as a potential wife, his partner Jim York had secured a copy of St. Joseph Academy's 1989 yearbook. He hadn't thought about that picture until he saw how Raine transformed herself from a naive college freshman in outdated hippie clothes to a stunning, sophisticated image of a Vogue-cover model almost overnight. Her fashion sense, her elegant walk—it was as if she was born to sashay down the Christian Dior catwalk in Paris. Peter's ego swelled as heads turned in their direction when she was on his arm. In glossy magazines, they were the perfect, most photogenic couple in New York City.

But he should have known that Raine would not remain content to be merely his arm candy. It all began with her sitting on the boards of various charities, befitting the station of a society wife. Peter was stunned to see her rise to executive roles at those organizations, raising record amounts at the fundraisers she'd organized. His friends often complimented him on having such an intelligent wife.

"Gorgeous and smart, you lucky dog," they'd say, slapping him on the back.

Peter was proud of her—except that wasn't part of *The Plan*.

Raine

SEPTEMBER 1995
NEW YORK, NEW YORK

Peter found it unsettling that I began showing interest in his company.

Branding. Positioning. Value statements.

I was fascinated by the excitement of creating an ad campaign, from developing a brand to making it a household name like Coke or Intel.

When Peter made calls from home, I sometimes heard him shouting, "Listen to me! I said, shut up and listen to me!"

Other times, his excitement was contagious. "No shit! We got the deal? We got the fucking account!" He'd throw his head back in unrestrained laughter.

I envied his energy and power, the life he led outside of our marriage. I wished I could work on something infused with that adrenaline high. I, too, wanted to punch my fist into the air and scream, *"Yes!"*

My big break came the day Peter asked me to attend a meeting with the National Multiple Sclerosis Society on his behalf. I was expected to sit quietly, smile, nod, and stay awake. But I was absorbed by the discussion on disseminating clinical trial data efficiently to doctors worldwide. My brain started turning, and I drew circles, arrows, and diagrams on my notepad.

Then I piped in, "What if..."

And that was the beginning of everything for me. I was pumped and raring to go.

I walked down to Peter's office. We could have lunch, and I could give him the news but he wasn't expected back until later in the afternoon. Disappointed, I turned to leave and ran into Jim.

"Hello, gorgeous," he greeted, kissing me on the cheek. "And what brings your loveliness to the salt mines?"

Since Helen's death, women had flocked to him, eager to be seen with the handsome widower. He played the role of a refined playboy, indulging in discreet affairs without hesitation.

"You look positively radiant this morning," he said, always the master of flattery. "Expecting some news?"

"Not that kind," I blushed. "I came from the MS Society board meeting, and I've been charged with a project that could potentially lead to something big for S&Y. I wanted to talk to Peter."

"I believe he's out golfing with Henry today?" Jim glanced at Rosemary questioningly, who nodded in response.

"Yes, I heard," I replied, unable to mask my letdown. "I guess it will have to wait until he gets home."

Sensing my disappointment, Jim took me by the elbow and led me into his office.

"Last I checked I still had some say around here. Why don't you come in and tell me about it?" he offered, closing the door behind me.

Peter

H is wife's career didn't just take off. It shot out from a cannon with a loud bang, and then money rained from the heavens. That was when his mother's disease struck him.

At a black-tie fundraiser Jim hosted for the MS Society, the organization unveiled Raine's brainchild, the clinical trial digital catalog project. It sounded complex but was stupidly simple. Take clinical trial data, visualize it with computer graphics on PowerPoint slides, and burn the files onto CDs. Physicians didn't need to read every detail. They just needed the bullet points to make informed decisions. The CDs could be distributed at medical conferences or by drug reps. No mailing, no faxing, no photocopying. S&Y would program the database, produce the CDs, and create the marketing materials. The revenue to S&Y? A cool million for one drug.

Peter's mind raced, calculating the potential profits from multiple drugs undergoing trials. Raine was fucking brilliant.

Tonight, she exuded confidence, her brainpower drawing admirers all evening. She basked in her accomplishments, unaware of the influence she held. She would be in demand, commanding large sums for her work. She wouldn't need him anymore.

"You okay, son? You look a little peaked," Jim asked, approaching Peter.

"I'm fine," he replied, sipping his drink. He shifted his glass to his left hand, flexing his right fingers to stop the tremors that had started minutes ago.

"Raine should work for us full time, not as a volunteer."

"No!" Peter snapped, hiding his trembling hand.

"I know how you feel about her having a career, Peter. Dammit, the client wants her as the lead project manager and account executive. It's a million dollars. Do you really want to pass on that because of your fucking ego?"

That stung.

Jim patted Peter's shoulder and walked away. He knew there would be no further discussion.

Numbness crept up his leg. Excusing himself, Peter pushed through the crowd, desperate for the elevator. Outside, he loosened his bow tie and unbuttoned his collar, gasping for air. He limped up the sidewalk, trying to shake his leg awake until he stumbled, scraping his hands to break his fall. Passersby walked around him, not offering help, for which he was grateful. He didn't want the attention.

He knew what this was. The gene that had been dormant was manifesting itself. For the first time since his mother died, Peter allowed himself to cry.

NOVEMBER 1995
NEW YORK, NEW YORK

We left the MS Society's fundraiser unusually early. It was the first time I'd felt Peter's cold side with displeasure toward me. His face was stony and distant, sending chills up my spine. Guilt gnawed at me, wondering what I'd done to anger him. But something else seemed to be bothering him. Once we reached the privacy of our apartment, he unleashed a fury that I could not calm.

"I can't believe you pulled a stunt like that, Raine. You embarrassed me!" he shouted as we walked into the apartment, throwing his tuxedo jacket over the couch. He looked back at me, his eyes demanding an answer.

"What? What did I do?" I asked, baffled by his outburst, shuddering at his outrage.

"Don't be stupid. You knew exactly what you were doing. You were trying to upstage me."

He sighed in exasperation, shaking his head mockingly as if I were nothing more than an empty-headed woman. Sweat beaded on his forehead and neck as he struggled to undo his bowtie. He didn't look well.

"Here, let me help you…" I walked toward him, but he batted my hand away. I had never felt such a direct and physical rebuff from him.

"Why did you go to Jim and ask him for help with your pet project? Why didn't you ask me first?" His anger filled the room.

I stared at him, unblinking, in disbelief.

"I did, and you'd said nothing. I thought you'd have been proud of me," I said quietly, retreating from him.

Except with my parents, I never played the wounded waif when someone called me out. I didn't fight back, either. I would calmly talk through the problem with logic and reason. But Peter's temper was murderous that night, and this was the first time he fixated his tempestuous ire on me.

"Proud of you? You flaunted yourself before everyone tonight. Do you think they were praising? They're making fun of you, Raine. You're my wife, for God's sake! Doesn't that mean anything to you?"

"But they were complimenting me..." I trailed off.

"Listen, Raine, don't think people were admiring you," he said, wagging a finger. "You were nothing when I met you. And you'd be nothing without me."

That felt like a slap. I turned and fled the room, locking myself in the bathroom before he saw my tears. I would not let him see me cry. I would not let him witness my crumbling to the floor like a rag doll silently calling for my Da.

Peter

NOVEMBER 1995
NEW YORK, NEW YORK

He struck the steel-reinforced front door of their apartment with his fist, a sharp crack echoing through the hallway. Pain shot through his hand, but he held it in check, releasing a litany of expletives as he stormed out of the apartment building. In the emergency room, as they tended to his broken hand, Peter could see his future crumbling. But when he returned home, hand splintered and cast, he found a new resolve. Maybe this was a fluke. He was tired and overworked.

Peter found Raine curled up on her side of the bed, hugging the edge as far as she could. The sight broke his heart. The codeine dulled the pain in his hand, but the grief and guilt inside him were unbearable. She had borne the brunt of his anger without understanding why.

Silently, he undressed with one hand, keeping his plastered fist away, then curled beside her. Her soft, hiccupping sobs still echoed in the quiet room, even as she slept.

"I'm sorry, sweetheart," he whispered, his voice cracking as he closed his misting eyes, hoping his apology would reach her.

CHAPTER 19

Luke

NOVEMBER 1995
NEW YORK, NEW YORK

U nlike his partners, who had executive suites along Mahogany Row, Silverman & York's third major partner and chief creative officer preferred to have his office on the opposite end with his team of art directors, artists, and graphic designers. They were rebels and nonconformists who didn't wear suits and ties, cut their hair, or sport clean-shaven faces.

Born in China and adopted by a Swedish couple, Luke Henes liked having his drawing table face the window to look out toward the south side of Manhattan and contemplate the beauty and architecture of the iconic Flatiron Building when he needed inspiration for his work.

He was not searching for inspiration that morning. Staring through the raindrop-covered window of his office, the image of his partner and best friend's wife came to mind.

When he'd first met her, he could not understand how Peter could have married such a shrinking violet who seemed to faint if one so much as said boo to her. Luke has tried to pull Raine into a conversation several times. Still, she would only nod and string no more than two sentences in response, which seemed orchestrated to follow through on whatever Peter had started to say as if she'd rehearsed the part and had practiced her cue.

Luke suspected an untapped personality beneath her timidity. But how could he get her to smile of her own accord if he only saw her when Peter was around? She would always withdraw behind Peter's shadow.

He sighed as the rain pelted against the window. Another day for lunch delivery, he thought. He wasn't in the mood for cold, chewy pizza or Chinese takeout, the standard staples for eat-at-your-desk days.

He wondered if Raine liked Italian. Would she enjoy Mama Rosa's?

"Luke, got a minute?"

He jumped at Jim's voice. Thank God it wasn't Peter.

"Sure. Come on in," Luke offered, motioning for Jim to have a seat. "So what's up?"

"We've got a big account coming in."

Luke sighed. "Good news for the agency, but bad news for me. I can't keep up with the hiring. Jim, we are so understaffed in the creative department. But feel free to ignore my bitching and moaning. Which account is this?"

"Drummond Pharmaceuticals."

"Shit!" Luke exclaimed, rubbing his temples. "I don't have any creatives with expertise in pharma marketing."

"Not to worry, I've hired a project manager to launch it and get the staffing. Since it is design work, she'll be a part of your department and will report to you as her supervisor. Anyway, she starts today. She's in HR right now, filling out paperwork. As soon as she gets done, she'll be right over," Jim said.

Luke's jaw dropped.

"*What???* Since when did you get involved in staffing matters? What's going on here?"

"Those comps you did for the MS Society?"

"Yeah? It was for one of Peter's nonprofits. That was gratis."

"That was Raine's concept. She landed Drummond for a solid million in fees. And we're already seeing other pharma companies lining up."

Luke held his breath. "Are you telling me..."

"Yes, Raine starts today as a full-time PM. She can take the office next door since it's vacant."

Raine Garvey? The same Raine Garvey who'd been flitting in and out of his subconscious since Peter brought her to New York? How did this happen? Did Peter agree to this?

Peter's wife. Dear God.

How would he get any work done with the beautiful Mrs. Peter Garvey working next door?

Luke sunk his head between his hands. He was in trouble.

"We, uhm, normally take new employees out to lunch on their first day," Luke said, filling the door of Raine's new office.

He watched as she carefully pulled some folders from her briefcase and laid them on the empty desk. Her hair was partly pulled back by a barrette, which revealed her forehead. But the rest of it hung loose down her back. Luke watched as Raine's fingers gently tucked the loose strands behind her ear.

There was something different about her today. She was dressed in a designer pantsuit, modestly cut and in black. Underneath, she wore a white shirt open at the collar, her neck bare and unadorned by jewelry. Luke could see—no, feel—her temple's pulse.

She radiated a quiet, tentative confidence. Was it because she wasn't playing coy wife and hostess to Peter?

"Sure, if you want to," she replied without looking up. "I mean, you're my boss, right?"

When she smiled at him this time, she stood tall, chin up, back straight. Peter was out of town.

"Right," Luke said. "Unless you'd rather not. I mean, the weather and all...."

"I don't mind the weather." She shrugged.

"Let me call Carty then," Luke offered.

"Why? Is it far from here?" She frowned at his suggestion. "If you don't mind, I'd rather not venture too far for lunch. I do have a lot to do on this project."

"Couple of blocks," he replied. "But they are long blocks, and it's pretty nasty out there."

"I don't mind walking. Pity to get a car for two blocks. I've got one of these big umbrellas we can share. What do you think?"

She pulled out one of the giant golf umbrellas that bore the agency's logo.

Share an umbrella, Luke thought, swallowing an imaginary lump in his throat. They would walk side by side, huddled under an umbrella. Their shoulders would rub against each other, maybe their heads touching.

"If you're sure..." He said then, quickly before he lost his nerve, "We'll walk."

Maybe it was the rain. Or the spaghetti Bolognese. Perhaps it was the fist-sized meatball she ordered with her pasta. Or the mountain of cheese she'd sprinkled on top. Or the Chianti.

She'd changed right before his eyes, emerged a different person. And when they left the restaurant, she suddenly fled from him. But before he could wonder if he'd said something wrong, she stopped, stretched out her arms and faced the sky, drinking the droplets of water, then twirled around, nearly bumping into a woman who scowled at her, but Raine paid her no heed.

Luke stood in awe, watching her. And when she saw him standing there, she threw her head back and laughed with wild abandon. He lowered the umbrella, stood amid the rain, and allowed himself to get soaked, laughing with her. He must have been a sight to her, drenched and dripping wet. But he didn't care if she didn't. Right then, he made a silent vow that even if he were nothing more than a friend to her, he would do everything to ensure that Raine remained as she was amid a New York storm—footloose, fancy-free, and happy.

Raine

NOVEMBER 1995
NEW YORK, NEW YORK

"I ... I'm so sorry, Peter. I didn't know you would be home..."

The apartment was filled with roses, and a candlelit dinner was set on the table. Peter sat on the couch with a drink in his hand. Dear God, how long had he been waiting?

"Honest, Peter, Rosemary said you weren't due back until the day after tomorrow... And Jim asked me to start work today. You're okay with that, right? He said he cleared it with you. I tried to reach you and left you a message that I'd work late tonight, thinking you wouldn't be home anyway..."

I covered my face, bracing for his rage. Instead, he came to me and gently pulled my hands away from my eyes, tilting my face to meet his gaze. I was startled to find no anger in them, only a soft, endearing plea.

"Shh," he said, brushing the loose strands from my face. "Raine, I love you. Let's start our family now," he said softly.

What?

I was stunned, my mind racing. "Oh God, Peter. Yes, of course!"

I should have been thrilled. I had so longed for him to want to start a family. But Peter's unexpected declaration threw me into emotional turmoil.

He pulled a box from his pocket and opened it before me. Inside was a diamond anniversary ring. Three diamonds—one for the present, the past, and the future. It didn't matter that it wasn't our anniversary.

"I think this is long overdue," he said, slipping it onto my left hand, joining my wedding band and engagement ring.

He said each diamond represented the number of children we would have. I couldn't stop the tears if I tried.

We ate our cold dinner by candlelight, hands continually held just like on our first dinner date, and talked about our future children—a girl, maybe a boy, then another girl.

"The girls will take after their mother's beauty, and our son will excel in academics and sports."

It all sounded so...matter-of-fact, like we were placing an order for dolls.

"I'm going to run for U.S. Senator of New York, Raine. And I want you there beside me." He kissed my hand gently as he said it.

I couldn't read his expression but felt he'd already planned this. His ambitions were to rise to a more powerful place, and he wanted me there. But not as his equal. Not as someone with a career alongside his. I knew then that my days at the agency were numbered. My heart sank with this preordained conclusion.

I was just beginning to discover who I was independent of Peter. And now, it would all end as we planned to start a family and he ran for public office. The thought disheartened me, yet how could it? Wasn't becoming a mother a dream of mine, too?

Lingering in the back of my mind, however, was the all-important question of why I never conceived in the six years of my marriage to Peter. I wasn't on birth control. What if I couldn't have children at all? It was a daunting thought because more than giving up a career, being childless would be the bigger heartbreak.

CHAPTER 20

Raine

JUNE 1998
NEW YORK, NEW YORK

Three diamonds. Three years. And I still couldn't get pregnant.

I gently tried to prod Peter to see a fertility specialist with me, but his response was to offer an excuse.

"Not now, Raine. This will be a heavy travel month for me." Or, "I have to start laying the groundwork for my campaign. Unfortunately, the timing to have kids is bad."

Eventually, the excuses wore on me, and I gave up. I sat in my office reviewing a new sales pitch for my client, wondering how Peter would react if I told him I was planning to pursue a new project. If he approved and I was awarded the account, it would mean another commitment of time that would push any plans of starting a family even further into the future. At least, in Peter's mind, it would be. *Well, fuck it.*

I twirled the three-diamond ring I'd been wearing on my left hand. So much for the three-children sentiment it held. I pulled it off and slipped it into my purse. Despite all the promises, I was convinced he had no plans to have children.

Peter

"I 'll have results in a day or two," said Jordan Horowitz as Peter dressed following a complete physical workup, which he finally scheduled after three years of indecision and Raine's incessant nudging.

He'd meant it when he told her he wanted to start a family. Part of his indecision was deciding which physician to confide the most private parts of his life and health. Something even his wife had not been privy to.

Jordan Horowitz was Peter's high school buddy and now a neurologist who was highly respected for his work in neurodegenerative diseases. They'd come a long way from their days at Valley Forge Prep, where he'd spent his last two high school years.

Peter remembered the isolation of his teenage years, the sterile smell of hospital rooms, and the relentless pain of skin grafts and surgeries. At seventeen, he had been a ghost among his peers, the agony etching lines of maturity into his young face. With his mother and father gone and his grandmother who raised him too cold, his only solace had been Jordan's unwavering friendship. Now, sitting in his office, the memories felt as raw as his reconstructed skin once had. Would his body betray him again? The thought gnawed at his optimism, turning his hope into a fragile facade.

"So if everything comes back normal, I can refer you and Raine to a fertility specialist. But let's cross that bridge when we get there. Hopefully, that flare-up you had three years ago— and I wish you'd have come to see me sooner—wasn't anything to worry about. You said you haven't had any since then?"

"No, I've been feeling great, in fact. Maybe tired and stressed from work, but nothing out of the ordinary."

"Then there's good reason to hope," Jordan said.

After leaving his doctor's office, Peter asked Carty to drive him to Washington Square Park South in Greenwich Village, where in the late afternoon, he entered the small chapel in the heart of the NYU campus. During his undergrad years, he would visit the little church to pray for his mother and speak to her when things troubled him. Such was the moment for him now.

Currently empty of congregants, he slipped into a pew and knelt in prayer.

Hi, Mama...

"Mr. Garvey, your wife wants a meeting with you. Your calendar is open at five. Shall I put her on it?" Rosemary asked, standing in the doorway of his office. Peter checked the time on his executive desk clock.

"Why don't you send her in now?"

Perfect timing, Peter thought. After seeing Jordan this morning, Peter felt confident all would be okay, and he wanted to tell his wife they could finally see a specialist and start the family they had long planned.

When he saw her enter his office, she was dressed in a simple cream-colored straight-cut dress that fell to her knees. They had been married nine years, and she never ceased to take his breath away.

In another day or two, Jordan would give him the all-clear, and he'd be free of the demons of his past. He couldn't wait to see his wife pregnant with his child.

When she walked in, Peter saw poster boards under her arms threatening to spill. He walked over to assist, but she waved him off.

"I want to show you these," Raine said, her eyes bright with excitement as she propped the boards against the back seat of the couch in his office's seating area.

"What's all this?" he asked, walking over to get a closer look.

"I comped an ad campaign for Drummond's Forenza. We created the drug's clinical trials database. They just got FDA approval, and it will hit the market next year. They invited us to make a pitch for the commercial marketing."

"You did this?" Peter said, his eyes still studying the posters. The message was clear, the image compelling, the design unified, and the tagline... *The Promise of Tomorrow.* Forenza was a drug to manage MS flare-up symptoms. This was his wife's genius. Because that was what she was—a genius at writing taglines and copy. But the ad's message also hit too close to home for Peter.

Suddenly Peter was scared. All the positivity he'd felt earlier seemed to be slipping as he looked at the drug ads for MS. As if it was an omen.

"Not only that," she continued, "take a look at these sample mini boards."

It was all Greek to him. Still, Peter couldn't help being impressed. His wife had learned the pharmaceutical advertising business in less than three years.

When they'd met, he never expected her to want a career, let alone one in advertising. Or that she would be a quick study—frighteningly quick study. She went on about the virtues of the new drug, its findings, and the product positioning she envisioned like a medical expert *and* a seasoned advertising pro.

But Peter could barely listen.

"If hard data supports the marketing, sales would be inevitable. The client will have a blockbuster drug with an eighteen-year patent, and S&Y can also lock in a contract on that term. I'm guessing another million in fees—per year!"

He usually would have perked up at the sound of the fees. Instead, he looked up, trying to bring back the reasons he had in mind earlier to talk to her, trying not to get irritated. Jesus, she wasn't supposed to be this... *brilliant?* And to pursue a career to boot. How exactly would this work out with him in public office and her with a career and kids in tow?

"Raine, you were supposed to wrap up the database and be done with it."

He heard an audible sigh escape his wife's lips while she crossed her arms impatiently.

"We didn't wrap up at one drug. We signed up to do databases for five other drug trials. That's seven million in revenue, and I know you see those numbers when Charlie runs the reports.

"Forenza is the first one that is ready for launch. Yes, that should be the end of that project after we hand the database over to the client, but why let it end when we can keep the revenue stream going with our traditional business? This is much easier than chasing the elusive Coca-Cola and Nabisco accounts that stress Greyson's team every time they pitch for new business or struggle to keep existing ones from walking."

Peter remained quiet long enough for his wife to sense something was amiss. When he walked toward his office door to close it, he was signaling that he was done listening and wouldn't provide further commentary. He noted her stiffening when he faced her.

He should have walked over to her, taken her into his arms, run his fingers through her hair, kissed her softly on her lips, and talked to her tenderly. Instead, he stood with fists on his waist, staring at her darkly, and spat, "So how exactly do you propose to do all this and still have a family? I thought you wanted to have a baby?"

For the first time in his life, someone told Peter to fuck off.

Raine

"*F*uck you!*"

That was what I said to my husband earlier in his office, and I said it to his face, firing daggers from my eyes. This time, I wasn't playing the simpering waif.

I was red-in-the-face pissed off, my hands trembling with unspent rage. The last time I felt this way, I had screamed at my father, then ran off and eloped with Peter. My anger propelled me to leave the office. I stormed into a nearby bike shop, not caring about the bewildered look from the clerk as I demanded the best gear they had.

Minutes later, I stood in full cycling gear—helmet, jersey, padded pants, gloves, shoes, and a seven hundred-dollar Thorn English bike. The absurdity of my spontaneous purchase barely registered as I pedaled furiously through the city, my anger fueling each push of the pedals. The rhythmic hum of the tires on the pavement did little to calm the storm inside me.

I had never biked in Manhattan or anywhere since leaving LA. That afternoon, I rode across town, the unfamiliar weight of the bike gear grounding me in the moment. I aimed to cycle from Chelsea to Grant's Tomb, a three-mile stretch that promised to be just long enough to burn off my fury.

But after about forty-five minutes, I felt my calves screaming, and by the time I reached Grant's Tomb on the Upper West Side, I collapsed onto the grass. I had painfully cramped one of my legs. And what with not having eaten since break-fast or brought any water, I started hyperventilating. I held my head forward to prevent from blacking out but was losing.

My vision started to fade, and a high-pitched ringing pierced my ears when I felt Peter's strong arms lift me, car-rying me to the car with Carty nearby.

He handed me a bottle of water, which I drank from thirst-ily. I'm sure the security detail he employed to follow me ev-erywhere let him know where I was.

This wasn't a matter of distrust but protection. I'd grown used to security, growing up in LA as the daughter of a famous chef and hanging out with the daughter of a movie mogul. Both my parents and Vivienne's father were paranoid about us getting kidnapped for ransom, so we were never without someone keeping an eye on us from a distance.

I was grateful Peter knew where to find me.

"Thank you for rescuing me from my stupidity and care-lessness," I said, trying to get him to look at me.

Peter said nothing as Carty drove along the West Side Highway. His gaze was fixed on the Hudson Bay, the sun set-ting over the New Jersey landscape. The silence between us grew colder, the air thick with unspoken words. Though he sat beside me, he felt miles away, an overwhelming distance I couldn't bridge. Tears welled up and spilled over as I turned my face away, my shoulders shaking with the effort to contain my sobs. Then, unexpectedly, I felt his fingers brush against mine, a tentative touch that spoke of apology and unspoken promises. It was a fragile connection, but it was all I had.

CHAPTER 21

Raine

MAY 2000

DURHAM, NEW HAMPSHIRE

"Hey, you okay?"

I jumped, snapping to my senses and taking several deep breaths to steady myself. I squinted toward the voice until my vision cleared, and recognized Ron.

"I'm fine. You startled me!"

"Sorry, I seem to be doing that all the time," he said, frowning. "But you look kinda pale. Shouldn't you go inside? It's almost too warm today."

I shook my head and removed my gloves, tossing them on the ground beside the hand spade.

"This happens when I get dehydrated and then stand too quickly," I said, squinting at the sun again. It was getting warm. "I think I've had enough gardening for the day."

I turned toward the house, unsure whether to say goodbye or invite him inside, but finally said, "I'm going inside. Would you like to come in for a cold drink?"

"Sure," he said, following behind.

"Watch yourself," I warned as we navigated the mess of cut shelves on the living room floor and various tools scattered about.

"Looks like you've got more shelves sawed up. You did a good job."

"Thanks, I had a good teacher." I smiled, remembering the day we worked together. Truth was I messed up the next batch I sawed but I wasn't going to admit that to him.

"You want help putting these up?" He looked around, eager to help.

"Thanks, but it can wait. I'm onto yard work now that the weather's nicer."

I walked to my new lemon-yellow Smeg fridge and pulled out two water bottles.

"I see you got your vintage fridge," he said. "It's quite unusual looking. Very retro and the color is striking. I don't think I've ever seen a yellow fridge before."

"Thanks. It's styled that way on purpose, and the color was popular in the seventies. I heard about it from Gordon, the guy who restored my range. It has modern features but fits in this corner nicely."

"It's a bold choice, but it works perfectly!" he admired.

With cold water bottles in hand, we headed for the backyard, where it was cooler beneath the shade of the now-leafy apple tree.

"I don't know what kinds of trees those are," I said, pointing to the wooded area. "But they look like hardwoods."

"Maple and oak, some apple," he said as we walked toward them. "I see an old locust. Must be about one hundred years, judging by the gnarly branches. Beyond the trees would be the Oyster River, and I'll bet you can walk down to it."

I noticed he was no longer stammering, which I hope meant I no longer made him nervous around me. "I think my property line runs straight down to the river. I haven't walked out that way yet, but I'm told you could get a canoe or kayak off the embankment."

"This branch," he said, pointing, "meanders toward the Great Bay before spilling into the ocean. It's more like a creek, though. Unless the water level's high, you'd be paddling over rocks and not going far."

"I don't think I'm going to be doing any paddling anytime soon," I said as we returned to the front of the house. "You know quite a bit about the outdoors,"

"It's what I teach. Geology."

"Jops mentioned you're a professor at UNH."

"Assistant professor," he corrected. "Just a fancy word in academia for teacher. I'm still working on my Ph.D. before I can get a full professorship."

"How far along are you in your dissertation?"

"Close. I'll defend my thesis in November, then hopefully graduate in December," he said, crossing his fingers. "What about you?"

I sighed.

"Nothing as impressive as being a professor with a Ph.D."

Ron chuckled, "I doubt that."

"What do you mean?" I frowned.

"You strike me as someone who's accomplished many things, including fixing this up?" He waved his hand at the house. "I don't know of any woman who would have had the guts to do what you're doing."

I shrugged. "I'm on sabbatical from my job in New York. The pressures got to be too much. I needed a break. Working on the house was therapeutic."

"What did you do?" he pressed without sounding pushy.

"Advertising? Marketing? Creating ads for products and stuff."

"That sounds like fun. And creative," he said with such innocence.

If only it had been...fun, I wouldn't have been here.

"Sometimes it was fun. Advertising is just a glamorous term for selling, and it can be a pressure cooker," I chuckled.

"Not all jingles and joy?" he teased.

"No, running a large public company is overwhelming. I had to step away, but I'll have to face it again. Hopefully, being here will bring clarity, and I can be a better leader."

Ron fell silent, and when I looked at him, his gaze was penetrating too deeply and seeing more.

"You're Raine Garvey, aren't you? Married to Peter Garvey?"

"I...was." I looked away briefly.

"Oh God, Raine. I'm really sorry... I didn't mean to bring it up...ah, I wasn't uhm, you know, trying to pry?"

He spoke haltingly again, endeavoring to process the revelation.

"It's okay. It is what it is," I said softly, trying to reassure him that I was still the same Raine he'd known for the past few months. However, I'm not sure I convinced him as he began walking backward.

"Well, uhm...I better go... Thanks for the water." He handed back the empty bottle. When our fingers brushed, we felt that spark again, which seemed to startle him.

I watched as he hurried away. The attraction between us was palpable. But how could I act on it? We were too different. My life was too complicated. Who would want to get involved with me?

If my musings hadn't been enough to remind me I didn't belong here, my phone buzzed. Chills ran up my spine when I heard the voice on the other end.

"Mrs. Garvey, this is Nick Coelho of *The New York Tribune*."

I might as well have scalded my hands when I heard Nick's voice because I dropped my cell phone like it was radioactive. Then I popped out the battery to prevent him from calling me back, drilled a hole through it, drove to Portsmouth and flung it into the ocean.

I'll admit, it was a little extreme, but once I'd calmed down, I ducked into the nearest Bell Atlantic store, picked up another one with a new number bearing a New Hampshire area code, and then called Vivienne, the only soul who knew where I'd holed up after leaving New York.

"So, you chucked your company-issued cell phone into the Atlantic, Nish? I wondered how long it would take before you changed your number. What happened now?"

"Nick called."

"Shit! Seriously?"

"I have no idea how he discovered my New York cell number, but I wouldn't put it past him. That guy's a snake. Anyway, take this new number down."

"What did he want?"

"I don't know. I hung up. I freaked out and crucified the phone with a nail gun."

"Jesus! Are you sure you're okay?"

"I'm fine. Now." I paused to gather my thoughts. "Vivi, can you call him directly and find out what he wants?" I bit my lip because tears were stinging my eyes. I just wasn't ready to deal with all that New York shit.

"I know I could call Greyson. Or Melissa in PR. But then I would have to make myself reachable. I really don't want anyone to have direct access to me. Except you. Not yet."

"I gotcha, babe. Not to worry. I'll make a few calls."

My eyes blurred. "Thanks, Vivi. God, I owe you so much."

Hearing my cracking voice, she asked, "Need some company? I can be there tomorrow if you want. Or tonight even."

How did I ever deserve such a faithful, loyal friend who always had my back?

"I'm good now."

"Well, don't worry about a thing. I'll get back to you on the snake."

I laughed, wiping my tears. "Love you, Vivi Girl."

Nick

MAY 2000

NEW YORK, NEW YORK

"So what exactly is this shit I'm reading?"

Anna Jackson's face was scrunched as she read Nick's draft on her computer.

Summoned into his boss's boss's office, Nick knew he was in trouble. Anna Jackson, executive editor for *The Tribune,* ruled over all things news. She was a tall black woman who'd clawed and scratched her way to the top post in a profession dominated by egotistical and blusterous white journalists and editors. Nothing got past her, no matter how "fit to print" the news was.

Nick had clashed with Anna in the past, fighting hard for stories he believed in. This time, however, he felt embarrassed that this draft had even reached her desk. He'd asked Sheila, the night editor, to see if the story had merit. Somehow, Anna got a hold of it.

Nick took a seat in front of Anna's desk while she read his headline aloud:

"Missus hangs up executive apron—finds kitchen too hot.

"Really, Nick?" But Anna kept on reading aloud.

"Glory Media CEO Raine Garvey plans to step down next year following her sabbatical, sources close to the company said.

"In January, York was admitted to NYU Medical with a stroke just two days before Garvey surprised the board with a request to take a belated year-long bereavement leave nearly thirteen months after her husband, former CEO Peter Garvey, committed suicide in their Upper East Side apartment.

"Investors are wondering, why now? Among speculation brewing is that the billionaire heiress and York had squared off over personal matters.

"One theory was that York was contesting the widow's claim to the firm, now worth six billion in equity. Others believe the argument may have stemmed from a silly incident at the company's Year 2000 bash at the Waldorf when York had embarrassed the CEO in front of clients."

Nick was visibly cringing. Hearing it from Anna made it sound like he was a greenhorn in undergrad school.

Anna finally stopped without finishing the rest of what he'd written.

"What Kool-Aid were you drinking when you wrote this, Nick? Because even as a draft, this doesn't sound like the guy who received a Peabody award last year."

"Anna, I tried to call Raine Garvey to interview her before you read that. It wasn't finished."

"And did you get Raine on the line?"

Nick hung his head.

"She hung up on you, didn't she?"

Nick nodded, staring at the ceiling.

"Nick, your obsession with the Garveys is getting out of control. Even if there was a fraction of truth, it's old news. York died six months ago. Drop it. Now, I will delete this story from the server, and I never want to see it again."

Nick left Anna's office with his head bowed. She wouldn't see that article again.

But drop the Garvey story? Never.

CHAPTER 22

Ron

MAY 2000

DURHAM, NEW HAMPSHIRE

"It was going so well."

"So what happened?" Ed asked, not looking up from the emails.

"It got awkward."

More like he got awkward and scurried off like a skittish chipmunk. God, what had he been thinking? Didn't he tell himself that Raine was out of his league? And now that he knew who she was, it felt worse.

"She's who?" Ed asked when Ron told him that Raine Garvey of the Callahan House was the Raine Garvey, billionaire widow of the late Peter Garvey.

"And this is a problem...why?" Ed asked, sounding frustrated. Ron leaned back in his chair, anticipating a lecture.

He couldn't explain to Ed why he bolted. Yes, Raine's status was overwhelming, but seeing her eyes matching those of the little girl in his vision a few months ago was more disconcerting. His granny's words echoed in his mind, *"All ye hae tae dae is look at yer daughter's eyes... Does she no' look like her mother?"*

It couldn't have been clearer. His "future daughter" was the spitting image of Raine. He pinched the bridge of his nose, trying to chase away thoughts of a nonexistent wife and child.

"I'm not a part of her world, Ed. Can you imagine me in New York as her boyfriend? Going to those glam fundraisers in a black tie? Being photographed wherever she goes?"

Ed gaped at him. "Aren't you getting ahead of yourself?"

"I'm so confused over what to do."

Ed finally looked away from his computer. "Ron, this is not a dissertation research question. Just decide and move on."

"You're right. This isn't going to work," Ron replied, shaking his head as he stood to leave. Undoubtedly, the faes were playing tricks on him. "There's no way she'd say yes if I asked her out anyway."

Ed snorted, "Fritzso will be happy to hear that."

Ron stopped by the doorway and glared back at Ed.

"Thought so," Ed said.

"What do you mean?"

"Ron, you're so hung up on her she's got your balls in a vise grip. You couldn't run away if you tried."

Ron raised a brow. "Wanna bet?"

Ron knew he'd made the biggest sucker bet of his life.

He should have just handed his twenty to Ed right then and there and walked around with the word "*Sucker*" tattooed on his forehead.

Damn the fae. He knew that his *An Dà Shealladh* and the vision that he and Raine were destined to be together made the bet folly. And it bothered him. Hell, it scared him!

It won't work.

She won't be happy with me.

I won't fit in in her world.

The next day, Ron threw his climbing gear in the trunk of his car and drove to Maine's Acadia National Park, seeking clarity. As he reached the Great Head rockface, the sun cast a warm glow over the rugged coastline.

Standing at the base, Ron considered his route. Checking his gear, he began his ascent. His fingers found familiar handholds, and his body moved with practiced ease. The climb was challenging but exhilarating.

Midway up, a strong gust of wind threw him off balance. Panic surged as he slipped, but he managed to grasp a small crimp. Dangling precariously, he heard a child's voice from the top.

"Come on, Da. You can do it." Ron looked up, seeing the image of the little girl from his earlier vision. Fear for her safety, not his own, gripped him.

"Jesus! Move away from the ledge, Mackenzie," he shouted, glancing around for Raine.

Where the hell was her mother?

He forced himself to breathe and focus. With deliberate movements, he regained his footing and climbed the final pitch.

Pulling himself over the edge, he looked around for the imagined girl. She was nowhere to be found.

"Are ye awright?"

Startled, Ron turned to see a woman in climbing gear, with two similarly dressed women beside her.

"Weel, tha' was daft, takin' a chance like tha' tae climb a rock ye'd ne'er scaled before by yerself, ken?" scolded another, with a hint of amusement in her eye.

"We were jist aboot tae come doon and rescue ye, lad. Right, ye had us worried, aye" Added the third woman.

Three older women, probably in their fifties, fit and trim, looked like experienced climbers judging by their gear. Two had short-cropped salt and pepper hair, while the third had hers all in gleaming silver swept up in a tight bun above her head. Despite their age, they were beautiful.

Standing a few feet away from them, Ron thought they might have been three of his grannies with their distinctive accents.

"Ladies, I'm fine," he replied, forgetting his earlier vision of a child calling to him. "You needn't have worried about me. It's not like this is my first solo climb."

"O' course, we were worried aboot ye. Ye've a wife and two bairns. Another on the wee. Ye had nae business danglin' on a rock scarin' them like that."

"Oh, I'm not married," Ron corrected, but the women chuckled as if sharing a private joke among them.

"Oh, ye will be. Shame tae miss oot on that, wouldn't it?"

Ron was getting annoyed. His life was none of their business. Christ, they just met. What did they know?

"Where did you all come from anyway? The park isn't open to the public yet," he asked.

"Same way ye came. We're professors from Uni in Edinburgh. Ye can tell by our accent we're from Scotland, aye?" said the third one with the bun, likely the oldest of the three, who stood up and approached Ron.

"Ah'm Leann. This here is Magda and Bobbie." The other two women nodded, smiling. Ron saw mischief in their eyes and wondered what they were up to.

"Nice to meet you all, but you already seem to know me. In fact, you sound like my Scottish granny. Have we met before?"

"Aye, we've known yer granny since we were wee lasses, lad," Magda said.

"We ken ye'd be an eejit tae make the climb by yerself and thought ye might need rescuin'. And ye almost did, aye?" said Bobbie, who looked the youngest.

That just did a number on his rock-climbing ego. Never mind that he was now even more confused than ever as to why these women were here expecting to save his butt from that accidental slip, which he recovered from nicely—by himself—thank you very much.

But before he could figure out what was happening, Bobbie walked toward him with a thermos from which she poured a hot liquid into its small cup.

"Here, lad. This'll dae wonders fer ye. It's a braw cup o' hot chocolate straight frame Cocoa Mountain in Balnakeil, wi' a wee nip tae warm yer toes. It's the finest ye can get, nae doot aboot it." She winked at him.

Ron thanked her, took a sip, and felt the magic of the sweet liquid calm every bone in his body and drain his mind of all his puzzled thoughts. He sunk to the ground with an indescribable serenity that wrapped around him like a warm quilt on a brisk New England morning.

He had no words.

As the women loaded their gear, Leann turned to Ron and said, "Ye can hike yer way doon this path here that we're takin', and ye'll be safe. Ye'll not rappel doon the way ye came, now hear?"

Feeling pleasantly calm, Ron could only nod reassuringly.

"Give yer troubles a rest, lad. Dinna fash yer destiny," Leann added just before the three departed by way of the hiking trail.

My destiny. Ha! What did they know about that?

Ron laid back on the ground to face the sky.

Leann, Magda, and Bobbie. Ah, crap!

Leannan Sith, Maighdeann-mhara, and Baobhan Sith

They were the fae who'd been dogging him to embrace his destiny.

Raine

MAY 2000
DURHAM, NEW HAMPSHIRE

Go away, Peter.
I whispered to my mind while huddled beneath my sleeping bag, struggling to keep the morning light from piercing my line of sight.

I was having the mother of all emotional battles because Ron was starting to crowd my mind and invading my dreams. I wondered what would happen if I acted on this attraction that seemed to be growing between us.

How should I not love thee? Let me count the ways.

You're too young. Three years my junior. Okay, that's not really a reason. It's an excuse.

You're a professor. An academic. And I am so not that.

You'll never fit in my world.

I can't leave my life in New York.

"He's not me, Raine," Peter interrupted my mind again.

Fuck you and all you male species. You're all jerks. You'll pretend to love, then leave.

"Give him a chance." Hearing Peter's voice was not helping.

But what about the future?

What happens after my year is up?

Finding no immediate answers, I gave up the fight and rose from my sleeping bag, grunting and groaning while I unkinked my stiff joints. It had been a good three months since the floors had been refinished, and I had no ungodly reason for continuing to camp on the bedroom floor. It was high time I got a proper bed.

Even if I wasn't staying permanently.

CHAPTER 23

Ron

"ANOTHER GLORIOUS DAY IN DURHAM, PARTLY CLOUDY WITH TEMPERATURES RISING TO THE SIXTIES BY MIDDAY BEFORE DROPPING TO A COMFORTABLE LOW OF 52 TONIGHT. IN OTHER NEWS..."

R on jumped from sleep to wakefulness when his clock radio blasted the morning news at full volume. Who the fuck turned it up to the max and... Wait a sec, where the hell was he anyway?

He should have guessed that seeing the three fae face-to-face (Was that a dream?) was a sign of his day going awry.

Before too long, he was faced with ankle-deep water at the geology lab in the basement of James Hall, where he was slated to give final exams. This meant he had to scramble to find a replacement classroom, which ended up at the other end of the campus. By lunchtime, he crammed grading his students' exams and then raced to submit them to the registrar for recording before they closed for the year.

Then his meeting with Dr. Murdoch to go over his research in Iceland just dragged on and on. He thought he'd never leave.

Dammit, he had to see Raine. Since he didn't have her number, he had to go to her house to ask her out before it was too late.

But his spirits sank when the red Jeep was missing from its usual spot under the carport and the house dark and silent. He rang her doorbell but there was no answer.

Tonight would have been the perfect time to see if she wanted to go out with him—before he left for Iceland.

Feeling defeated, he headed toward Joplin's Jazz, where he knew everyone would be celebrating the end of the school year. Between the noise and the booze, he could forget about this day, which had begun so miserably anyway.

Thank you, Leann, Magda, and Bobbie.

"Ron!" Ed waved to him as he approached their usual spot at the end of the bar. "I thought you'd never make it. Where the hell have you been?"

The din was almost unbearable when Ron pushed through the tavern, squeezing between the bodies of students and faculty.

The place thumped with live music from Mister G, who played covers of jazz greats Thelonious Monk, John Coltrane, and Miles Davis. The dance floor overflowed with bodies gyrating to the sensual melody of Keith Scott's soprano sax.

"Dropped the final grades off. I am done for the year," he exclaimed, offering his buddy a high-five and signaling Jops for a beer.

"This day has sucked since I got up this morning." Ron gave Ed a deflated look.

"Yeah, well. You're not the only one who suffered through the flooded basement."

"I really wanted to see Raine and catch up with her today before I left, but she wasn't home," Ron said, trying to hide his disappointment behind a casual shrug as he tipped his beer for a long sip.

"Wait, I thought you said you weren't gonna ask her out anymore?"

Fritzso, who was busy chatting up a coed beside him, turned around when he heard that.

"What? When did this happen? How did I not know this?"

Ron turned to Fritzso and gave him a smug look. "Forget it, Fritzso. You wouldn't know how to handle a woman like Raine."

"Hey, did I just win a twenty?" Ed smiled.

Fritzso looked at Ed then back at Ron again, mouth gaping. "Hang on a sec... I'd been giving you a wide berth, buddy," he said, poking Ron in the shoulder.

Ed jumped in. "Our pal here said he'd give you the green light to ask Raine out, and we bet that he wouldn't be able to because he's too whooped over her. But since he's leaving tomorrow..."

"Shut up, Ed," Ron muttered while pulling out a twenty from his billfold and slapping it on the counter.

Fritzso shook his head. "If I'd known about this, I'd have snatched Raine away before you changed your mind. And then you would have kept your twenty. God, you are an idiot, Ron."

At that moment, the coed who was with Fritzso, grabbed her beer and stalked off. She'd overheard them discussing dating bets that didn't involve herself. Ron watched her walk away in a huff.

"Smooth move there, buddy," he said, turning back to Fritzso and then to Ed. "I rest my case."

"I'm confused," Ed frowned. "Are you or aren't you asking Raine out? Thanks for the twenty, by the way."

Ron motioned for a second beer.

"I *intend* to," he replied, knocking back the rest of his first brew and then picking up the second one before him.

"Ron, dammit! You've had all goddamn semester to close on this deal. I'll give you tonight and tomorrow, but the minute your flight takes off and you haven't made a move, I'm going in for the kill," said Fritzso.

With that, Ron watched him walk toward the long, leggy blonde who had marched away from him only a few moments ago and was now asking her to dance. And there was no hesitation as she smiled and joined him on the dance floor.

Ron shook his head in amazement. Only Fritzso could diss a girl and then make up with her minutes later. Ron watched Fritzso do a fast dance with the girl. She looked none too bruised about the earlier jibe. There was no way Raine would go out with someone like *him*.

"Buddy, you better do something, or Fritzso *will* make a move on Raine while you're gone."

"I'm not trying to be cocky, but as far as Fritzso's concerned, I doubt Raine will go out with him," Ron leaned forward, swaying his bottle then tipping it back for a swig. "Bet me on that and you'd lose."

Ed watched Ron guzzle the rest of his beer and signal for a third.

"Think we should order some quesadillas or something?" Ed suggested.

"Sure. Whatever. You can spring for it since you're now twenty bucks richer," he teased, taking a long pull on his third beer, intending to down it all in two gulps.

Ed signaled the order to Jops. The three amigos have been coming to Joplin's for years, and hand signals were all they needed to place an order. And when the night was hopping like it was, short gestures in the air were the quickest way to get your order in.

Ed also made a different gesture to Jops, who nodded and then turned to make a call.

"What was that about?" Ron noticed and looked confused. He certainly didn't understand *that* hand signal.

"Nothing. So what makes you so sure I'll lose this bet to you?" Ed asked, changing the topic quickly as a server set another beer in front of Ron.

"You and I both know what a player Fritzso is. Knowing what I know about Raine now, that she's this billionaire CEO from New York, you don't walk up to her and say, 'Hi, can I buy you a drink?'" Ron said, picking up the new bottle.

A jumbo Mexican appetizer combo arrived. Quesadillas, nachos oozing with cheese, beans, and corn, jalapeño poppers, and mini tacos were artfully arranged on a large platter placed on the counter between the guys. Ron reached for some food and guzzled the rest of his beer—then called for a fifth. He was feeling no pain now.

Ed shook Ron's shoulder. "Listen, I've always known Fritzso's not her type. He's too immature for her. Now you, my friend... *You...* are perfect for her. The bets have always been about getting your damn act together because I get the sense that she likes you, and she's been waiting for you to make a move."

"She's only here for a year, Ed. If I ask her out and it works out, then what? I want a future with her, but what happens when she returns to New York?"

Ed picked on the food and spoke in between mouthfuls of nachos. "Why are you worrying about that when you haven't even asked her out yet?"

Ron downed the rest of his sixth beer, then swayed slightly.

"Whoa, buddy. I think you've had enough," Ed said.

"Shit. You should have stopped me sooner. I'm gonna need a ride."

"Uh-uh. Ginny's off tonight, and no one's sleeping on my couch."

Ron snorted. "Where's Fritzso?" He scanned the crowded dance floor.

"I wouldn't rely on him. Chances are he's going home with that chick he was with and getting laid."

Ron shook his head. Fritzso wanted to ask Raine out but was looking to get laid with someone else tonight? Ron *had* to get to Raine before he left for Iceland. Even if he wasn't too worried that Raine would take Fritzso seriously as a date, someone else might ask her out.

"Don't worry. Something will turn up," Ed said with a glint of mischief in his eye.

That was when Ron *felt* her walk through the door, making him look up.

"Oh fuck! She's here."

Great! Great timing.

He was smashed and smelled like a brewery. Couldn't the fae have at least warned him?

Ed snickered, "Say hi to your designated driver."

Raine

MAY 2000

DURHAM, NEW HAMPSHIRE

J ops called in a favor for helping me paint. And since I owed him, I agreed to rescue one drunken puppy named Ron.

"Sure, no problem," I readily agreed to Jops.

But when I walked in the door of the tavern, I saw Ron blanche as if he'd just seen a ghost. When our eyes met, I knew he was thinking about the last time we saw each other. The time he figured out who I really was and then bolted.

Not wanting to embarrass him further, I approached Ed instead, who wound an arm around my shoulder and planted a noisy kiss on my cheek. I could feel Ron's eyes burning a hole at us.

"Thanks for coming," Ed whispered.

"No sweat," I said, taking the barstool he'd offered.

I turned to Ron and casually said, "Hey."

He smiled crookedly, his face flushed. He was about to lean over for a hug when we heard a shout.

"Raine!" It was Fritzso making his way back from the dance floor.

"Hey, big guy," I greeted, slipping into his embrace and peck on the cheek. I could hear Ron gritting his teeth above the loud music.

"I see you're working the room," I laughed.

"Yup. And you're next." He smiled, tugging me to the dance floor.

After three fast numbers on the dance floor with Fitzso, I broke out in a sweat but felt exhilarated. I returned to the bar and signaled Jops for a glass of water. I watched him spritz a wine glass with the water hose and drop a slice of lemon, mouthing a thank you when he set my drink on the counter.

Noticing Ron wasn't around, I scanned the room when Ed said, "He went to the little boy's room. He'll be right back."

I nodded, taking a sip of water.

"Thanks for doing this again, Raine," Ed said. "Ron doesn't usually get drunk. He rarely drinks beyond a couple of beers. Don't worry, he's stopped after he went through a six-pack, but we didn't want him driving home."

"What happened? Is he okay?"

Ed shrugged. "End-of-year decompression. We're all blowing off steam. He didn't realize he'd had one too many."

I nodded again, looking in the direction of the bathrooms.

"He's a good guy, Raine. I can vouch for him. If anything, he'll just be a goofy drunk. And then he'll pass out." Ed said, rising to leave. "If you don't want to make the twenty-minute round trip to Rochester for him, you can leave him in his car. But take his keys away so he doesn't try to drive off."

"He can crash at my place. I've got a sleeping bag and an extra bedroom. I don't mind. Where are you off to? Hot date with the wife?"

"You bet. We don't often have evenings together because of her shifts at the hospital. But tonight, she's home, and I don't think she'd appreciate me bringing a tipsy Ron home to crash on our couch."

"You gonna be okay driving?" I asked, peering into his face with mild concern.

"I'm good. I only had two beers and quit hours ago. I don't have far to drive, but thanks for asking."

"Anytime. Tell Ginny I said hi. And don't worry," I chuckled. "I'll take care of our errant child."

Ed laughed, pulled me in a hug, and then left.

While I drank my water thirstily, strains of *Try A Little Tenderness* started from the band as they neared the end of their set. Fritzso was about to pull me back when Ron appeared and rather firmly said to him, *"No!"*

Before I could say anything, he pulled me to the dance floor and folded me in his arms as we swayed to the slow rhythm of Joe Cocker's soulful song.

He smelled of fresh soap, and his breath was minty. I appreciated his effort to clean up before pulling me in for a dance. The feel of his hard body against mine sent shivers down my spine, prompting him to pull me closer. Perhaps he thought I was cold. I couldn't help but rest my head against his shoulder, his lips touching my temples, the warmth of his breath against my skin. We said nothing as we moved in unison to the song's melody, conflicting emotions rioting within me. We didn't need words. Perhaps it was because it all felt so natural.

After the bar closed for the night, I had to shove Ron into the Jeep when he resisted coming home with me, insisting he would sleep off his intoxication in his car.

"Are you kidding me?" I argued. "You can't sleep in your tiny clown car. You won't be able to unfold yourself in the morning."

"I'll be fine. And the pumpkin is not a clown car," he argued, taking deep breaths of the cold night air to sober himself more quickly.

"Ron, I promised Jops and Ed I'd take care of you and let you crash at my place."

"Raine, I can't go home with you. It's a university policy."

Huh?

"A university policy? What? No fraternizing with the village people?" I laughed.

He wasn't just being a goofy drunk. He was being silly.

"Look, I'm five minutes away. I have a sleeping bag. Granted, it will be on the floor, but it will be way more comfortable than your car. After all, *I* slept in it for three months. Plus, the guest bedroom has a lock. I promise your virtue will be safe with me. So, will you get in the Jeep and stop arguing."

When we got to my place, he draped his arm over my shoulder while I wrapped mine around his waist. There was nothing romantic in that gesture. I was trying to keep him upright, but he was swaying wildly.

"Ron, if you fall to the ground, I'm leaving your ass out in the front yard."

"Aw, come on, Raine. Have mercy on me," he slurred, giving me a lopsided grin.

We made it inside the house and up the stairs without falling. I won't deny that the sexual charge between us hovered thickly in the air. Our closeness incited a desire I hadn't felt in a long time. And when he sniffed my ear, for God's sake! I had to scold him.

"Hey, you're not Goober, pal. Keep that up, and I'll let you fall backward." We broke out in side-splitting laughter again, making it up the stairs without incident.

"Raine, you smell so good," he whispered. "Wait, did you just call me Goober?"

Truth was, his warm breath in my ear felt so electrifying. Had I turned my head slightly, we would have been lip-locked on the stairs, and with a few steps, we'd have tumbled onto my new bed and gotten naked within seconds. Yes, hell of a way to christen the mattress—but no. I'd never done a one-night stand and wasn't about to start one. Not with Ron.

Somehow, he tugged at my heartstrings as someone special, and I didn't want to sully it over one drunken night's imprudence where regrets would inevitably embarrass us the morning after. More importantly, I did not want a panacea for my broken heart.

When we reached the landing, I left him to use the bathroom while I ran downstairs to retrieve some pillows and blankets for the sleeping bag. When I returned, I found him—not in the guest room—but on my *new* bed, lights out. Oh, well. What's another night on the floor for me?

CHAPTER 24

Ron

MAY 2000

DURHAM, NEW HAMPSHIRE

The aroma of coffee brewing stirred Ron awake. As his brain registered his surroundings, he realized he was in a strange bed with a comforter over him. Where exactly was he? He heard a shower running and a woman's soft crooning.

He sat up quickly, only to be nearly floored by a pounding hangover. Groaning, he clutched his head, fearing his brains might spill out.

What the hell had he been up to last night?

His eyes felt sticky with sleep, his mouth filled with cotton, and his clothes reeked of last night's beer. Since he was still fully clothed save for his shoes, he was glad he didn't have sex with a stranger.

Ron groped his way down the stairs, following the scent of fresh coffee in the kitchen. On the counter, he spotted an empty mug and a bottle of ibuprofen. He looked around the kitchen, saw an unusual-looking yellow fridge, and remembered the only person he knew who owned one like it. When he heard a voice, his heart stopped.

"Hey," Raine called, coming down the stairs, hair still damp from the shower.

What the hell was he doing in her house? Waking up in her bed? Fuck! This was worse than the throbbing inside his skull.

She was wearing snug jeans and a fitting T-shirt that showed off her small but curving breasts. She wore no makeup and smelled fresh of soap and water. There was that heather scent again. A hint of a tiny waist peeked from above her waistline when she reached for another mug from a shelf.

Don't look... Otherwise, another part of his anatomy would notice. Ron shifted his stance and glanced away quickly.

"Judging by how you look, you probably have a smashing hangover this morning," she said, pouring coffee into the cup she'd set out for him.

"Ahh...I'm sorry. I'm sure I look like hell," he said, combing his fingers through his hair as if that would have groomed him to look better.

"Cream or sugar?"

He shook his head. "Thanks," he muttered, sipping the dark brew and downed a couple of Advils.

"You conked out last night."

"Uhm, yeah." He cleared his throat again, trying to find the right thing to say without making an even bigger ass of himself.

"About, uhm, last night..." His voice faltered.

"What about it?" She took a sip of her coffee, raising her eyebrows.

"No," he said, "I mean, uhm, I'm sorry..."

"Forget it. I wasn't about to let you sleep in your car."

What? Why didn't he remember that conversation? He frowned into his coffee, desperately trying to remember something. *Anything!*

"Your car's still back at Joplin's, and I put your keys in your jacket."

Ron gulped down the rest of his coffee and his pride.

"Thanks," he muttered.

She smiled at him, her eyes meeting his. In that moment, he glimpsed a future intertwined with hers, both thrilling and terrifying.

He covered his face and rubbed his eyes as if he couldn't bear to see much more of his fate entangled with hers.

"Headache still there?"

"W-what? Ah, no. I'm fine... But I need to go." He set his mug on the counter and turned to grab his jacket hanging on a peg near the backdoor.

"If you hang on a second, I'll give you a ride back to your car. I need to head down that way and do some errands."

"No... no, that's okay. I can walk. I've troubled you enough already," he said, hand on the knob.

"Listen, thanks again. And I guess I'll...see you around," he said, then bolted out the door.

When he returned to his car, he started the engine but sat there for a minute, staring over the dashboard, then slapped his hand against the steering wheel.

That was when it all came rushing back like an avalanche.

Every...single...minute.

Every...ticking...second.

Every move he made. Slow dancing with her... and *she* was holding him up because he was too... How much had he drunk anyway? Six beers, as best he could recall. God, he was such a lightweight when it came to his liquor.

Every...word...he said.

Raine, I really like you. You can trust me not to do anything you don't want me to.

He cringed. Wait, when did he say that? Were they in her house already? What did that even mean?

Every touch... Ohmigod, did he... sniff her ear??? He was drunk, she smelled good, and he was horny.

But then she said, "Okay, you're not Goober, pal." Great. She'd just compared him to Murdoch's dog.

Ron rubbed his face hard, willing the memories to go away and not be true.

He let out a big sigh. He remembered her touch and how he felt her pain. But it also shot a heroin-high of desire right into his loins. He wanted her. He craved her so much that he remembered his erection rising when he smelled her.

"Raine, you smell so good," he'd whispered. Good thing she stopped him. And if she hadn't said something about him tumbling backward and breaking a leg, he might not have controlled himself.

And then, when she'd left him upstairs, he purposely crawled into her bed, hoping she'd snuggle next to him. So he could hold her, kiss her all over, slowly peel off her clothes, feel her naked body against his, and take away the hurt. He wanted to drive out the nightmares and fill her with nothing but all his love for her.

Oh God... Ron rubbed his eyes again. Was he falling for Raine? Already? He hadn't even gotten to first base, and with his record, he might never get there.

Of course, instead of waiting for her to return upstairs so he could sweet-talk her into joining him, he'd passed out, which meant she must have slept in.... *Nooo!!!* The sleeping bag that was meant for him?

Idiot, idiot, idiot!!! He said while banging his head against the steering wheel as if that would jettison his stupidity.

And if all that wasn't enough for Raine to never want to see him again, he'd scurried away again.

"Ladies, just leave me alone. Please? You are not helping me at all," Ron pleaded aloud to the fae inside the deafening silence of his car.

His buddies were right. He was a class-one moron.

Ron threw his suitcase and backpack into Ed's Bronco's cargo space and jumped into the passenger seat.

"How'd it go?" Ed asked.

"How'd what go?"

"You know, last night?"

"What about last night?"

Brows furrowed, Ed glanced at Ron, turning the ignition.

"Well, what happened? Did you end up sleeping in your car...or something?"

Ed was clearly fishing.

"Or something..." Ron said.

"And?"

"Nothing happened. And I know what you're angling for, Ed."

But Ed was undeterred. "Was it good?"

"None of your beeswax, buddy."

Ron quickly changed the subject as Ed entered the highway ramp and merged into the interstate.

"Looks like traffic's moving. We're going to make good time."

Ed glanced back at his friend, then shook his head. Ron pretended not to notice his friend's eye roll.

"Okay, okay, the whole thing was awful. Happy now?"

"Sex was awful?" Ed snickered.

"What the fuck, Ed?" Ron rubbed his eyes. "First of all, it's really weird that you're asking me about my sex life. Second, you and Jops set me up with Raine when you knew I was pickled. How did you expect that to turn out? Do you have any idea how humiliating this was for me? Thank God she was nice about helping one sorry drunken sop. That was so, so embarrassing."

"Hey, we did not set you up." Ed pretended innocence. "Jops called because you were going through a six-pack so fast. We knew you were going to be soused and would need a ride. Seriously, bud. You know I'd have taken you home to crash on my couch, but you also knew I had a rare date with my wife last night. You'd have been sleeping on the bar room floor if Raine hadn't arrived."

Ron shook his head, still annoyed about his friends setting him up at the wrong time and place.

"Look, nothing happened. Okay? I crashed on her bed and woke up this morning without knowing where I was or what happened. She offered me coffee, and I graciously accepted. Then I left as quickly as possible."

"Whoah, whoah... wait..." Ed's jaw dropped. He glanced around at the slowing traffic, looking confused.

"You... were on...*her*...bed," he said, enunciating each word as if Ron was in kindergarten. "And *nothing* happened?"

"Ed, I passed out."

Ed had to shake his head in disbelief. "And so this morning, you woke up sober and then ran out. Did you even at least kiss her? Tell her you'll miss her and can't wait to see her when you return. Give her some idea that you *want* to see her again?"

Ron froze.

"Shit!" He smacked his head with the heels of his palms, startling Ed. He hadn't told Raine he was leaving for Iceland for a month. She'd think he'd blown her off after everything she'd done.

Ed was incredulous. "Wait... I get it. You're making this up. You have to be making it up."

But Ron wasn't listening anymore. How was he going to fix this 2,500 miles away? In another country?

"So you gonna at least email her and beg for forgiveness? This way, you can stay in touch even while you're gone. It'll probably keep Fritzso from swinging for the fences."

Ron leaned forward and rested his head in his hands. He didn't have her email address. When he returned, he would have no chance.

Red taillights started flashing ahead, slowing down traffic.

"Don't worry, buddy," Ed reassured him. "This is a minor slowdown from congestion ahead. You'll make your flight with plenty of time to squirm over how you'll fix this."

There was only one thing Ron could do while he was in flight. Pray to the fae who have set his destiny. Beg for help so he wouldn't stumble so much in his pursuit of love.

Finally, Ron was ready to embrace his destiny with Raine. Now, he just had to convince her they were meant to be together—forever.

Fuck!

Raine

MAY 2000

DURHAM, NEW HAMPSHIRE

"*He left? For fucking Iceland?*"

I looked at Ed, Fritzso, and Jops, who were speechless at my reaction to the news. They seemed to assume I knew about it.

I went to join the three amigos the following Thursday, hoping to see Ron again and try to make him feel more comfortable around me. But when they'd said he left for Iceland, it stung. I felt left out. Snubbed. As if I wasn't a friend worthy enough to share that he was leaving town, even if it was only for a month.

"Well, fuck that piece of shit. That'll be the last time I'll ever do anything for him," I said, storming out of the bar.

The next day, after stopping in Tye's True Value for a new floodlight fixture for my backyard, I walked to Joplin's Jazz for my usual burger lunch, setting the shopping bag on the counter.

"He just fucking left, Jops," I said, perching on a stool.

"I mean, I played nice and offered to let him sleep off his alcoholic over-indulgence at my place so he wouldn't have to fold himself into his car. I didn't have an extra bed, but I had a sleeping bag, which would have been infinitely more comfortable for him than his car. And then I went to get sheets and a pillow, and when I returned, he'd passed out. On. My. New. Bed. *Diagonally*. I had to sleep in the sleeping bag again. And this is the thanks I get?"

"Oof," Jops scrunched his face.

"Right?" I replied, taking a bite of my burger. "He dissed me. Made me feel like I'm not a friend. Sucks."

"That's cause he likes you." I wondered if Jops had heard me.

"Riiiight," I drawled out.

"No, Raine. I mean, he really, really likes you. He's been trying to get up enough nerve to ask you out."

"I never would have guessed."

"Raine, you have to understand something about Ron. He's painfully shy around attractive women. You, mainly. Bet he stutters when he has to talk to you."

"You, Ed, and Fritzso don't treat me differently. You guys aren't afraid of me, are you? I don't think I've been acting like my old New York highfalutin' society self or a bitch-face CEO since I've moved here. I hope you don't think I'm a snob just because..."

"No one here thinks you're a snob," Jops said, cutting me off. "Even without your famous father or your high-powered job and wealth, you are also one drop-dead gorgeous babe, and that alone will trigger what Ed calls Ron's 'attractive woman anxiety syndrome.'"

"Hah! That's an excuse if I ever heard one."

"He'll be back at the end of the month. Give him another chance."

"I'm not trying to get into a relationship with anybody, Jops. I'm too complicated, but it would be nice if he didn't run off whenever he saw me."

"Listen, Sunshine, on his idiotic behalf—thank you for your kindness. I hope he didn't try to do anything weird, did he?"

I shook my head. "I don't think he could have. He was too far gone." I omitted the ear-sniffing part.

"I'm always here for you to bend an ear. I am sorry you've had it rough the last few years, but it's time you gave yourself a chance at happiness. That's why you came here to live in Durham, right?"

"Hmmm..." I mumbled, finishing off my burger.

"I wouldn't worry about things you can't control. Let whatever happens happen."

Then he straightened up and peeked into the shopping bag I'd brought in.

"Now, you want some help installing that light? Or were you going to try and electrocute yourself?"

As spring mellowed into summer, the campus emptied its grounds of students, leaving a quiet hush over the town. Bookstores, souvenir shops, and hot dog stands boarded up for the holidays gave the community a sense of abandonment. But many of the locals didn't mind this time of year as they headed off to their mountain cabins further north for a well-earned vacation.

It was the end of May, and the day's unseasonably hot and humid temperature sent me indoors. Although much of the house was shaded with leafy maples and oaks, the sultry air lingered inside. Thank God new insulated windows and a state-of-the-art ductless air-conditioning system were installed a few weeks ago.

I poured myself a glass of iced chamomile tea I'd made earlier and retreated upstairs to the back bedroom, where the squatty apple tree shaded the room.

Everything that belonged on a desk was still on the floor, as I hadn't yet considered furnishing the room. I squatted down, folding my legs beneath me, yoga style, and powered up my MacBook. I dialed into the ISDN phone line to launch the Netscape browser and check the stock prices.

As soon as the graphics were rendered on the screen, I couldn't miss the glaring headline from *The New York Tribune*.

"Glory Stock Slips On Rumor Of York Estate Shares Sale"

By Nicholas D. Coelho

CHAPTER 25

Raine

DECEMBER 1998
NEW YORK, NEW YORK

"About time a damn woman took over."

Lenore Bliss's voice rang in my head when I asked her what she thought of me taking on the role of acting CEO. As the CEO of a major cosmetic company and one of S&Y's biggest clients, I greatly valued her input.

When Jim suggested I take over the agency's leadership, I called a few clients to gauge their opinions.

"Martin, Jim's making me acting CEO. What do you think, big guy?" I asked the founder of Drummond, my biggest pharmaceutical client.

"Seriously, Raine?"

"Might happen if I get enough support."

"Lady, you've got my vote. You would be great for S&Y."

Really?

Then from JJ Rheems of Hanover Bank. "Raine, I signed up because of you, not Peter."

What?

After getting the consensus, I dropped my head into my hands. It was time to get to work.

Walking along the hushed corridor toward Peter's office early in the morning before others arrived was unnerving. Peter had only been gone a week. It was a surreal, out-of-body experience, and I struggled to process the reality of what had happened, so I welcomed the opportunity to work.

I unlocked the door and turned on the lights. The windows overlooking the northern Manhattan skyline were shrouded in mist from the December rain.

The memory of the last time he held me in his arms right in this room, looking so sad, threatened to overwhelm my composure. Had that been the last time I saw and felt him... alive?

I should have lost it and melted into a puddle of tears. Instead, I impassively sat behind his desk, contemplating what else I might find, checking each drawer—nothing to see other than a few pens and a pad.

On the large credenza behind me was a pull-down door revealing a collection of top-shelf liquor and a crystal decanter with matching lo-ball whiskey glasses from which to serve. And just beneath, a built-in mini fridge blended seamlessly with the furniture. I opened it to retrieve some water when I noticed a prescription bottle and a blue plastic box tucked in the back of the top shelf.

I pulled both bottle and box and looked at them. The bottle prescription sticker read: *Baclofen*, with Peter's name— twenty milligrams, prescribed by Jordan Horowitz, M.D. "Take one dose three times a day for three days."

The blue box was labeled *Copaxone*, twenty milligrams, twenty single doses, to be administered by subcutaneous injection once a day and kept refrigerated. Jordan Horowitz also prescribed it. The blue box was filled the day Peter died. *Baclofen* was a few weeks before, with a few remaining tablets.

I flipped open the box, revealing vials and sterilized syringes. A doctor's card fell out, listing an address: 299 Park

Avenue, Montclair Building. My heart raced. This was where Carty said he'd dropped Peter the morning of his senate announcement. A web of questions tangled in my mind, hinting at secrets yet to be uncovered.

I heard people stirring from down the hall. Despite the early hours, the office was already coming to life. I stashed the drugs back into the fridge, making a mental note to deal with it later.

As the months passed, I became more deeply entangled in Peter's world, navigating meetings, conferences, and new challenges. By May, Jim finally came to my office and closed the door.

"I take it you're here to tell me who the next CEO will be?" I asked. Why else would he close the door?

"What's the matter? Anxious to get rid of yourself already?"

"Jim, it's been five months! We can't keep the firm in limbo like this. Aren't you worried?"

"Why should I be? You've been doing a stellar job at the helm yourself."

"You know what I mean," I sighed in exasperation.

"Raine, I can have someone with twenty years of experience to head this company. But that won't mean they'd be any better than you."

I blinked hard at the man who was looking at me deadpan. "What the hell does that mean?"

"The partners' quarterly meeting is coming up. I want you there." Jim's tone shifted to one of command, as if he saw in me something of Peter's drive and ambition. Or maybe it was his unwavering belief that I was the company's future.

This meant meeting with other executives who headed up regional offices around the country and from our offices in London and Paris. And they were all men—back-slapping, cigar-toking, good-ol'-boy's-club guys with golf handicaps in the single digits.

"Why?" I asked while my brain scrambled for some rational thinking.

"To your point, we want to settle on a CEO quickly. Frankly, Raine, you're the only logical choice."

The thought of stepping into Peter's shoes permanently made my stomach churn. Was I ready for this? Could I handle the weight of the entire firm on my shoulders?

"Have ye gone daft, man?" I couldn't help emulating my mother's Scottish accent. Jim thought I was hysterical.

"Why don't we have breakfast tomorrow and talk about new business? Future directions. Growth projections," Jim said, rising from his seat and concluding our conversation.

He was about to open the door when he turned to me and said, "I want you to interview for Peter's job. Put together your vision for S&Y and present it at the meeting. Make it like you want this job because I want them to vote for you as CEO. And I want nothing short of a unanimous decision on this, Raine."

No pressure there.

Vivienne

MAY 1999
NEW YORK, NEW YORK

When Raine eloped with Peter, she'd severed all contact with Vivienne. And Vivienne might have moved back to Paris had it not been for Auntie Rae and Uncle Tono, who reassured her that fate would reunite them. The hurt and loss were so deep that she didn't think she could live in LA or New York without the constant reminder of their friendship.

Oh, she'd tried to reach out. She called the agency. She tried to hang out near the office building. But she never heard back. She didn't know if Peter had been vetting her messages, keeping Raine isolated.

Auntie Rae had shared a vision with Vivienne, promising they would meet again and their friendship would be stronger than before. But she needed to be patient. Very patient.

"Vivienne, ye'll have to stop trying, lass. 'twill happen. Besides, ye're fated to bring her home to us," Auntie Rae reassured her.

Well, she didn't think it would take *years*. But sure enough—it happened.

The building was easy to overlook, tucked between a coffee shop and a souvenir store in the heart of Manhattan's Koreatown. Inside, the lobby offered little reassurance, its drab gray and cream tiles looking worn and tired. A disinterested security guard sat at the desk, barely glancing up. The stainless-steel elevator, pocked with dents that resembled bullet holes, suggested a hint of intrigue worthy of a bestselling mystery novel.

One would never have guessed that the Incheon Spa on the sixth floor was an oasis that mimicked a lotus flowers and bamboo garden, artfully designed with rocks and stones strategically placed to represent mountains and hills. Bridges and stone paths led to a sauna, a steam room, massage rooms, and a fruit and juice bar. Whirlpool tubs with waterfalls were focal points symbolizing the dynamic flow of life in a harmonious environment within a structured space.

This was Vivienne's secret hideaway—her sanctuary. Here, she could escape from the pressures of her job and the sting of not being named partner again. She closed her eyes and tried to release the tension building around her neck and shoulders as the dry heat of the sauna coated her skin.

This morning's announcement still gnawed at her. Despite being the daughter of a Hollywood mogul, New York bankers saw her as an outsider. Her hard work and talent didn't matter. They only cared about money. She needed to bring in a new client, a mega deal that would net the firm not less than a million in fees. The injustice of it all simmered inside her as she perched on the top step of the sauna benches, the heat doing little to soothe her frustration.

Leaning against the wall, her eyes closed and basking in the warm mist, she tried to shake off the morning's disappointment. She felt adrift, yearning for an anchor. Little did she know that anchor was about to walk through the door.

The creak of the door opening pulled her from her thoughts. As she opened her eyes, she saw none other than her long-lost best friend—Raine Nishiseki, or Raine Garvey now—draped in a large white Turkish towel.

"Holy shit!" Raine cried out, her eyes wide with shock.

Vivienne stared, mouth open, before breaking into side-splitting laughter.

"Jesus, of all places..." Raine said, laughing along as she sat on the platform across from Vivienne.

Soon, they faced each other, grinning and shaking their heads in disbelief before falling into each other's arms.

"So you come here often?" Raine joked, taking a seat next to Vivienne.

"Quite often, actually. I won't run into anyone I know or who knows me," Vivienne replied.

"Except me. What were the chances? But even though we haven't seen each other in almost ten years, Vivi, I'd know you anywhere. You haven't changed."

The elephant in the room suddenly came crashing in and loomed large. From Vivienne's viewpoint, Raine had abandoned their friendship.

"I have no excuse, Vivi, for not reaching out," Raine began, covering her face.

They were silent for a while, with only the heat rising from the fired coals hissing quietly.

Ye're fated to bring her home to us.

Vivienne replayed Auntie Rae's portent in her head and knew the Scottish fae was a powerful force to be reckoned with. But truth be told, Vivienne missed her friend. She had desperately wanted Raine back in her life. She had prayed for this moment. Now that Raine was here, Vivienne would move mountains to make sure they would never part again. As far as she was concerned, there was nothing to forgive.

When Vivienne offered her pinky, she felt like she'd found her anchor at last. "Nish, *yubikiri* will never be broken between us," she said softly, invoking the Japanese promise they'd made when they first met in fifth grade.

She remembered that first day at St. Joseph's. Raine approached Vivienne, the new kid at school. She'd felt lost, angry, and brooding after her parents split up. But with Raine's cool detachment and those strange lace-trimmed socks in boy shoes, she'd had cut right through Vivienne's defenses.

"*Yubikiri*," Raine whispered, her eyes filling with tears as she hooked her pinky with Vivienne's. "Best friends forever—or suffer a thousand needles."

"You remember when Sister Felicity called our parents in for a conference after they caught us linking our pinkies, and they thought we were doing some kind of demonic ritual?" Vivienne said, adding levity to the solemnity of their reconciliation. Then she broke out in stitches again.

"Oh my God, I'd forgotten all about that!" Raine exclaimed, following Vivienne in giggling uncontrollably as they reminisced about that memory and other shenanigans they got away with in school. Soon, they were both lying on the bench with their sides splitting and tears in their eyes. They felt like twelve-year-olds again.

Finally, they fell silent, the air thick with the warmth of the sauna and Eucalyptus calming their senses. The years melted away, their bond as strong and unbreakable as it had been in those early days.

Raine stretched her picky toward Vivienne once more. "*Yubikiri*. And this time, I swear, Vivi, I'll never do anything to hurt you again."

Raine

The sauna's heat wrapped around me like a cocoon, but it couldn't stifle the whirlwind of thoughts in my mind. Seeing Vivienne after all these years felt surreal, like stepping back into a life I'd almost forgotten.

No one had called me Nish since high school, and hearing Vivienne address me by my pet name melted all the time we had lost between us. I watched the sweat glistening on her well-toned body. She looked great. Not fat, but God, she had curves I'd always been jealous of. I sensed the high-powered success behind her poise and grace. I, on the other hand, felt inadequate and tightened my towel around me. She'd done what she set out to do: become a lawyer. She had a bachelor's degree from Harvard, a law degree from Columbia, and an MBA from NYU.

Now, she was working at one of Wall Street's prestigious investment law firms. Me? I up and married. I was widowed before turning thirty and faced with the daunting task of running a giant company. Unlike Vivienne, I didn't have a lick of credentials to warrant being in this position.

"What's it like being a lawyer on Wall Street?" I asked.

Vivienne shrugged. "You remember those pony rides at St. Joe's annual fair?"

"Uh-huh."

"It's a little like that. Scary at first, but once you get on it, you love it. You love it so much that you want more. You want to go faster. And then you get on the bigger horses because those ponies can't run fast enough. I'm riding a wild appaloosa that makes me want to scream, yeehaw! But falling can break your neck and kill you. So, I don't think about it. Instead, if I'm lucky and play this out smartly, I'll reign in my appaloosa, slow him down to a stop, and get off. One day... someday..."

"Why would you want to get off? It sounds like fun!"

"You can't run forever, Nish."

I guess she'd been riding her appaloosa for a while. On the other hand, I was just about to mount my horse.

"The senior partner wants me to take Peter's place as CEO, Vivi. I don't know. It's embarrassing that I don't even have a bachelor's degree."

"Nish, you're so full of shit. Of course, you can take on the job of CEO. Do you remember me telling you that a tennis match can teach you more about business than an MBA?"

Yes, I remembered. Tennis was strategy, execution, and gameplay. You anticipated your opponent's moves and quickly decided on a response stroke—baseline forehand, backhand, top spin, drop shot, volley, and cross-court. Strength was a requirement, but speed, accuracy, and control were more critical. You kept your eye on the ball, watched your opponent's body language, and knew when to play conservatively or go in for the kill.

"I take it you haven't played in a while?" Vivienne challenged.

I looked up in defiance. "Are you challenging me to a match?"

"What do you think?"

As Vivienne's dare hung in the air, something shifted inside me. I felt a spark of the confidence I thought I'd lost forever. The old Nish. The confident Nish. It was time to reclaim it.

CHAPTER 26

Raine

"Hey, stranger!" I called cheerfully from the doorway of Luke's office.

"My, what blew you to this side of the office? Is there a hurricane outside?" he replied without looking up from his drafting table.

It sounded like a snark, and I was taken aback but let it slide, dropping the computer printouts on a nearby table.

"I could've sent Timmo to bring these to you, but I thought I'd stop in and say hi for a change. I guess I wasted my time," I replied tartly. "Could you get someone to draw up some charts for me? Somebody who understands visualizing data. My notes and drafts are right there. The reports should have all the numbers. It's for the partners' meeting next month. Would be great if I could get some comps by tomorrow. I know it's short notice, but I have no choice."

He finally looked up, adjusted the glasses over the bridge of his nose, and said, "You're going to have to let go sometime, Raine. This can't be healthy for you."

"What?" I feigned ignorance.

"This business of putting in eighty-hour work weeks. You're killing yourself slowly, and you don't even know it."

"Who made you my guardian angel?" I snapped.

He winced, and I immediately regretted my remark.

"I'm sorry," I said, avoiding his eyes. "That wasn't necessary."

"Don't shut me out, Raine. I know you're still hurting."

"I don't have time to hurt, Luke. There has been so much pressure Jim put on me. So much expectation, and I'm terrified of failing."

I looked around Luke's office as if seeing it for the first time. His collection of Smurfs, crammed onto a single bookshelf, caught my eye—a quirky reminder of his creative spirit.

"I was there with you, remember?" he continued while I studied one of the little blue men. "When you found Peter. At his funeral. And ever since, all you've done is push me away. I've watched you run yourself ragged. I've tried to talk to Jim about it. It isn't fair of him to give you so much responsibility. You're still mourning, but you won't let yourself go. You don't have to take his offer to be CEO."

I swiftly turned to face him with a tilt of my head. "You don't think I'm qualified for the job?"

"Listen to me," he started, rising from his desk with his face hard as stone. "You know damn well that's not what I meant. Jim's pressuring you, and you feel you have no choice, but you do, Raine. You may think the old man is a benevolent mentor with your best interest at heart, but Jim wants only what's best for Jim, and I wish you'd see that he's taking advantage of your vulnerability. One day, he's going to break you, and you'll end up in the hospital with a nervous breakdown."

"Luke, the work has been cathartic, and I have Jim to thank for that. It keeps me from obsessing over Peter's death. This is how I've been able to move on."

He turned away from me and angrily ran his fingers through his hair. When he turned back to look me in the eye, I saw his sadness. I could tell he was still mourning Peter.

"Raine, this has to be eating you up inside. One day, the real you will disappear. I don't want to lose the real you."

I cupped his face with the palm of my hand.

"Thanks for the concern, sweetie, but really, I'm fine," I said and walked away.

Back in my office, I couldn't deny the truth of what Luke said. I was exhausted, but my mind had been racing with ideas for the future of S&Y— *Lots* of ideas. The most ambitious of these was to take the company public, fulfilling Peter's vision.

Execution, however, was daunting. My eyes fell on Vivienne's business card tucked into the side pocket of my desk blotter. I picked it up and dialed the number.

"Hey, girlfriend. Wanna take on the world with me?"

Raine

JULY 1999
NEW YORK, NEW YORK

2000 and Beyond:
- *Go Public*
- *Acquire the competition*
- *Become a global media powerhouse*

T he boardroom buzzed with quiet anticipation as I clicked through the slides, each bullet flying in from the right as I discussed briefly what they were about. And then came the pivotal slide, *"Glory Media, Inc."*

"By definition," I began "Glory means magnificent. Splendor. Brilliance. Exultation. Grandeur. Wonder."

My voice was steady, my gaze unwavering. I spoke with confidence, leaving little room for doubt.

"Why now? Why not wait?" John McGee's British accent cut through the room.

"We have the valuation now that will net us proceeds to grow through acquisitions. Without acquisitions, we'll stagnate. We can't count on just landing new accounts. That's not a good strategy for growth."

I saw a few nods and a few taking notes. Jim's eyes gleamed with pride. Luke, however, looked bored, tapping his pen against the table.

Nate Jackson, head of the LA office, spoke up next, "Trying to buy companies now when the market's so overheated is insane. All those tech companies have no profit and have ridiculous valuations."

"I'm betting in 2000, tech stocks will go through a bust. A Big Bang. And when that happens, we'll shop for bargain basement deals," I responded. "Oh, and I'm not making a risky bet. Your ring binder will have the data supporting the projections about where those bloated tech stocks are headed."

Pelletier from Canada leaned forward. "And our own stock price?"

"I want steady growth, not a spike. We're not going to lump ourselves with the ballyhoo of the dotcoms. We're an established company. We've been around for more than fifty years, right, Jim?" I looked at my mentor and saw him nod. "We have no debt. And we have plenty of cash on hand. That's our advantage over the tech startups."

Brian Cranston, an outside trustee, chimed in with skepticism. "We could lose control as a public company."

"When we become public, Jim, Luke, and I will have the controlling majority and vote. The splits are also detailed in your ring binder. You will all have significant stock ownership when your partnership units convert."

After answering all the questions, I stepped out so the partners could vote. They had two options: vote me in or buy me out.

The latter was not really an option. Still, I wanted them to vote yes because they had confidence in me.

As I paced my office, minutes felt like hours. When Jim finally walked in, my heart was pounding.

"Well?" I asked, trying to keep an expression of indifference as if daring Jim to tell me otherwise.

"Well, congratulations, Raine. You're our new CEO."

Relief and triumph washed over me. Maybe—just maybe—I could do this.

I rose to hug Jim. Instead, he pulled me in and gave me a kiss behind my ear that felt far more intimate than appropriate, and I pushed him away discreetly. Last thing I wanted was to abruptly show hostility, especially after all he'd done for me. Disquiet washed over me, but I refused to mar my moment of victory.

"Thank you, Jim," I said warily.

He merely nodded with a foreboding grin, then walked out.

That afternoon, I was lying on my side of the tennis court at New York Racquet Club as if I'd just won the U.S. Open, breathing hard, hands on my face, but I wasn't crying. I was elated.

"I let you win," Vivienne said as she approached me and gave me a hand to get up.

"Bullshit," I shot back.

Vivienne laughed. My breathing was still labored even after dousing my face with water from my bottle.

I had beaten her 7-5 and 7-6 in straight sets. Not only did I win against Vivienne, who held the title of team captain all through high school until I took it away from her in the last semester of our senior year, but I was also voted CEO of my company. Unanimously.

Once my heart rate slowed and my breathing evened, we packed our equipment and headed for the showers. As we stored our stuff in the lockers, I stopped Vivienne momentarily.

"I want you to be our investment counsel of record for our IPO."

Vivienne cracked a smile. I knew she needed this for her career as much as I needed her help for mine. She was a critical partner when we strategized for my presentation. She was a part of my win.

"After the IPO, I want to retain you as our independent investment counsel ad infinitum."

Vivienne threw her head back in pure joy, letting out a loud whoop, not caring there were women in the room.

"This makes losing to you so worth it, Nish," she said, pulling my sweaty body into a tight hug.

"We're doing this together, Vivi," I said, then broke into Rick Astley's song, *Together Forever,* and danced my way to a shower stall.

"We're gonna rule the world. We're gonna be the badass bitches of Wall Street and Mad Ave."

CHAPTER 27

Raine

DECEMBER 1999 – NEW YEAR'S EVE
NEW YORK, NEW YORK

H e was drunk.

"About time you got here," Jim greeted me with a slight slur and a lopsided smile. By the looks of it, he'd been tippling for hours, and I should have trusted my gut feeling that trouble was brewing.

After a grueling international schedule for most of December, my flight finally landed at 10 p.m. on New Year's Eve. There was enough time to rush home, change for the evening celebration at the Waldorf, and join the company in toasting our successful IPO—plus the end of the millennium.

"How are you, doll?" Jim leaned in to kiss my cheek. Boy, did he reek! I'd never known him to be sloppy with his drink, and we were due on the podium shortly for the honorary speech and toast.

"Hello, Jim. You're having a blast. Have you seen Vivienne?" I asked, pulling away from his inebriated face.

I scanned the ballroom for Vivienne and Luke but couldn't find them in the sea of faces. God, there too many people here tonight.

I was about to call Vivienne from my cell to find out where she was when Jim pulled me next to him, his arm around my waist.

"Fuck 'em! They're missing the best party of the century," Jim said, pushing a champagne flute into my hands. "Come on, time for us to ring in the New Year."

I kept my best smile on while we did the countdown on stage before business associates, clients, and a few colleagues. After finally toasting to 2000—and the world didn't implode as predicted—I pushed toward the exit when Jim found me. He took my elbow and ushered me out of the ballroom, dodging more well-wishers, excusing us with vague promises to return.

Instead, we left the building and hailed for Carty, sitting not too far behind the line of limousines parked in front of the hotel.

"Let's go down to Gateway, Carty," he ordered from behind the dividing glass window before sliding it shut.

"Ugh! Thanks for the rescue," I said in relief. I wished he would have dropped me off first instead of going downtown to the corporate apartment opposite my own. But I let it go. I was too exhausted to argue.

"That's okay, babe, I understand. Must be overwhelming for you," Jim said, covering one of my hands, squeezing it lightly, then throwing a protective arm over the seat above my shoulders. "Did you just get back from London?"

I nodded, stiffening slightly at his gesture, but with jet lag catching up, I rested my head against it.

As Carty pulled up to the complex, I shook myself awake, having dozed during the short ride downtown.

"Happy New Year, Jim," I said, bidding him goodnight and making no move to leave the car. "I guess I'll see you at the office in a couple of days."

"Listen, why don't you come up for a few minutes? We can have one quiet New Year's drink together. We deserve to celebrate in peace, don't you think?"

Alarm bells clanged loudly in my head, and I was conflicted. This man was technically my boss. I owed him my career and its success. Because of Jim, I had moved past Peter's suicide, and the year had flown by without me dwelling on his death and the loneliness since.

It's Jim, silly. You've known him for years.

"Okay, one drink. Then I have to go."

As we exited the car, I quickly signaled Carty to wait. He understood.

The corporate penthouse at Gateway Nine in Battery Park City felt more like a hotel room, distinctly appointed but lacking the warmth of a human resident.

Jim's eyes showed an unmistakable glint when he held out a champagne flute for me and raised his own in a toast. They were bloodshot and glassy, but there was something else. I'd seen eyes like those in high school—kids who did cocaine.

"To us, Raine," he said, raising his glass. "To our empire."

"Hear! Hear!" I said, raising my glass to my lips. I took the tiniest sip, aware that he was raking the length of my neck with his eyes.

I set the glass down on the coffee table and moved to pick up my coat and clutch. "Okay, time for me to go, and you need to get some rest as well."

He walked toward me, closing the space between us and blocking my move. Before I knew it, he was inches from my face, his hand cupping my chin. He assaulted my mouth with his. I stood numbly, too stunned to react as his tongue invaded mine. I turned my face away and shoved my fists against his chest to push him away.

"Raine, darling," he began. "We'd be so good together."

What the hell was this about?

"No, Jim... please," I said. He wasn't just kissing. He was biting my lower lip—hard.

"Ouch, that hurt," I said, squirming to get free, but he made no move to let go. The man worked out regularly, and I felt his hard muscles imprison me.

"Think about it, Raine," he said, slamming me almost violently against his hard chest. "You and me. If we combined our fortunes, we'd be one of the ten wealthiest families in the country. We'd plunder and pillage the industry. Rock the markets. And then we could take the company private. And while we're gathering wealth along the way, we could have mad, passionate sex. We'll have our cake and eat it too."

I resisted the urge to panic and needed to keep my wits.

"You've got this all wrong, Jim. You've had too much to drink, and you're not thinking straight," I said, staying calm and diplomatic despite the fear creeping up my spine.

This was tricky. I wanted to believe this was all a misunderstanding and that he would be embarrassed and apologize once he sobered up in the morning. But first, I needed to get away.

"Trust me," he groaned as he licked my neck. My stomach lurched in disgust. "You've trusted me before, and I've not let you down, Raine. You and I can make much more money... more than you'd ever dreamed. More than Peter could have ever dreamed. But this time, I'll have you on my arm, darling."

He rattled a sickening chuckle, his noxious breath heavy with liquor.

"Jim..." I shook my head to get that repulsive tongue away from my skin.

"Come on, love and money don't go together. I learned that being married to Peter," I said, trying to laugh it off.

"Who said anything about love, Raine? We're both adults. We'll leave love to those who believe in the mushy stuff. They rarely succeed in life."

"Jim, I'm sorry if I gave you the wrong impression before, but I'm not interested in having an affair with you."

Staying unfazed was challenging once I realized the man wasn't just drunk. He was intent on forcing himself on me.

"Let me go, Jim. Now!"

I struggled to push him away, but he tightened his grip, refusing to release me.

"You know, Peter was blind. He never saw in you what I see. You are both ruthless and savvy. Peter felt threatened by you. Did you know that? He was selfish and didn't want to share the limelight. He never wanted to acknowledge that you have what it takes to be a successful CEO. Think about it, Raine. I was the one who gave you the chance to soar. And look at us now, my gorgeous."

His arms further tightened around me.

"Know what else he didn't see?" Jim further taunted.

I didn't want to know. But he held my gaze. "Under all that ice and frost you put on as a front, you're one hot little number, babe. And I could tell Peter never really satisfied you, did he?" he growled.

His tongue, again, on my face, his saliva smearing my skin. It was sickening. I yelped when he slammed and pinned me against a wall, imprisoning my hands above my head. I felt his erection grinding against me. I wriggled in protest without much success.

His lips traveled lower, nearing the exposed cleft of my breasts. I felt my flush rise, and I knew Jim felt it as he inhaled the heat, thinking it was my body responding to his touch. That he was turning me on. My survival instincts kicked in.

I started breathing hard, letting him think I was getting horny, grinding my pelvis against his thickening penis.

"Oh yes," I moaned, lengthening my neck and inviting him to graze it. When I heard him growl with increasing need, he released his grip on my hands to raise my skirt. I saw my opportunity to squirm away.

I ran for my purse and made for the door. But he caught my arm, and I squealed as he pushed me to the floor. Hard. My face hit the corner of the coffee table as he pounced to land on top of me. All I could think was the pain.

"Don't even think you're getting away. You owe me this, Raine," he said with pure evil.

He crushed his mouth against mine again, this time cruelly, biting again until my lip bled. I realized he had some perversion with sadism and punishment.

I started flailing with my arms and legs to wrest myself free.

"I see why Peter would never leave you for that slut." he teased. "You're a fighter, and it's such a turn-on. Go ahead, fight me, baby."

I froze.

Slut. Peter and slut in one sentence.

What... the... hell!

This time, my cunning mind took over with raging anger.

"Well, then... I might as well enjoy this. Take off your pants, baby," I purred, working to pull his shirt from his waist, feeling his skin, which I knew would make his dick throb even more with anticipation.

"That's my girl," he said, easing himself up to release his belt buckle.

That's when I saw my chance to make my move with a groin shot. I shoved my knee against his dick hard enough to feel perhaps a small bone crack, sending him stumbling backward in shock and shouting in excruciating pain.

Yeah, he didn't need his family jewels anyway.

"What the fuck, Raine?"

He hollered with labored breath then groaned louder. His eyes were shut tight as he groped the carpet, making his way toward the couch, cradling his balls.

I was now in control, but I was raging inside. Rendering him immobile, I took my time slipping on my shoes and gathering my coat and clutch while I narrowed my eyes at him in disgust.

"Raine," he spat, squinting in pain and rasping between breaths, "your husband slept around. He's got a kid with that woman who filed a paternity lawsuit against him and the firm. He settled it because it's true. He's got a kid out there because you...couldn't...give...him one."

I tried to block out the ramblings of a drunken, vindictive man as he hissed each word. But it was too late. Jim was determined to hurt me where it mattered most—my barrenness.

As I slammed the door behind me, still within earshot, I heard him call out, "If you don't believe me, ask Luke."

Luke

DECEMBER 1999 – NEW YEAR'S EVE
NEW YORK, NEW YORK

Raine had been hurt. Really, *really* hurt.

"What the hell happened?" Luke asked as Raine stumbled out of the elevator, collapsing into his arms. She was sobbing against him.

When he'd buzzed her up, Luke suspected something was very wrong. But he had not expected to see Raine in such a state—her tear-streaked face, mascara-smeared eyes, swollen lip, and, Jesus, was that a black and blue bruise by her eye?

"Shh..." he comforted, stroking her hair and kissing her temple, taking care not to touch her bruise.

She pulled away from him, still sobbing.

Luke reached for a Kleenex from a side table and handed it to her while he went to get her a drink of water. She blew her nose softly, drank slowly, and then handed back the glass, muttering, "Thanks."

She'd been crying so hard her shoulders shuddered with each sob.

"Raine, who did this to you?"

But she ignored his questions.

Instead, in between hiccups, she spat, "Tell me."

Her voice had a hard edge. She was angry. *Furious*.

"Don't talk now," Luke said, trying to pull her back in his arms, but she resisted, shaking her head.

"Tell me about Peter. Tell me it isn't true," she demanded. Her eyes looked violent, her lips tight.

Luke gasped. He knew exactly what she was asking about, and a chill ran up his spine because there was no hiding from it. How had she found out? Who'd told her?

He said nothing, struggling to find a way to answer her honestly without distressing her any more than she already was. He looked at her earnestly, then looked away and raised his eyes to the ceiling.

"Oh, God," she whispered.

"Peter received a lawsuit..."

"What lawsuit?"

Luke wouldn't look at her. "A woman had filed a paternity suit claiming Peter's the father of her child. It was a nuisance suit, Raine. It's not uncommon for these suits to come about, especially against a wealthy guy. He told Jim and me at one of our partners' meetings because the firm was also named. The woman sought millions, including a part of his equity in the agency. But I was surprised when he said he settled and had it sealed."

"I know Peter. If there hadn't been any merit to the suit, he'd have fought it tooth and nail. He'd have crucified the bitch."

"My understanding is that settling would have kept it quiet. Otherwise, the press would have had a field day if he fought it, and with his campaign gearing up..."

"Was that all Peter cared about? The publicity?" Raine was now looking at him in disbelief. "Was that all you and Jim cared about? His reputation? The agency's reputation? Did Peter have a child, Luke? Or was it a nuisance lawsuit?"

He saw her plea, but he couldn't lie.

"Honestly, I don't know. Not for a fact."

"But if Peter had settled the suit, that most likely meant...," her voice trailed off.

Luke covered his face, then rubbed it hard, trying to wipe away whatever nightmare he was floating in.

You sonovabitch! he cried out in his mind, cursing his dead friend.

"Why didn't you tell me?" she whispered, gazing at Luke with eyes pained with what she saw as his betrayal of trust. It was as if he'd stabbed her in the back.

"Raine, it was Peter's wish. But it's all in the past now."

She laughed. "In the past, for whom? You? Why didn't anyone tell me, for God's sake? Peter's been dead for a year. Don't you think I should have been told? The firm was named in the suit, and you didn't think I should have been told? When was I going to find out? From the press?"

Luke ran his fingers through his hair, grasping at what he could say to comfort her. But he had none.

Her breathing came in rasps said. He went to refill her glass of water, but when he handed it to her, she grabbed it and hurled it against the wall, shattering the tumbler into shards across the room.

They were both silent for what seemed like an interminable moment. Then she started for the elevator to leave.

"Raine, Peter made us swear not to tell you. Especially you. He was trying to protect you."

Raine turned back at him. "Jesus, Luke, from what? His philandering?"

"Raine, you're understandably distraught..."

"I thought you were my friend," she said through her tear-streaked face.

"I am, dammit! I didn't say anything because I didn't want to believe it either. I still don't!" Luke began to pace, feeling helpless.

"You didn't think I could handle the news, did you? Well, fuck you, Luke."

"I wanted to tell you, but Peter was adamant about it. Raine, we'll figure this out together. We'll find out what the facts are. Right now, you're hurt and should see a doctor. Who did this to you anyway?"

But Raine had turned around and stepped back into the elevator, cranking the gates down with such force that steel ground against steel, echoing around the building.

"Raine, wait ... Shit," he muttered as he tried to go after her but stopped when their eyes met. As the elevator slowly descended, Luke saw the searing accusation of duplicity through her cold, black stare—from Peter. From Jim. And most painfully from him.

CHAPTER 28

Vivienne

S he howled, choked, and spilled her guts.
Vivienne allowed Raine to release the hurt and the pain until nothing was left.

She set a mug of freshly brewed chamomile tea by the bed where Raine was sleeping, still hiccupping from her crying spell.

After leaving Luke, Raine went to Vivienne, who had been nursing a mild cold that New Year's Eve. Raine said she didn't care if she caught Vivienne's bug. So Vivienne let her stay for as long as she needed.

Detective Rich Molino had come by her studio apartment to take Raine's statement about what had happened. After all, Raine had a bruise on her forehead and appeared disheveled and tear-streaked when she'd arrived at her doorstep.

Vivienne sat on the couch next to Luther, her black cat, licking his paws as he lounged quietly. When the phone rang, she quickly lifted the receiver, not wanting to wake Raine.

"Hey," she whispered. It was Luke, who was probably calling to get an update on Raine. Instead, her eyes widened in disbelief over what she was hearing.

"What? Oh my God!" Vivienne struggled to keep her voice low despite the shock of what she'd just heard.

"This is such a shock." Vivienne covered her mouth as it widened with every word Luke told her. "She's sleeping right now... Yeah... I'll let her know.... Sure, keep me posted."

Vivienne didn't mention to Luke that his asshole of a partner had tried to rape Raine. That was not for her to divulge to anyone, especially not to Luke, considering what happened between them early New Year's Day, and Raine hadn't mentioned the sexual assault to him.

Jim had suffered a massive heart attack on New Year's Day, probably shortly after Raine left him. And this morning, after three days in a coma, Luke told Vivienne that the old man had died, never regaining consciousness.

Still, she worried that when Raine awoke, her friend would be so empty with nothing left to give.

Raine would be changed forever.

CHAPTER 29

Nick

MAY 2000

NEW YORK, NEW YORK

I t was all about connections.

"Any interesting claims crossing your desk these days?" Nick asked, signaling the bartender for a brewsky as he sat beside Brad.

As a reporter, Nick's carefully cultivated network granted him access to information beyond what the Freedom of Information Law could provide.

So when one of his insurance buddies from the behemoth brokerage firm of Martin and Mather, Ltd. loosened his tongue one evening over drinks at the Bull and Bear on Wall Street, Nick's scoop antenna rose.

Brad was a beefy guy who made a career in large commercial insurance broking. His tie hung loosely at his collar, shirt rumpled, and face flushed, indicating he'd been at his beers long before Nick arrived.

Nick always thought the best news scoops came from the insurance guys. They knew who was about to go belly up, who was getting sued, and who violated laws long before anyone else did. To Nick, they held the *Open Sesame* key to the Alibaba cave of rich news stories.

"Usual stuff... Workers comp, environmental claims, hurricanes..." Brad shrugged with indifference.

But then the insurance man turned quiet, staring into his beer, which to Nick meant Brad might be brooding about something—his recent divorce and how his wife was sending him to the poor house—or simply the intense pressure of working for a known sweatshop.

"Something bothering you?" Nick sipped his Corona.

Brad shook his head. "I dunno, I really shouldn't say anything."

Nick stayed quiet, biding his time.

"It's just that..." Brad grimaced. "Well, there's something that's baffling me."

Nick leaned in, all ears.

"You know that guy who was one of the bigwigs at Glory Media? The one who died earlier this year?"

Nick nodded.

"You know, Glory Media's one of our largest accounts, but we're also handling the old man's estate. Now, you can't use any of this, but this is something that came to me from third-party sources.

"One of our attorneys had heard from another attorney, and I don't know who, but they were asking about the viability of filing a personal injury and wrongful death lawsuit against Glory and Raine Garvey personally. Mind you, it's not a criminal charge they're making. And they haven't done anything—yet. But they wanted to know how likely Glory's insurers would settle for something like this."

"Whoah! Buddy. You can't just spill something like that to me and expect me not to do anything with the info."

"Nick, I've got nothing, and I'm going to deny this on the basis that I am now legally under the influence," Brad started cackling as he tipped his beer for a sip.

"Well, you're right. That is baffling. I mean, do you have any idea why this would have come up? Is this just a rumor you heard?"

Brad looked around the bar to see who might be within earshot.

"I swear, Nick, if you breathe a word about this, I will kill you. But listen to this..." Brad looked around once more, then leaned into Nick's ear.

"It's about the cause of death—a penile injury."

Brad broke into a boisterous laugh, the kind that was loud and rowdy after one had a few drinks. It was as if he'd been dying to tell someone about this, and the hilarity finally just exploded like an overfilled water balloon.

"Seriously?" Nick laughed along, but his mind raced.

"I mean..." Brad was still splitting his sides as he wiped his tears. "Somebody must have kicked the old man in the nuts so hard that it killed him. So apparently, the estate thinks Garvey—the widow—is responsible."

Brad started pounding on the bar counter, hooting uncontrollably, and patrons began turning to him as if wanting in on the joke. "Hahhhh... can you imagine that, Nick? Glory's CEO finally giving that snake his comeuppance?"

Brad was clearly six sheets to the wind.

"I mean, everybody in the conference room was just hysterical over it. Of course, it was just us guys in sales, so you know..."

"So, really, you didn't just hear this from somebody. It's true enough that you guys talked about it in a *meeting*? That's sick, dude."

Nick felt his Blackberry vibrate with a message, then frowned when he read the email. Slapping his buddy on the back, he threw some bills on the counter, enough to pay Brad's tab.

"I swear, Nick, you can't say a word..."

But Nick was already walking out the door.

Back in the newsroom, the rumor that the York estate "might" be considering a wrongful death suit against Glory and Raine Garvey had already reached *The Tribune*.

Fancy that being a coincidence, Nick thought.

No one knew who the source was or where it came from. Nick was only aware that it had come from *"upstairs,"* and he was assigned to look into the story.

There was something just so hokey and far-fetched about an estate that was already richer than sin to want to file a wrongful death lawsuit to squeeze even more money out of the company and the widow herself. *Why?*

But thanks to his connection to Detective Rich Molino, Nick learned that the old man had suffered a penile injury very recently before his coronary event. Molino had also shared the police report the widow filed for sexual assault against York just hours after she left the old man in the company apartment—three days before the old man died.

"Jesus, Richie, are you serious?" Nick was stunned as he read the faxed report.

"I wish I wasn't, Nick. It was pretty ugly. She had a fat lip and a bruise on her forehead. She said she'd fallen against the coffee table when the old man pushed her. That's when she hit her head and bit her lip."

"Oh my fucking God!"

If Nick had thought the lawsuit absurd, this revelation was appalling.

"So, she kicked him in the nuts? Hard to believe she injured him enough to kill him."

"Well..." This time, it was Richie who cleared his throat. "Are you aware that Ms. Garvey has some training in mixed martial arts?"

"*What*???"

"She said she knew enough jiu-jitsu and kickboxing because she trained under Sebastian Taylor."

"Are you fucking kidding me? The two-time UFC champ? *Shiiiittt!!!* I'm blown away by this, Richie."

"She said she took it up as a form of self-defense. Smart on her part because that's what she did to him. She pulled a groin shot on him that can be devastating to the family jewels. If you know what I mean."

"A groin shot? Wow, dude. That's a move that was banned from the sport, you know," Nick suddenly had a profound respect for Raine Garvey. Maybe even feared her.

"How many people know about this, Richie?"

"Just Ms. Garvey, Ms. Oliver, and me. Garvey didn't want to file anything, let alone press charges. It was Oliver's insistence because, at that time, she feared the old man would exact vengeance against Garvey. Probably ruin her reputation.

"Mind you, this was all before we knew York was being transported to the hospital."

After he hung up with Molino, Nick quickly called Henry Barton, York's estate lawyer. And he was right.

The attorney knew nothing about the complaint.

CHAPTER 30

Raine

MAY 2000

NEW YORK, NEW YORK

Glory Stock Slips On Rumor
Of York Estate Shares Sale

By Nicholas D. Coelho

Shares of Glory Media, Inc. (GLOR) fell sharply in early trading after reports surfaced that the estate of former chairman James P. York might sell its stake.

"We're reviewing our First Right of Refusal agreement with Glory. If the company passes, we'll pursue a market sale," said Henry Barton, attorney for the estate.

The stock drop adds to concerns over leadership stability following the departure of several creative directors. CEO Raine Garvey's bereavement leave in January has sparked speculation that major shareholder Luke Henes might launch his own firm.

"I wouldn't be surprised if Luke goes independent," said Angel Fusseli, Glory's former multimedia director, now running her own Hollywood firm.

Glory Media did not respond to requests for comment.

Fund managers are shorting Glory stock, expecting further declines. Meanwhile, British rival Sherman Holdings has been quietly buying shares, leading analysts to predict a potential takeover. Sherman generates over two billion in annual revenue.

"It will be interesting to see how this unfolds," said a source familiar with the matter. "Garvey, York's estate, and Henes still control the majority of shares and board votes."

Since when did Nick write stories based on rumors and speculation? Why was *The Trib* publishing stories with unnamed sources?

Wasn't it just a couple of months ago when Vivienne called The Tribune's chief editor, who had assured her the paper wouldn't print anything without thoroughly vetted sources?

Well, this one slipped by Nick's superiors. I was disappointed that I'd appointed Greyson as acting CEO, and he hadn't said or done anything. He should have made a statement or, at the very least, reached out to me. Instead of calling him, I dialed Vivienne's number directly.

"I guess that snake slithered this article past his editors," I said drily.

"Don't sweat this one, Nish. Any stock drop will always be news. If *The Trib* didn't write about it, the *Journal* would have. I'm just as surprised as you at how sloppy Nick's story was."

"What a jerk," was the only appropriate response I had.

"It's all just shock tactics, Nish. However, I am curious why Barton would go to the press. I asked Heywood if Barton might have inquired about selling. Not a peep.

"This is something that should have been highly confidential. Seems a petty way to manipulate the stock price, and he should know it wouldn't have any bearing on the estate's sale because of the First Right of Refusal clause in the closing documents."

"I smell a rat, Vivi, which means Coelho knows something. We need to nip this business of shorting our stock in the bud. The arbitragers are leaping from their cushy armchairs on this bit of news, whether or not there's a lick of truth to it. I'm so pissed I want some people to lose their shirts on this."

I gritted my teeth as I spoke. "You ready for a bit of adventure?"

"Always am, girlfriend. Let's get started."

"First off, let's buy it all, Vivi. Luke and I can buy Jim's stake based on a fixed price plus a percentage. It was all part of the IPO agreement."

"I remember," Vivi replied. "I drafted that agreement myself."

"We'll offer one hundred percent cash. I want them out of my hair and out of my life."

"That should shoot the price up tomorrow. You're right. A bunch of somebodies will lose their shirts."

"I have to talk to Luke to get his approval."

"Good, you're finally going to call him."

"Of course. This is too important. It's just business, Vivi."

"Still, he'll be happy to hear from you."

"Let's move on," I said, brushing off that last remark. What happened between Luke and me was still a sore subject.

"Once we get the estate's go-ahead, let's move on to John Jay Agency. Their bond matures this year, so they'll be desperate. If it looks good, make an offer. You have my power of attorney.

"If they say yes, get a due diligence team together fast. I want this to go before the board by the end of the month. That's three weeks from now. After that, we close."

"You realize the acquisition will put you over the top," Vivienne said. I could hear her excitement. "Glory will be number one, Nish. You'll own the world's largest advertising and media company. Sherman won't have a prayer to buy you out, and there aren't too many other agencies for them to merge with."

"Good. That's the plan," I said with conviction. "Well, my lovey, it's time for you to get to work. Sorry, you're going to have a few late nights."

"Not to worry, Nish. My law firm has great people we can pull together as a team. I'll loop in Grey, Luke, Charlie, and Heywood as soon as we hang up. Then I'll have a chat with Barton. If they're serious, and I feel they are, we can have the transfer of shares concluded by the end of the week. Friday next week at the latest."

"Fabulous, girlfriend. I knew I could count on you."

"Not so fast, Nish. Let's close the John Jay deal in Boston, so you won't have to return to New York."

I paused in thought. Boston. Too close for comfort. But better than driving back to the city.

"And, Nish," Vivienne added. "You're going to be there. In person. Because I want to see you, and you're going to tell me what the hell is going on in your life."

Luke

MAY 2000
NEW YORK, NEW YORK

Hearing her voice after months of silence disturbed him. He'd envisioned being with Raine many times, even though she'd gently made it clear the feeling was not mutual. Nothing was more deflating than hearing the woman you fantasized about say she loved you like a brother, though she had trusted him implicitly.

And then he betrayed that trust.

He needed a drink with a friend. But with Peter gone and now Raine, he felt lonelier than ever. When the phone rang, he had contemplated letting it go to voice mail. He felt too broody to speak with anyone. But he picked up anyway.

"Hi, Luke. It's Vivienne. Remember me?" Of course, he remembered Vivienne, although they hadn't spoken since Raine announced her sabbatical.

"Hey, long time no talk. How's it going?" Luke said.

"Have you checked your stock lately?"

"No, it's too depressing," he replied, frowning at the thought of the market battering his shares.

"Check the ticker. Late-day trading. You may end up with a record high before the bell rings."

He made no move to check the ticker on the Internet. "Well, that's good news for a change," he said.

"Have you heard from Raine about buying Jim's estate holdings?" Vivienne asked.

"I have. She was still rather cool towards me. All business. I'm sure she hasn't forgiven me, but I agreed to her plans."

"Great! I'll be over this afternoon to get your signature on the paperwork."

"Why not messenger it over."

"That's gonna take too long. How's five o'clock?"

"Sure," Luke muttered indifferently, then quickly added. "Hey, Vivienne? Instead of coming over, let's meet for drinks. You can bring the docs, and I'll sign them then."

"*Tonight???*"

Luke heard her astonishment. His heart sank and prepared for disappointment.

"Earth to Luke. Did you not hear what I just said? Do you know what I need to do for the next forty-eight hours?"

"Vivienne, please. I need to talk about Raine, about what happened. I'm not asking you on a date, just as a friend." Luke pleaded and then hoped during the silence.

"Alright. I'll meet you at the Hudson Bar and Book in the Village at six for *one* beer. Sign the papers first, and then we'll talk." she replied, then hung up.

Oh God. Luke pushed his hair back.

He must have sounded pathetic. He hoped Vivienne hadn't agreed to meet just because he was a client and she felt sorry for him. Turning to Raine's best friend for company felt desperate.

Still, he was glad he picked up the phone. He was no longer brooding.

Vivienne

MAY 2000
NEW YORK, NEW YORK

Vivienne wasn't sure meeting Luke for drinks was a good idea—even if he was a client. But he sounded so heartbroken over losing Raine and their friendship. The bond and trust between them was severed because of Jim. And Peter. And now Luke felt lost and guilty. So Vivienne would have one drink while he signed the documents. Maybe she wouldn't mind some alone time with him, even if he would only talk about Raine.

Luke would never see Vivienne as more than Raine's friend, certainly not as a woman who liked him—a lot.

CHAPTER 31

Luke

MAY 2000
NEW YORK, NEW YORK

T he usually hopping English pub on Hudson Street was quiet, making it easy to spot her from his seat.

After almost two hours and three beers, he saw her rush in, burdened with a bulging briefcase and laptop case. She had sent Blackberry messages that she'd be late, but he assured her he'd wait since she needed his signature.

She wore a clinging cream-colored silk dress, showcasing her curves and long legs, with matching sandals. Her look was seductively businesslike.

Luke felt a knot in his gut as he took in her flushed face, glistening with a sheen of perspiration. It made her look quite...hot...literally and figuratively.

Vivienne wasn't model-thin but had a figure a man could embrace, with some softness to squeeze.

"I'm so sorry," she said while trying to catch her breath as she climbed the stool beside him.

"Don't," he said, covering her hand. "I'm glad you came to keep this sorry client company."

"I wouldn't consider you a sorry sop of anything, Luke. I'm a terrible lawyer for keeping you waiting," she smiled. "But... grateful you waited for me."

"Of course."

She grasped the hand that touched hers as if to respond in a handshake, then let it go as she settled her things on the counter. A move that was not lost on him that this meetup was strictly business.

Still, he continued his appraisal of the woman who had perched next to him, subtly taking in her big blue Kewpie doll eyes and a mop of cornsilk hair styled in a bob. Her mouth was a tad too wide, but she had a pretty smile. Now, her lips...those lips were seductively plump and pouty, thick with red lipstick that he knew would get all over his collar if he kissed them.

Those sensual thoughts of Raine's best friend assaulted Luke with a jumble of emotions he found disturbing. He cleared his throat and signaled for two Sam Adams

"First things first," Vivienne said, pulling documents from her briefcase, then marking lines where he needed to sign with an X.

"We're going to offer..." Her voice trailed off as he grabbed her pen, waved her off, and quickly scribbled his signature with his left hand.

"You can't just sign without knowing what it says," Vivienne said, exasperated.

He shook his head. "What for? None of it's going to make sense to me anyway."

"All the more you should listen," she insisted.

"I find it hard to believe we could just walk into John Jay's and offer him money, and he says yes, just like that. What's the catch?" Luke asked.

"They've been looking to merge with an agency for a couple of years now. The problem with Jay's business is that it's all internet advertising."

As she crossed her legs, the hem of her dress inched higher, baring a sliver of her thigh.

Luke noticed.

"Glory needs a new avenue for growth besides bringing in more clients. The world's changing, and money can be made if you're not asleep at the wheel. And Raine never is, even if she may be away on sabbatical."

Luke munched pretzels, listening to Vivienne explain the deal in plain English. But why did she have to sound so sexy? How had he never noticed how sensual her voice was?

After putting away the documents, she raised her bottle. "Here's to your first acquisition."

"Save that toast for when Raine's around and let's not talk business," he said.

"You said you needed to talk." Vivienne set her drink on the counter.

"How is Raine?" Luke asked, watching her gaze shift to the liquor shelf behind the bar.

"You spoke with her, Luke. Didn't you ask her?"

"I don't understand her anymore, Vivienne. Peter's death has changed her." Luke stared at his beer, debating ordering another.

"She's fine," Vivienne replied, not offering much of an explanation for the change Raine had just undergone.

"I think Jim attacked her. And had he lived, I might have…" Luke's voice was tight. "I have a feeling she's never coming back. Is she coming back?"

"Luke, when Raine commits, she keeps it. She won't abandon the agency."

Vivienne's tone was defiant, chiding Luke for not believing Raine would be back.

"Where can I reach her?"

Vivienne fell silent and looked at Luke in empathy, but then her gaze floated away, this time to the books that lined the tavern's walls.

"She never told you where she is, did she?" Vivienne asked, watching him shake his head. "She's not far."

"I'm sorry." Luke could no longer hide his disappointment that Vivienne wouldn't be more forthcoming about Raine's whereabouts. "I just want to make it better between us. I want to restore that trust and friendship we had. I don't know... I've been trying to reach out...I've emailed but unless it's business, she won't respond."

"Give her time." Vivienne reached for his hand. "Heck, Luke, she's even pushed me away. But I know Raine. And with her, you need to let her bide her time."

Feeling the warmth of her hand, Luke drew her to her feet. "Let's grab a bite to eat. I'm starved.

Vivienne

MAY 2000

NEW YORK, NEW YORK

They shared a white veggie thin-crust pizza at Mappa Mondo, their knees bumping and fingers brushing as they pulled slices from the tin platter. Their foreheads almost touched as they ate silently. She worried about the garlic-laden topping, thinking it would not be appropriate to have such offensive breath. Not that she expected him to kiss her since he was still far too besotted with Raine.

Vivienne suddenly felt unattractive, embarrassed by her hope that Luke might see her differently. She wiped her mouth, not caring that the last hint of lipstick had disappeared on her white paper napkin. She passed on dessert, and he asked for a cannoli. They sipped cappuccinos laced with amaretto before she finally declared that she was tired.

"I'm sorry. I should have known you'd be exhausted." Luke hailed the waiter for the check.

"Here, let me get this," Vivienne offered, reaching for her pocketbook.

He reached for her hand and stopped her. "I dragged you to join me," he said quietly.

"No, really, I can expense this..." she mumbled.

"Vivienne," he said, this time tenderly. "Let me do this, please. It wasn't all business. I'm glad you came. Joined me for a pizza."

A lump caught in her throat. If he talked endearingly to her one more time and then followed it up with another Raine memory, she'd croak and lose all that professional composure.

Outside, they debated hailing a cab.

"I can walk," she said. "It's less than five blocks. You go on and get a cab."

"Chrissakes, Vivienne, it's eleven o'clock. I'm not going to let you walk alone in this neighborhood," Luke cried as he scanned the area.

"Luke, I've lived here for five years. I know this neighborhood, and I've walked home at night alone before," she insisted, wishing he would get in a cab and go. She needed the solitude. She didn't want him to walk her home if she wasn't attractive enough for him. If he only felt pity.

But there was no arguing with him. He grabbed her laptop case to ease some of the weight she was carrying, then followed her as she headed toward her Horatio Street apartment.

They walked in silence, the blocks falling away. When they reached the front door of her apartment building, they stopped and looked at each other for a moment. Luke made no move to hand back her laptop, and Vivienne was in no rush to fish for her keys.

"I'd like to come up," he whispered.

"It's late, Luke," she said, avoiding his eyes. What for anyway? To talk more about Raine, "I have an early morning tomorrow with a lot of work ahead."

But she handed him her keys, letting him unlock the door and follow her to her apartment.

"Let me make you some coffee," she offered, tossing her bags on the couch.

But before she could turn for the kitchen, he caught her arms and drew her in.

Luke

MAY 2000
NEW YORK, NEW YORK

She tasted of Amaretto and espresso, and a deep longing crept inside Luke. She didn't withdraw from his kiss. Their tongues danced, and her nails ran down his spine, making him ache for more. But before his hands could explore further, he gently pushed her away. They were adults, single, but they did business together. Not the best timing.

"I better go," he whispered.

Vivienne said nothing. He kissed her forehead and let himself out, hearing the door close behind him. He lingered outside, listening to the click of her locks before heading down the staircase, unaware of her silent tears.

CHAPTER 32

Raine

MAY 2000

DURHAM, NEW HAMPSHIRE

"Holy Mother of God. Where have you been? Did you run off with a Latin lover and your husband's millions?"

"Really, Nick? That's the best you can come up with?" I rolled my eyes.

"What really happened between you and the old man on New Year's Eve?"

Goosebumps rose on my neck. Why ask about New Year's Eve when his story was about Jim's estate selling its stake in Glory? Nick was baiting me, and I wasn't going to bite.

"Do you want a scoop or not?" I pressed.

"You gonna tell me where you're hiding?"

"Trace the call if you're that curious."

"It'd be quicker if you just told me."

"But not as much fun."

"So, what do I owe the honor?"

"I bought York's share of the company yesterday. The price is undisclosed but based on IPO terms."

"No shit!" He paused. "Why are you telling me this your-self?"

"To ensure you have the facts. It's not like you to write garbage. Who's your unnamed source?" I asked.

"How do you know it's not true? Feeling insecure?"

Typical reporter ploy. Answer a question with a question. Well, two can play that game.

"I'm not stooping to answer that. Do you want the next scoop or not?"

"There's more?"

"Glory made an offer for John Jay Advertising. It'll be official tomorrow morning. Both scoops are accurate, and you'll beat *The Journal* if you run it tonight."

"Why now?"

"The acquisition was part of our IPO strategy. We've been in talks with target firms for almost a year. You can quote me on that."

"Who were the others?"

"Doesn't matter."

"Why John Jay?"

"Their core business is an area we would like to expand in. They complement our business strategy nicely. Another quote for you."

"Nothing to do with their bond maturing soon?"

"You need to ask Jay about that."

"How many people are getting gassed?"

"John Jay's a very lean operation, and they run a tight ship. We like the talent they have. Right now, no one's going to get laid off. We'll make decisions when we've had a chance to look at the operations and the redundancies and determine where we can cut costs. We've never laid anyone off at Glory, and I'm not about to break that tradition."

"But you'll do it with Jay's shop?" He asked, still baiting.

"Like I said, we'll see first."

"What's this going to do to your stock?" I could hear a keyboard's fast and furious clicking in the background.

"We'll find out tomorrow, won't we?"

Nick

MAY 2000

NEW YORK, NEW YORK

"Dammit!" Nick stared at the phone. He'd finally gotten the widow Garvey on the line, and she'd hung up before he could get the answers he needed.

"How'd you make out?" asked Sheila, his editor, as she approached his desk.

"She's buying out the York estate's share. That's not news. She also mentioned an offer for John Jay. Big whoop!" Nick shook his head.

"Maybe not, but you got an interview about the estate selling its stake, and that's pretty big. We'll run it on page one of the business section."

"Yeah, but that's not the story I wanted," Nick said, pounding his desk. "I wanted to know what happened between her and Jim York on New Year's Eve."

"Just write today's interview and forget the lawsuit. They never filed it anyway."

"Yes, thanks to me. I could have withheld the police report and let them proceed with the suit. It would have humiliated the estate and led to a countersuit from the widow Garvey herself, bankrupting York's entire estate. The greedy heirs would have had nothing."

"Why didn't you?"

"As tough as I am about news, I have scruples. I didn't want the scandal to hurt Raine, especially after what that jerk York did to her."

"Wait, I thought you wanted to write about the lawsuit?"

"No, Sheila, the lawsuit's tabloid stuff. I'm talking about something bigger that forced Raine to leave town. I think she discovered something about her husband, and maybe that's why he killed himself. But his history before his senior year at Valley Forge Prep is a mystery."

"Why are you so obsessed with this story?"

"Sheila, it isn't about one news story. I think I knew this guy before he moved to New York but I can't seem to place him in my memory. I think there's a whole series of stories to be written about him, if not a book. If only Raine would talk to me. Wouldn't she want to know why her husband committed suicide?"

"Nick, when you did your research, you found the story of Garvey's grandparents. That's much more interesting. *The Tribune's* book division would love it, and the royalties would be huge."

Peter's grandparents, the Van Rostums, pioneered the plastics industry in the early 1900s. But by mid-century, their company was mired in lawsuits for polluting rivers and causing cancer. They funneled billions to the Cayman Islands, evading claimants and the IRS.

Sheila was probably right. Nick should focus on the Van Rostum story. For now, he would call John Jay and finish today's article.

But Nick knew the mystery behind Peter Garvey would continue to haunt him. He had every intention of solving it.

Raine

"Charlie?"

"Listen, Raine, I'm sorry—"

"Charlie, listen to me..." I cut in before he could say the dreaded words, "I quit."

In addition to everything else happening at the agency, I didn't need to hear that from our long-time financial and operations officer.

I needed to psyche myself back to the Raine of New York. CEO of Glory. Bring that confidence and bravado that I was known for, which was important—no, urgent. The staff has been showing signs of fraying and talent has already begun leaving. But more importantly, I needed to keep my executive team intact. I needed Charlie, the CFO. The money man.

"I can do better than your million-dollar bonus offer from *Global Telecom*. How would you like a major cut of Glory? We'll still need board approval, but I don't foresee any major issues."

"That's one hell of an offer, Raine. But this place just isn't the same anymore. When you turned the agency into a public company, the culture changed. Now it's all about profit."

"Charlie, I've always thought you were with me on this. We made decisions together. If you think the culture is changing, let's do something about it. With your stake, you'll be part of the controlling interest. You'll have a say, Charlie—a bigger voice."

"Raine, right after we went public, you up and disappeared. I've been doing my job, the COO, and your job in your absence."

Oh God. What would Peter do? What would Vivienne do? Fuck that. What would Raine do?

"But you're family. We've been behind you every step of your career growth with us. *Global Telecom* is a new venture. Right now, you know the dot-com fire alarms are everywhere. The stress alone will kill you. Don't do this to your family. You've got a couple of kids who will be headed to college in a few years.

"I'm asking you not to blow it all on the wad of money they're offering you or the CEO title. You're at the pinnacle of your career. No one could offer you the kind of challenges we can with the kind of security you've always had. You've got to think long-term on this one," I urged.

When he finally spoke, he said, "You gotta come back, Raine. I'll stay if you come back."

"I swear... I won't abandon you or the agency. Have faith in me. The same way you did with Peter."

I should have breathed a sigh of relief when I hung up after I got Charlie to stay. Instead, I put my head in my hands. After promising Charlie that I would return, I had just increased the size of my inner conflict.

CHAPTER 33

Ron

JUNE 2000
SKALAFELL, ICELAND

He was more than three thousand nautical miles away from New Hampshire. Yet Raine stayed on his mind. Every morning. Noon. And night.

He saw her face everywhere he went.

Amazing that he'd been able to concentrate on his work. God, he'd missed her. Painfully so.

He'd emailed Ed to see if he could somehow get Raine's contact info so that he could stay in touch.

From: rmm28@unh.edu
To: er460@unh.edu
Date: June 15, 2000, 9:45 a.m.
Message: Raine's Contact Info
    Hey Buddy
    Can you do me a favor? Can you ask Raine
    for her email address? I want to apologize
    for the ass-holey way I left her house.
    Ron

But he got no help from the guy he thought had his back.

From: er460@unh.edu
To: rmm28@unh.edu u
Date: June 15, 2000, 10:15 a.m.
Message: Raine's Contact Info
    Nah-ah. I'm not getting between you and
    Raine. You're on your own on this one, bud.

Ron had implored Ed several times, but Ed wouldn't budge. And Ron knew better than to ask Fritzso. Well, fine. In less than twenty-four hours, thirty minutes, and... Ron flicked his wrist to check the second hand on his watch. Nine seconds. Eight... He'd be on a flight back to Durham. To Raine.

One last trek to the Moberg Ridge this morning to check the strain meters and record any activity.

"Let's go, Ronald," Rolf teased, patting Ron on the back and disrupting his daydream. Ron's research partner, Rolf Magnusson, knew he'd been pining for a girl back home.

Every morning for the past four weeks, Ron and Rolf had scouted the ridge from a helicopter, looking for signs of breakage—cracks, fissures, anything to signal that Mt. Hekla might soon vent its wrath. On this final morning in Iceland, Ron scanned the rift's surface with high-powered binoculars while Rolf piloted the bird.

After spotting a stable area around the mountain's north face, Rolf touched down and switched off the helicopter. Ron leaped out, bucket in one hand and video camera in the other, while Rolf grabbed the rest of the equipment. As Rolf went to read the strain meters, Ron gently scooped ice into his bucket, then added hot lava, careful to avoid a sudden steam explosion. The sample would be crucial for his dissertation on volcanic impacts on climate change.

Ron looked up and sensed Rolf's unease. His partner was staring at the smoking crater, eyes narrowed.

"There's activity below," Rolf said, his voice tight. "Enough for another mild eruption, I think. Why didn't we catch this earlier?"

"Sensors were down, remember? The software update," Ron replied.

The ground shook beneath them.

"Shit! Let's get out of here!" Rolf barked, rushing to the helicopter. Ron followed, racing over the uneven terrain, his camcorder still rolling. As soon as they were airborne, Rolf circled the smoking ridge.

Ron leaned out, legs dangling as he filmed. "Can you get behind the wind pattern? There's too much smoke!" he shouted over the rotors.

"No! We're out of here," Rolf snapped.

"Wait! Just a few more minutes!" Ron pleaded. "Let's get some fire out of this monster's belly!"

But Rolf's instincts prevailed. "Ronald, get inside and shut the door! The smoke will kill us."

Ron slammed the door shut just as the volcano erupted, fiery debris shooting skyward. The helicopter rocked violently as sonic booms echoed through the sky. Ash and smoke engulfed the helicopter as they flew southward, escaping the worst of the ash cloud. When they landed, they were covered in soot, the taste of volcanic grit still in their mouths.

Ron wiped his face and laughed. "Shit! That was close."

"Too fucking close," Rolf muttered.

Later that evening, despite his stomach still unsettled from inhaling ash, Ron joined his research team for dinner and a beer. It was his last night in Iceland, and they had gathered to give him a proper send-off. But feeling queasy, Ron made his excuses and left early. He wanted to rest and ensure he felt better for his flight the following day.

This should have been a high point of his trip. The data he gathered and the experience of being so close to an eruption was something he had hoped to witness while he was here. Tonight, however, he missed his father deeply.

The last time he was in Iceland, he had been in the first year of his master's degree. It was cut short by his father's unexpected death. Ron was mad that his father had died too soon and even angrier that the fae of *An Dà Shealladh* had never sent him a vision. Otherwise, he'd have gone home sooner to spend a few more days with his dad. That was when he stopped believing in his gift.

After the funeral, Ron lost all desire to return and finish his studies. He bummed around aimlessly in Ann Arbor, mooching off his mom and sister, wasting six months hiking, rock climbing, and brooding.

It wasn't until Ed and Fritzso dragged him to New Hampshire that he took a job as a graduate assistant at UNH while finishing his master's degree in geology. When he was accepted into UNH's esteemed accelerated Ph.D. program and promoted to assistant professor, Ron finally found his grounding. He returned to Iceland during the summers to continue his work on volcanic activity and climate change, which was the crux of his dissertation. This would be his last trip.

"Stars live for millions of years." His father's voice was crystal clear in his memory. When he was five, he remembered his father showing him the constellation through a high-powered telescope.

"How long will we live, Dad?"

"Compared to the stars, our lives are too short."

"But you're a doctor. You make people live a long time," he had replied with youthful innocence.

"The heart is the center of a man's life," his father had told him. "I help people keep their hearts beating. But I can't keep it alive forever. That's the way life works. We live for a while and then die like the stars up there. That's why you must live well while your heart's beating strong."

"How do I do that?" Ron had persisted.

"Always keep love in your heart, Ronnie," his father had advised. "It's what keeps it strong for a long time."

On his last night, Ron dreamed of Raine. She was in a conference room with several men and women in business suits and piles of documents on a conference table. Did this mean she was already back in New York?

Shit! Ron panicked.

But then the dream dissolved into a camping scene in the mountains. Raine was playing a guitar and singing to his two girls while he roasted marshmallows over a fire. After she sang, Mackenzie turned to him and said, "Tell us a story, Da."

In that toddler lisp, Amee said, "Yes, Da. Please tew uth a stowy,"

"Alright. Once upon a time, there were three faeries. Leannan Sith, Maighdeann-mhara, and Baobhan Sith."

And as he told the story, Raine rested her head on his shoulder.

The dream lingered in his mind throughout his flight home. He wanted that dream. And he believed it would happen. Because it was his destiny, and Raine was meant to be a big part of it.

He vowed to do anything to convince her they belonged together. No more fumbling. No more excuses. He had to do it *now*. Because, as his father said, life was too short.

CHAPTER 34

Raine

JUNE 2000
DURHAM, NEW HAMPSHIRE

"Ready to do this?"

"Yep. Let's do it," I replied.

Vivienne stood outside the Parker Meridien in Boston, wearing a striking Donna Karan powder-blue suit and to-die-for Christian Louboutin double-strap pumps. A stark contrast to my casual clothing from Kmart—just a simple white shirt and a black pencil skirt. I looked like a restaurant server. Vivienne took one look at me and raised a brow.

"I could've worn jeans, you know," I muttered while pulling her in for a hug.

"Maybe you should have," she laughed. "It'll be the most exciting topic among the lawyers today."

It had been six months since I left her apartment—the day I made the life-altering decision to leave New York. At that time, I swore I would never return. And yet here I was, getting sucked back into my former executive life. But Vivienne's embrace felt reassuring. That whatever I decided in the end, she'd understand. I'd missed her.

Charlie came up from behind Vivienne and gave me the biggest, tightest bear hug.

"Do you know how much I love you?" he quipped as he released me.

"Too much, Charlie. So, how's our new president doing?"

"I'll be better after the closing, and we can reassign Jay's COO and CFO as part of our executive team. The stress level should ease up after that."

I nodded, agreeing with the strategy. "Where's Greyson?" I asked, wondering where the acting CEO was.

"Inside with the sharks," Vivienne remarked. "I'm going to rescue him. He's never been to a closing and looks piqued and overwhelmed."

Once Vivienne had disappeared through the conference room's double doors, I turned to Charlie.

"Are you happy? With everything, I mean?"

"Fabulous. You were right. I'm glad you insisted that I take a look at their financials. Global is leveraged to the eyeballs with no cash to save them. My wife is so relieved I didn't take that job. Let me tell you, she said I'll be paying for your next pair of Manolo Blahniks. Thank God for women who rule the world and lord over their spouses. We, men, would never be able to carry on the next species without making a mess. What about you, Raine?"

Laughing, I said, "I'm getting there, big guy." We walked arm in arm toward the conference room where the closing was being held, but Charlie held me back before we entered.

"You know, she's amazing. Vivienne," Charlie said, tilting his head to point at the conference room. "I don't know how aware you are, but she's the one who's been keeping the agency together, even if it isn't in her contract. Greyson's doing a good enough job, but he was the reason I wanted to leave. I hate to say it, but he's ineffective—and very unhappy—in this role.

Mind you, I didn't say incompetent. He's still our best sales guy. I would hate for him to leave."

"I suspected that. But he was Peter's right-hand guy, and I thought he was being groomed to succeed him after Peter went into politics. I thought it only natural to hand him the reins while I was away."

"No, Raine. Peter was grooming you."

"What?"

"It was pretty obvious when he kept deferring major decisions to you. Even Luke noticed. Didn't you?"

"Jim hadn't said anything when he asked me to take over."

"Yeah, Jim..." Charlie cringed as if saying the man's name was so distasteful.

"Well, that's a conversation for another time. Preferably over a shot of single malt. Or two."

Charlie laughed. "You got it, boss."

"Tell you what, though. Let's schedule a conference call this week and decide what to do with Greyson."

"Are you sure?" Charlie peered at me. "I mean, I don't want to interrupt your sabbatical."

"Charlie, I promised you I wouldn't abandon the agency. And I meant it. This needs attention."

Leaving so soon after the closing was challenging, but I finally found escape when my phone rang. It was Vivienne calling, intuitively guessing I needed a distraction to slip away.

"A door to your left leads to the ladies' room. If you exit that way, another exit will get you to the front desk. I'll meet you outside in five minutes."

When I exited the hotel, I ran toward the valet, slipping him a twenty to snap to it before Vivienne arrived.

But she caught up to me while I waited by the curb.

"Hey, where are you off to in such a rush? You weren't going to take off without me, were you? Let's grab a bite somewhere. I'm starving."

"You mean you're not going to go to the closing lunch? Don't you think you should be there?"

I was gently prodding Vivienne to return to the meeting so I could leave—by myself. I had a crew of workers rebuilding my front porch with Jops supervising. I wasn't sure I was ready to explain all this to her.

"Are you kidding me? That crap they serve during the meetings is disgusting."

Her casual tone belied the worry I saw in her eyes. I swallowed hard, feeling a wave of guilt. When the Valet pulled my Jeep around, I turned to her and said, "I gotta get back, Vivi. I've got some urgent things I have to take care of. Thank you for everything. I owe you so much."

"What?" She gaped at me as I rounded toward the driver's side. When I slipped inside, Vivienne jumped on the passenger side and then lit into me. "I don't want your Goddamn thanks, Nish. I mean, Christ! This is my fucking job. It's why you pay my employers obscene amounts of money. So drop the act, you miserable brat. Forget the closing. Charlie's got that under control. Let's just be ourselves right now. I want the real Raine Nishiseki. Is she still there? Are you home?"

Jesus! After that verbal blistering, I caved in. "Okay, where do you want to go, Vivi?"

"At the end of the ride, Nish. Show me *you*." she challenged. Vivienne wasn't giving up.

Part of me had feared this, so I had kept parts of my life in Durham from her, reaching out to her only when it concerned business and my company. But a voice nagged, "*Yubikiri*." I was reminded of my promise never to keep her away.

"Alright, buckle up. It's a long drive," I sighed, gunning the engine, and headed for the interstate.

I had removed the Jeep's top, allowing the wind to whip our hair into tangled knots. But neither of us cared. I felt myself letting go and opening myself up to Vivienne.

When we crossed the New Hampshire border, we pulled off the highway and slowed our drive through the picturesque countryside, taking the same route I had taken when I first arrived.

"Toto, we're not at UCLA anymore," Vivienne remarked, gazing at the sprawling UNH campus as I pulled into Durham.

"You can say that again," I muttered, heading for my house.

"So, this is where you've been hiding?" She gazed at my house as I pulled into the driveway,

"Yes, I've completely lost my mind," I said.

"Well, I am impressed, girlfriend."

I wasn't lying when I said I needed to get back. I had workers rebuilding my front porch, and I didn't want to leave them unsupervised for too long. After giving her the ten-cent tour of my house, which was nearing completion, we had a late lunch at Joplin's Jazz, devouring the lobster roll special and a Mad Viking on tap.

"So, what's next on Vivi's agenda?" I asked, switching to business topics. "What's the next big thing you're lawyering in investment banking?"

"What's not happening is Raine Garvey leading Glory as she should be," she replied, eyeing me with that not-buying-your-bullshit look. "How are you? I mean, the *real* you. I haven't had a chance to ask since you called earlier this month."

"I'm better." That was about as honest an answer that I could give.

As our server set our plates in front of us, I picked a few of Rosie's fries while they were nice and hot.

"Try these. They're the best fries ever."

"What made you decide to do house renovations?" she plowed ahead with her lawyer style third-degree line of questioning.

"I know, it's crazy. The idea came to mind after my three-day crying binge, and I just went for it, and the consequences be damned."

"How come you never told me?" Vivienne sounded hurt, and I felt guilty.

"I'm sorry. But if I'd told you I was buying a fixer-upper in the middle of nowhere and would rehab it myself, you'd have stopped me—you and Luke. You both warned me about my impending meltdown. You were right. And this respite has been the best therapy for me—working with my hands, the trials and errors, the physical pains and aches... I needed to do this on my own. Without yours or Luke's influence."

Vivienne's eyes softened, but I caught the flicker of something else—maybe fear or doubt. She squeezed my hand, her voice barely a whisper. "I just don't want to lose you again, Nish. Not like before."

"Oh hell, knowing you, you'll hound me to my grave," I teased.

Satisfied with the reassurance that I would *try* not to shut her out, I switched topics. "Enough about me. You haven't answered my question."

She grinned and raised her frosty mug. "Well, you're looking at the newest partner of Dortmund Woodson."

"*Aaahhhh!*"

I screeched across the bar while Vivienne winced, covering her ears.

"Jesus, Nish. It's not like Eminem just walked into the room."

I ignored her comment and called out to Jops. "Hey, Jops! A round for everybody in here. My friend just got a huge promotion."

Everyone in the tavern cheered while a couple of tables with undergrads were drum-rolling on their tables.

Vivienne turned beet red and hissed at me. "I did not tell you this to make a spectacle of me."

"You should have said so earlier. I'm so happy for you, but this falls nicely into my plans," I smiled like a Cheshire cat.

"Why do I not like that look you have on your face?"

"Oh, I think you will *love* what I have to say."

I watched Jops saunter over to serve our drinks himself.

"Well, congratulations, Vivienne. I'm sure it was well deserved," Jops cheered.

"Thank you. I couldn't have done it without my best bud here," Vivienne acknowledged.

"You know, we all love Raine here in Durham," Jops said to Vivienne, patting me on the back. "We're hoping you're not here to take her away so soon."

Vivienne's eyebrows rose.

"Don't worry, Jops," I replied before Vivienne could speak. "I'll be around a while yet. I grabbed his hand and patted it. Thanks for the drinks."

When Jops left, I returned to her questioning look. "Alright, let me put on my glory leadership hat. I know you just got your promotion, but would you mind stepping away from lawyering for about six months?"

"*What?* I made partner only yesterday, Nish. You want me to give it up already?" Vivienne's brows furrowed.

"I want you to take over as acting CEO of Glory."

CHAPTER 35

Raine

JULY 2000

DURHAM, NEW HAMPSHIRE

I t was a warm, mildly humid day before the Fourth of July. I wore denim shorts and a halter top, relishing the cool breeze on my skin. I sat barefoot on my new double porch swing, enjoying an ice cream cone, pushing the swing gently with my big toe, reveling in a moment of no renovation projects beckoning, no crises in New York.

That's when I heard the pumpkin growl as it crawled up Mill Road before I saw it pull into my driveway.

Ron shut off his car, jumped out, and strode up the porch. He was taking in all that had been done while he was gone—a new porch, painted siding, a newly paved concrete walkway flanked by flowers in a riot of color. Even the lawn was freshly mowed by yours truly.

"Hey," he called out as he climbed the porch. "You've done quite a bit since I was last here."

"Uh-huh," I said, licking my ice cream, determined to ignore him. *Sorry, bud, but I'm not welcoming you back with open arms after the way you left last month. Humph.*

"Are you going to share that?" he asked, leaning closer with a teasing grin.

He seemed different, more confident in his stride. Gone was the awkward, gangly guy I had known. He had a quiet assurance in the way he moved. His hair was shorter, neatly cut, and he wore a Henley shirt with a Nautica patch on his left breast, cargo shorts, and...boating deck shoes? It was a far cry from the faded Radiohead t-shirt he used to wear. Iceland must have worked some magic on him.

"No," I said.

He grabbed my hand, started licking my cone, and then licked the drips on my fingers, which gave me a jolt. Then he grabbed the whole thing, and in just a few bites, he'd finished it all.

"What the hell? That was mine!"

"Not anymore," he teased. His confidence was disarming.

"What are you doing here anyway?" I huffed.

"Come here," he said, pulling me to my feet and tugging me toward his car.

"What? Where're we going?" I asked, scampering barefoot across the grass.

"It's a surprise," he said. He opened the passenger side door and shoved me in.

"Wait! I don't have any shoes," I cried. "Let me slip on a pair of sneakers? They're right by the door."

"Nope," he said.

"What do you mean nope? Why not? If we're going somewhere, I also need my keys, sunglasses..."

"Wait right here," he interrupted, shutting the car door firmly, then sternly looked at me. "Don't move."

Who the hell was he talking to, Goober?

He returned with my sneakers, sunglasses, and keys in less than a minute.

"Are you kidnapping me?" I asked half-seriously.

"Maybe," he said as he backed out of the driveway, and we headed out of town.

"I'm serious, Ron. Where are you taking me?"

"You'll see."

I lifted my chin and tightened my lips in defiance.

I studied his profile. With his shorter hair, I could see a more defined jawline. Ron looked younger than his twenty-seven years, but something else had changed in him.

"Where the hell is Ron, and what have you done with him?" I shouted above the roaring wind ripping past us.

"Killed him, buried him. Never to return. Ever." He peered at me through sunglasses. I couldn't see his eyes but felt them smiling even if his lips weren't curled.

"I like this one, I think."

He glanced at me momentarily. "Yeah?"

"Yeah. Much better than, uhm...the one I knew. Uhm...you know...he didn't say much... Uhm, the other one, uh...the silent one..." I threw shifty looks his way, twirled my hair, and shrugged, which drew a quiet laugh from him.

We reached Portsmouth harbor within a few minutes and then crossed the bridge to New Castle Island. Then, he pulled into the gravel parking lot of the Portsmouth Yacht Club, a small marina.

The clubhouse was an unassuming building no bigger than a fisherman's saltbox, looking a bit tired on the outside. Gauging by the vehicles parked in the lot—no European imports—its members were local boaters and recreational fishermen.

Ron came around and helped me out of the car while I looked at him with questions. He tugged me along the quay until we reached a small two-sail sloop bobbing in its slip. My eyes widened.

The name Skye was painted in swooping script strokes on one side of its bow.

"Is this yours?" I asked, eyeing it for seaworthiness, which was unnecessary since it looked new just from its appearance. It was beautiful.

"No, I stole it for the sole purpose of kidnapping you," he joked. "Come on, do I seriously look like a kidnapper to you?"

He grinned, offering his hand to help me board. Then he motioned for me to sit in the sunken cockpit toward the stern, next to the wheel, while he ducked inside the tiny cabin and emerged with a tube of sunscreen and a bright yellow windbreaker.

"I thought you might get chilled once we're out on the water and the wind kicks up," he said, scanning my skimpy halter top with an appreciative eye.

As I applied sunscreen, I watched him check the rigging and sails, easily navigating the boat out of its slip and into open water. He was no novice.

After hoisting the main sail and jib, it caught the wind and sailed northward.

"You doing okay?" he asked. "I've got one of those sea-sickness bracelets if you want one."

"So far so good," I assured him.

I watched him steer the tiller to steady the boat forward and admired his leg muscles as they flexed and tightened with every purposeful move.

"How long have you been sailing?" I asked.

"Since I was ten. My family has sailed every summer for as long as I can remember. But on my tenth birthday, my father showed me the ropes. He died a few years ago and left me this sailboat. He loved to sail."

I saw sadness shadow his face at the memory. He must have been very close to his father.

"I'm sorry to hear that," I said, thinking of my Da. Even if we hadn't spoken in more than ten years, it made me ache for him.

"Thanks. It took us by surprise, his death. He had a heart attack, and it was fatal. He had just turned sixty. Ironic because he was a cardiologist. He was the healthiest person I knew."

"Mom's still alive?"

"She is. She's the arts and science dean at Michigan—University of Michigan at Ann Arbor. My dad also taught cardio-thoracic surgery at the medical school."

I watched him tack with each shift of the wind, releasing and trimming the sheets with impressive movements. I was in awe.

"Any siblings?" I asked.

"A sister. Still in Michigan. A pediatrician. Married. I have a two-year-old nephew and another on the way. And then there's unimpressive me. A geology teacher."

"No way. You're going to be a doctor soon. That's nothing to sneeze at." He snorted.

"I'm sorry I never told you I was leaving for Iceland. I was humiliated the day I left your house after being blitzed the night before. I couldn't even bring myself to show my face afterward to apologize." He grimaced, looking contrite and imploring forgiveness.

"You don't owe me an apology," I quickly said.

"Of course I do. You were so nice to rescue me from my..." He hesitated as he thought of the right word to use. "Crapulence."

We both had to laugh. "Did you just make that word up?"

"Nope. You can look it up."

"Okay, I'll have to remember that. For next time." I smiled and winked.

"I hope never to have a next time. You were a good friend, Raine. I never thanked you properly."

I shrugged. "I'm sure the guys would have helped you if they'd been available."

He chuckled while he simultaneously steered and adjusted the sail's trim. "No, they wouldn't have. That was a setup, Raine."

My eyes widened.

"My buddies have been trying to get me to ask you out, but I'm such a dork with women. They set us up that night, and I knew nothing about it. I was so surprised—and mortified—when you walked into Jops's and I was in such a sorry state."

"Did they set us up for this sailing date?"

Ron shook his head.

"God, no! I've had enough of their meddling."

"Oh, so you decided you'd go from being shy to being bold enough to kidnap me? That is some bipolar disorder you have, Ron."

He laughed. "I was afraid you'd say no, especially after I acted like a jerk the last time I was with you. So, I'm apologizing for the way I left your house that day and forgetting to mention that I was leaving for Iceland. Not really like me to do that, except there's something you do to me, Raine. You unnerve me and make me act like a clumsy teenager."

Ron was anything but the shy, socially awkward guy from a month ago. Instead, he moved with confidence as he worked the sails.

God, he was sexy hot!

"So how was your trip? Ed said you were researching volcanoes."

"Iceland's breathtaking. Mount Hekla erupted on our last day. That was quite an experience. I've been studying volcanic activity and how it impacts the Earth's climate for my dissertation. I did several experiments on the ice and lava to see if the chemical reaction could predict the rate of the changing atmosphere. I know I'm spouting a lot of scientific gibberish, and sometimes I get carried away. Stop me if I'm boring you."

"Not boring at all. Maybe it's the way you lecture. If that's how you speak to your class. It's almost seductive. I bet a bunch of your female students have crushes on you. I've seen how they ogle you at Jops.'"

"Oh God, that has always made me uncomfortable, and I will forever be the butt of Ed and Fritzso's jokes. I'm easily intimidated, especially around attractive women."

I tilted my head and asked, "Do I intimidate you?"

"Horribly so. You are the most intimidating woman I've ever met. You're different. You have a lot of maturity about you, like a big career, and I'm sure you've been to places and seen and done things more than I have. You've also experienced tragedy and handled yourself with grace under pressure. Me? I'm just a timid midwestern guy pretending to be a professor at UNH.

"So the next best thing was not to think about asking you out but to drag you to come along with me. At least I didn't have time to think about being nervous that you'd say no."

I felt that flutter again, and I had to look away because now I was blushing. I was glad he returned to tacking the sails and letting the boat pick up speed. I watched him concentrate on navigating the rocky coast of Maine, picturesque with its cliffs and towering granite formations.

"We should reach the Nubble Light in York in a few minutes," he said while securing the mainsheet and other controls. "We can drop anchor there and maybe have a picnic lunch?"

I nodded. "Sounds nice."

He smiled in agreement.

"We've been doing studies at UNH on that nub of land. That's what the lighthouse was named after. There has been some erosion, and we're trying to figure out the rate and how much longer it will be before the structure crumbles and the ocean reclaims that piece of land."

"There's that lecture voice again. You're making me swoon, you know," I teased, resting my chin under a fist, looking up, and fluttering my eyes at him. I was being playful, but I could feel my heart skipping beats.

"Raine, Raine, Raine..." he teased back, launching into the nursery rhyme.

"Don't even start..." I warned playfully.

He laughed and shook his head.

"I like saying your name," he said with tenderness. There was that jolt in my gut again, stronger this time. I wrapped my arms around my waist to stop the quivering.

"How'd your parents come by your name? It's not very common," he asked.

"It was a dark and stormy night..." I started, and his eyes narrowed in skepticism.

"Seriously, it's true. According to my father, it was almost midnight and raining like mad when my mother went into labor. Thankfully the hospital was nearby."

I stopped and contemplated his expression. "Are you okay?"

He threw his head back in laughter.

"Yes!" he exclaimed. "Go on. The suspense is killing me. What happened?"

"Okay," I said, taking a deep breath. "My father, who is Japanese American, wanted to name me after the weather—in Gaelic, no less—and my Scottish mother thought he was insane."

Ron's brows lifted.

"I know what you're thinking. And yes, my parents are a bizarre combination of Scot and Japanese. But anyway..."

"So, what name did he come up with?" Ron asked, dying with anticipation.

"*Ouisgé.*"

CHAPTER 36

Ron

*H**er name is Ouisgé, and she has Highland blood like yours. But her heart is full of hurts. Ye'r fated to heal her first, Ronnie. Help her find the way to yer heart. Believe in yer gift of the sight, child.*

Ron's grandmother's words echoed in his brain. If he had doubts about who his 'wife' was in his vision, they dissipated when Raine revealed her Scottish middle name.

"Ouisgé," he said softly, feeling a breath catch. "Water of life, rain from the heavens. Without it, humanity wouldn't exist."

"More like the water used in Scotch-making," she joked.

"Even more important," he laughed.

Amid the Atlantic, the revelation overwhelmed him. It stung his eyes. Raine was his destiny. And here she was, next to him, telling her story.

He felt goosebumps—not from the ocean spray. She seemed oblivious to his emotions. How would he explain his *An Dà Shealladh?* Would she understand?

He put the brakes on his thoughts, still unsure if she even liked him.

She continued to talk, but he felt something pinging inside him wildly, like a pinball in play.

"My mother put the kibosh on that real quick," Raine laughed and mimicked her mother's accent.

"'Are ye daft, Tono? Ye're no' gonna name oor poor bairn a word nobody can pronounce and hae the other weans make fun o' her. We're no' in Scotland, aye? If ye're set on namin' her after the weather, we'll name her Raine. Plain and simple.'"

"I love your Gaelic accent. Like my grandmother," he said.

"Your grandmother's Scottish?" She lit up.

"Yes, my father's side, first generation from Thurso. In the Highlands. Born from the original MacKenzies.

"What a coincidence. So you're part Scottish also."

Yes, just as his granny had said, he would marry a girl with Scottish blood.

Ron nodded, his heart bursting with joy. Unable to resist, he closed the distance, cupped her chin, and gave her a lingering kiss. He dared to run his tongue over her lips, which was a terrible idea because he sensed her hesitation and the assault of painful memories. Ron pulled away slightly but held on to her.

"What...was that about?"

"Raine," he whispered, leaning his forehead against hers. "You are so irresistible. So desirable. I'm sorry. I couldn't help myself."

No, not sorry at all.

He felt her squirm. Once she calmed, he tugged her back to the seat. She wasn't ready. Her heart had a "do not enter" sign. He went below deck to grab some fruit and brie cheese from the compact under-cabinet refrigerator. Then he pulled a sourdough baguette from a paper bag.

He sliced a wedge of cheese, tore off a piece of bread, and gave it to her.

Easing away from the heat of his desire, he changed subjects. "I read a few articles on the public offering of your company and your recent acquisition. I was impressed. I couldn't even imagine how to pull off something like that."

She nodded, studying the wedge of brie she'd just bitten into. "I also read those articles about your husband. I am truly sorry. That was such a tragedy."

"I hope you didn't believe all the stories. Some can be so outrageous and trashy," she said with concern.

He contemplated the apple he'd shined against his shirt then bit into it.

"I can't imagine the trauma you experienced. You loved him deeply, didn't you?"

He broached the subject carefully. He wondered if she was still mourning Peter. It hadn't even been two years since he died. Maybe she was still in love with him and hadn't gotten over him. It didn't matter to Ron. He'd give her the time and space she needed. He would help her heal. Wasn't that what his granny had told him? That he was fated to heal her?

"I...did," she whispered.

"You don't have to talk about it," he said tenderly, seeing her crestfallen face. "I mean, it's none of my business. But if I can help in any way..."

Ron quietly reached for her hand and held it, respecting her silence. From his fingertips, he felt the jumble of emotions she wrestled with—confusion and indecision.

"Ron, I'm not a good person to be involved with," she said, looking away. "I'm too complicated."

That was when she opened up to him and shared that part of her life—the good, the bad, the ugly. Jim's assault, Peter's death, his infidelity, her infertility...everything. All that had cut her to the core, leaving her bitter and mistrustful.

There was so much weight on her small shoulders, and he marveled at her strength and resiliency.

"I have to go back to that convoluted life at the end of the year, and I don't want you to get caught up in all that. It's... too messy."

Ron studied her pained expression. She was right. Why take on all that emotional baggage? Instead, he moved closer and threw an arm around her shoulder, pulling her in to lean on his strong shoulders. In her ear, he whispered, "I don't care."

Ron felt the gentle rhythm of the waves pulling them into a peaceful silence. Raine's warmth resting against him was grounding, a soothing contrast to the turmoil he sensed she usually carried.

When the sun dipped below the horizon, Ron rose to haul in the anchor, and Raine stood to join him.

"Teach me?" she said, laying her hand on his. Ron felt his heart squeeze. It was a small gesture. She'd opened a tiny crack of her battered heart, enough to let a little bit of him in.

He'd shown her how to steer and had her steady the tiller as he adjusted the sail trim.

"Look." Ron pointed toward the setting sun. The big yellow ball had cast a shimmering pathway on the water's surface, creating a captivating trail of golden light as they sailed back to shore.

He would teach her not just how to sail but to trust. To let go. To fall without fear. So she could learn to love. Again.

CHAPTER 37

Raine

JULY 2000

DURHAM, NEW HAMPSHIRE

Conflict.
Complications.
Stress.
Pointless.
No future.

I shut the door behind me. Desire...the big D word...was banging against the door of my heart, begging to be let in.

Desire was overwhelming. It lodged in my throat, making it impossible to swallow. My heart hammered so loud that each beat felt like a drum in my ears. I was so, so afraid. Memories of past heartbreaks and broken promises flashed in my mind, fueling my hesitation.

When Ron dropped me off, he'd kept the engine running, hinting he wouldn't see me to my door. While inside his car, he turned to me, cupped my face, sighed, and kissed my forehead.

"Raine," he murmured while the engine idled. "Our time together today was indescribable. I'm so in awe of you. I'd like to see you again."

My heart had screamed yes, but fear clamped down. Instead I said, "Thank you for a wonderful time."

I jumped out and ran inside the house. Like the first day I met him.

I made no commitment to see him again. How could I? I had to go back, and that was my reality. Durham was a respite. A sabbatical. Never meant to be permanent. No, it was best if I didn't encourage him as much as it was tearing me apart.

I listened for the car to pull away, watching for the headlight beam to fade away from the window.

But as the tears started to sting my eyes, I heard the engine cut off and the sound of steps walking up my front porch. Before he could knock, I opened the door. He walked in and kicked it shut. Without a word, his mouth devoured mine. Tenderly but with intensifying heat, daring me to build the flame I'd been trying to tamp down. I felt Ron falling in love with me. And taking me with him.

Ron

JULY 2000
DURHAM, NEW HAMPSHIRE

They made love that night, rolling over and over on her bed, limbs tangled, breathless sighs quickening as the fires that raged between them burned hot and bright. And when he entered her, he felt all of her—heard the voices in her soul.

"Raine, what do you want?" he whispered, thrusting slowly, more deeply, coaxing her to match his rhythm, feeling the carnal power rise between them. He struggled to hold back his own intensifying storm, the hunger threatening him to lose control. But he wanted to...give. Give her everything she needed. Wanted. So he asked again.

"Tell me what you want."

She grabbed his face, her breath feathering his cheek until she reached his ear, whispering, "I just want to be loved."

Ron felt her breath quickening, her hips wildly pushing with speed and urgency, and when her body tightened, gripping his shoulders, digging her nails into his flesh, feeling her peak and tumble, over and over, he plunged deeper, faster, the world narrowing to this singular moment of connection until he too lost all of himself and moaned.

"I love you," he whispered, spilling himself into her. To join with her. To become one. To fall irrefutably and eternally in love.

CHAPTER 38

Raine

"Ron?" I muttered in that raspy, not-quite-awake voice, spooned in his arms, listening to the calming drumbeat of the rain against the roof.

"Hmm?" he said, feeling his whisper caress my shoulders.

"Did you remember to pull the top of your car last night?"

Ron bolted out of my bed so fast as if it were on fire. I lingered for a while, savoring the sweet soreness between my legs, a delicious reminder of our night-long passion. Even when I'd lost my virginity, it hadn't felt this...achingly exquisite.

Peter had been my only lover for so long, and with him, I often felt myself disappear, swallowed by the sheer force of his presence. He always took the lead, and I followed, more a shadow than an equal. But with Ron, there was a balance between us—a rhythm, a give and take. I knew what I wanted for the first time, and I felt truly heard. My orgasms became more intense, more real because I wasn't just following. I was fully present. I was *there*. And afterward, in the quiet of his arms, I felt something I had craved for years. A deep, lasting peace that was beginning to heal my battered heart.

I finally rose and went downstairs to brew coffee when Ron burst through the backdoor, dripping wet. He was bare-chested, wearing only his cargo pants.

My eyes raked over his naked chest with admiration. Last night in the dark, his body had astonished me with its raw masculinity and strength. In daylight, he looked every bit like the young Greek Adonis, revealing abs of corded muscle.

"I can't believe I forgot to pull up the roof last night," he announced.

"You were otherwise...distracted?" I teased.

I tossed him a kitchen towel to dry himself off, then handed him a mug of coffee. He murmured a thanks while taking a sip.

"I don't want to drip all over your house, but these pants are soaked, and I haven't got a change of clothes," he said, remaining rooted to the doormat, looking helpless.

"Why don't you run to the basement and toss your pants in the dryer?" I suggested, pointing to the door just a few steps away. "I can get you a towel to wrap around your waist."

"Okay," he said when a smile tugged at his lips. "Although, I think we can skip the towel."

Romance writers have got it all wrong. Sex in a tub was nothing like what they'd written. It was foreplay on steroids if you didn't mind the bumps and bruises sloshing around like kids playing catch-me-if-you-can within the constrained space of the tub. Our bodies slipped and slid as I tried to slither away from Ron playfully, shrieking as his hands always managed to find me. And then there was the matter of "find the soap," which always seemed to end up between my legs.

"Hey, no tickling," I squealed and squirmed, half the water now outside the tub.

"Ow!" he cried when I knocked him sideways, his elbow hitting the faucet.

I froze with concern. "Are you okay?"

Within a second, he'd pivoted me around, pinning me underneath him, his mouth on my nipples.

"Uhm, Ron..." I replied breathlessly. "I'm not sure that's part of the cleansing ritual."

"Says who?" he gurgled. I giggled.

"Says my knee that's right in your groin. You might want to move off me."

He shifted his body, releasing my elbow, allowing me to dunk him.

"What the f..." His voice drowned underwater while I giggled. But he was just as quick when his thumb slipped inside me, forcing a moan of heat and desire and rendering me immobile.

He dove for my mouth, seeking my tongue. His thumb continued to flick while my hips ground against it.

"Inside me. Now," I muttered with breathless urgency.

Despite the awkward and contorting position, he finally slipped inside and drove into me with a madness to match the heat I felt. When I came, I felt my muscles grip his penis, squeezing, throbbing with excruciating ecstasy, and I felt myself...freefalling. Yet never once did I feel Ron letting me go. He clung with his own desperation as he released himself inside me and whispered once again, "I love you."

We spooned on top of each other while the pounding of his heart against my back slowed in rhythm with mine. Neither of us seemed in a hurry to move, even as the water grew tepid.

His words, "I love you," ran circles in my head.

What have I done? I would break this poor man's heart, eventually.

We both were caught up in the romance of our date on the ocean, the palpable heat of desire between us. Having sex seemed the only way to find gratification. But love? As in with a future? I started to feel a gnawing inside of me.

"Raine, your brain is making so much noise. What are you thinking of?" he asked.

I felt his deep empathy reading my mind.

"That I think your clothes are dry now," I teased, shifting in his arms.

Then he asked, "What's your favorite food?"

"What?"

"Your favorite food," he repeated.

"Spaghetti," I uttered, not because it was necessarily my favorite, but because it was the first thing that came to mind. Where was he going with this? "What's yours?"

"Spaghetti," he whispered while I chuckled. "Tell you what, let's get stuff to make spaghetti for dinner tonight. I'll have to stop by my place to get a change of clothes, though."

I twisted my head to look at him. "Hmm... angling to stay over another night?"

"Raine," he whispered, "a thousand nights with you won't be enough."

I felt my "no future" stance careening toward "relationship." I waited for warning bells. There was only silence.

Ron

"*R*onald *Mackenzie Mitchell, if you pick up that jar of spaghetti sauce, you're sleeping on the couch!*"

Raine yelled down the supermarket's aisle of jarred sauces.

He slowly turned and walked toward her, holding the jar up like a guilty verdict.

"But you don't have a couch," he said in a lowered voice.

"No, but I have a sleeping bag," she hissed, crossing her arms with a smirk.

And so started their second date that didn't involve a kidnapping.

"How the hell does one make spaghetti without spaghetti sauce?" Ron looked at the jar of Rao's marinara sauce and wondered if he'd mistakenly picked up a cantaloupe. Was this about to be their first argument? Already?

"The garden's bursting with Roma tomatoes, and there's basil in the greenhouse window," she said, pulling out her cell phone.

"Hey, Jops, it's Raine."

What the fuck was she calling Jops for?

He caught a mischievous glint in her eyes.

"Is Rosie there?" Raine paused for a moment. "Hey, Rosie, listen, my date wants to impress me with a spaghetti dinner, but I think he needs some help... Yeah, your Bolognese is amazing. Do you mind sharing your recipe with him... Who's my date... Well, here, you talk to him..."

"Hey, Rosie" Ron said, keeping an even tone as he watched Raine walk away to get things for a salad. "Yep, it's Ron..."

He felt a flush creep up his neck, then his face, when Rosie's teasing began.

"So how'd your sailing date go? What happened? Did you sleep over? Are you staying over again?" Rosie interrogated with Jops cackling in the background.

Ron groaned. "Knock it off, Rosie." He'd never understand why his love life was a source of endless entertainment for his friends. "Can you please just tell me what I need for this spaghetti dinner that I'm starting to regret I ever suggested?"

Oh, God! Ed and Fritzso would hear about this, and he'd have a hell of a time explaining without the endless razzing. Ron was going to kill Raine.

Front page of *The Boston Globe?*

"Young professor slays billionaire lover over spaghetti sauce."

CHAPTER 39

Raine

"You had morning sex, didn't you?" Vivienne groused loudly over the speakerphone as Ron descended the stairs, making me spew coffee.

I grabbed the handset before she could make any more inappropriate remarks while Ron was within earshot. I watched him warily as he poured himself a cup of coffee, struggling to control his snigger. He heard.

"Good morning to you too, bitch. Snarky this morning?" I greeted Vivienne.

It was her first day as acting CEO of Glory, and we made an appointment to speak first thing.

Ron had been sleeping over nearly every day since we started dating a week ago. Experiencing sexual satisfaction just minutes before the call was an entirely new experience, and I wasn't sure how to deal with it. I must have sounded throaty and purring to Vivienne.

I raised my brows as Ron approached me with a fresh cup, swapping out my spilled one, then gave me a quiet kiss. A wet one. On my mouth. Tongue and everything. Which made me sigh contentedly.

"Did I just hear kissing?"

"What?" I stiffened and elbowed Ron away.

"Don't mind me, I'm just jealous. My sex life is nonexistent. Can I live vicariously through you?"

"Who said I had morning sex? Can we get started, please? The time's a-wasting," I replied, ignoring her question. "So, how are you settling in?"

"I'm meeting with Charlie and Heywood this morning to discuss staffing and operations. Raine, your shop is so understaffed. We'll need everyone at Jay's to lift this place. No savings there, I'm afraid."

"That's okay. I'm glad to hear no one's getting laid off."

Ron kissed my neck, making me catch my breath audibly.

"Uhm, are you listening? You sound distracted," Vivienne said.

I turned to Ron, glaring with tight lips.

"Just sipping my coffee. What else?"

"Analyst call on the first quarter results is coming up. Despite being understaffed and you being away, we've exceeded expectations. Your team is amazing. This reminds me, I'll need your statement on the agency's future directions. Oh, and you really need a new headshot."

Earnings call? Future directions? *God, not yet. Please.*

A pit knotted in my belly. My New York life suddenly loomed large, disrupting my recently acquired balance. I could hear the loud ticking of my sabbatical clock winding down. I twisted my neck around to try to loosen the building tension.

"Ugh! No headshot. Not now. Let's get a call with Charlie on the calendar, and you guys can give me the rundown on the numbers. Then, we'll decide together how to handle the analysts. Is that it?"

I felt Ron's strong hands on my shoulders, gently kneading away my anxiety.

"I'm sneaking out at lunchtime to get some flowers. This office needs a little cheering up," Vivienne said.

"Feel free to make it your own, Vivi," I encouraged.

Ron continued to press small circles into just those right spots knotted at the base of my neck.

Vivienne pressed on. "I also think we should move Charlie into Jim's office if that's okay with you. It's so dark and empty. Since you've made Charlie the third largest shareholder and president, I think he should be next to the CEO's office."

"Great idea," I said, luxuriating in the chair massage I was getting. Could I hire Ron to be my office masseuse when I return to New York?

"This afternoon, I'll stop by Luke's office."

"Sounds like you have things under control. Just call me if you need anything," I said, hinting the end of our call.

"Yup. I see some lights down the hall, so I'll skedaddle. Later, babe," Vivienne said, signing off.

I was surprised at how eager I was to get off the call.

"Seriously, Ron, you need to make yourself scarce when I'm on a business call." I tried to mean it and failed.

He grinned, setting his coffee cup down and pulling me into his arms.

"No," he breathed into my ear, grazing his lips along my neck and shoulders.

"No?"

"You want me to stop?" he asked while his hands found my nipples, hardening instantly with his touch through the thin t-shirt I had slept in. *His* Radiohead t-shirt, which I had claimed to be my favorite sleepwear since he started spending nights with me.

"I think you got up too early. You need to come back to bed," he said, gently pivoting me toward the stairs.

JULY 2000

DURHAM, NEW HAMPSHIRE

When Raine had asked Vivienne to take over as Glory's acting CEO, she was stunned. Yes, making partner at Dortmund Woodson was exhilarating—something she'd worked so hard for. But CEO? She remembered biting her lip to stop herself from squealing like Raine had when they were at Jops's. Instead, she'd excused herself to the restroom, pretending to need time to think about it. In the privacy of a stall, she stifled a giggle, bubbling with unabashed excitement. Who would turn down the chance to be CEO, even if only temporarily? It had been one of her wildest dreams back in MBA school. This stint would boost her resume and open new doors for a more permanent leadership role in another megacorp.

On her first day, after a smooth phone call with Raine—and she knew the bitch had sex; way to go, girlfriend—Vivienne was raring to go. She met with Rosemary to go over her schedule, then Charlie, who gave her the ten-cent tour and introduced the other managers. She was about to leave for lunch when Luke appeared at the doorway.

"Hey," he said.

"Hey, yourself. Come on in." She motioned for him to have a seat.

They hadn't spoken about that kiss at her apartment since it happened. Not even a phone call under the pretext of business. She wasn't surprised—Luke never involved himself in executive matters. Still, she'd hoped. And just when she'd dismissed the whole incident as a moment of weakness, they met again.

She recalled that conference call when Glory's executive team had gathered in the conference room to hear Raine announce that Vivienne would take over as acting CEO. Luke hadn't joined the team's collective sighs of relief or their banter afterward. Had she imagined the flicker of disappointment in his eyes? Did he not think she was qualified? Should Raine have consulted with him first? After all, he was the second-largest shareholder.

Vivienne tried to read his expression but still steeled herself for a blistering confrontation in her new role.

"Something up?" she asked coolly.

"Yeah, well... about this afternoon's meeting..."

"If that doesn't work, we can change it—"

"We kind of left a lot unsaid the last time," Luke interrupted, stunning her into silence. He wasn't referring to the conference call.

She hadn't expected him to bring that up now. Quickly, she gathered her thoughts before she could lose her composure. Damn it. It was her first day.

"Forget it. Just a lapse in judgment."

Luke hesitated, his gaze locking onto hers. "It wasn't. Not for me. There was something there, Vivienne. And I think you felt it too."

She suddenly felt like she was walking on eggshells. Things were still strained between Luke and Raine, and Raine was her best friend. It would feel like a betrayal, and she'd never do that to Raine.

Vivienne crossed her arms. "Luke, I'm sorry, it'll be too complicated, and not just because we're colleagues now. You know why."

"Vivienne, I know things are still weird between Raine and me, and it's been killing me. But that ball's in her court now. I don't know what more I can do to make things right with her." He hesitated, seeing the tension on Vivienne's face.

Luke shoved his hands in his pockets and shrugged casually, trying to soften the moment. "I don't know, maybe after our meeting this afternoon, we could grab dinner? You know, just to talk? I'd like the chance to clear the air between us—and see if there's maybe something more?"

Vivienne reddened.

What? He likes me? Oh, this is such a terrible, terrible idea.

He closed the distance between them but didn't touch her. Instead, his eyes pleaded.

"Can we at least...try?"

He'd said dinner "just to talk." That was it. Luke had chosen The Clam Hut, where they slurped on mussels in hot sauce with their fingers. It was so "un-C-suite" that Vivienne found herself charmed by his easygoing nature. She'd opened up more than she thought she would, sharing stories of growing up in Hollywood's shadow, her summers in France, and her famous father. In turn, Luke had surprised her, talking about his adoption from China, his diplomat parents, and his life in Sweden. And my God, he spoke French! Was she dreaming? *Pinch me now.*

There had been no mention of work, no serious talk about Raine—just the two of them, peeling back layers as they walked through Chelsea, sharing ice cream and stealing glances.

And when Luke pulled her closer, his arm slipping around her waist, she hadn't resisted. By the time they reached his loft, any thoughts of keeping things professional had long since melted away.

Vivienne thought she was dreaming in Luke's arms, content from a night of lovemaking when a bluish light of dawn filtered through the large, expansive window of his bedroom. She was about to close her eyes again when she realized what had happened, checked the time, and bolted out of his bed.

Oh my God! Oh my God! Oh my God!

"What are you doing? It's too early," she heard him murmur in that husky, just barely awake voice she found so sexy. *No, not dreaming. Shit!*

"It's five o'clock, and I have barely enough time to get back to my apartment, shower, and head for the office before anyone finds out I've just slept with one of the company's major shareholders on her first day as acting CEO. Do you know how bad that looks?"

Luke raised his head, propped it with an arm, and peered at her through sleepy eyes. "Looks good from over here. Please come back to bed," he begged.

"Love to but can't. It's an ethics thing, and you know it. I'm not about to set that bad example, and if I do the walk of shame straight to the office from here, there will be a scandal."

They gave each other a deep, long kiss with the promise that last night wouldn't be the end, which was the only reason Luke grudgingly let her go.

When she returned to her apartment, Vivienne sank into her couch and buried her face in her hands.

Oh God, Raine, I hope you will forgive me but I like him—like, I might actually be falling for him. Please don't hate me.

Luther looked up at her, then purred around her legs, clamoring for breakfast.

CHAPTER 40

Raine

AUGUST 2000
NEW YORK, NEW YORK

"Rock climbing?" My eyes widened at his suggestion. *Did I hear him right?*

"You want me to rock climb with you for your birthday?" I asked again.

"We'll pick an easy rock face. You'll enjoy it," Ron assured.

We were just a month into our "relationship," and I had wanted to do something special for his birthday—fly him somewhere he'd never been—Paris, Rome, Vienna. Anywhere his heart desired.

"It's *your* birthday. Don't you want something you've always wanted for yourself?

"You've been what I've wanted all my life. Now I want more of you."

I had assumed Ron would be dazzled by the luxury of being flown around the world in a private jet, staying at penthouse suites at five-star hotels, dine with celebrity chefs, just as it had been with Peter when we first met.

But no—Ron's idea of adventure was taking me rock climbing in the White Mountains. That revelation grounded me, pulling me away from the high-flying lifestyle I had known and underscoring how different he was from Peter.

I shook my head doubtfully. "What if I slip and fall? I'll be a nuisance."

"Raine, I take my class on expeditions all the time," he said as we pulled into the lot of the L.L. Bean outdoor sports outlet in Kittery. "Come on, it'll be... amazing."

We began our hike at Crawford Notch State Park, stopping after a few miles at the New Zealand Falls. The twenty-foot-high waterfalls thundered over granite ledges, their roar enveloping us. We sat on a rock shelf beneath the spray, the power of the water surrounding us. Instead of fear, I felt renewed as the cool mist kissed my skin.

We continued our hike, and Ron, ever the professor, would keep lecturing on the landscape around us.

"Look at these rock formations," he'd say along the way, pointing to the granite and syenites, cooled from magma and solidified over millions of years. "See this foliated texture? It's made of layers of schist, slate, and gneiss..."

When we stopped before a sheer metamorphic rock face, my eyes traveled upward, and doubts crept in. Unlike the rock-climbing center at UNH's gym, which had the safety of padded floors, this natural rock looked imposing, even threatening. One slip-up meant a bunch of broken bones. I envisioned my body mangled and contorted in a shape beyond healing. For the past two weeks, I trained with Ron at the gym. I had been open to the challenge and willing to try it. But was that enough time?

"Yes, you can. It's only about twelve feet to the top ledge. You've scaled this height at the gym. You can do this," he reassured me.

"I dunno, Ron. Training at the gym is different. This is scary, babe."

"This is the practice rock I bring my students to," he explained.

But as we slipped into our harnesses, I began to shudder visibly.

Ron moved me against the rock and whispered, "Relax against the stone for a while. What do you feel?"

I closed my eyes. I felt electrical currents travel inside me. "It's buzzing like it's alive."

I squirmed in his arms to move away, but his body kept me still.

"Don't be afraid. Feel it. Fill yourself with its energy," he whispered, touching his forehead to mine. "Let yourself go. I'm right here."

Buoyed by the granite's energy, I secured my helmet while Ron fed the rope through the belay, locking the carabiners for added security and attaching a chalk bag to my harness.

"Go ahead and chalk up your hands. Don't forget to reach for more as you go up," he instructed.

We performed a buddy check as we had in training, then started our climb.

Ron turned my face to him and said reassuringly, "I'll be right behind you. Trust that I won't allow you to fall and get hurt, alright?"

I nodded, took a deep breath, and reached for the first hold. The rock's rough texture felt foreign and unforgiving against my fingertips. My legs wobbled as I searched for secure footing.

"That's it. You're doing great," Ron cheered on.

Each step upward was a battle, each grip a tenuous hold on my mounting panic.

All I could think of was slipping and plunging both of us to our deaths. I was tempted to look down to convince myself he was still there, but I focused on reaching the top. How far up had I climbed, and how much more was there to scale?

As if reading my mind, Ron called, "Almost there!"

I took another deep breath and reached for a crimp. My foot moved into the next foothold, lifting me. After an eternity, I reached the ledge and hauled myself up with trembling arms. Relief washed over me, but several unsettling emotions overwhelmed. I was furious because a man dared push me to do what I deeply feared, even after making that fear known. Panic because it cracked open a vulnerable piece of my soul. I hated the experience. But most of all, I hated that it was Ron who challenged me.

I unlatched my harness and tossed it aside, and moved as far away from the edge and didn't stop, leaving Ron several paces behind. It was a clear violation of safety rules. Of course, I needn't worry because Ron scrambled up like a spider and then chased after me. He didn't need me. I, on the other hand, had to get as far away as I could.

"Hey, what's wrong? You made it. I told you it wasn't a hard climb," he said, catching up to me, and grabbing my hand, jolting me back to stop.

"Okay, but I'm not doing that again," I said, abruptly dropping his hand.

"Oh, you will. Next time, twice as high," he teased. He still didn't get how deep-seated my anxiety was.

It wasn't the height I was afraid of. I've often stood in front of my office window, twenty-eight floors above the ground, and looked down at the world below without it bothering me.

"No. Fucking. Way!" I spat.

Grabbing my shoulders, Ron turned me around and kissed me. Hard. Insistent. Almost angry.

"Raine, as long as I'm with you, you never have to be afraid. I promise. If you fall, I will always be there to catch you." His face darkened, incensed that I didn't have enough faith in him. We both glared at each other, surprised to see the fury in his eyes. "Now, let's go back and properly pack up our equipment and talk about how you should never leave your climbing partner like that because this is a two-way street."

Ron

He hadn't expected the extent of Raine's fear to overwhelm her after they'd scaled an easy wall. She was visibly shaken. And even after he'd infused his chi to calm her down, he couldn't settle the anxiety in her mind.

"Uhm, maybe you should stay over at your place," she said, looking away after they'd returned to her house and unloaded their gear from the Jeep.

"Raine, sweetheart, I'm sorry," he said, his heart sinking. "Please don't let this come between us. We won't do it again."

"I need some time alone, Ron," she said, pulling away from him when he tried to enfold her in his arms.

He looked up at the sky, the light just now fading. He had no one to blame but himself for fucking up his own birthday celebration. They were supposed to meet with the guys at Joplin's for a beer and pizza to celebrate his birthday and Raine's first climb. He had thought she would have felt triumphant. He was clearly mistaken, and now he wasn't in the mood to face his friends alone. Not without Raine.

"Alright, but please don't give up on us already?" he pleaded.

She didn't reply, leaving Ron no choice but to hop in his car and drive away.

Raine

AUGUST 2000

DURHAM, NEW HAMPSHIRE

I felt like a jerk for telling him to leave. It was a terrible way to end his birthday. But I was terrified by the experience, and I'm not sure he grasped the magnitude of my fear that sent me panicking down the mountain. Despite promises that he'd never hurt me, I wasn't ready to trust. Didn't Peter promise the same thing?

Nearly every night since our first date, I'd fallen asleep in Ron's arms. That night, I never anticipated how empty I would feel without him beside me. It was worse than the day Peter died. Losing Peter left me stoic and numb, but without Ron, the ache stabbed deeply.

The next day, I walked down to see Jops at the tavern. His brows rose when he saw me walk in.

"I know. I'm sorry we didn't show up last night for Ron's birthday," I began.

"Well, that long face of yours tells me it wasn't because you blew us off for mind-blowing sex," he teased. "So what happened?"

I wasn't laughing.

"I got scared," I replied, avoiding his eyes while he squirted water in a tumbler from his dispenser and set it before me with a slice of lemon.

"Why do I get the feeling it wasn't just rock climbing that scared you?" he said. "Did you chicken out and fight about it?"

"No, I climbed the whole fucking thing," I said, then sighed. "Jops, what am I doing with Ron? You know there isn't any future I can envision with him. I never intended to get this deeply involved with him."

"You planning to sell your house then?"

I shook my head.

"Then what? Leave it to ruin like Mrs. Callahan did?" he remarked tersely.

I stared at my drink, thinking I needed something stronger, but resisted and stuck to water.

"I have no idea what to do, Jops."

"Don't you still have about four or five months of your sabbatical? Do you have to decide now?"

I sighed. "What difference does it make? I still have to leave in the end."

"So you return to your job and have a long-distance relationship. You could see each other on weekends. Why isn't that doable?"

"Not with my job." I shook my head. "I need to stay involved, and doing it from this distance is too difficult. When I go back full-time, there will be no getting away. Somehow, I can't see Ron moving to New York. That's not him. He loves the mountains, sailing, rock climbing... He freaking loves living here so much. Have you seen how much work he's been doing on the house? He doesn't even own it. If he lived in New York, he'd be too unhappy and grow to resent me."

Jops leaned over the counter, his eyes locking onto mine.

"Listen to me. I was in the Navy for five years, and Rosie and I would only see each other six months out of each year I served. You can't tell me a long-distance relationship won't work. What you fear is the past repeating itself. You've got to take a chance, Raine. It's scary, but it's worth it."

I exhaled and looked away.

Jops grabbed my hand and held it tight.

"You still have five months before your time here ends. Give Ron a chance to prove he's not Peter."

That afternoon, I trudged across the campus lawn toward James Hall, where I knew Ron would be finishing up his last class. I walked down the hall of laboratories in the basement, poking my head in each one searching for him, when class suddenly let out and the corridors filled with bodies milling around. I was afraid I'd miss him.

Then our eyes met. He shoved his way toward me between the crowded hall, lifted me off my feet, and drowned me in his kiss.

"Get a room!" Fritzso hollered as he passed us. Behind my back, I felt Ron flip Fritzso the bird but kept his lips on me.

We crossed the campus lawn arm in arm, heading for home, my head resting on his shoulder. As we approached the house—our house—a pang of trepidation hit me. Despite my growing closeness to Ron, the looming end of my sabbatical continued to ache inside.

The wounds from Peter's infidelity were still raw. It felt safer to hold back, to protect my heart a little longer, even as I knew I was falling for Ron more and more with each passing day. I wished I had my mother's *An Dà Shealladh* to see beyond this year. God, I missed her so much, but I couldn't bring myself to call home.

I held on to Ron tighter. Sensing my thoughts, he kissed my temple and whispered, *"Bidh a h-uile càil ceart gu leòr, mo chridhe."*

His tender words in Gaelic made me shudder. But there was a nuance that couldn't be translated into English. It wasn't only his assurance that everything would be alright—but his conviction. It felt like he, too, had the gift of foresight my mother had. The air around us seemed to shimmer, a subtle reminder of the magic that bound us together.

It was both exhilarating and terrifying.

CHAPTER 41

Ron

A s August waned, the campus transformed. Banners welcoming the Class of 2004 adorned Main Street's lamp posts. Upperclassmen and graduate students had already moved in.

For Ron, this was an exhilarating time. He had to defend his dissertation research, and then, fingers crossed, he'd graduate and get hooded for his doctorate. Excitement mingled with nerves, a familiar cocktail of emotions.

Nevertheless, something elusive hung in the air—perhaps foreboding. No visions had been revealed to him—yet. His thoughts drifted to Raine. Despite his declarations of love, she had never reciprocated those three words. But his gift of empathy reassured him. He felt her love buried deep within her soul. He strongly felt that together, they would endure.

Ron hummed Radiohead's *Creep* as he crossed the lawn toward home.

As he unlocked the front door, he slipped off his shoes and set them on the mud tray. The house felt eerily silent.

"Raine?" he called, frowning. Her jacket was missing from its usual peg. Her laptop sat on the dining table, the screen still glowing, but her keys and phone were there. When he peered out the window, he saw that her Jeep was still in the driveway, parked next to his Pumpkin. Usually bustling with dinner preparations, the kitchen was still devoid of something fragrant and exotic from her cooking.

She'd probably walked into town. It was a beautiful fall day for a stroll, he thought. She might have stopped at Tye's to pick something up for the house.

He climbed the stairs to change from his work clothes into a more comfortable Henley t-shirt when something caught his eye. He noticed the open top drawer of the bureau they shared, her neatly folded underwear now disarrayed. It was not like she'd rifled through them in search of something. More like she'd grabbed a few things to take on a trip, which baffled him. A photograph tucked at the back caught his eye.

Ron picked it up. A young Raine, about ten, smiled alongside her father in a field of Scottish heather. The landscape sloped toward the sea.

Kirtomy, Scotland. Summer 1980 read the back. He'd never been to Scotland, yet the place felt hauntingly familiar.

Where could she be?

He went back downstairs to where she'd left her phone and scrolled around for the last number she dialed. It was her office—Vivienne. He pushed redial only to get her friend's voicemail.

He considered that she might have her Blackberry. If she did, she'd get emails. He went to his laptop to type out a frantic email. If there was one thing she did constantly, it was to check her Blackberry. If she had it, it would buzz. Surely, she would get his message.

He decided to head out the backyard and walk down the thicket of woods. It had once been impassable and now had a path he'd cleared not long ago. It gave them a place to walk toward the river, where they set an old rusty wrought-iron bench—a place to find peace and solitude.

But she wasn't there. Ron stood with his hands on his hips, deliberating where else she might have gone when he saw movement from the water. A canoe floated by, its paddler waving to Ron as he glided past him when he realized he may have inadvertently invited intruders and trespassers by opening a path from the river embankment to the house.

Could she have been kidnapped? As the thought crossed his mind, his chest tightened with panic. Her wealth, though never flaunted, was substantial. Outside their close circle—Jops, Ed, and Fritzso—no one in Durham knew her true identity, let alone her net worth. Durham was a small town, and nothing so sinister was ever expected to happen. But with Raine, she'd be an easy target if anyone knew of her whereabouts.

"Hey, Jops, is Raine at the bar with you?" Ron asked on a call to the tavern.

He listened to Jops with mounting anxiety. "So you haven't seen her at all today? Her purse and Blackberry are gone, but her keys and cell phone are here... And her car's outside... No, we didn't fight," he said defensively. "Yeah, yeah. I'll call the cops and report her missing."

Ron's fingers began to tremble. "Yeah, that would be great if Ed and Fritzso could walk around the campus to see if they spot her before it gets too dark. Thanks, Jops."

The cops arrived and took his statement, then left with assurances that they'd start investigating. But they were too damn calm about it.

An hour later, Ed called to let him know that he and Fritzso had combed the campus and checked every shop on Main Street but found no sign of her.

Ron's anxiety grew as the minutes ticked into more hours. What if she was hurt and unable to call for help? Unconscious somewhere?

Desperation clawed at him.

Could he call on his gift of sight to *see* where she was? Of course, *An Da Shealladh* never worked that way. Visions came to him unbidden, never called up as a psychic medium would have. Where were the fae when he needed them? He would try anyway.

Where are you, my love?

Ron reached out with intense concentration.

Are you okay? Or in trouble? Are you mad at me? If you are, I'm sorry. Won't you come home, please? I'm getting really worried.

But instead of hearing Raine, Ron heard his granny's voice.

"Her heart is full of hurts. Ye're fated tae heal her first, Ronnie. Help her find the way tae yer heart. Believe in yer gift of the sight, child."

He thought he had been healing Raine's hurts. Making her forget her past and promising to love her forever. But after pushing her to rock climb with him, he realized she hadn't been ready to let go. Yes, she loved him, but not enough to trust her heart to him. Would she have gone back to New York without telling him? Did he matter so little to her?

Ron walked outside and sat on the front porch steps, looking into the darkness, seeing the campus now quiet save for a few undergrads still enjoying their first day in college.

He bent his head into his arms, letting the tears flow, calling out:

Raine, don't leave me, my love. I can't stand being without you. Please come home.

"Ron! Ron!" he heard her voice echo from a distance. *Thank God!*

"Raine, love, where are you?" he called out, arms flailing until a hand shook his shoulders.

"Ron, wake up." Raine's voice, strong and urgent, pulled him from his sleep.

He jolted awake, disoriented at first. But he clutched Raine tightly when he saw her eyes peering into him.

Had he been crying in his sleep?

"You were having a nightmare," she said.

He shivered as goosebumps prickled his skin. It was no nightmare. It was a vision portentous of that mystical 'something' lingering in the air.

"Shh... It's okay," Raine comforted, pulling him closer and warming his chilled body.

"Don't leave me, Raine, please?" he pleaded in a whisper against her hair.

His hands roamed around her body, feeling her flesh as if to convince himself she was real and lying next to him.

"I'm not going anywhere," she reassured. "Wanna talk about it?"

Ron shook his head. It was too soon to tell her of his *gift of two sights*. The last thing he wanted to do was frighten her into leaving.

Raine

SEPTEMBER 2000
DURHAM, NEW HAMPSHIRE

That was one hell of a nightmare Ron had, thrashing about and screaming for me. Groping as if he'd gone blind and I'd been lost at sea or something. He was calling out, "Please don't leave me." And I sensed a foreshadowing because, damn it, I still had to return to New York at the end of the year.

Cuddling in the dreamy afterglow of our lovemaking, I asked lightheartedly, "So you wanna put in a change of address, Luv?"

Ron turned and peered at me through half-closed eyes, too languid to consider that I might be serious. "You want me to move in with you? As in, give up my apartment and live here?"

"Uh-hm," I said. "You've been living here nearly every day since our first date. Now that the school year has started, wouldn't it make sense for you to move in officially? Your job is right across the street—a five-minute stroll to your office. Half your stuff's already here. In fact, how about I make you co-owner of the house."

"*What?*" He shot up in disbelief, hesitant to smile. "Seriously?"

"Yes," I said. "You should have half the vested interest in this house as I do."

I had thought about this for the past few days. I wanted to show him how deeply committed I felt about our relationship even if I couldn't see past December 31. And whatever happened beyond that date, I would gift him the deed to this house.

"I can't!"

"What do you mean?" My eyes widened, not sure I heard him right.

"I can't accept it for free."

"Why not? I'm giving it to you."

"I don't want your charity. It wouldn't be right. Let me buy my half from you then."

"Okay. Fifteen grand would be exactly half."

"Are you kidding?"

"Remember, this was a dump when I bought it."

"Yeah, but you've already put in so many improvements. That wouldn't be fair."

"So have you since you've started staying over. You should own half. Take it, or you can go back to commuting from Rochester."

He settled back down, staring at the ceiling.

"You're sure?"

"Are you trying to change my mind?"

"Okay, I'll talk to my bank about getting a mortgage." I finally heard the excitement in his voice, the trauma of his nightmare erased, at least for the moment.

Then he rolled on top of me and started kissing me all over. "I need to thank you properly."

"Na-ah. You're going to be late," I said, gently pushing him away, but his hands kept roaming.

I maneuvered into a kickboxing move to gently shove him off the bed, where he landed on his back with a thud.

"Arghhh... What the fuck, babe?" he groaned, though I knew he wasn't hurt.

"Ron, you barely have time to shower and grab a cup of coffee," I said as I rose from the bed. "If you plan to get a mortgage, you better keep your job."

"Ugh!"

"Now get up!" I said, smacking him with a pillow. I slipped on a robe and padded down the stairs to make coffee when I heard him holler back.

"I love you!"

I paused, feeling the warmth of his words wrap around me like a soft blanket. How does he know? How can he feel so sure that we had an eternal future together? I wanted to say it back, to let him know that I loved him too, but the words stayed locked inside. Was it because my time here and with him would have to end? Or I still had one foot out the door, ready to bolt at the first sign of heartache.

Ron

They closed on the Callahan house, officially making him a co-owner. Sitting in his windowless office, Ron stared into space, recalling one of his earlier visions. The one he'd had long before he'd met Raine. He was lying in front of the fireplace, making love to a woman who would become his wife. She was faceless then. When fate led him to Durham and he saw the Callahan house, he knew he was meant to be here. But being with Raine... This was beyond his wildest dreams, even if they hadn't yet made love in front of the fireplace. Maybe with a fire crackling this Christmas, they'd fulfill that vision.

Shaking himself back to the present, Ron packed up his things to head for a meeting at the provost's office where he would propose a whole new degree concentration to teach for next semester—environmental geology. An advanced master class for when he got his Ph.D. and could teach grad students. He was so excited for his future.

As he made his way across the campus toward Thompson Hall, something caught his eye—Raine on the tennis courts. She was a vision of focused energy, her hair held back by a headband, every movement deliberate as she volleyed back and forth with her partner. Ron had never seen her play before. Tennis was one of those things about her he hadn't known, a side of her he was now discovering. Maybe rock climbing wasn't her thing, but seeing her in her element on the court, so driven and competitive, gave him a new appreciation for her athleticism.

But as he watched her rally with a guy who could easily be mistaken for a young Andre Agassi—earring and all—Ron felt a twinge of something he wasn't used to: Jealousy. Not the same kind he had against Fritzso. This one felt mildly threatening. It was irrational, he knew. She was his, and he had no reason to doubt it. Still, the sight of her with someone else, sharing this part of herself, made him pause.

"Hey!" Raine spotted him, waving him over with a bright smile that made his heart lurch. That smile reassured him.

Ron pushed open the chain link gate, jogging over to her. Without thinking, he scooped her up in his arms, planting a deep, possessive kiss on her lips right in front of Agassi Junior. Maybe it was a bit alpha male of him, but he didn't care. He wanted the world to know she was his.

Raine pulled away and introduced him to her partner.

"Ron, this is Colin. He coaches tennis here at UNH."

"Colin." Ron nodded, trying to keep his tone neutral. "You giving private lessons or something?"

"Only for special people." Colin winked at Raine, making Ron twitch. But Raine just poked him in the side, her laughter bubbling up.

"What?" Ron looked at Raine.

Instead, Raine turned to Colin and said, "Next week? Same time?"

"I'll be here," Colin smiled at Raine, then turned to Ron. "Later, man."

Ron ignored him while Raine laughed.

"Why do you find this so funny?" Ron asked, half-annoyed, half-charmed by her reaction.

Raine finally let out the giggles she'd been holding back. "Colin's married with a kid on the way, Ron. He agreed to be my hitting partner to make some extra money. There's no need to be jealous, my love."

"Well, that doesn't mean he hasn't got the hots for you," Ron muttered, though the tension in his chest was already dissipating.

"Where'd you find him, anyway?"

"In the Love Connections section of the Durham Daily, dork," Raine teased, grabbing her towel and racquet. "But seriously, you're cute when you're jealous."

"I am, huh?" Ron grinned, feeling his jealousy fading, her amusement a balm to his insecurities.

He playfully lifted her again, this time aiming to give her a hickey. Raine shrieked with laughter, her voice echoing across the court.

"Hey, stop it!" she cried between giggles. "Don't you have to be somewhere important?"

"Oh shit! I'm supposed to be at the faculty senate meeting in..." He checked his phone, panic flashing across his face. "...five minutes. I gotta run."

As Raine swung her tennis bag over her shoulder, she called after him, "Want me to walk you to school?"

Ron threw his arm over her shoulders as they walked together, pulling her close. He turned to kiss her moist temple, savoring the simple joy of being together. In that moment, nothing else mattered. Not the nightmare that had shaken him nor the looming end of her sabbatical. They were happy, and that was enough.

As they walked, arm-in-arm, toward Thompson Hall, lost in their happiness, neither noticed the figure hidden in the distance. A photographer's high-powered zoom lens clicked away, capturing their private moment, unveiling Raine's whereabouts to the world.

And who she was with.

CHAPTER 42

Nick

OCTOBER 2000
NEW YORK, NEW YORK

"Coelho," Nick barked through the receiver.

"It's Tanya."

"Hey, what's cooking at the courthouse, kiddo?" Nick asked.

Tanya was the staff court reporter who spent most of her days in the dismal basement of City Hall sifting through lawsuits filed—and there would be dozens of them each day—in search of juicy cases that would warrant a salacious story—divorces, lawsuits, and other frivolous complaints.

"You might want to come down and look at this, Nick."

He prodded her on, "Whatya got?"

"Well, I was looking at this lawsuit, Nicky. Been here a couple of years now. Dunno how I coulda missed it. If I'm reading this right, it's a paternity lawsuit against Peter Garvey and his company. Says here that a Maria Gonzales is claiming Peter Garvey's her baby's papa, ya know what I mean?"

"So what? Tanya, Anna's already busting my balls for not letting the Garvey story go. And a dead man's paternity suit?

Sounds like a stretch. Lots of rich guys get bogus paternity suits. Why is this one different?"

"Maybe it's nothing, Nicky. But you wanted me to tell you if anything on Garvey or Glory Media came up."

"When was it filed?"

"October '98. That was just a couple of months before the guy killed himself, right?"

Nick tapped his pencil furiously, his mind racing back to the countless dead ends and frustrations tied to Garvey's case. The man was dead, but his shadow loomed large over Raine's life. Why did this matter now? But if there was a secret worth keeping... who else might have a stake in it?

"Nick, you still there?" Tanya asked.

"Yeah, what else?"

"Well, it's weird because the suit was settled, but the terms were sealed. If Garvey wasn't the papa, why'd he settle?"

Nick glanced out his office window, the chaotic energy of New York City mirroring his turbulent thoughts. Maybe... just maybe, there was something there. He had to investigate.

"Hang tight. I'll be right down." Nick said, hanging up and reaching for coat.

Probably another dead end, Nick thought. But he was never one to leave a stone unturned. Not if it involved Garvey. And with this lead, his gut told him there was something there. Nick intended to find out before anyone else did.

CHAPTER 43

Raine

"I love, love, love trick-or-treating. Halloween's my favorite holiday," Ron declared.

"Aren't you a little old for that, love?" I teased, though the joy in his eyes was infectious.

"Never!" He thundered, shaking his head vehemently.

The truth was, he wanted an excuse not to go to Jops's Annual Halloween Costume Party.

"I hate dressing up in silly costumes for those parties," he admitted, a pained expression crossing his face. "Last time, Ed and Fritz talked me into going, and the only costume I found was Snaggle Puss. And, of course, klutzy me, I tripped on my tail in front of a group of my students."

I couldn't help but laugh, even as he scowled. "Oh, I would have paid to see that."

"Thanks a lot!" He grumbled.

I didn't mind staying home with Ron on Halloween night, as he took charge of handing out the candy. He was so excited to see the munchkins in costume, and I watched how he leaped every time the doorbell rang. He would oooh and aaah over the kids' costumes—fairies, princesses, ballerinas, Pokémon, Darth Vader, Yoda, and lots of monsters. He was in his element, which made me sad. This man was meant to be a father, and for all the wealth I owned, that was something I couldn't give him, and it broke my heart. It hurt to think I could never be a mother.

"Growing up in Beverly Hills, trick-or-treating wasn't the same," I said.

He gave me a puzzled look. "What do you mean? How can it not be the same?"

"I had only one opportunity to dress in costume and go trick-or-treating. With Vivienne, we were chauffeured to carefully vetted homes."

"Chauffeured?" His brows rose, and then he shook his head. "You mean like in English Royalty? Uniformed driver and Bentley?"

"Pretty much. The Bentley was Vivienne's dad's car, and they kept a full-time driver on staff to chauffeur her anywhere she wanted to go."

"That is some wealth you grew up around," he exclaimed with widened eyes.

"For the record, it wasn't me who grew up in wealth. That was Vivienne."

"Okay, so your house had what? Seven bedrooms instead of twelve?" He teased.

"Nope, we lived in the gardener's residence of the Ito mansion. An unassuming three-bedroom ranch. I bet your house in Ann Arbor was larger. Didn't you say your family house had a pool?"

Ron ignored my question. "There's more to that story of your house, isn't there?"

"Yeah, a sad one, actually. The Ito family were wealthy industrialists but had to abandon their home during the World War II internment. The city of LA owned it for years, but because of the anti-Japanese sentiment, no one wanted to buy it, even if for just the back taxes. When my father heard it would be demolished, he saved it and turned the mansion into The Shogun Restaurant and Tea House. Our house was just your typical suburban house. But we had an amazing view of the city and over two acres of hillside that we used to cultivate all the produce that went into the restaurant."

"And here you are in Durham, living with a poor, starving assistant professor."

"You are hardly starving. I bet you got to dress up as a kid and came home with bags of candy."

"Oh, you poor deprived soul," he ribbed, grabbing me and kissing my temple. "Don't worry, when we have kids, we're going to walk around with them trick-or-treating in the neighborhood dressed up in costume."

He'd said it so pragmatically. As if our having a family together was a given. A destiny. But that 'when' wasn't in any future I could envision.

"Ron," I began.

He stopped me, pulling me to my feet. "Want an espresso? I think we've seen the last of the candy beggars."

I wondered if he heard me as he went to the kitchen to make coffee, so I called him again, louder. *"Ron!"*

"What?" He finally stopped and turned to look at me.

"I can't have children."

Ron

OCTOBER 2000

DURHAM, NEW HAMPSHIRE

"What do you mean?"

"Ron, I've told you. I can't have children. Have you forgotten?"

No, he hadn't forgotten. He just never took it seriously—because of the fae. Because of destiny. He was meant to marry Raine and raise a family with her. But how could he convince her without scaring her?

"I was married to Peter for nine years and never got pregnant," Raine said, her voice tinged with bitterness.

Ron pulled her close, kissing her forehead softly. "But what if it was Peter's problem?"

Raine shook her head. "No, Ron. Peter had a child with another woman." She recoiled slightly as if embarrassed by the admission.

"Raine," Ron said, holding her gaze, "you've told me about Peter and how much he hurt you. But do you remember me telling you I didn't care?"

"Ron, you've always wanted a family. And you deserve to have one."

"No, Raine. I've always only wanted you." The words were true and settled deep in his heart.

He had already planned to take her to Michigan for Thanksgiving, where he'd retrieve the two-carat garnet ring his grandmother had given him. "For your future wife," Granny had said. He'd imagined proposing to Raine in front of his family, surrounded by love. But now, that vision felt more distant.

Taking a deep breath, he turned her to face him. "Raine, let me tell you something. Remember when you told me your mother had the gift of two sights? Do you believe in it?"

Raine nodded slowly, her head resting on his shoulder. "Yes. I wish I had the gift. I'd like to see beyond this year."

"I have the gift, Raine. I inherited it from my grand-mother," Ron whispered, gently moving a strand of hair from her face. "You are my destiny. I've seen it—us—long before I met you. I'm telling you this so you won't worry about the future. It will be you and me—always."

He felt her breath catch. "What? What did you see, Ron? How did you see us?"

So he told her about the visions—the glimpses of a future they were destined to share. "I saw us in our house long before I even moved to New Hampshire. I didn't know it was you because the woman's face wasn't clear.

"And then another time, before you even moved here, I saw a woman—again, her face wasn't clear—but there were two little girls with us. We were camping in the mountains. The woman had a guitar and was singing to me and the kids.

"The third time was right after your birthday. When I held you for the first time and felt all the hurt inside you. In that vision, I was walking down a hillside covered with heather. A child was walking with me, and again, a woman whose face I couldn't see was further behind. She held the second child and was now pregnant with our third. This time I saw my grandmother. She told me all I had to do was look into my daughter's eyes, and I would see that she looked like my wife. And, my God, Raine. Our first child will look so much like you. And when my granny said my wife's name was Ouisgé, there could be no doubt. It could only be you, Raine. You're the one in my vision. This is our destiny, Raine."

Raine stilled, processing his words.

"So don't worry so much, my love," Ron said, trying to reassure her. "Somehow, I know these logistics will eventually work themselves out. We'll figure it out. We'll make it work out. For us. Please believe."

But when Raine turned to face him, her expression wasn't one of relief—it was disbelief.

"Raine, what's wrong?" He reached out to her, but she stepped back, raising a hand to stop him.

"Oh my God, Ron." Raine covered her face, pacing with a hand pressed to her forehead.

"Raine..." he called, desperation creeping into his voice as he walked toward her, but she kept her distance. When she finally looked at him, the fear in her eyes was unmistakable, piercing through him.

"Ron, how can I be that woman in your vision when I can't have children? It can't be me, even if I wished otherwise."

"No, no, no, Raine. You've got this all wrong. Love, it is you, and I've never been surer about anything in my life. Whatever your biological makeup is, this isn't going to change. It will happen. You said you believed in the two sights."

Raine shook her head, tears welling up. "How? How is it possible? It can't be me in your vision, Ron. That's someone else."

"Because that little girl looked just like you. Because your name is Ouisgé. How many women do you think I might meet with that name?" Ron argued, his grip tightening on her arm, forcing her to look at him. He held her face in his hands, trying to make her see what he saw.

"You have very distinct features, Raine. The way your eyes crease when you smile. It's that rare combination of Asian and Scottish roots. No one has your eyes, Raine. Only you. And that little girl—our girl—was a mirror image of you. Do you play the guitar, Raine? Do you sing along when you play?"

Raine bit her lip, looking away, clearly battling with herself. But one look into her eyes, her expression, Ron knew, his vision was right. He just hadn't seen her play a guitar or sing. Yet.

"You're looking into things that aren't there," she said, her voice shaky but resolute. Ron couldn't understand why she was so convinced of her infertility even as he told her about their destiny.

"Ron, I believe your vision. But that's not me you saw. It's someone else and you need to find her. She's meant to be with you. To have your children. To give you the life you want, deserve, and are destined for. I need to let you go," Raine said, her voice cracking.

"Jesus, what do I have to do to convince you that our destinies are intertwined?"

"I'm not her," she whispered again, her voice thick with anguish.

Ron's heart broke as he watched her struggle. He regretted telling her about his foresight. The timing wasn't right. How could he have been so stupid? He should have trusted that it would all work out without overwhelming her.

He was about to pull her into his arms when the house phone rang, shattering the tense silence. Hesitating, he loosened his grip on her, and she quickly moved to answer it.

"Hey. What's up?" Raine's voice sounded croaky, her face still pale from their conversation.

"What? Oh no... Vivi... How bad... Of course, I need to go to him."

Ron's stomach twisted as he watched Raine's eyes widen, her fear escalating with every second. He knew something terrible had happened, but he was helpless, trapped in his growing panic.

"What time?" she asked, her voice tight as she listened intently.

"All right. I'll be there. Yeah. See you soon then," she said, ending the call.

Raine turned to Ron, her eyes filled with a fresh wave of worry. "That was Vivienne. It's my father. He had another stroke."

Ron pulled into the Portsmouth airport and parked by the private hangar off the main terminal. It was a small regional airport that saw few flights and at that time of night, the place was deserted save for the lights from the small control tower nearby and the blinking ones that lit the short landing strip.

She didn't resist when he reached for her.

"I'm sorry," he whispered. "About tonight. I don't want you to go feeling sad. We're not ending what we have, Raine. I'm not letting go without a fight. You'll return, won't you?"

Raine stayed silent. Ron could feel her thoughts were far, far away. He leaned his temple against hers to fill her with all the love he could give, hoping it would be enough until she returned.

Standing on the tarmac, they watched the sleek twin-engine jet land on the short runway, graceful as a heron.

"Got room on that thing for one more?" He quipped as the door opened and a small stairway unfolded. If she would let him, he'd board with her this instant.

She didn't smile at his light humor. And though she hadn't wanted him to hold her or even respond to that searing, desperate kiss he gave her, he felt her cave in.

"Come back to me, Raine," he whispered.

But her only response was, "Bye, Ron," and she gently pushed him away. Without looking back, she ran toward the plane.

He stayed until the jet's thrusters fired back up, inched forward, and then pivoted as it righted itself in the other direction, readying for takeoff. As the jet engines began to rev higher and higher to that ear-blasting pitch, Ron waved as it lifted off and disappeared into the night sky.

He couldn't help the avalanche of tears that streaked his face. The pain in his heart was so great that he wondered how it would be possible to go on living without her.

CHAPTER 44

Ron

OCTOBER 2000

DURHAM, NEW HAMPSHIRE

T he drive back to Durham felt endless, each mile stretching with the weight of his thoughts. Halloween was in full swing, with students swaggering in costume, their laughter echoing in the crisp night air. The parking lot at Joplin's Jazz was packed, but Ron wasn't in the mood to stop by. Ed and Fritzso were probably there, but tonight, he wanted nothing more than to get home and drown in his sorrows.

Home. The word felt strange now as he unlocked the door and stepped into the silence. Without Raine, the house felt like a shell—empty, cold. He missed her presence, how she looked up from the dining table with a sweet smile when he came in, or how he'd find her in the kitchen, fixing dinner. It was domestic, warm. It was Raine.

He thought of calling and leaving her a voicemail she could listen to when she landed. Even if it was two a.m. Eastern Standard Time, he just needed to feel reassured that he was still a part of her life, that she would come back home.

Ron pulled his cell phone from his pocket and hit speed dial. But instead of hearing it through his phone, it rang in the house. His heart sank as he followed the sound to the dining table, where her cell phone lay next to her laptop. She'd forgotten it, along with her keys.

Shit. Now what?

She likely had her Blackberry with her. He could send an email. He quickly skipped up the stairs to the guest room that was now his office, turned on his laptop, and launched his email.

From: rmm28@unh.edu
To: rgarvey@glorymedia.com
Date: October 31, 2000, 9:45 p.m.
Message: Raine, my love
Hope you landed OK and your father gets
well soon. Please write back because I'm
missing you terribly already, *mo chridhe.*
I love you.
Forever. -Ron

As he hit send, a shiver ran down his spine. The eerie sense of déjà vu washed over him. It was too similar—coming home to an empty house, Raine gone, that cold, empty feeling in the pit of his stomach. Her cell phone, keys, Jeep still in the driveway... He slammed his laptop shut, trying to shake off the dread that lingered like a shadow in the room.

The fae must have taken pity on him because instead of reaching for the bottle of single malt scotch to drink himself to a stupor, he reached for the can of Scottish chocolate from Cocoa Mountain and made himself a mug.

"Here, lad. This'll dae wonders fer ye. It's a braw cup o' hot chocolate straight frame the Highlands."

The voice was so clear that he looked around and saw... his daughter, Mackenzie, now five, wide-eyed with excitement, standing beside him as he stirred the chocolate. He could hear her giggles, feel her tiny hands tugging at his sleeve.

"Hold on now, Kenz, it's still hot. You gotta blow on it first," he warned, smiling as she clapped her hands and jumped in anticipation. In the living room, Raine was nursing baby Amee in a rocking chair.

All felt right in the world for Ron, even though he'd gone to bed alone. And just as he closed his eyes to sleep, he heard his fae comfort him.

"Give yer troubles a rest, lad. Dinna fash yer destiny."

Raine

OCTOBER 2000
FLIGHT TO BURBANK, CALIFORNIA

I boarded the jet, and Vivienne hugged me tightly, whispering, "It's going to be okay."

"Thanks for doing all this, Vivi."

She nodded. "Your father's going to be fine. I spoke with your ma before we left. The stroke wasn't as serious as it could've been."

I sighed, trying to relax as I sank into the plush seat and buckled up. But my mind was tangled with anxiety and guilt. I glanced out the window at Ron, still standing on the tarmac, watching as we lifted off. My heart ached, thinking of the hurt in his eyes when I left.

"You've had a lot on your mind," Vivienne said, breaking into my thoughts. "We'll be in Burbank by three a.m. A car will take us straight to the hospital. Your ma's probably staying there."

I nodded, though the thought of seeing my parents again after all these years filled me with dread. How could I ever make up for the lost time? The anger and bitterness of our last conversation had dulled, leaving only sadness and regret.

"Can I really walk back into their lives after all these years?" I wondered aloud.

Vivienne's voice softened. "I saw them that Christmas after you left. They were devastated, Nish. They blamed themselves for pushing you away. It broke my heart to see them so lost without you."

I winced. I knew they had tried to reach out, but I'd ignored them. I shook my head at the wasted years. "I should have called them after I spoke with you."

"Your ma tried earlier, but it went to voicemail."

I rummaged through my tote, realizing I'd left my phone on the dining table in my rush to leave. "Dammit."

"Don't worry about it," Vivienne said gently. "Focus on the present. You'll mend things with your parents, and your da will be fine."

I exhaled slowly, some of the tension easing. Vivienne had been a rock through all of this, and I couldn't help but feel a pang of guilt for how absent I'd been in her life during my marriage to Peter. I wasn't even there when her mother died.

I had apologized when I found out. It was only recently that she and I had rekindled our friendship, and I caught up on all that had happened during our time apart. But she brushed it off. "It's okay, Raine. My dad and I had each other. They never divorced, you know. He never stopped loving her," she'd said.

The guilt had stung, yet she forgave me, as always.

Staring out the window into the dark sky, my thoughts drifted back to Ron and his words about destiny. The idea frightened me more than I cared to admit. I couldn't see a future for us.

Not with children.

Sensing my distraction, Vivienne turned to me. "Alright, I know you're not worried about your dad anymore. Spill it. Who is he?"

"What?"

"I saw you on the tarmac with Robin Wilson. And then you two shared this searing kiss, like parting was such sweet sorrow," Vivienne said, mockingly quoting Shakespeare.

"Who the hell is Robin Wilson?" I asked, utterly baffled.

"Frontman for Gin Blossoms? Alt band from the nineties?" Vivienne looked at me, exasperated. "Nish, did you lose all sense of yourself when you married Peter?"

I flinched at her words.

"You used to know all the latest bands, and we'd sing along while you played guitar," she said, reaching across to hold my hand. "Surely you remember when we snuck off to Phoenix to see Gin Blossoms when they were still unsigned, and you said you wouldn't mind losing your virginity to the singer."

"Vivi!" I shushed her. The pilots couldn't hear us, but there was a flight attendant within earshot. "We were seventeen!"

"You know, when you said that, I was hoping you'd finally gotten over Robert Redford."

I sniggered. "Yet I ended up marrying his look-alike."

I paused, contemplating my words. Had it been fate? Why else would I have made such a choice—one that, as Vivienne warned, was so out of character for me?

"Well, you've been spending your sabbatical reconnecting with the Nish you'd lost, right?"

I smiled and squeezed her hand back.

"What would I do without you, Viv?"

"You'd die! Now, tell me about Mr. Gin Blossoms."

I pinched the bridge of my nose. I couldn't keep it from her anymore. "His name is Ron Mitchell. He does look like he belongs in a band, but he's a professor at UNH."

"Ooh, a professor. Why didn't you tell me sooner?"

"Because it wasn't serious. It's a sabbatical fling. It's over."
The words felt like a lie.

"Why?" She asked with some incredulity.

I told her about Ron's vision and his certainty that we would be together, and I explained why I thought he was wrong.

Vivienne looked thoughtful. "Robin Wilson told you you're his destiny and you told him to find someone else to have babies with? Are you nuts?"

"For God's sake, Vivi. Be serious!"

"I'm serious! If he's gifted then why don't you believe him?"

"Because I can't have children," I said quietly, the old wound reopening. Peter's betrayal still haunted me.

Vivienne sighed, shaking her head. "You're thinking in absolutes. Even if you can't have children naturally, there are other ways."

I shook my head. "I don't want to hurt him any more than I have to. No, I'm not going back to him."

"You will," she insisted.

"You sound so sure."

"I am because you're not fucking a coward."

CHAPTER 45

NOVEMBER 2000
LOS ANGELES, CALIFORNIA

I t didn't matter how modern and state-of-the-art a hospital was; it still smelled of sickness, of desperate hopes and prayers. Even the swanky cardiology wing on the tenth floor, where celebrities and VIPs stayed in enormous suites, reeked of antiseptic.

As we entered the lobby, Vivienne searched for coffee, giving me time to see my parents alone. But it made me nervous. Butterflies fluttered in my belly when I took the private elevator to the top floor.

When I exited, I saw my Ma and ran to her.

"Oh my God, Mama! Mama!" I squealed, crying like a five-year-old lost in an amusement park. I clung to her, bawling like a baby and sobbing nonstop.

In my arms, my mother felt slighter. Silver streaks framed her face, highlighting her unfading beauty. Her eyes were soft and glassy when she saw me and quickly folded me into her embrace. She rocked me back and forth, like when I was younger, not wanting to let go.

"*O mo leanabh. Tha thu air tilleadh. Tha mi cho toilichte ur faicinn. Tha mi air do ionndrainn gu mòr,*" she whispered amid a free flow of salty tears.

In her sweet Gaelic voice, she said, "Oh, my child, you have returned. I am so happy to see you. I have missed you very much."

I laughed and cried, feeling transported back in time when the sound of her lilting Scottish accent was so comforting.

"My lovely lass. My Rainey. Hae bonny ye've become," she said, switching to English and breaking away to get a better look at my face, cupped with her hand. "The magazine pictures hae not done ye justice t'all."

Oh God. She was referring to a time when I used to dress glamorously. At the moment, I was a mess.

"How's Da?" I finally asked, wiping away my tears.

"Yer Da's back tae bein' stubborn, so he must be gettin' better. He's been fightin' the doctors every time they show up."

"Is he awake? I mean, it's almost midnight."

"Och, ye dinna think he'd sleep when he learnt ye were coming home, *a ghràdh*."

"W-will he want to see me, you think?" I asked tentatively.

"Oh, Rainey, he's missed ye, *mo ghràdh*. O' course, he wants tae see ye. When I telt him ye were comin' home, his eyes brightened."

She pushed a few stray hairs from my forehead as if needing to touch me to believe I was finally home again. I caressed her face, missing her touch, the feel of her skin, her motherly smell.

"Ye go on." She pushed me gently toward the door. "He's been waitin'."

I pushed the door open and went inside. My father was reading an issue of Cordon Bleu magazine, his glasses perched at the edge of his nose.

"Good, you're here," he said when he saw me, setting down the magazine and removing his glasses. "Maybe you can talk some sense into these doctors and get me out of here."

I smiled and shook my head. "You haven't changed," I said, standing at the foot of his bed, giving him a look my mother always said mirrored his when he was being haughty and pig-headed.

He looked thinner, a little tired, older, with grayer hair, but his eyes held that vigor and determination. When he smiled, my heart melted. I fell into his arms gently, careful of the IV drip. He tugged me into his embrace, squeezing me as his tears wet my cheek, his shoulders shuddering with emotion.

After visiting my father for about an hour and seeing how well he was doing, I left his room feeling relieved. Then I felt slightly dizzy, probably from not sleeping since I left Durham. It was nearing six a.m. East Coast time. My mother noticed I had paled and suggested that Vivienne and I grab a bite at a nearby diner before going home to sleep.

"This must be a huge relief to know they're releasing him in a few days," Vivienne said, munching on a bagel with veggie cream cheese and sipping her coffee.

"It is. There's some nerve damage in his right leg, but nothing that physical therapy couldn't fix. Might have to walk with a cane for a week or so. But he'll be home before Thanksgiving," I said, tucking into the eggs, breaking the runny yolks, smearing the yellow goo over the corned beef hash and hash browns, then scooping mouthfuls with a slice of toast.

"I'm going to stay for Thanksgiving, Vivi. I'll fly straight to New York from here in December. Then I'll be back in the office on the second of January, as promised," I said, gulping the rest of my orange juice.

I wasn't sure if she heard me. She seemed focused on my plate.

"My God, did you really eat all that?"

I rode back from the hospital with my mother, feeling slightly uneasy about returning to my childhood home.

"You left everything the same," I whispered, taking in my old bedroom, each detail familiar yet distant. I never realized how much I had missed it.

My mother's eyes softened. "I kent ye'd come back, *a leanabh*."

"You did?" I asked, disbelief tinged with longing.

"Aye, I had nae doot. Ye were meant tae leave, but I kent ye'd find yer way hame."

Confusion flickered across my face. "I was fated to leave you? Why hadn't you told me?"

Her smile faded. "Ye'll no' remember the day ye left. Yer Da tried tae warn ye. He telt ye Peter would break yer heart, but ye wouldnae listen. Ye were as stubborn as both a Scot and Japanese could be, Rainey."

The memory surfaced, and I remembered it very well. Still, I would have made the same choices. I just wished it hadn't been so hateful and hurtful. "I'm sorry, Ma.'

"And sorry I am, ma bairn. Yer da and I never meant to hurt ye. But we canna change the past. Only learn from it. Tis what I always hoped for ye, Rainey. That ye'd learn and come back tae us."

I swallowed hard, the reality of our lost time pressing down.

"I wish I had your gift."

"Rainey, ye dinna need a gift tae see yer own destiny, lass. It's often right there, plain as day, in front o' yer eyes. But folk, they refuse tae see it. They turn away, blind tae what's guid and true. An' in doin' so, they make choices that lead them straight intae the very fate they were meant for. It's no' that ye canna change yer path, but sometimes, ye're guidin' yerself right back tae where ye were always supposed tae be."

Her words were a balm, soothing the ache of years lost. She was right. I'd been determined to marry Peter, ignoring every warning, every plea. And yet, my choices led me to where I was meant to be. Oddly, I had no regrets.

As I changed into my pajamas and crawled into bed, I noticed the old movie poster of Robert Redford still hanging on the wall. His smile and blue eyes stared back at me, triggering memories of Peter.

Sleep pulled at me, but before I succumbed, I rose, took the poster down, rolled it up, and stuffed it in the closet where it belonged—in the past. As I closed my eyes, I saw only one pair of eyes—warm brown ones—filled with love, waiting for me.

The next morning, I rocketed to the bathroom, heaving my gullet and retching loudly, losing every bit of that enormous breakfast I had eaten.

"Rainey, are ye all right, *a leanabh*," my mother called from down the hall.

I couldn't answer without provoking another round of puking. Somehow, I made it back to bed, feeling slightly better. Maybe.

She rushed in to check on me and felt my face, but I wasn't feverish or clammy.

"Ye want water, aye?" I nodded weakly.

When she returned, she looked at me tenderly, helping me sit up to sip some water.

"I think I ate way too much this morning. My system isn't used to so much food. My fault. I hope it's nothing more than gluttony on my part. Maybe some Pepto Bismol might help."

She tipped my chin and leaned her forehead against mine, trying to heal me with her empathetic power. But when she lifted her head, she gave me an unreadable expression.

"What, Ma?" I asked, fearing she saw something serious.

She didn't answer. Instead, she went to the kitchen and returned with saltine crackers and a can of Sprite.

"Take a wee sip o' the soda, then nibble on the crackers. It'll settle yer stomach."

I didn't argue. "I hope I didn't catch anything from the diner yesterday. It would be miserable to be laid up for days."

"Are ye cramping?" She continued to caress my bangs and finger them away from my face while I lay back in bed with my knees up to my chest.

"No. Just nauseous. I'm sure it was something I ate."

"Come, sit up, child," she said, pulling me toward her.

She hugged me tightly, peppered my face with kisses, held me at arm's length to look at me, and then kissed me again as she whispered, "Rainey, *a ghràdh,* ye're wi' child."

CHAPTER 46

NOVEMBER 2000
BEVERLY HILLS, CALIFORNIA

O*h no! Nope, nope, nope, nope, and again nope.*
No way in hell.

Not possible.

Not happening.

"Rainey, when was the last time ye had yer bleedin'?" my mother asked with that soft, gentle gaze but was dead serious.

"Ma, if this is one of your visions, I'm not listening. It can't happen. No way, no how."

"Ye haven't had one in two months, nae?"

How the hell does she know this?

I shook my head, resisting a giggle. I was maybe a few days late? I really couldn't remember, and it shouldn't matter.

"Ma, it's impossible. I can't have children."

I told her about Peter, our inability to have children, his infidelity, and his illegitimate child.

Ma pulled me against her shoulder.

"I'm sorry about all the pain ye had tae go through wi' Peter. I ken 'twas a rough journey for ye. But I'm yer mother, aye? And a mother kens her own bairn. Ye're pregnant, and I canna be happier ye're makin' me and yer Da grandparents."

Did she say grandparents?

"Ma, have you not been listening? Argh!" I groaned.

"Rainey, hae ye been telt by a gynecologist that ye canna hae bairns, *mo chridhe?*"

"Well, no, but... I was with Peter for nine years!" I cried, nearly shouted. Why couldn't I get this through to her?

"Dinnae fash yersel'. I'll run oot an' fetch ye a test kit if it'll set yer mind at ease. But I'm tellin' ye, I only hae to touch ye, and I ken it.

"No, Ma. I'm not going to pee on a stick. I know you're my mother, but this is my body. I know my own body."

"Sae, what's the harm in makin' sure?"

As she walked away, I slumped back on the bed. Fine. Bring on the stick.

Later that morning, in the bathroom, I sat on the toilet waiting, praying for that second blue line not to appear. By then, I knew. Moreover, I knew my mother's empathetic ability to read people was uncanny. It was real. As that second blue line slowly appeared, I started sobbing uncontrollably with the reality.

Oh God! Ron. How would I tell him? *Sorry, I was an idiot for doubting you.*

"A *ghràdh,* I hope ye're crying because ye're happy, no?"

"Ma, I don't understand how this could have happened."

"It happens in the usual way, aye?"

"Mother!" I whimpered. "Don't you see? This adds another layer of complication to my already complicated life."

"Rainey, a bairn is no' a complication. 'tis a gift."

I dropped myself on my bed and stared at the ceiling.

"The man ye were with, ye love him, nae?"

I swallowed a lump in my throat. "Yes, with all my heart."

"And he loves ye? Will he no' be chuffed he's goin' tae be a Da?"

"Yes." I felt optimistic that Ron would be overjoyed. I recalled our last night together when he was giddy handing candy out to trick-or-treaters. It was almost as if he couldn't wait to be a father. Yeah, he's gonna be *chuffed*.

"Well, there now, Luv."

I turned to my side and curled into a fetal position, feeling a different kind of queasy.

"I'm going to the hospital to see yer Da. Are ye coming along?"

I shook my head. I seriously did not want to face the world at that moment.

"I'll be off then, and ye rest yerself. I'd like tae tell him, *mo nighean gaoil*. I'll no' be able tae keep it tae me self," she said with an excitement I wish I could share.

"Fine. I hope he doesn't have another coronary when you tell him. I'd rather not be there."

"Ha'e faith, me love. He'll be verra happy. I ken it in my heart."

When I heard her car drive off, I picked up my old pink Princess telephone and dialed the number I still knew by heart.

"Vivi, I'm pregnant."

CHAPTER 47

NOVEMBER 2000

BEVERLY HILLS, CALIFORNIA

"Looks like my best friend is going to have a baby Gin Blossoms frontman," Vivienne grinned when I answered the door.

"Oh, for God's sake, Vivi!" I grumbled, rolling my eyes.

She'd picked me up in her old Porsche and drove me to Bel Air to see her gynecologist.

"About four weeks, give or take," the doctor confirmed after a quick exam.

Afterward, we picked up my prescription for anti-nausea and prenatal vitamins. And then we swung by the AT&T store to activate my new cell phone before returning to her house for lunch.

Vivienne pulled into their four-car garage and parked next to Stanley's Maserati.

"The old Maz is still here," I commented, admiring the red Italian racer that had once severely grounded us when we loudly raced it up and down our neighborhood's steep, curving roads as if we were racing in the Le Mans.

Thinking alike, she said, "I'll never forget that time. We hadn't had our licenses for thirty minutes before it was taken from us." Vivienne remarked as we walked through a side door into the cavernous kitchen. We smiled together at the memory.

In the past, whenever I visited, I was so impressed—and jealous—of Vivienne that I knew it partly influenced my decision to marry Peter. I wanted to live with the same wealth and social standing as her.

"Do you want to lie down and rest?" Vivienne asked, eyeing me with concern.

I shook my head. Despite the morning's ordeal and the doctor drawing what felt like a quart of blood, I felt surprisingly good. Everything was normal so far, and the baby was due in June. My mother wasn't hallucinating, and that pregnancy test wasn't lying.

"Cheese omelet okay for lunch? Can you eat?" Vivienne asked as she pulled out eggs and cheese.

"Sounds great. I am hungry," I said, wondering how I could think about food when I had sworn off eating anything this morning. I perched on a stool at the expansive kitchen island. "This brings back memories of you cooking at our house."

"Your mother taught me how to make omelets and pancakes. I can still make her mean shepherd's pie."

"I'm glad you're putting those skills to use. You'll have to invite me for a home-cooked meal."

Vivienne set a plate of grapes before me, cracking eggs into a bowl. "You don't have to make any big decisions right now, Nish," she said, whisking the eggs and adding ricotta cheese. "Except for one."

She glanced at the new cell phone I'd placed on the counter. "You're calling Robin Wilson to let him know he's going to be a daddy."

I groaned at her insistence on calling Ron Robin. "Vivi, I'm not telling Ron I'm pregnant over the phone. He deserves to hear it in person."

I thought back to yesterday when we landed, and I had checked my Blackberry. Seeing Ron's email checking in on me made my heart flip. But the hours that followed had been so emotionally charged that I hadn't had a chance to reply. And now, I sure as hell wasn't going to tell him I was pregnant—not by phone and certainly not by email.

Vivienne said, "If I were him, I'd want to know now. I don't care if you sent smoke signals. Otherwise, I'd wonder why you kept it from me."

"If I told him now, he'd get on the first flight out of Boston. He'd be sitting on my parents' doorstep before I knew it."

"Exactly!"

I shook my head, reaching for a grape. "He has his doctoral defense next week. I don't want him to lose focus."

"He's probably already lost focus since you said you dumped him. Come on, if you tell him, he'll be ecstatic and ace his defense."

"I will, Vivi. I know I can no longer argue that the woman in his vision wasn't me because now I'm pregnant with his child. But I can't reconcile our careers. I don't want him to give up something he's worked so hard to achieve. But my obligations and commitment not to abandon the agency... Come on, Vivi. You're both my lawyer and CEO. I'm counting on your ideas. Got any?"

"Why don't you let Ron know first? His input is as important, especially if he's going to be a part of your life regardless of where you live. Fly back to New Hampshire after Thanksgiving and have reunion sex. I'll bet the answers will come to you in an instant."

I threw her a furtive look to gauge her seriousness.

"All right, all kidding aside, let it lie. As I said earlier, don't make any decisions right now. It will come to you soon enough," she reassured me.

And then I heard my mother's words again.

Ye dinna need a gift tae see yer own destiny, lass. It's often right there, plain as day, in front o' yer eyes. It's no' that ye canna change yer path, but sometimes, ye're just guidin' yerself right back tae where ye were always supposed tae be.

I hoped she was right. I could let this lie and let fate work its plan for me.

CHAPTER 48

NOVEMBER 2000

BEVERLY HILLS, CALIFORNIA

"My girls are here!" My eyes lit up when I heard Stanley approach us.

Vivienne and I were sitting on the patio with our herbal teas when he gave Vivienne *bisses*—kisses on both cheeks, the French way—and me a peck on my forehead as if I was still ten.

"What a blessed surprise. My goodness, Raine. It's been way too long, but you are looking enchanting, I must say," he said, pulling off his sunglasses.

For a man in his fifties, Stanley looked remarkable. He still had that full head of hair, gray streaks framing his face. He was California-tanned but flaunted none of the leathery wrinkles most bronzed celebrities sported.

"Raine's pregnant, Dad. That's why she's glowing."

Reflexively, I kicked Vivienne under the patio table.

"*Ow!*" She yelped.

"Oh, I'm sorry. I didn't mean to," I said, shooting visual daggers at her.

Stanley rolled his eyes. "You're both CEOs, and you still act like fifteen."

His remark made me laugh. Ever discreet, he offered his congratulations, gave me a peck on the cheek, and inquired about my father's health, having heard about his mild stroke.

"You don't mind if I join you? I'd love to spend a few minutes catching up."

I sipped my chamomile tea while he sat across from me. Sunlight painted golden streaks on Stanley's hair. His natural furrowed brows, often referred to by photographers as "the scrunch," made him look slightly mysterious behind those eyes as if to say, "I'm more than what you see."

"Uncle Stanley, you look scrumptiously handsome. How is it a babe hasn't nailed you down yet?"

"You know I'm a hard one to pin, Raine. I move too much," he said, raising his glass to a toast and sipping his martini.

The truth was Stanley never fully recovered from losing his wife. He believed no one could compare to his Claire—a devotion rare enough in any world, let alone in Hollywood's glittering circles.

"Looks like you two have hooked up quite nicely again—both chief executives? When you guys were in high school, I never thought you'd mature—especially this one here," he teased, thumbing in Vivienne's direction. "But seriously, I'm proud of you both."

"We'll drink to that," Vivienne said, raising her mug of tea in response.

"So, what's in your hopper these days, Uncle Stanley," I asked with genuine interest.

"I'm taking a break," he said. "Like you, taking a bit of an extended sabbatical. What about you guys?"

He asked as he glanced at me first, then over to Vivienne.

"I'm supposed to be back at the helm of Glory after the New Year, and I can't decide if I'm looking forward to it."

"I suppose I'll return to the legal salt mines of Wall Street," Vivienne followed up. "Which I'm sure will be so dull after having had a taste of heading a company. I'm considering putting out feelers for my next act now that I have some experience under my belt—thanks to Raine."

I turned to Vivienne with a puzzled look. "Wait, seriously?"

"I am. I've been thinking about it as my contract winds down, Nish."

Stanley's gaze shifted between me and Vivienne.

"Then why not stay on as CEO at Glory? You can buy me out." My own words surprised me.

Vivienne was stunned, speechless.

"*Are you serious?*" Vivienne asked, hand over her chest.

"You just handed me the ideal solution to my dilemma, Vivi," I said straight-faced. "I know you love the job. You're so good at it. The staff already respects you. Charlie will forgive me if I don't return because he loves you. Grey seems happy he's found a mentor in you. I'm sure Luke would genuinely support you stepping into this role."

"What?" Vivienne asked cautiously, her cheeks flushing slightly.

I smiled and wondered if my best friend had a crush on Luke, but I hadn't wanted to bring it up in front of her father. Instead, I said, "Why wouldn't he be supportive? You've earned everyone's respect. So, what do you say?"

"Nish," she started, seemingly at a loss for words. "Oh, sister, I can't believe this. I need to think this through."

"What's to think through?"

"Well, for starters, I'm not sure I can afford to buy you out—yet. Wow! I need a stronger drink," she said, rising to get something alcoholic from the bar.

Stanley cleared his throat.

"Well, isn't this fortuitous? Raine, I want in on that deal you're offering Vivienne," he began, tipping the last drop of his drink, then followed Vivienne to make himself another. "I'll back her up."

"Seriously, Dad?" Vivienne said as she returned to her seat with a glass of Chardonnay.

"You guys are killing me with your drinks," I said, mildly jealous.

"This certainly opens up a lot of windows, doesn't it, Dad?"

"Honestly, I've been looking around for my next act too. Something that would depart a bit from filmmaking. The world is trending toward media technology, and I think Glory would be a perfect fit for what I have in mind." Stanley took his daughter's hand and kissed it. "Think you can stand to have your old man as a business partner?"

I stood up and faced Vivienne. "Since you're acting CEO and will remain so until you take over officially, you can work out the details with Stanley. Meantime, this pregnancy thing is making me sleepy. If you don't mind, I'll tuck myself into one of your guest rooms and nap while you talk."

While I settled in one of the guest rooms, I drifted off to an enchanting sleep, dreaming of my baby's father lying next to me, his head on my belly, feeling his child alive and kicking. As I had begun to trust my mother's wisdom, I also made a solemn promise that never again would I doubt Ron's Scottish fae.

CHAPTER 49

Raine

NOVEMBER 2000 - THANKSGIVING
LOS ANGELES, CALIFORNIA

"Ye'll not be racing my new car now, *a leanbh*."
I heard my mother bellow as Da and I walked out the door, ignoring her as I twirled the keys to her new sporty SLK Mercedez Benz.

Ever the pragmatist, my mother insisted that father and daughter needed to spend time together. After our quiet, intimate Thanksgiving dinner, she shooed us out the door.

Her "new-ish" car, which she bought used from a friend, was her very first "feckless" purchase. The five-year-old two-seater roadster was hardly broken in. Insanity for her, but she drove it like an old lady.

With thoughts of mischief, I winked at my Da, gunned the engine, and burned the tires to a screech when we took off. We navigated a couple of hairpin turns at high speed as we drove down the hills. Oh, to hear my Da go "Whoooo!" was priceless.

Once we hit Sunset Boulevard, I slowed down and headed toward the Santa Monica Boardwalk. The ocean air brought a rush of nostalgia—the salty breeze, hints of marine life, and the scent of roasting peanuts and popcorn from the pier's amusement park. Da used to bring me here on his rare days off. I could still picture him chasing me as a five-year-old, squealing excitedly as I darted through the crowd. Playing skeeball and winning me a giant stuffed panda, or quietly cussing as he tried to clean cotton candy off my face, worried about my mom's reaction to my sticky fingers and chocolate-stained clothes.

The wind whipped our hair as we strolled down the stretch of the pier, taking slow, careful steps so my father wouldn't trip with his cane over the uneven planks.

At the end of the pier, we settled on a bench facing the Pacific, its thundering waves crashing against the shore. The ocean breeze was light, but temps were cooler. Save for a couple of fishermen with poles cast over the railing, we were alone. Sunset would come early this time of year, but we had an hour yet before the light faded.

We were silent for a few minutes as if nature had asked us to revere the moment's beauty without words or thought. And then my father spoke.

"Your Ma and I are retiring next year, Ame," he began, calling me by my Japanese name, pronouncing it Ah-meh, which in Japanese meant rain. So, my name in English, Scottish, and Japanese is Raine Rain Rain Nishiseki. My parents had a weird sense of humor.

"It's about time, Da," I agreed. "You've worked so hard for so long, and the stress of running a restaurant is taxing your health."

He nodded. I knew what he meant. After achieving the third Michelin star, he was ready for his next adventure, likely to be a departure from restauranteurdom. I was so excited for him.

"Your cousin, Naomi," he continued, pronouncing my cousin's name in Japanese, Nah-you-mi. "I've already made her executive chef. We're selling both the house and The Shogun to her and her fiancé. They're getting married next year and will move into the house. This would keep the entire property in the family. I'm sure you'll get an invitation to the wedding."

My da circled his arm around my shoulder and said, "Your Ma and I will travel a bit, but we will hang out in Edinburgh for a while. Your grandda is still alive, and your ma wants to spend time with him as he may not have many years left. But he'll be tickled to death to learn he'll be a great grandda. This time, you won't stay away from us so much. I expect you to visit Edinburgh with your family as often as possible. Spend summers in Kirtomy."

Hearing him say, "my family," squeezed my heart because I knew he meant Ron, me, and our baby. And summers in Kirtomy? Wasn't that Ron's vision?

"You know, da, I wish it didn't take your stroke for me to come home. I wished I'd listened to you. Spared us all this heartache."

My Da shook his head vigorously.

"Rainey," he said, pulling me away to look at me. "You married Peter against my better judgment. But you married for love. You fought for love. The same way your Ma did when she came after me. She had the same bitter fight with her da."

"Yes, but you didn't break Ma's heart," I argued. "You married Ma. You had me. You've never been unfaithful to her."

"You forget I left her without saying goodbye. I was such a coward," he said.

I argued that Peter had broken my heart when he had a child with someone else. How much that had cut me to the core. "You had warned me that he would hurt me."

"No, Rainey. I was angry Peter was taking you away from us too soon. And I was too proud to admit it. I've been wanting to ask your forgiveness all those years. I missed you so much, Rainey.

"Da, I love you. No forgiveness is necessary. From now on, we'll be together again as a family. You'll come to visit me in New Hampshire?"

"Of course, sweetheart."

My father kissed my temple and drew me against him.

I had meant to share what had happened between Peter and me—for closure. But my Da stopped me.

"You've been searching for answers since Peter died, *uchi no musume.* One day, you'll learn why. Right now, let's look ahead."

Da took my hand in his, and I leaned against his shoulder.

"I'm selling my stake in the company, Da."

He nodded but listened quietly.

"I'm going to settle in New Hampshire. My life is there now."

"Of course it is, sweetheart," he said, kissing my temple and squeezing my shoulders.

"You know, Ron's also from a long line of Scots." I pulled away to gauge his reaction.

"I know. Your Ma told me," he replied with an amused crease in his eyes. "But for heaven's sake, Rainey, haven't you learned something from me about living with a Scot?"

I had not expected to laugh with my Da.

"Not only that, Da. He's also gifted. Like Ma."

My father raised his eyes to the sky. "God help you!" He continued to laugh.

"You know, the night you came home and slept in the house again, she said she had a dream. That was before you even woke up puking. It was one of her visions. She said she saw you on your wedding day, walking up to meet your groom, and he was wearing a kilt."

"What?" I shrieked into the wind, unable to control the laughter that burst with wild abandon. Somehow, I couldn't see Ron wearing a kilt. Not on our wedding day or any other

day for that matter. Did he even own one? I put my head in my hands, thinking how bizarre this trip had turned out when I landed in LA and reconciled with my parents.

When we returned to the house, we savored my mama's clootie dumplings, a cake bun she makes with pumpkin spice and English marmalade, drizzled with Scottish cream sauce and topped with shaved chocolate from Cocoa Mountain. What pregnant woman wouldn't be in heaven?

"I talked to your Ma about this," Da said as he licked his spoon. "Since we planned to spend Christmas in Edinburgh, we'll fly back to New York and celebrate New Year's Eve there. After we settle the house and restaurant, we'll come out to New Hampshire and rent an apartment or house near you for a while. We want to be with you for the birth of our first grandchild."

How was it that I had the best parents one could ever have and not known it for so many years?

My face crumbled into tears as I felt the last decade I'd spent away from home melt away. There was only today and tomorrow—the gift of the two sights. That was a destiny I could see without the gift of foresight.

CHAPTER 50

Nick

"Don't forget those two boxes with old clips from the *Courier Post*. They're in the garage," Nick's mother called out from the front door as he was getting ready to leave. "If you don't want them, we'll take them to the recycling center next week."

While at his folks for Thanksgiving, he was reminded that they were preparing the house for sale. It felt bittersweet to know the humble Levittown house he'd grown up in with his brother would be gone.

"Anything left behind is going to the dump or Goodwill," his father said.

Of course, he wanted his old clips. They were all the articles he'd written while interning as a journalism student.

They unearthed the two boxes from the garage stuffed to the rafters with even more memories from his and his brother's childhood. He carried them to the trunk of his car and bade his parents goodbye, promising to return to help them move.

But as he drove around his old neighborhood, something moved him to make a side trip down Magnolia Lane. Though the street looked like any other, he was struck by a modern white split-level house with blue trim, a high, sloping roofline suggesting a vaulted ceiling, and a two-car garage. Whoever built this house would have had to raze the former home to the ground. Not a trace of the old house from the seventies remained. Something about this street, this house, felt familiar.

Nick frowned in frustration. He was only forty-seven, and already he couldn't remember shit. New York did that to you, Nick sighed.

Exposed to the uglier violence of the big city, everything else he'd written for his small hometown paper—vandalism by wayward teens, a drug dealer hiding out in one of the houses, homes damaged by a hurricane. And the fires... God, he'd written enough about fires—cigarettes left burning, stove burners left on, candles—all paled compared to the bigger stories he'd written for *The Tribune*.

The trip down memory lane and the thought that his parents would be moving depressed Nick as he gunned it for the Jersey Turnpike, suddenly anxious to get home.

When Nick returned to his apartment, the last thing he expected to see was a FedEx envelope slipped under his apartment door. He picked it up and tossed it carelessly on his coffee table.

He would crack open a cold beer first. Once he had his first sip, he felt human enough to open the large cardboard envelope, wondering who would have sent him something urgent over the Thanksgiving holiday. Inside, an issue of *The Hollywood Talebearer* slipped out. A Post-it stickie was pasted on the front page.

"Check out page 58. -Lena."

Lena was the editor at the gossip rag on Sunset Boulevard. She knew Nick had been sniffing around for news—*any* news—on the Garveys. Hell, he'd said he would even consider rumors and then follow up on them. When Nick flipped to page fifty-eight, under the headline "Caught in Passing," his eyes bugged out at the photo that stared back. Then he read the caption.

"Was Gin Blossoms Frontman Robin Wilson spotted kanoodling with billionaire widow Raine Garvey at the University of New Hampshire?"

CHAPTER 51

Nick

N ick knew for sure it was not Robin Wilson who was with the widow Garvey. The mystery man could easily be mistaken for the band's lead singer from the early nineties—if Robin Wilson was still in his twenties. But Nick knew it was the publication's way of hyping the photo. They didn't know who she was with, but Nick was determined to find out.

This time, he knew what had happened to Peter and the scandal he had created. But Nick wasn't chasing Raine for that story anymore. He remembered his silent vow to himself all those years ago as a rookie reporter that he would never forget—and he would keep it.

Pulling into Durham, Nick felt transported in time to a Christmas picture postcard of vintage shops lining Main Street blanketed with fresh snow that had fallen the day before.

If Raine was here, where would she be living? Maybe she'd rented an apartment or perhaps a house. Would she have bought a house?

While at the county office of the Registry of Deeds, Nick discovered that one house near the campus sold on January

5th this year, about the time Raine left New York. The deed was under ROAN LLC. But then it was later resold to a couple: Ronald MacKenzie Mitchell and Ouisgé Amé Nishiseki.

Nick remembered that Raine's maiden name was Nishiseki. ROAN... Raine Ouisgé Amé Nishiseki. Hot damn! She and this guy, Ronald Mitchell, were living together as a couple.

Nick was surprised to learn of Raine's involvement with a new guy. Nothing wrong with that. She was single. But after a call to the office to check out who this Ronald Mitchell was, Nick learned he was local professor at UNH. He knew the tabloids would have a field day with this. His editor would freak out. They would all put two and two together and assume the professor was Raine's rebound lover interested in her money. After all, she hadn't been a widow *that* long. And she had *all* that money. It would be a media circus. Still, he reminded himself that he had a different mission.

After ringing the doorbell several times, Nick gave up. No one was home at the house on Mill Road despite a red Jeep and vintage Miata under the carport. He headed back toward Main Street and pulled into a tavern, figuring he'd catch some locals and make inquiries. Besides, he was starving, having missed breakfast, and it was well past the lunch hour.

"Hey there. What can I get you?" the bearded bartender asked as Nick perched on a barstool. Save for a waitress refilling the ketchup bottles on the tables, the place was deserted.

"A Bud Lite on tap and a burger. Looks like you guys got some snow last night," Nick said, making small talk.

"Yeah, a little. But it's supposed to warm up this weekend. Should melt all this stuff off," the bartender said, pulling a draft for Nick.

As Nick took a sip, a group of loud and boisterous young men ribbing each other burst in, disrupting the peace of the tavern as they strolled up to the far end of the bar.

He watched as the bartender greeted them as if they were close friends. That was when he recognized one of them. Nick took out the article from his breast pocket and studied it, stealthily glancing at the one with long hair and then back at the sheet again.

Then the bartender asked one of them, "Hey Ron, you heard from Raine yet?"

Bingo!

Nick made his move. Torn page in hand, he rose from his stool.

"Hey, can I ask you something?" Nick asked Ron.

But then all three—including the bartender—looked at Nick questioningly.

He set the page on the counter in front of Ron.

"Is this you?" Nick asked, pointing to the picture of Ron's arm around Raine, kissing her temple.

If Ed and Fritzso hadn't been quick on their feet, Nick's nose would have cracked under Ron's knuckles.

"Whoa, whoa..." Everyone hollered while Ed and Fritzso held Ron back, pushing him toward the kitchen while the bartender walked Nick out of the bar.

"Listen, I take it you're a reporter or something. I'm sorry, but I can't let you back inside."

"Look, I'm not the paparazzi. I didn't take that picture. I'm from *The New York Tribune* and just wanted to..."

"Beat it, man. I mean it. Or I'm calling the cops."

"Why? I didn't do anything. He's the one who came after me."

"Come on, you came here sniffing around for something. Just leave, and we'll forget this ever happened." The bartender turned and headed back inside.

Nick would never have made it to the top of his career if he'd turned his heel whenever somebody told him to beat it.

This time, it wasn't about the story. It was about getting the truth to Raine. But first, he needed to find her.

Huddled inside the warmth of his car with the engine running, he waited for Ron to exit Joplin's Jazz. It wasn't long before he emerged, zipping up his coat, and crossing the parking lot.

Nick chased after him and called out, "Hey, Professor Mitchell."

Ron looked back. "I have nothing to say to you."

But Nick was quick and caught up to Ron.

"I just need a couple of minutes to talk to you. I'm not after any scandal," Nick quickly added before Ron could bolt.

"Well, I don't," Ron said, turning away, quickening his steps, but Nick kept up.

"You think you can keep living this quiet academic life with her in your cute little house? You have to let me talk to her before your picture gets to the tabloids because they will tear you both apart."

Ron's stopped in his tracks. His reaction was immediate, defensive. But Nick could see the fear in his eyes.

"They don't care about the truth. But I do," Nick said.

For a moment, he thought he'd gotten through. But then Ron turned away, refusing to listen. Nick watched him go.

His lips tightened. His fists curled in frustration. He couldn't walk away from this, not now. He needed to get to Raine before somebody else got a hold of what he knew.

CHAPTER 52

Ron

DECEMBER 2000
DURHAM, NEW HAMPSHIRE

The minute Ron slammed the door behind him, tossing his snow boots on the tray, he knew his temper was spiraling out of control. What Nick said kept gnawing at him. Was he ready for this? The media, the scandals, the relentless scrutiny of his private life? Raine had warned him about her complicated life, but he hadn't cared then. Now, he had no choice but to care. He was due to defend his dissertation, and his lifelong goal of getting his doctorate was within reach. He didn't need any scandal to rock that boat.

What the almighty fuck was he going to do about it now? He needed to blow off some steam. So Ron put on his gardening boots and grabbed his chainsaw from the garage. He would pick out a dead tree from the backyard, cut it down, and then chop the logs into firewood for the winter. It was a chore he'd meant to do anyway. Why not let his aggression out while he was at it? Handling a chainsaw when pissed was probably not a good idea, but it was better than getting drunk and feeling sorry for himself.

Still, as the axe fell against each log, he felt his heart fall. Raine was right. Her life was too complicated. This probably wasn't going to work out between them. The thought made his eyes swim with tears.

That was when the fae thought he needed a reminder about his destiny.

In his dream, Ron was stroking her belly, distended and hard as a watermelon. Her skin was taut and dry even though he knew she applied lotion daily after her shower. She was almost due. She would have their baby in a few weeks. He felt the little life jabbing beneath his palm, announcing her presence, her identity, her tiny soul. His hand traveled upward, brushing against his wife's breasts, imagining his baby suckling on her swollen nipples.

He leaned into her to kiss her shoulders but instead felt the empty bed and awoke with a start and a painful erection.

Great! Just great! So, it was just a dream. A vision?

How the hell was Raine going to get pregnant if she wasn't even here with him? She hadn't even called or responded, no matter how many emails he sent. He'd told himself he would give her the time she needed when she left. However long it took. But damn it! The fae had to stop sending him visions that left him horny and frustrated.

Resigned to another day without her, he rose and dressed into his running gear. The workout would surely clear his head.

He paced his breath as he ran the perimeter of UNH's campus, starting on Main Street and then cutting through the athletic field before heading for the woods by the Oyster River.

It was the weekend after Thanksgiving, and some students had started returning to campus, though it wasn't yet in full swing. He hadn't expected to run into anyone, not in the woods. Yet there was this dude who seemed to appear from nowhere.

He didn't look threatening as Ron took in his height and build. He was tall, good-looking, fair-skinned with blond hair and blue eyes, dressed in expensive designer hiking threads. He looked like he should be trekking with a luxury expedition team somewhere in Patagonia, not the Oyster River in Durham. Probably a professor who was new in town, Ron thought. From the business school, for sure. He looked like one of those MBA types.

Ron hadn't intended to acknowledge the stranger beyond a nod, but the man's gaze locked on Ron's as if he'd been waiting for him.

"Are you lost or something?" Ron finally slowed to a walk, wiping moisture from his forehead. The man strode next to him.

"No, I was waiting for you."

"Oh? Do I know you?" Ron asked cautiously, curling his fist just in case the man planned on jumping him.

"Maybe you know of me. I'm Peter Garvey," he said, looking away beyond the thickly wooded area. Ron stopped in his tracks, and so did the man.

"Peter," Ron started, tilting his head at the man, his brows now drawn together in deep skepticism. "As in Raine's... late husband?"

The man merely nodded and tucked his hands in his pant pockets.

But Peter was dead. This guy had to be an imposter. Ron played along to see what this was all about.

He set his hands on his waist and chuckled in mild amusement. But first, he swiftly swung his fist around and popped the man in the mouth.

"You're supposed to be dead," he said to the imposter, wondering how far the charade would go.

The man touched his lip and tasted his blood.

"Did that feel like I was dead to you?"

Okay, so the dude's not a ghost.

Ron rubbed his knuckles. His whole hand was starting to sting. But Garvey was still dead, and what the fuck kind of sick joke was this?

"Who are you really? And what do you want?" Ron asked. He was getting tired of this game.

"Take care of her for me," he said, moving his sore jaw from side to side.

"You mean Raine." Why was he still talking to this jerk? "If you're not dead, you should go back to her."

He was done. Ron turned and started walking away. But the ghost followed alongside.

"You're fated to be with her. I wasn't."

He stopped dead. Oh hell! The fae. The fae sent Raine's husband to him. His ghost?

Ron knew his gift allowed him to see the realms beyond the living. But it had never happened before. Did the fae send him Peter's ghost? Ron shook his head and sniggered.

"Dude, she left me. How the hell am I supposed to take care of her if she's gone? She doesn't believe we're fated."

"Give her time." Peter's ghost turned to meet Ron's gaze.

"Time? She's been gone for more than a month. And I don't even know when she's coming back. If she's coming back," Ron yelled, throwing his arms at the stupidity of it all.

"Of course, she's coming back. She's your destiny," Peter's ghost said.

A ghost, for fuck's sake. He was having a conversation like he was real. Could the fae be any more mischievous?

"You're a fucking coward. You broke her, dude. I'm supposed to be fated to heal her from the shit you left her with, but she's so wrecked I don't even think I can," Ron yelled, his temper rising. "And as I said, she's not here anyway."

Peter's ghost hung his head in sadness. "I should have told her everything."

"Don't give me your goddamn regrets. You offed yourself, and now she won't stop blaming herself until she knows why. And what's with you fucking around on her, having a child with another woman, and then you leave that child an orphan? And now you want me to clean up your shit?"

It was all he could do to keep his temper from boiling over because he had an overwhelming urge to beat the ghost to a bloody pulp. Kick him senseless. But what good would that do? The man was dead. Instead, Ron threw his arms in the air.

The ghost nodded. "But if you understood desperation, you would feel empathy toward those who decide to end their lives. We're not all cowards."

Peter held his hand to Ron as if offering a handshake. "Take my hand. You're an empath, and I'm real to you right now."

The ghost's hand was warm as any living being, his grasp firm. And then Ron saw into Peter's mind, felt the inexorable hurt he suffered, the disease that was going to eventually cripple him, destroy his health, a slow and long painful death. He also saw Peter's trauma from the tragedy he'd been through as a young man.

Ron withdrew his hand abruptly. "Holy shit!" He'd seen enough.

"If it were only for my sake, I would have lived my life until it was time to go. But not with Raine. I couldn't enslave her to my illness. That's not her destiny, Ron. Think what you want. It took a lot of courage for me to leave her."

"You still made her suffer."

"I loved her with all my heart, Ronnie. I wish my life would have turned out differently. And Raine and I would have lived the happily ever after life I had promised her. Then she wouldn't have needed you."

Okay, the jerk had a point.

"Believe in the fae, Ronnie. You and Raine are fated. You don't know how lucky that makes you."

Ron watched the guy stroll away and then disappear. He turned his head up to face the sky. God, he hated it when the fae fucked with him.

And then his alarm went off, blaring Journey's "Don't Stop Believin'" so loud that when he rolled over to hit the snooze button, Ron fell off the bed.

CHAPTER 53

Raine

DECEMBER 2000
NEW YORK, NEW YORK

When I left the city last January, I'd forgotten that I had my apartment renovated so I could sell it. It looked so different, and had Johnny, the doorman, not been standing next to me with my luggage, I'd have thought I was on the wrong floor.

"It's gorgeous, ma'am. There were lots of workers here. It's the first time ye're seeing it?" he asked with a hint of an Irish accent.

"Yup. Thank you, Johnny. You can leave the suitcases by the door. I'll get to them later."

"By the way, this came today, Mrs. Garvey. I was told to give ye this personally."

Johnny handed me a yellow manila envelope, and I tossed it on the nearest counter.

"Thanks for everything, Johnny," I said.

Only after he left and closed the door behind him did I take stock of my newly redesigned apartment, which was now twice its former size after acquiring the one next door and joining the two. When I hired an interior designer to reconfigure the entire space, I wanted no shadow of its former self since I had planned to put it on the market. With people likely knowing what had happened here, I wanted to ensure the place was beyond recognition.

I was happy with the results because, this time, there were no ghosts. No sad, sordid memories. But it didn't matter. This was no longer my home.

Home was the little old house in Durham that I made my own with all my imperfect handiwork. And with Ron. It made me miss him terribly. A few more days and this co-op would be on the market, and I would leave for good.

I rummaged around the fridge and was pleasantly pleased to see it stocked with a few provisions. I made a mental note to call the cleaning lady and thank her for the extra thoughtfulness as I made myself a PB&J sandwich.

Settling on a bar stool by the new kitchen island, I opened the envelope that Johnny had handed me. Three old newspaper clippings spilled out. I picked up one clipping and unfolded it, and my heart stopped.

June 15, 1970
Deadly Fire Kills One, Another Critically Injured

By Nicholas D. Coelho

A fire that broke out just past midnight in the Pine Ridge section of Levittown has left one person dead and another critically injured.

According to witnesses, fifty-year-old Eliza Garvey of 24 Magnolia Lane did not survive. Her son Peter Garvey, 16, suffered multiple injuries and was transported to nearby Albert Einstein Hospital's burn unit in Philadelphia.

CHAPTER 54

Nick

"What the fuck do you mean by sending me this shit?" Nick saw the rage on her face when the widow Garvey approached his desk and dropped three balls of crumpled paper.

Her voice was even but loud enough to carry to the other reporters on the floor who turned toward the raucous.

"I thought it was important for you to know about it," he said calmly, throwing glances around the newsroom and feeling heat creep to his ears while others watched and listened.

"Are you suggesting that the young man in your story was my husband? Is that what you're going to write about? If you publish this, or even so much as imply a connection, I'll sue *The Tribune* for libel, and you won't be reporting the news for anyone for the rest of your life."

The top boss must have heard the rumblings because Anna Jackson flew from her distant office to Nick and Raine to diffuse a situation that sounded like it was about to get ugly.

"Hi, I'm Anna Jackson. Mrs. Garvey, right?"

Nick blew an audible sigh of relief.

"I'm the executive news editor. Why don't we go to a conference room and discuss this there? I'm sure there's a logical explanation to all this."

Anna led Nick and Raine to a modest-sized conference room, but before entering, Nick took Anna aside and spoke with her in undertones. Anna turned to Raine and said, "Nick would like to speak with you privately. If you want me to join you any time, pick up the phone in the room. My extension's on the list."

Saying nothing, Raine walked inside the windowless space and sat as far away from Nick as possible.

"I wrote those articles back in 1970 at a small daily paper in Philly," he began. "*The Tribune* will not run any story about that fire or tie your husband with it."

"And I'm supposed to believe you?"

"Ask Anna," Nick challenged as he sat down. "This is all on me. My own time, and I spent the better part of this year piecing together what happened because I felt your husband had a story that even you knew nothing about. Something about Peter Garvey seemed vaguely familiar, and it bothered me that I couldn't complete the picture. I tried to reach out to you, but you wouldn't talk to me, so I had to do the research independently, using other avenues."

"Nick, you're a rat. You thrive on scandal. You would twist untruths to make headlines."

"I don't care what you believe, but that boy whose mother died in the fire was your husband, Raine."

He studied her expression, and something told him she believed him. But she mistrusted his intentions.

"How can you know that for a fact? Peter Garvey is not an uncommon name."

"The boy in the story was taken into custody by his grandparents, who lived in Radnor, Pennsylvania. You knew Peter came from the Main Line, didn't you?"

This time, Raine looked away.

"Not close enough for you? His grandparents' names were Ed and Lila Van Rostum. Garvey's public bio reveals that he's from the Main Line, has no parents, and was raised by his maternal grandparents. The Van Rostums. He graduated from Valley Forge Prep, then NYU, then Wharton. It matches what you know, right?

She remained silent, tight-lipped, and deep in thought.

"I also know about the paternity suit..." Nick knew he'd hit a nerve, and it struck home because before he could say any more, Raine stood up and headed for the elevator.

"Wait..." Nick couldn't afford to lose her again. "I'm coming with you."

He quickly grabbed his coat and charged after her. But he'd just missed the elevator she got on. He painfully waited for the next one, praying there would be time to catch up to her.

She was walking through the revolving doors when Nick reached the ground floor. He yelled, *"Raine! Raine!"*

Dammit.

Nick ran after her to the street as she headed toward her waiting limo.

"Raine!" he roared above the din of traffic, loud enough to ensure she would stop and turn around.

"There is no child!"

CHAPTER 55

Peter

OCTOBER 1998
NEW YORK, NEW YORK

He had to see her. She was just misguided in filing that lawsuit. Some seedy lawyer must have put her up to it, using fraudulent DNA testing, and if he didn't straighten it out with her in person, he knew his lawyers would crucify her in court. That was the last thing he wanted to do for the woman who'd mercifully helped him when he suffered an MS flare-up in the middle of Washington Square Park.

It was summer last year when the numbness started on his right calf, buckling his knees and making him fall helplessly while rank homeless vagrants stood around and watched. And then she came to his rescue. She had helped him up, let him use her as a crutch as they both ambled to the nearby Washington Square Hotel at the edge of the park and checked into a room, thinking he could ride out his symptoms where no one would know.

He remembered her mass of dark curls, heavily made-up eyes, and blood-red lips. He didn't think she was a hooker, only a nice ordinary working woman who was on her way home from her job and played the Good Samaritan.

She'd followed him to the room, wanting to make sure he was going to be okay because he'd begged her not to call the police or 9-1-1 or any doctor.

"Don't worry," he'd said. "This goes away. I'll pay you... to thank you."

Between his quivering fingers, he opened his billfold and handed her all the cash he had—a thousand dollars.

"That's all I have. If you need more, let me know." He remembered handing her his card, telling her she could call anytime for help.

She'd tried to decline, but he was too weak to argue.

He had fallen asleep while she was still in the room with him but was gone when he awoke. She didn't steal anything. But she took the money he had given her.

She should have called him, Peter thought.

He rapped softly against the apartment's dirty, paint-chipped metal door of one of the housing projects just south of Alphabet City. When she opened it, he heard her gasp, eyes wide in shock and panicked.

"I can't see you. You have to talk to my attorney," she said, keeping her eyes away from his, pushing the door shut, but Peter stopped her.

"Maria, I need to talk to you," he pleaded. "I'm not here to harass you. I haven't forgotten how kind you were to me. But you need to hear me out. This lawsuit you've filed will ruin your life. I'd rather help you if you need money."

Peter heard her sigh, and after a few minutes, she stepped outside, closing the door behind her.

They headed away, silently plodding through the darkening streets of the seedy Lower East Side.

Peter wondered what she was thinking, her face expressionless, her stride not breaking.

"I don't know what you and your lawyer have cooked up, but you can't win. Not only will my DNA disprove your claim, but it's biologically impossible for me to have children because I have multiple sclerosis. That day you rescued me was a flare-up of my disease. And it's getting worse. I don't have long to live," he said to her, mist curling from his breath as they continued walking west along Delancey Street.

"Fraud is a criminal offense. If the court discovers you've filed a fraudulent claim, you won't just lose. You would go to jail. You and your lawyer."

"Shit," she finally mumbled.

Maria stopped and broke down.

Peter shoved his hands in his pockets and sucked in a breath. He handed her his handkerchief when she started wiping her eyes and nose with her coat sleeve.

"I was already pregnant that day I saw you fall. A pregnancy mistake. I was raped." Maria sniffled, lowering her eyes in shame. "I didn't want to do it. The lawsuit. The cash you gave me... I was grateful for that. It was enough for me to get an abortion."

Peter listened as they continued their walk along Delancey for a few more blocks until they reached Allen Street, just at the perimeter of Chinatown. Already, the air wafted with sesame oil and stir-frying.

"And then everything went wrong."

She was furiously dabbing the tears away again with his handkerchief. "I don't know what happened. All of a sudden, I was transported by an ambulance to the E.R. They were hooking me up to all these machines, poking everywhere with needles. There was a lot of blood. I thought I was going to die. I was so scared, Mr. Garvey," she wailed.

They crossed the intersection and settled on a bench on the center divider, where, in the shadows, they could talk without anyone noticing—not that anyone in New York paid attention.

"It's the hospital bills, Mr. Garvey. I owe over one hundred thousand dollars and have already been sent to collections. I lost my job after taking too much time off to recover, but now I can't get a job with my credit in the toilet. I was a teller at Astoria Savings, and no bank would hire anyone with bad credit. Even if I got work, they would only take the money away to pay the debt."

She'd stopped sobbing and started fidgeting with the hanky.

"I didn't know what to do. I went to an attorney to sue the clinic. But somehow, when I told him how I got the money for the abortion, he said I should file a paternity suit because I would get more money from you than the clinic that did my abortion. The lawyer said that he could get records of our stay at the hotel since we were together and that he could get DNA proof, and no one would bother checking because you would settle out of court to keep it quiet. God, that was so stupid. But I didn't know what else to do."

Peter shook his head. A backstreet operation that did abortions for a thousand bucks. A sleazy attorney who thought to make a quick buck from a monied dude who wouldn't want the media to know and would, therefore, settle quickly and quietly—because Peter was running for office. And after her attorney's fee, she'd get nowhere near enough to pay her debt. Peter lamented the state of a society full of predators who preyed on the less fortunate—the desperate.

Maria looked away from him. She was just someone who'd made bad decisions, misguided and desperate.

"Listen. I promised I'd help you. I'll pay off the hospital bills and give you a cash settlement—enough to buy a place away from the projects and maybe go to school. And I'll call somebody who can give you a job. You're going to withdraw your lawsuit and fire your attorney. He's bad news all around. Stay away from him. You'll have to sign a sworn statement not to disclose the settlement as part of the deal. You can't talk to anyone about it except my lawyers."

Maria nodded in defeat. She had no choice, and what Peter was offering was a heaven-sent miracle.

"I don't know how I can thank you. You are so nice. And I'm sorry. I hate being so helpless."

Maria returned Peter his hanky when he said, "Not as helpless as me."

Luke

NOVEMBER 1998
NEW YORK, NEW YORK

Luke trudged along Mahogany Row toward the elder part-ner's office for an emergency meeting. He hated being here because it was so staid. So formal. So... corporate. And he was underdressed with his NYU hoodie, jeans, and sneakers. He couldn't imagine what the damn emergency was this time.

Luke entered Jim's office and joined him at the small conference table. Peter walked in and dropped a pile of legal documents on the table with a thud.

"I wanted you guys to know about this," Peter began but kept pacing.

"What is it?" Jim asked, picking up one of two batches of documents. Luke could tell they were lawsuit documents from the first page with the New York Justice Department logo and seal. Jim hadn't bothered reading all of it when he handed them to Luke.

"Is it true?" Jim asked while Luke skimmed the pages. He didn't need to read it closely to know what it was about.

"Hell, no," Peter responded firmly.

"I don't understand," Luke said, flipping the pages back and forth. "You have two things here. The lawsuit and the settlement. This says you settled it out of court. This is not a 'go away' settlement either, Peter."

The more Luke read the settlement, the lower his jaw dropped.

"Three hundred thousand in cash and a million in a trust? And you're not the father?" He looked up at him, raising his glasses. "Are you fucking insane? If you're not guilty, this settlement says otherwise."

"Trust me on this. I called you both in because it named S&Y as a co-defendant. I made sure the suit dismissed the agency of liability, and the settlements were all from my personal accounts," Peter said, waving his hand impatiently.

"How's this going to affect your political campaign?" Jim was more pragmatic and less concerned about the incident itself.

"It won't," Peter said confidently. "I had it sealed."

"Wait, what exactly happened anyway?" Luke asked incredulously.

Peter shook his head. "I'm not going to go into the details, Luke. It doesn't matter. There is no child, and that's all you need to know."

Jim seemed satisfied with Peter's response and didn't care to know more.

"Thanks for trusting me, Jim," Peter replied, glaring at Luke.

Luke snorted, shaking his head. Leave it to Jim to *not* worry about the fact that Peter might have been fucking around. The more he thought about it, the more he believed Peter was guilty as hell and the angrier he got. And, *Oh my God. Raine!* This would surely break her heart.

Peter grabbed the documents and went next door to his office. Luke followed, shutting the door behind him.

"So, were you intimate with this woman?" Luke started.

Peter glared at Luke.

"None of your fucking business, Luke," Peter spat out in disgust.

"You know, because you're still my friend, I'll give you the benefit of the doubt that you weren't fucking around. Either way, you'll have to tell Raine about this lawsuit and your insane settlement offer and then explain that you don't have a bastard child out there."

Luke felt Peter was hiding something, not just his indiscretions. His health, for one thing, was evident to everyone in the office, with whispers and speculation brewing. Cancer? AIDS? But Peter had not breathed a word. Now this?

"Peter, talk to me," he begged. "This is Raine we're talking about. You can't do this to her. It'll kill her if you don't say anything and she finds out. And she will find out. Eventually."

Peter walked over to his office door and opened it, gesturing for Luke to leave. There was nothing more to say on the subject. Case closed.

CHAPTER 56

Peter

DECEMBER 1998
NEW YORK, NEW YORK

Jordan wouldn't look Peter in the eye.

Sitting across the polished cherrywood desk, Peter looked at his former high school buddy struggling to keep his expression neutral.

"Peter, I'm sorry. But fulminate multiple sclerosis is the worst type," Jordan said. "It's the same type of MS your mother had. I don't know if you've experienced more than the one flareup you mentioned, but your MRI shows even more scarring than last summer. Best case scenario? Five years."

The flare-ups were more frequent. Soon, he wouldn't be able to hide it from Raine. His body was failing, and eventually, he would be trapped in it—paralyzed, blind, unable to speak. He hoped his heart would give out before too long for her sake.

Peter didn't respond. Instead, he ran his fingers through his hair, which had once been soft and blond and was now wiry and thinning with streaks of gray.

They'd tried—months of testing, X-rays, and MRIs—leaving no stone unturned, hoping the results would prove wrong. Jordan had given the slightest hope for remission. But once the results came in, Peter knew, and Jordan could see with his eyes.

"And worst case?" Peter asked.

"A year? We don't know. But you've always been in excellent health. You may have a good chance of going for five years—maybe more. The downside is that it will progressively impair your mobility. I won't lie to you. Campaigning for office is out of the question.

"Meanwhile, there are new drug therapies we can start you on to manage your symptoms. Slow the progression," he added, trying to find something encouraging after the devastating news he had to deliver.

Yes, Peter knew about the research. Dammit, his wife, worked on the research for the MS Society, of which Jordan was the executive director. They had worked together in the planning of the database.

He had already started Peter on other drugs, which had miserable side effects. Baclofen made sleep difficult, while Hydroxyzine, meant to counter the sleeplessness, knocked him out cold, which had him oversleeping this morning. *Oversleeping, for God's sake!* When had he ever done that?

"What about Forenza? I hear it's been FDA approved," Peter asked.

"Forenza's not going to help you—not with Fulminate MS. I'll get you started on Copaxone shots. I have several patients on this medication, and they seem to be doing very well with it. It's not interferon. You shouldn't get any flu-like symptoms. Several of my patients have reported a marked reduction in flare-ups," Jordan said.

When Peter walked out of the building, he squinted against the sun reflecting against the high-rises on Park Avenue. A strong breeze from the East River blustered down the sidewalks, stinging his cheeks. Carty was nowhere in sight, probably stuck in traffic. He rummaged through his coat pocket for his cell phone, only to realize he'd left it inside his briefcase in the car.

Trudging along the gridlocked avenue, he allowed himself to recall the fire that claimed his mother's life. The faulty wiring had sparked the blaze, but her cause of death read "fulminate multiple sclerosis" on the certificate. In his mind, however, the real cause of death was his negligence. Had he been awake, he'd have put out the fire before it raged out of control. He blinked back the tears—he had let both his parents down and refused to forgive himself.

He thought of Raine and cringed to imagine her by his side, watching him turn into a crippled, useless mass, her young life wasted in servitude to be with him till he died.

Five years—if he was lucky.

As soon as he entered the agency, he felt relief. He spotted Rosemary standing by the doorway of his office, ready to give him a rundown of the earlier morning's events.

"Mrs. Coyne called a dozen times already," said Rosemary.

"I thought Raine was supposed to take care of it?" Peter asked.

"Mrs. Coyne said she wanted to speak with *you*, Mr. Garvey," Rosemary said. "And Angel Velasco called to ask if you can attend the World Gymnastics Conference next summer in Atlanta."

"Send Angel's call to Raine. Send everything that has to do with the accounts to my wife. She'll know what to do," he said dismissively.

Rosemary made her notes while following him inside his office.

"The first quarterly partners' meeting next month is all set," she said, reading off her notes when Raine barged in unannounced, interrupting their conversation. They both stared at her as she excitedly propped the Read Aloud and his campaign posters on the windowsill.

He should have been annoyed, but after the morning he had, he didn't have the heart to dampen her exuberance.

"What do you think?" Raine beamed. "Luke's a genius. I gave him my vision, and he came up with this. See the light blue single brushstroke silhouette of a mother reading to a child? That's the brand's logo."

Her finger traced the brush stroke.

Every night, read them a story, read the tagline in bold serifs.

"And then these are your campaign posters."

He studied the photo shoot results with him in a living room, reading a storybook with a child on his lap.

Championing future generations. Garvey for Senate.

It wounded him to see the image of the child on his lap. That should have been their child—his and Raine's. But the reality was that the Garveys would have no future generations. His family line would die with him.

Peter looked away. It had hurt too much to think about what could have been. When his intercom buzzed, he returned to his desk to pick up his phone. He quickly glanced at his wife, steeling himself of emotion.

"That will do," he said, dismissing her.

"I'll take the call, Rosemary," he said over the speaker, watching his wife's crestfallen face as she picked up the posters and walked out the door.

By the time Peter finished his round of meetings, it was close to five p.m. He had two hours to go before the cameras. With the phone tucked between his ear and shoulder, Peter opened his briefcase, removed the medications Jordan had given him this morning, and shoved them deep inside the mini bar fridge in his office, where no one was likely to see them.

"I cleaned out your e-mail, but there are five high-priority items I think you should look at," Rosemary said. "And Rick Wolcott called. He said it was urgent and wanted you to call before you left for Read Aloud tonight."

Rick Wolcott, his campaign manager, was calling about something urgent before tonight's press conference, and it didn't sound good.

"Now what?" he muttered. "Rosemary, you go on. I'll be all right."

"Hey, Rick," Peter said when his manager picked up.

Suddenly, he could feel his face flushing, but he pushed on. "About tonight..."

He fell silent, listening to Wolcott. As his eyes widened with fright, Peter walked to his office door to close it.

"What? What are you talking about?"

Sweat broke on his forehead. Had someone turned up the heat? He listened to his campaign manager over the phone while he loosened his tie slightly and unbuttoned his collar. He swallowed hard and breathed deeply. He combed his hair back with his fingers to calm his nerves. He felt a flare-up coming on and regretted that shot of scotch Jim insisted on when they met earlier to toast a new account. His medication specifically warned against consuming alcohol while on it.

"Are you serious?" Peter's eyes widened. "Wait...that can't be. Who the hell told you that?"

He started panting as if he'd run a marathon. Tingling started on his arm.

"What private investigator? You had me investigated? Why?"

He was getting angry, and soon, he was gasping for breath. He needed water. He reached for a bottle from his fridge and guzzled it.

Breathe. He slowly willed his heart rate to slow and the tingling to calm down.

"Rick, keep the damn thing out of the press. I don't care how you do it."

His hand began quivering, causing him to drop the receiver. He fell to the carpet as he felt weakness in his legs. Then, one of his eyes started twitching. His vision doubled.

He groped his way toward the air conditioning unit, fumbling for the knobs to turn it on high. When he felt the cold air blast through the vents, cooling his clammy forehead, his breathing eased.

"Peter, are you listening to me? This paternity suit is public court record. We can't keep it out of the press."

He heard Rick's voice over the receiver lying on the floor a few feet away, too far for him to reach it. "Peter, are you there?"

He heard a click. Rick had hung up.

Let it pass. Get to someplace that's cooler. Splash water on your face.

Peter recalled Jordan's advice. He stayed by the vents for a while longer. The settlement was sealed, but the suit would remain in the public domain. And if his manager had unearthed it, then, yes, the press surely would find out. The publicity would be insane.

It wouldn't matter if he announced his withdrawal because of his illness, which was what his plan was for tonight. The press wouldn't believe it.

Luke was right. Raine would find out in the worst possible way. How the hell was he going to explain this to her?

Still on the floor, Peter covered his face. He'd tried so hard to make everything perfect for her for so long. He was tired now and missed his parents.

Peter stood to check his legs, and when he'd found them steady, he walked back to the mini bar, took out another bottled water, and poured it over his head over the sink in his executive washroom. He styled his hair back, checking his reflection in the mirror. He returned to his desk, picked up the phone off the floor, and called the firm's general counsel, Marc Heywood.

Marc would know what to do. He'd figure out a way to bury the demand suit. At this point, he no longer cared about the press finding out. He had to find a way to keep it from his wife.

That was when he saw her standing by the doorway.

"Heywood, come see me in about ten," he said over the phone, then hung up.

He ushered Raine in, closing the door behind her, then taking her in his arms. She gasped in surprise, dropping her briefcase. He held her tightly, longing for the connection they once had. How long had it been since they made love? The memory of their last time together, the rhythm of their bodies in sync, was distant and painful. His disease had taken that away, leaving him numb.

"Are you alright?" she finally asked in a barely audible whisper, caressing his damp hair and sensing his melancholy.

She was feeling his sadness because he would have to leave her much too soon. But better while she was still young. If there were an afterlife, he'd ensure she would never be alone. Someone out there would be able to give her the love that he couldn't provide—the happiness she deserved.

He nodded in response, then bent to give her what he knew would be his last kiss. The kiss lasted only a fleeting moment, his lips barely touching hers, and then he slowly released her.

"What time are you leaving," she asked, feeling somewhat bemused.

"Soon." He smiled back.

"Why don't I wait for you? Then we can leave together. Make an appearance together?"

"No, have Carty take you to the library, and I'll meet you there."

She was about to object, but Peter cut her off. He gave her a cold, distant stare.

"Don't argue with me, Raine," he snapped. "I've got way too much to do before I have to leave. On the other hand, *you* need to be there. Now go."

When Peter opened the door, Heywood was waiting outside.

"Come on in, Marc. Raine was just leaving."

He watched his wife walk away, her eyes mirroring his own disappointment. It would be the last time she would see him alive.

CHAPTER 57

Raine

DECEMBER 2000
NEW YORK, NEW YORK

Today, my head exploded.

I had gone from a commercial redeye that landed at 6 a.m. to Nick dropping several bombshells about Peter's past. After we parted, I called Vivienne to meet me at the bistro on the ground floor of our office building. ASAP.

Despite my mind reeling from shocking information overload, I had one immediate priority—feeding the ravenous peanut-sized beast growing inside me. According to my child, that PBJ I had for breakfast was now a distant memory.

Vivienne sat across from me, reading Nick's articles while I devoured a turkey club and shoveled freshly fried hand-cut potato chips in my mouth by the handful.

"Jesus, Nish! This is a lot to process," she said, putting down the articles and removing her reading glasses. "Was this really Peter?"

"That's why I asked you to meet me," I said, washing down my food with an herbal iced tea.

Vivienne placed a Manila envelope on the table, followed by a small gift bag with colorful balloons and a Happy Birthday printed on it.

"Sorry," she said. "That was the only bag Rosemary could find for me to use, and I didn't want to carry the drugs in my hand since they're rather personal."

"Thank you," I said, shaking off crumbs from my hands.

I picked up the envelope first and pulled out the documents it held—the paternity suit filed against Peter and the company and the settlement terms negotiated.

When Nick discovered the paternity suit, he tracked down the plaintiff. Somehow, with his charm and savvy, he convinced her to share her story despite the strict confidentiality of the settlement. Afterall, *The Trib* wouldn't run any story that would have violated court orders and privacy laws.

"I should have asked Marc Heywood about this suit earlier this year when I found out about it. I hadn't considered that since it involved the company, he'd have a copy," I said, shaking my head at my lack of forethought.

The plaintiff's statement that there was no child and her withdrawal of the suit was proof enough that Nick wasn't lying.

"You were not in the right headspace then," Vivienne said.

"Yeah." I scowled at the memory. Jim dropped that bomb on me out of spite because I wouldn't fuck him.

I slipped the suit papers back into the envelope and then pulled out the contents of the gift bag—Peter's medications—the ones I discovered in his refrigerator on my first day back after his funeral.

"I can't believe I didn't connect the dots when I saw Jordan's name as the prescribing physician and his office in Montclair," I said, studying the box again. "I mean, I worked with him on the MS project. He was the client. I could have saved myself nearly two years of heartache and regret had I contacted him when I first found Peter's medications. Peter's mother had MS, and according to Nick, the woman who filed the suit also knew about it. I'll contact Jordan to confirm this, although I have a feeling..."

I shook my head, shoving the drugs back in the bag. Vivienne reached for my hand.

"Nish, it's in the past. Leave it there."

"Right." I took a deep breath. "By the way, did you know anything about Jim's estate attempting to sue Glory for wrongful death? Nick mentioned it to me. How he gets his news boggles my mind."

Vivienne nodded. "Barton called and asked me if I had seen Jim's autopsy report, and when he hinted something about you causing Jim's penile injury, I laughed so hard. My sides were splitting. I faxed him a copy of the police report you filed. He called me back so fast and said, 'This conversation never happened.'"

"Yeah, that's what Nick told me as well. That man, if nothing, is thorough, and I badly misjudged him. He is one hell of a reporter," I remarked in admiration.

"One of the heirs hoped to squeeze a liability settlement from the agency's insurance because he knew the agreed sale price of Jim's shares was nowhere near market value," Vivienne explained.

"I guess the press was Barton's way of putting the screws on us if we were to fight it. And as always, you were right when you said this could come back to bite me. I'm glad you insisted on me filing the police report," I said, pursing my lips.

"When we filed it, Jim hadn't died yet. I was more worried about his revenge. He could have fired you, destroyed your reputation, and caused you to lose all your holdings. This thing from Barton, however, I had not expected. It was mind-boggling."

"Yeah, the stupidity of it all."

Vivienne rolled her eyes in agreement.

"It was greed. You didn't know this, but Jim's wanted you ever since he met you when you married Peter. Jim was so jealous of Peter. I sometimes wonder if Peter hadn't killed himself, the old man might have had him assassinated. It was convenient for him when he was widowed and then Peter died. He wanted you, your wealth, and world domination."

"How did you know?"

"Luke."

I was stunned by that revelation. I hadn't thought about Luke in a while. I missed him as my dearest friend and closest ally. I recalled his warning me about Jim, and I hadn't listened. Instead, I pushed Luke away. I couldn't understand why he'd kept Peter's infidelity from me, that he could choose his loyalty to Peter over being honest with me. But now, he deserved to hear Peter's truth and nothing but my full pardon.

"Come upstairs. He'd love to see you," Vivienne pleaded. There was something in her eyes and voice that told me this was important to her. Vivienne had done so much for me, how could I deny her this request?

I smiled and nodded. "And I would love to see him."

CHAPTER 58

Ron

DECEMBER 2000
NEW YORK, NEW YORK

After shoveling the driveway of last night's snowfall, Ron walked back to the house for another cup of coffee. Pulling off his winter hat and gloves, he heard his cell phone jangle inside his pocket.

Not recognizing the 2-1-3 area code, he answered cautiously.

"Hello?"

"Hi, Ron," said a gentle voice he'd recognize anywhere. Raine's. He closed his eyes and released a deep sigh of relief, needing to lean against the kitchen counter to keep him from falling to his knees.

"Raine! Oh my God! It's so good to hear your voice. How are you, *mo chroí?*" he exclaimed in one breath, calling her sweetheart in Gaelic.

"I've missed you," she said softly.

"Not as much as I've missed you." He started to blink back tears, glad she couldn't see him ready to lose it, but his sniffle gave him away.

"Hey, are you crying?" Her voice was like honey dripping from the comb.

Who me, cry? Oh yeah. Every night. Jesus! If Ed and Fritzso knew that I cried myself to sleep over you all this time, they'd have kicked the shit out of me from here to Michigan.

Ron wondered when he'd developed such a low threshold for tears. No one ever made him cry this badly—until Raine.

"No," he lied, tearing off a paper towel to blot his face as his tears flowed freely. He was hopeless. Ron knew he would do anything to have her back in his life. If he had to suck it up and wear a tux to her fundraisers, so be it. If it meant the paparazzi hiding in bushes to take his picture unsuspectingly, bring it.

She was silent over the phone for a while, and then he heard strings from a guitar. He listened to her sing Journey's "Don't Stop Believin'."

He might hate the song, but her voice clutched his heart. His vision was right. She did play guitar.

"Raine, sweetie, that was so beautiful, but did you have to sing *that* song?" Then, he laughed through his sniffles. They were happy tears, he told himself.

She laughed too.

"I brought my guitar back with me from LA. I plan to play and sing a lot more from now on."

"You're back?"

"In New York," was all she said, and then she was silent.

Ron waited for her to say more. He wondered why she'd gone to the city instead of back to Durham. To him. Her sabbatical wasn't supposed to end until New Year's Eve.

As if reading his thoughts, she said, "I have some urgent matters to take care of right now. But I'll come home, my love."

He felt his heart soar. "When?"

"Soon as I resolve some things here."

"Alright, how about I take the train to see you then? I got my doctorate. That's done and classes end in a couple of weeks."

"Woohoo! Congratulations, Dr. Mitchell. When I return, we'll have a big celebration," she cheered. Ron noticed how she'd avoided his question.

"How about we celebrate in New York? Spend Christmas together?"

"No, Ron. I won't have time. Besides, you're going to hate being here."

"How could I hate it when you're there?" He was baffled by her answer. It didn't sound like she'd wanted him around.

"Not now, please," she pleaded. But he didn't understand. *Why the hell not?*

She'd said she was coming home but didn't want him to join her in New York. That made no sense. *What was going on?*

Ron began pacing in frustration.

"Love, it's been so hard without you. I don't know how much longer I can hold on before I go insane. Please, let me come see you," he pleaded.

And then she crooned the song's refrain again. "Don't stop believing..."

Ron groaned. "I love you, Raine. I always will. And I'll wait forever. I won't ever stop believing. Sing some other song, please?"

She laughed. "Good. Won't be long, I promise. Once I settle some things, I'll call and tell you all about it."

He hesitatingly let her go, waiting for her to hang up first. He should have felt better after hearing from her. Instead, he felt unsettled. She was keeping something from him, and he sensed it—strongly.

Ron decided he was done sitting around and waiting. He would figure out something. If he had to kidnap her again, then so be it. As he headed for the shower, his cell phone rang again.

"Dr. Mitchell?" It was a man's voice he didn't recognize. It felt weird to hear someone address him as "doctor."

"Yes, this is Ron Mitchell."

"This is Norm Alverson, the dean of environmental sciences at Columbia University. I read your dissertation, and I am greatly impressed with your work. I was wondering if you'd like to come down and talk to us about an opportunity you might be interested in?"

Well, if the mountain won't come to Mohammed, then Mohammed will have to go to New York. Thank you, Leann, Magda, and Bobbie.

CHAPTER 59

Raine

"*The Rise and Fall of Peter Garvey?*"

Nick raised a brow, giving me a dubious look, wondering if I was being facetious on purpose.

"The title has a bestseller ring to it, don't you think?" I was dead serious when I suggested that Nick write a book about Peter.

I had asked him to meet me again at the Starbucks in Hell's Kitchen, where we last spoke.

"It's not for me to write your husband's story, Raine. It's yours." Nick held my gaze in all seriousness. His response caught me by surprise.

I shook my head. "No, you were the one who went in search of answers. You were there to witness his tragedy."

I mentioned that he should also write a fiction novel about the Yorks, starting with their estate in Jardin Malanga and the slaves they owned to work the plantation. Imagine the controversy that would emerge. It would have all the elements of a bestseller—murder mystery, greed, and intrigue.

He laughed at my suggestion. "Raine, I'm a journalist. You're the one with the bigger imagination. Ever thought about writing fiction?"

"Maybe," I replied honestly. I had attended an elective class in creative writing while at UCLA and loved it. Even got a short story published in their prestigious literary magazine. I remember planning to write more short stories and maybe attempt a fiction novel. Why had I forgotten about that aspiration?

"By the way, this boyfriend of yours in New Hampshire might need protecting from the vicious press who'll headline him as a gold digger."

I gasped. "What are you talking about? How did you even know?"

Nick pulled out a copy of *The Talebearer*, flipped the pages toward the back, and showed me a picture of Ron and me taken last September. I should have been mortified. Instead, I laughed when I saw that the publication had identified Ron as Robin Wilson. Oh God, Vivienne would get a kick out of this.

"He didn't think it was funny when I showed it to him," Nick replied, unaware of the private joke I shared with my best friend.

"Wait, when did you see him?"

"Just after Thanksgiving, I'd been trying to find you and was surprised to learn where you'd been hiding."

"I wouldn't worry about tabloids thinking Ron's after my wealth because I won't be near as flush when all is said and done.

"What do you mean?" I saw Nick's eyes light up. "You got something juicy?"

I held up my hand, beseeching patience.

"Which brings me to why I wanted to meet with you today. First, can you tell me where Peter's parents are buried? I want to reinter his ashes with them. In return, and for everything you've done to find the truth about Peter, I'll give you the exclusive scoop on some really *big* news happening at Glory and what I'm about to do with all of Peter's money. I promise this one is page-one-centerpiece worthy."

CHAPTER 60

Raine

DECEMBER 2000
NEW YORK, NEW YORK

"Raine, *mo chroí.*"

I jerked my head to look in the direction of the voice that addressed me in Gaelic. I would recognize that voice anywhere. And...*What. The. Fuck?*

Vivienne and I were in her office reviewing our slide presentation for this morning's board meeting. I was perched on the desk, peering into her laptop, and when I saw Ron standing in the doorway, looking lost and perhaps embarrassed but sheepishly hopeful that I'd be happy to see him.

I wasn't. Damn it! I was supposed to surprise him, not the other way around. I'd planned to fly up to Portsmouth right after the board meeting. Captain Chris was already waiting for me at Teterboro.

Vivienne excused herself, leaving us alone. Ron laid his backpack on a nearby chair, shoving his hands into his pockets. God, he looked even sexier than the last time I saw him. He was dressed in Ivy League fashion—tan khakis, an English tweed jacket with leather elbow patches, a white shirt, and... a tie? *Uh...why?*

I should have been thrilled to see him. Instead, I stayed perched on the desk, deliberately crossing my legs and hiking up my skirt to mid-thigh.

"What are you doing here?" I asked, crossing my arms.

"Uhm, a job interview."

Ron

DECEMBER 2000
NEW YORK, NEW YORK

"Columbia."

Ron quickly tried to explain his unanticipated arrival. From the time he stepped into the lobby of the advertising behemoth's imposing offices to walking down the deep plush carpeting of the executive wing, Ron felt as if he'd walked into Dali's painting, *The Persistence of Time,* with clocks melting around him. It was surreal.

And now he stood before her, taking in her seductive pose, sitting on a desk, legs clad in shimmery gray stockings tucked into long black leather boots. She had them crossed, which hiked her dress to near scandalous levels, and... He was speechless for a moment. He really should close his mouth and focus on what he had planned to say when he saw her.

"I interviewed with Columbia," he started, clearing his throat, willing himself not to stutter. "Great opportunity. It's an assistant deanship, and I'd be heading up their new environmental research center. Comes with an amazingly huge apartment in Morningside Heights. Has a bay window overlooking the Hudson. You can see the George Washington Bridge in the distance. They made a mind-blowing offer."

Columbia had been his last chance to convince her he was willing to move to New York so she could stay as CEO of Glory. He would proudly stand by her side, his arm possessively around her. And he wouldn't even care if a dozen lightbulbs flashed on them. He would do it.

"Raine, I know you've been trying to figure out how we could be together. With this job, I can live here. Be with you. You won't have to give up what you have because I know this is important to you," he explained.

"What? No!"

Did she say no? Ron suddenly felt fear spiraling through him.

He walked toward her, looked into her eyes, and tried to read her but couldn't. Where was his magic when he needed it? Where were the fae? He felt the waterworks coming on. *Dear God, do not make me cry.*

"Raine, please, I just want to be with you. Be near you. I'd do anything, give up everything."

Then he went down—not on one knee but on both—and laid his hands on her lap. He looked straight at her, swallowed hard, and said, "I came to ask you to marry me. Will you?"

With his heart banging in his chest, he waited for her to reply.

"What? Crap! No..."

Her words hit him like a punch to the gut. Ron swallowed hard and clenched his jaw, fighting against the rising panic and the tears that were about to flow. He dropped his head, pressing his forehead against her knees to keep her from seeing how pathetic he'd become.

"Wait... Ron. You've got this all wrong."

She shoved his hands away, leaped off the table, and lunged into him.

"You idiot," she said, slapping his chest. "I love you. What were you thinking? Do I have to sing 'Don't Stop Believin' again?'"

He nearly tripped over himself when she'd flown into him. All he heard was 'idiot' and 'I love you.' He lifted her off her feet, twirled her around, and kissed her senseless. He'd been waiting for her to say those three words for so long that he lost it and let the tears flow.

Then he abruptly pulled away because he heard something—felt *something*—strange and wonderful. He leaned into her forehead again to listen.

It was deep inside her. This was the secret she'd withheld from him.

Woosh-thump-woosh-thump-woosh-thump.

He dared ask, "Raine, I can hear another heart beating next to yours. A tiny one. Are you..."

"Yes, I'm sorry. I should never have doubted you," she babbled, wiping his wet face, then hers. "I know we've only been together for a short time... I didn't mean to get pregnant so soon. I should have been more careful. You know, go on the pill or something..."

"Raine, shut up," he said softly, drowning her mouth with another long, wet kiss, his hand resting on her belly. "How could you think I would be anything but ecstatic that you're pregnant with our child?"

He heard her sigh, resting her head on his shoulder, her breath warm against his neck.

"Before I forget," he said, pulling away while fishing in his pocket for something until he found it.

"Say yes?" he asked, offering her his grandmother's garnet ring.

"Oh my God, *yes!* Of course, yes." She placed her hand over her heart in awe, then threw her head back in unrestrained laughter, expressing her consummate joy as he slipped the ring on her finger.

"My grandmother wanted you to have this. It's ancient. Passed down through generations of MacKenzies."

"Ron, this is beautiful and so symbolic," she sighed, caressing the square-cut blood-red gem. "The highland uprising. The bloodshed."

"Yes, but now we are continuing with a new generation of highlanders," he said, touching her belly.

Slowly, he lowered himself to his knees until he was level with her womb and rested his ear against it, where only he, with his gift of *An Dà Shealladh,* could hear that swooshing heartbeat of his child and whispered, "Hello, Mackenzie. It's your Da."

CHAPTER 61

Ron

DECEMBER 2000 – CHRISTMAS MORNING
DURHAM, NEW HAMPSHIRE

O*h ye of little faith.*
The fae were scolding Ron because now, next to the Christmas tree adorned with paper ornaments and a string of twinkling miniature lights, he was lying naked with Raine asleep in his arms, maybe not on a plush rug, but on comforters and pillows strewn on the floor, just as he'd seen in his vision.

He rose gently so he wouldn't wake her and walked to the kitchen to brew her chamomile tea. The fireplace still had embers and kept the house toasty warm. In a little bit, he would goose it back up to a roaring flame as they celebrated their first Christmas together.

While waiting for the kettle to boil, Ron watched as his fiancée slept peacefully, his heart bursting with love. He remembered how he'd been in New York three days ago, walking into her office and seeing her dressed so sexily. He had tried to envision himself as her boyfriend—or husband. And it was tough. Even with the exciting job offer, he couldn't imagine working in a big, noisy city, away from the mountains, the river...his sailboat.

He shook his head and wondered how lucky he was that *she* didn't want that life either. She had wanted to come *home*— to this old house that was *theirs*. She'd even sold off her stake in Glory and then donated the proceeds to establish a foundation in Peter's name to support MS research.

"I won't be a billionaire anymore," she'd teased him as if he cared about her money.

She did this all for him. And when she'd told him that her new partners, Vivienne, Charlie, Luke, and even Vivienne's father, Stanley, who would become the newest major shareholder, all agreed to move the company headquarters to Portsmouth, it blew his mind.

Favorable tax climate, lower cost of living, and a better, healthier lifestyle for the staff with families. But that wasn't it entirely.

The fae. Yes, the three ladies had a lot to do with it.

"Good morning," she greeted, all throaty with sleep, stretching her naked, curvy form like a sleek female panther.

He handed her the mug of tea and kissed her after she'd taken a sip, tasting the fragrant herbs on her lips and tongue.

"Sleep well?" he asked, running his hand through her tangled bob.

"The best," she said, giving him a quick peck on the lips. "Why do you look like a child who's been up since four on Christmas morning and now can't wait to open presents?"

"Looks like Santa was here because two presents are under the tree. Wonder what they are?" he smiled.

"I want you to open yours first," she said, reaching for a small box and handing it to him. Feeling its weight, Ron shook it, trying to guess.

"This feels like a lump of coal," he laughed.

"Close," she laughed with him. "But not quite."

He tore the box open and saw a rock. But he knew it wasn't just any rock. He could feel its pulse when he picked it up.

"When I found out I was pregnant, I remembered what you'd told me, that if I was ever troubled or felt unsettled, I should find a rock and draw energy from it. To calm myself. So I drove out to the San Andreas fault. I figured the Earth couldn't be more alive than at an active fault line. So I hiked along the Pushawalla Trail. The place was deserted."

Ron's face was suddenly etched with concern.

"Oh, don't worry. I just hiked the five-mile trail and was mindful of the safety you've instilled in me—brought a big jug of water, wore loose clothing, and proper hiking boots. I knew I was carrying our precious cargo." She cupped his face gently and smiled at him.

"The place was throbbing, Ron. I'd never experienced anything like it. It hummed. I felt such clarity and peace. I was no longer afraid to love you. So I picked up this rock."

"Thank you. I'll keep it with me always," he whispered, kissing her forehead. He held the stone against the window light, noticed bits of garnet, and showed her.

"Best present ever. I'm glad you didn't give up on us," he said.

"As if I could," she teased, poking his side to tickle him. "We're fated, remember?"

He kissed her again, then reached under the tree for the other box wrapped in red.

"What's this?" she asked.

"Open it," he urged.

Raine ripped the paper and gasped as she unfurled a long woolen tartan sash with its striking combination of colors—blue, green, back, and white. Its pattern intersected lines and squares in a design that represented the heritage and tradition of the Clan MacKenzie.

"Oh, Ron, it's gorgeous," she said with breathless admiration, touching its softness to her cheek.

Ron took the sash from her, wound it around his wrist, and then wound it around hers.

While their hands were bound, he turned to her and recited his handfast vow. "Raine, I promise to love you without reserve, to take care of you, to be by your side, always to make you laugh, and if you're sad, I'll be there to wipe your tears. I'll forever be devoted to you and our child. For the rest of my life, I'm yours."

"Ron, thank you. That was beautiful. Thank you for my present. Thank you for loving me. For never letting go. For believing. Thank you for making me a mother and soon your wife. From now till whenever I promise it will always be us."

They kissed again, their lips lingering longer as if they hadn't just spent last night ravishing each other.

"Now that we're handfasted, we need to make it official with a wedding," he said, unbinding the tartan.

"I think I'm supposed to wear this at my wedding," she said, carefully rolling it up and putting it back in its box.

"When?" he asked, rising to toss another log in the fire and then goosing it up with the poker.

Raine lifted her brows. "When?"

"New Year's Eve," Ron said. He wasn't suggesting either.

"New Year's Eve? As in six days from now?" Raine blinked warily.

"My Catholic altar-boy conscience doesn't want our daughter to be gestating a day longer than she has to with unmarried parents."

"Seriously?" Raine rolled back in giggles. "Hmm...I don't recall any evidence of your 'altar-boy conscience' last night."

Ron reached for her fingers and kissed them.

"You can't be serious." Raine frowned.

"Oh, but I am," he said, pulling his face to touch her forehead and feel her thoughts. "What do you think? We can do this."

"Well, my parents are arriving in New York for New Year's Eve in a few days. This means you and I need to return to the city tomorrow—yikes! And my father wants to host a New Year's Eve party. I don't know if we can squeeze in a wedding on the same day, my love. Can you even get a license in such a short time? Will the courthouse be open? Jeez! I'm getting stressed out just thinking about it," she cried, rubbing her face.

Ron kissed her temple and quickly filled her with his chi to quiet her mind.

"Shh-shh... I've got this," he whispered.

He would call Raine's mother, and between them and their gifts of *An Dà Shealladh*, they would put together a small, intimate wedding on New Year's Eve—as their fae had willed it.

CHAPTER 62

DECEMBER 2000 - NEW YEAR'S EVE
NEW YORK, NEW YORK

"A proper Scottish wedding would nae be complete without at least one piper."

So said my mother, who had commandeered the wedding plans with the help of my Da, Vivienne, and Luke. And Ron, who'd kept his promise that I would have little to no involvement apart from showing up for a marriage license at city hall.

"You can put up your feet and eat strawberries all day," he declared, knowing I would do no such thing.

My mother's cousin, Margaret, whom I hadn't known existed until this week, was an accomplished piper. I'd never heard her play, but I trusted my mother implicitly. Finding Aunt Margaret, who happened to live in Greenwich Village, was fortuitous—or perhaps it was fate.

I still didn't know how we organized a wedding in less than a week. That Christmas Day, after we had opened our presents and had breakfast, we made a whirlwind of phone calls. I called my mother and Vivienne. Ron called his mother and sister.

When we called Jops and Rosie, they had been amid a noisy Christmas present-ripping frenzy with their two kids. Ed and Ginny were having a lazy morning in bed.

"You have two days to get a bag packed and leave with us on the private jet for New York," Ron had trumpeted to his friends.

He told a stunned Fritzso, who was with his mother in Michigan that he could hitch a ride on Stanley's private jet, which was picking up his mother and sister's family.

Jops had to do the most scrambling because the bar held an annual New Year's Eve bash, his biggest moneymaker of the year, and he needed to find someone to step in and take charge. Rosie snagged her parents to watch the kids.

Then, somehow, we managed to find them all hotel rooms despite the height of the holiday season.

Some people would spend lavishly on their weddings for a spectacle. Me? I spent it on our closest friends and family. The cost to shuttle them on a private jet and cover their hotel stays was enormous, but they were all worth it. And in turn, they pitched in, offering resources and services. Rosemary turned out to have a creative flair for event planning. With my apartment as the wedding venue, she'd organized all the decorations and even designated a suitable space for a DJ and a small dance floor in a corner of my apartment. Good old Carty cobbled together a group of Long Island Scottish friends who weren't booked for New Year's Eve to provide *craic*.

Of course, my father handled the catering, although I insisted that he not do any cooking. I hadn't wanted him stressing out so soon after his stroke. It would all be a very simple (maybe even low-brow) Scottish fare with clapshot, black pudding, and oatcakes. But I was looking forward to the tipsy laird, a Scottish version of trifle with layers of sponge cake, whisky, custard, and fresh fruit, serving as our wedding cake. I couldn't wait to smash that mess on Ron's face.

The best part of my big day? Wearing my mother's wedding dress. The one she wore when she married my father in a civil ceremony at an LA courthouse. When I was ten, she let me play dress up and wear it. It was a simple ivory sheath dress with a flowing skirt, very much in the tradition of a Scottish wedding dress with the Clan MacDonald tartan as a sash around my waist. She'd even clasped the Celtic knot necklace around my small neck and put the crown of silk thistle and heather on my hair.

"Look how bonny ye look, Rainey. Ye'll be a braw bride when ye grow up, ma bairn," she'd said while we both stood in front of her long mirror, even if the dress had been too big at that time and the crown sat lopsided on my head.

This time, Vivienne was with me when I tried it on as a grown woman getting married in a couple of days.

"Oh God, Raine," she said, breathless and in awe.

This was the childhood dream I had of my wedding day. A dream I thought I had lost. Not this time.

Ron

DECEMBER 2000 - NEW YEAR'S EVE
NEW YORK, NEW YORK

He only had eyes for her when she walked toward him, Aunt Margaret's bagpipe wailing "Highland Cathedral." If Ed, Fritzso, and Jops hadn't been there making bets on how long before Ron started sniffling, he would have been one bawling mess when she entered the room dressed in her mother's wedding dress. She just took his breath away. No words could describe how stunning she looked.

Following the Catholic blessing of their marriage, they performed the Scottish tradition of drinking from a quaich, a two-handled cup symbolizing the sharing of their lives. Then, they reenacted their handfasting vows, as they had done that Christmas morning.

Afterward, she slipped off her mother's tartan while Ron replaced it with the MacKenzie tartan, the same one he gave her for Christmas, which matched the kilt he was wearing. She now belonged to him.

As the hours ticked toward the New Year countdown, everyone had gathered by the big expansive window facing south, with a perfect view of the Brooklyn Bridge, to witness the fireworks that would fly to welcome 2001.

But before it began, no one noticed Vivienne and Luke slip away except for Ron, who smiled knowingly.

Luke

DECEMBER 2000 - NEW YEAR'S EVE
NEW YORK, NEW YORK

"Come on, you've got to see this from up here."

Luke was coaxing Vivienne, who wasn't crazy about having to go outside in the frigid New Year's Eve air despite the clear evening, up the creepy staircase leading to the rooftop. Holding her hand, he carefully helped her navigate the short but narrow steel steps wearing stiletto-heeled shoes.

"We had a perfect view from inside the warmth of Raine's apartment," Vivienne whined. "They're going to miss us. Raine will put two and two together and guess that we're involved, you know. She's going to kill us because we haven't told her."

"That's why I brought you up here. So we can be alone."

"Luke, this is her wedding day. I don't want to take this away from her." Vivienne started to shiver, pulling her fur-lined coat tightly around her.

"You worry too much."

"Of course, I would. She's my best friend."

Luke pulled the collar of Vivienne's fur coat to her ears and whispered, "Babe...she knows."

Vivienne's eyes widened. *"She what???"*

"Now turn around. It's about to start," Luke said, turning Vivienne to face the Brooklyn Bridge.

"Oh, I am going to kill her. No, I'm going to kill you both."

"Shhh... Ten, nine, eight..." Luke stood behind Vivienne, whispering the countdown, his arms wrapped around her to keep her warm. And just when he reached one, the sky lit up with shards of fiery light shooting to the sky.

"Oh my God, this is amazing!" she exclaimed, finding herself speechless as the splendor of the pyrotechnic display continuously pierced the sky.

"Je t'aime de tout mon cœur, Vivienne," Luke whispered in her ear. *"Bonne année, ma cherie."*

"Bonne année, Luc," she whispered back, saying his name in French, then turned to him for a long, burning kiss that created its own fireworks between them.

"I love you too. But okay, darlin', this L.A. girl is freezing," she said, breaking away from him to head back downstairs. He stopped her and turned her around to face him.

On the darkened rooftop, with only their silhouettes carved against the fireworks that continued to blaze the skies, Luke got down on one knee.

CHAPTER 63

Raine

JANUARY 2001
NEW YORK, NEW YORK

T wo days after our wedding, Carty drove Ron and me to the Sunshine Cemetery in Levittown. It was the last thing I wanted to do to close out this chapter of my life—to move Peter's ashes and lay him to rest next to his parents.

I held his urn while I stood by the new granite monument with his name and dates—1954 - 1998. Ron stood behind me, his arms around my shoulders as if the strong winter wind might topple me any minute. I stood quietly and whispered my last words to Peter.

"I'd been angry with you, Peter, for leaving me the way you did. For hurting me so badly. I wondered why for so long. But it's okay now, sweetheart. What you did took a lot... And because of your courage, you left behind a legacy. I'll make sure it lives on forever through a foundation with your name. It will fund research for MS. I think you would have liked that so people with this disease won't have to suffer the way you did. The way your mom did.

"You know, there's a saying that first love never dies. You will always be that—my first love."

And then, very briefly, I was transported to the past, and I was nineteen again, feeling Peter's embrace the first time he held me. I would always know the feel of his arms. It was definitely, if not eerily, Peter who I felt. And then he was gone.

I set his urn by his headstone to finally bid him farewell, the mist from my breath curling into the breeze and hoping that wherever he was now, somewhere out there, he heard me.

Godspeed, Peter. Sleep now, my beloved.

Ron

JANUARY 2001

NEW YORK, NEW YORK

Ron's arms were wound tightly around Raine's shoulders when he saw Peter in the distance—not as an apparition but as a man. He doubted Raine could see him as she was deep in thought and prayer.

He knew Peter was here for Raine's final goodbye. He wished Raine could see him or at least feel his presence. That was when he saw Peter make a final request, and Ron needed only to blink in response despite knowing it would deplete him of his energy.

He closed his eyes and held on to Raine more tightly as Peter's spirit entered Ron.

It was over in a flash, but it was enough for Ron to stumble backward. He reached to grab onto the granite headstone to steady himself, drawing energy from it. Looking up in the distance, he saw Peter mouth a "thank you" and then walk away, fading into the light.

Ron knew he had finally healed Raine.

Raine

"Are you okay?" I asked Ron, kneeling beside him and feeling his face flush with sweat.

"A little dizzy, but I'll be okay in a minute," he said, catching his breath as if he'd just run a marathon.

"I felt him. Peter," I said. "You let him in, didn't you?"

He nodded, breathing deeply to slow his heart rate.

"Thank you," I whispered, leaning my forehead to his, hoping to give him some of my chi.

It had been a profoundly selfless act for Ron to allow Peter's spirit to take over, even if for a second, because he might have lost consciousness or, worse, gone into a coma.

Carty rushed over with water bottles and helped Ron stand. When he emptied the bottle thirstily, his color returned.

"I'm good now," he said reassuringly, then turned to me. "Let's get you inside the car where it's warmer."

He shifted his arm around my shoulder as we walked toward the car.

"I love you, you know," I said, leaning against the man who was now my husband, feeling all the ghosts that have imprisoned my heart gone.

"And I love you," he said, kissing my forehead and then touching my belly, "How's our little girl doing?"

"Starving."

Author's Note

Raine

DECEMBER 2011

DURHAM, NEW HAMPSHIRE

It's hard to believe that ten years have passed since I began writing this book—a journey that began in grief and ended in hope.

Nick Coelho and I had originally planned to write Peter's story together. With his investigative brilliance and my insight into Peter's life, the publisher said it would be a bestseller. But when Nick tragically died in the September 11 attacks, his loss felt like another cruel twist of fate. It also pushed me to pick up the pen, not just for Nick or Peter, but for myself.

Peter's story was not easy to tell. I fictionalized it to protect those involved, but the pain and truth behind it are all too real. Peter struggled with the darkness of his past—watching his mother suffer and burn alive—and then becoming an invalid like her when he too was diagnosed with MS. These were burdens he carried in silence, and they ultimately became too much for him to bear.

For a long time, I saw Peter's suicide as a selfish act, a final blow to our life together. But now, I understand it was more complicated than that. In his own way, he was trying to protect me, sparing me from the life of being a caregiver to a man he feared would become a shell of himself. It was an act of despair, yes—but also an act of love.

Peter's death forced me to confront parts of myself I'd been avoiding for years—the estrangement from my parents and the distance I'd created between myself and those I loved—Vivienne and also Luke. His death, though tragic, set me on a path of self-discovery, forcing me to heal, reconcile, and find my way back to love.

It was during this journey that I met Ron. He entered my life at my lowest and taught me that love doesn't always follow the path we expect. Looking back, I see now that fate and free will are not mutually exclusive. They work together in ways we can't always foresee. I made choices of my own free will, but perhaps they were part of a larger design.

Peter's death, as painful as it was, became the catalyst for my transformation. It helped me forgive and open my heart again. In the end, Peter gave me the greatest gift—he set me free to live the life I was destined to have.

***

If you or someone you know is struggling with thoughts of suicide, help is available. In the United States, you can **call or text 988 the Suicide & Crisis Lifeline**, for free, confidential support 24/7. You are not alone.

Acknowledgments

To all the folks in the Reading Nook Discord server who enthusiastically guided me through my journey in helping me make this book a reality, I can't thank you enough. Most especially, Kristen Colern, for creating the Discord Nook Writers server.

To my beta readers: JP. Chapleau, who gave so many insightful critiques, encouragement when I would run into the dreaded block, and most especially for putting the bro in Ron and his buddies, I am forever grateful, *merci beaucoup*. Nicole Born, who was the first to slog through the original draft, which was a whopping 177k words, I owe you, girl. Raymond Paquette for following me from the Coursera Novel Writing Course to the Nook server and reading every revision I made, *Arigatou Gozaimasu*. Shannah Foo, for loving Raine and Ron and their romantic journey; Dee Ann, for her eye on all the nitty grammar and punctuation; Janice, for her hard-ass comments that punched up the story arcs of this book. Sabina who can't wait to read Fritzso's sequel. Blessings and RIP to Dottie

Soules, my centenarian beta reader, thank you for being so enthusiastic with your feedback.

To Jordan Sloan (aka "Shoo"), with gratitude and appreciation to include your poem as the epigraph to this novel, and for all your critiques that helped shaped the final stages of the book.

To my editors Jason Letts, Gage Saylor, and Elizabeth Kulhanek, and my agent mentor from MSWL, Nour Sallam.

My family for their love, support, and encouragement, most especially my dad in heaven, a journalist and photographer. He was my biggest influence and inspiration.

And lastly, my husband, David, for believing throughout the twenty years of stops and starts to create this book that I should, could, and would be a writer. ILHT.

About
R. MB. Pearson

Arriving in the U.S. from the Philippines at nineteen, I set my sights on becoming a published writer. Though my path was anything but direct, I pursued my passion relentlessly, ultimately earning my bachelor's and master's degrees in my forties and building a career in professional writing. Over the years, I've worked as a journalist, a writer in higher education, and a marketing research administrator at NYU, where I spent nineteen years before retiring.

Now a freelance writer and photographer, I live in Marlton, NJ, with my husband and our twenty-five-year-old peach-front conure, Peejay.

If you enjoyed reading Bound by Destiny, please consider leaving a review on Amazon.
https://www.amazon.com/dp/B0DRVQVHGD

Like and follow me on Facebook
https://www.facebook.com/rmbpearsonbooks

Get news and updates from my blog
https://www.rmbpearsonbooks.com
https://substack.com/@rmbpearson

Coming Soon

Legacy of the Gift, Book One:
Goddess of a Thousand Eyes
How secrets from the past threaten
to reshape the future.

To learn more, visit *http://www.rmbpearsonbooks.com*